LIMERENCE

Book 5
The Limerent Series

LS Delorme

Published: 2025 by Limerent Publishing LLC
Florida, USA

ISBN: 979-8-9924855-2-3 – Paperback Edition
ISBN: 979-8-9924855-4-7 – Harback Edition
ISBN: 979-8-9924855-3-0 – eBook

Cover Design by Brittany Wilson | Brittwilsonart.com

Table of Contents

This book is dedicated to the people who have been brave enough to walk with me in this life, and on this journey. Fearlessness is not bravery, it's usually stupidity. Bravery is the ability to look into the abyss, knees shaking, and not let it consume you. So, this is for the people in my life who understand that, sometimes, momentary madness is the only sane reaction.

You are my "home" and I love you all.

Author's Note (Trigger Warning)

Limerence is a cross-genre novel blending speculative science fiction, metaphysical fantasy, psychological romance, and existential horror.

This book also contains content that may be distressing for some readers, including psychological trauma, emotional manipulation, chronic illness, medical experimentation, grief, sexual content, references to suicide, and past abuse. It also explores intense themes of consciousness, memory, and soul-level transformation. Some scenes involve metaphysical horror, particularly the unmaking and resurrection of identity.

This story doesn't shy away from depicting intense or disorienting experiences, because these are essential to the emotional and philosophical journey of its characters.

As always, reader discretion is advised.

Chapter One

Recurrence

Dante stood still and silent between the resonances of the world. At this moment, it looked like a beautiful blooming meadow surrounded by forests and fields. Dandelion seeds danced on a gentle breeze that sang as it passed through trees and grass. It smelled of mint with an undertone of jasmine, but jasmine did not grow in this part of the world. It was one of many small signs that this place was a lie.

What Dante saw before him was not a physical place, or not yet. It was the idealized blueprint of a place, and in the present moment it was horror wearing a mask of beauty. It was a leprosy victim slathered in makeup. Descending into the truth of it would feel like ripping his skin off, nerves exploded and unprotected by the illusion of its ideal state.

In the physical world, and in its blueprint, this was a field that led up to the parking lot of Pineville K-12 School, in Manassas, Virginia. Pineville was just one of many schools in Northern Virginia. And, sitting as it did now, in this beautiful meadow surrounded by forest, it seemed nothing extraordinary. When Dante had received the call to come here, he hadn't recognized it by name, but as he materialized, he remembered this place. It was the scene of a slaughter eighteen years ago, and had been on the bleeding edge of a new and dangerous period of contagion.

For hundreds of years now, since the time of a particularly gruesome contagion in Brazil, there had been a remission. The waves of sickness that had crested in that time had obscured whole resonances in this story. So those infected resonances had been cut and burned away until no sliver of them remained. After that, all had been calm for a long while. Even two world wars had done nothing to tarnish this golden time. In fact, said wars had pulled together humanity, and all things with consciousness, to stand against the forces that threatened to infect not just this world but this entire story. The creatures at the heart of these wars, the ones posing as men, had been altered by outside forces. These particular creatures had been taken down by *humanity*, with no assistance needed. After the wars, hope had bloomed, like this meadow filled with wildflowers, but in the past eighteen years there were signs of a sickness returning.

Dante looked at the scene in front of him, taking in the tranquility. He could not linger in the idealized version of this place. He knew the dangers of staying too long at such a high resonance, even for him. If he had any doubts of that, the burning that was starting in his fingers was a tactile reminder. He was hesitating because he knew how jarring and painful the first few breaths would be after he descended to the normal resonance level of the physical world. Still, it had to be done. He took one more look at the green field, the leaves dancing on the wind and the trees swaying gently in the forest. Then he closed his eyes, dropped his resonance, and the world immediately came crashing in around him.

He kept his eyes closed at first to minimize the impact. No such luck. The noise was the first thing to hit his senses, like a sonic boom exploding in his ears. Shrill sirens were wailing. Someone was screaming, others were shouting, but beneath them was the ragged sound of weeping. Dante began running equations and formulas in his head to solidify his presence as quickly as he could, like ripping a bandage off. It worked, but with this solidity came smell: car fumes, bile, and fear, with a trace of wood fires that seemed to mock him.

The screamer had the voice of a woman; she was screaming a name over and over, *Adrian!*, with such panic and grief that Dante knew this was a mother. This stabbed at his heart, and he opened his eyes.

He had been a witness to scenes of violence like this thousands of times—no, hundreds of thousands of times, and yet the visual horror of it never dulled. It was different every time but yet the same. This time the horror was being played out in the parking lot of a school instead of at the foot of a burning idol, but it was the same at the core. The parking lot was filling up with emergency vehicles and police cars. There were officers and emergency rescue people everywhere. Zones had been set up for triaging patients, one for initial assessment, one for treatment, and one for the staging of transport. In the triage, EMTs were running toward stretchers that were being carried out of the building area. Those showing signs of life were taken to ambulances to determine the level of urgency of the patients' conditions. The ones that were beyond help were laid on the ground and covered with blankets. Some looked painfully small. A child's hand stuck out from beneath one. Dante turned away, his fury building. There was no time for anger now. That would come later. Still, the people of his time knew better how to deal with such monsters and monstrosities.

Taking a few unnecessary breaths, he turned away from the school. He would come back to this, but for now he preferred to walk the periphery.

Dante made his way through the emergency workers, down the driveway and past the yellow police tape barriers. Across the main road, a crowd had gathered. No one even glanced at him. In truth, his invisibility was a good thing, but even after all this time, he still found it disconcerting, particularly in moments like these. Even more disconcerting was his inability to touch or be touched in any normal way. Even in this cold and impersonal age, grief and horror were communal things. Touching healed and softened the intensity of pain. But, for him, there would be no sharing and no softening.

As he neared the crowd, the sounds of sobbing grew louder, as the few terrified parents who had found out about the tragedy waited to be alerted as to the well-being of their children. Their eyes were trained on the emergency vehicles, where some of the children were being checked. As Dante made his way through the throng, he heard a cell phone ring. The mother who had been calling out her son's name now grabbed her phone from her purse.

"Adrian?" she gasped into the receiver. A second of silence before she dropped to her knees.

"Oh god. Thank god. Thank god. Are you okay? Are you hurt?" She sobbed, cradling her phone between her shoulder, cheek, and hand, as if it were her child.

Dante walked by and touched her shoulder. A strong electrical buzz of emotion hit him. It was a boiling mixture of relief, fear, grief, and anxiety. But beneath the message that this current carried, its code was clean. Other parents had taken out their cell phones and were staring at them, willing them to ring. Some were crying but others had a slack-jawed look of shock. Dante walked among them, briefly assessing the energy of each person he passed. From each it was the same, electrical currents reflecting intensified emotions but emitted from a clean code.

It was too early for him to feel relieved, but at least this wasn't following the same pattern as Jonestown, Heaven's Gate, the Order of the Solar Temple, or that god-awful mess all those years ago in Brazil. He had been present for the aftermath and cleanup at all those tragedies. But so far this incident was not like those. There were no widespread infections. No well-formed viruses. No zombies. So far, so good.

On the periphery of the school grounds there were several news vans. A few reporters were standing at the edge of the road, microphones in hand, giving on-screen reports. At least they hadn't begun interviewing parents yet, though they were certainly already planning it. Dante watched as pale green tendrils of energy began pushing out from the vans toward the crowd. He wondered if these people knew the extent to which they actually fed off the grief and horror of others. He also wondered for the millionth time if working in media drove people to become parasites or if only parasites were drawn to such a career.

"... example of child-on-child killing in yet another in a series of senseless school shootings that is reaching epidemic proportions in this country," said a youngish, dark-haired reporter in a red coat, with a look of grave concern. She was standing in front of a van with WRLD plastered across the door.

Epidemic. Dante snorted softly to himself. People threw this word around for effect without having any real idea what it meant, what it looked like. Physical epidemics were bad enough and the reality of them, the blood, stench, and death, would touch the lives of mercifully few if viewed as ribbons across time. But there were other types of epidemics that were far more dangerous. These were the sort that, if allowed to spread, would consume much more than just a few human lives. This was why he was here.

The reporter had just finished her piece and was standing with her cameraman next to the van.

"Can we talk to some parents now before the police get involved? And if you see a child, make sure we get to them first?" The woman's face was soft and pretty, but her expression was hard and hungry.

"I don't know, Grace," the man replied. "We can't talk to the kids without the parents, or some adult."

"Ugh. Really, Mick?" she said, rolling her eyes with disgust.

"Yes, really, Grace. It's the rules," he said, pursing his lips.

"Fine. Fine. Then go find a parent who is willing to be interviewed or something." She waved him off and then turned to inspect her reflection in the window of the van. As Mick walked away, she called after him.

"And Mick, try to grow a pair."

"What a bitch," Mick muttered under his breath, as he shuffled away with the camera.

Dante walked over to her as she was primping. He ran his hand above her arm. As he suspected, the electrical energy that came from her was different from the others he had encountered today. It felt weaker and it had breaks in it, as if it were a note being played staccato. Dante grimaced, pulling back his hand. He could see infinitesimally small sheer particles on his palm, wriggling, searching for an entrance they would never find in him. He wiped his hand on his khaki jacket with disgust. This one was certainly infected, but probably not recently. He didn't know the extent of her infection, but he spat in his hand and touched her shoulder again, marking her. Grace shivered slightly.

There was a scream and a sob from the crowd. Another woman was on her knees holding her phone in her hands and weeping. Grace motioned her cameraman forward to capture the footage. Dante turned away.

He continued making his way through weeping parents, more parasitic members of the media, and the gawkers. He stopped before each and every person, looking deeply into their faces, looking for traces of infection. There were probably thousands of tiny symptoms that might signal trouble. The change of the electrical current indicated a longer-term infection but there were other, earlier signs. A slower than usual blink reflex, a slight over-production of saliva, the smell of tar on the breath, a narrowing of emotional range that was sometimes hidden with showy overtures of emotion. All these things could indicate the beginnings of unnatural infections. So he was thorough in his examination of people. When he found someone with symptoms, he marked them, as he had marked the reporter, Grace. While he found lots of signs of minor infections, he found nothing too alarming here. Grace was the only one that would probably require attention.

More phones began to ring and news of the dead and the living made its way through the crowd. There was more crying, in grief and relief. More people were showing up, more media vans parking nearby, but Dante needed to concentrate on those immediately in the vicinity during the tragedy. So, when he finished with this group, he moved back toward the school building.

He walked slowly through the shell-shocked school staff, the glassy-eyed survivors, the grim but focused emergency workers, and the forcibly detached police officers. Most of these people were clear. Just as he was about to decide that there was nothing of note here, he heard a small voice coming from inside a parked ambulance.

"The monster is still looking for us."

Dante immediately moved toward the voice, which turned out to be that of a little blonde girl. She couldn't have been more than six years old. Her eyes were red and wet, and her face was splotchy. But she wasn't crying anymore. She was sitting on a stretcher in the back of the ambulance and being attended to by a pretty, petite, dark-skinned medic.

"Don't you worry, you're safe now," the medic said, as she put a blood pressure cuff on the girl.

"No, we're not."

"The boy who did this is gone."

"The boy wasn't the one who did this," the little girl said. "It was the monster inside the boy. It scared him and then it killed him."

The girl was clearly Cambion and needed to be assessed. There might be something here after all. As Dante touched the girl, her eyes turned toward him and widened before turning back to her nurse.

He left, and walked toward the main building. Instead of entering, he walked around it. The shooting had occurred in one of the classroom buildings in the back.

It wasn't hard to determine which building was ground zero, as the doors were open, and medics were coming in and out. There was a covered stretcher near the wall just inside the entrance, with two medics and several police officers standing near it. As another police officer came in, the first two subtly stood up straighter. It was obviously a senior officer.

"Is this the shooter?" he asked the men, pointing to the stretcher.

"Yes sir."

"And he's dead?" He turned to one of the medics.

"Yes, he's very dead," one of the officers replied through clenched teeth. This young man was angry. He was angry enough that he could have possibly helped speed up the shooter's death. Dante ran a hand over his back. Slight tremors. He was angry but that was all. There was no infection, or not yet. The other two men were clean as well. The superior officer nodded, but then got a call on his cell phone and turned to leave the building. The other officers relaxed.

Dante turned to the body. He hated this bit. If there was any residue of the person left inside, it would cling to him and that was always unpleasant. Still, he had to check. He touched a finger that was sticking out from under the sheet. There was nothing there. Absolutely nothing. Dante sighed.

Suddenly, he caught a glimmer of motion down the hall. When he turned toward it, at first he saw nothing. But when he looked away, something appeared in his peripheral vision. It was something he was always on the lookout for but was afraid to find. At first glance, he could have mistaken it for a small child, but only for the merest of moments. It was dark against the brightness of the daylight that was streaming in from the window, but transparent, like smoke. It was drifting back and forth in front of the emergency exit, with vines of smoke reaching out like arms whenever someone walked by.

Shit, the thing was an airborne.

Dante moved slowly toward the creature so as not to alert it to his presence. But as he watched, someone opened the door, and the thing reached out tendrils toward a school official who entered. The man shuddered and involuntarily pulled away. Then it drifted past him and out the door. Dante followed swiftly.

This thing was a surprisingly well-formed virus, and it was very advanced. He had seen only a few hundred of these over his lifetime and they could be tricky to catch. He certainly wouldn't be able to contain it while it was this incorporeal. It would have to infect someone substantially before he could lock it into a physical form. And it would take a special type of human to host such a developed monstrosity. It would take someone with a defective code.

"Of course," Dante muttered to himself, immediately heading out the door.

As he came out, he saw that the thing was making a beeline for a group of reporters now huddling on the school side of the road, just inches from the police barrier. It had smelled the presence of what it needed. As it passed people, it would drag a tendril over an arm or around a leg. The person touched would cringe, or shudder, but for the tiniest moment. It would only be later that they would start feeling poorly. Some people would develop a fever. Others might develop a headache or chills. For most people this was as much as they would ever know. Their lives would go on as normal. But inside them, a battle would continue to rage throughout their lives. And with something this advanced, it could be a serious battle. Many times, this would result in a chronic disease, most likely of the mental variety.

The shadow moved through the crowd, caressing those it passed, growing more solid, more visceral as it went. It did not move swiftly but it moved steadily, reaching with grasping arms, full of desire and need. It was looking for a home.

Across the street, Grace, the dark-haired news reporter, had cornered a man next to her van. The shape moved toward her; it was moving more slowly, but its tendrils were now waving frantically in the air. It was close to its target.

Dante slowed down as he approached the van. He wasn't sure if the shadow had spotted him, but if he was still enough, it was unlikely that it would. He was not alive enough to register as a victim or food for such a creature. As Dante neared, he could hear the exchange between the reporter and her interviewee. He would need to be able to work quickly if the thing made its move.

"So your son goes to this school?" Grace asked the tall, skinny man with graying hair and outdated corduroy pants.

"Yes, but he wasn't in school today. God …"

Dante cupped his hands together. A small ball appeared between them. It looked like a dirt storm caught in a snow globe. In truth, it was a frozen time signature, a marker of sorts.

"How old is your son?" Grace asked.

The shadow had stopped and was now hovering at one corner of the van.

"Seventeen."

"So he was in class with the killer then?" Grace probed, her face full of concern and eyes full of desire.

"What? The shooter was someone from the school? I didn't know … I need to go." The man turned but Grace grabbed his arm.

The shadow moved in closer and slid beneath the van.

"I understand, of course, but the name of the shooter hasn't been released yet. It must be unnerving to think that your son might have been friends with a child who would do this," Grace said, leaning in close to him and turning to give a knowing look to the camera.

At this moment, the darkness slipped from beneath the van and briefly brushed the parent.

"Leave me alone," the man cried suddenly as he pulled away. He was tall enough and it was forceful enough that Grace was momentarily knocked off balance and staggered back, falling against the van.

"We'll cut that last bit," she said curtly, straightening and dusting her hands. She did not see the shape as it came up behind her. It slid up her leg and seemed to disappear underneath her skirt.

Suddenly, Grace doubled over and began to cough. Mick came up and put his hand on her back, but she waved him away as she took some deep breaths. Mick went back into the van. Grace's body suddenly shuddered.

When she stood back up, for just a second, there was a look of terror in her eyes. But then her face went completely slack. The terror was replaced by something else, a look that Dante had never seen before. The muscles in her face began to move at unnatural angles and her eyes looked in slightly different directions—like an insect. One side of her mouth was turned up in a smile, the other side stretched wide enough to see her back teeth. One eyebrow arched while the other remained still. The lack of symmetry of all these facial moments gave the impression of a doll being manipulated by a bad puppeteer, or a rubber toy being stretched. In short, it looked inhuman.

Dante had been taken off guard for a moment by this, but now he moved quickly. He walked directly up to the woman. She seemed to be able to see him. Her face distorted yet again into something that looked like rage, but it was replaced by fear as he threw the bubble in her direction. It expanded outward, becoming a brown net of dust that surrounded her. As it hit her skin, it sank beneath it, trapping the virus inside her. Grace stepped backward, flapping her hands around her head. Dante stepped away as the reporter's face went blank for a moment. Then, suddenly, a normal expression returned. Her cameraman stuck his head out of the van and gave her an odd look.

"I thought I saw a bee." She shrugged. "Have you got that footage ready yet?"

Dante allowed himself to pull back from the scene. For now, he could relax. There was much here to be concerned about, and a few small things to celebrate, but nothing could be done until he saw Kara.

She would decide who would live and who would die.

Chapter Two

Eighteen-Year Cycle

The woman sitting on the infamous *Exorcist* stairs in Georgetown was physically perfect. Her heart-shaped face held sapphire-blue eyes and small but perfectly formed lips that could only be called rose colored. She was wearing a retro black dress circa 1958. She looked like some strange mixture of Marilyn Monroe and Audrey Hepburn. Marilyn's coloring and face, but Audrey's body and eyebrows. Her platinum hair was pulled up in a ponytail high on her head. She was tapping narrow feet that were encased in black ballet slippers and she was breathing rather heavily. In her hands she held a small, black-beaded handbag. In the fading light, she looked like a 1950s screen goddess excitedly waiting for a date. Her sparkling eyes were locked on Dante with an eerie sort of intensity.

Dante knew that he was a far cry from the Cary Grant or Tony Curtis that one might have expected to be the consort of this woman. He was too weird. He was dark, tall, and thin, but broad across the chest and shoulders. Wavy hair framed a face that had full lips, high cheekbones, and a jawline sharp enough to cut glass. His almond-shaped eyes had an upward slant, making him look slightly Asian but their shocking blue color put that assumption to rest.

It wasn't his body that marked him as weird, it was what was adorning it. On his head he had an unusually tall but dingy black stovepipe hat with a maroon band. Stuck in the band was a seven of spades Bicycle playing card. When this was added to a khaki army jacket that had seen better days, it screamed *I dug my clothes out of garbage bins.* His trousers were black and tight with a rather ornate codpiece that was in fashion for about fifteen minutes in Italy roughly five centuries earlier. While it was true that his overall attire was nothing short of hideous, he was proud of it. He had earned every single article of clothing on his body over the centuries. Ghosts were usually either consigned to the clothes that they died in for eternity or something basic and bland appeared on their bodies. However, in Dante's case, each article he wore was something that he had managed to take from Malkuth, the physical world, and adapt to his in-between existence. As he forced himself to learn how to move up and down levels of existence, the clothes had followed. In all his travels, he had met no other ghost who could do what he did. So, yes, he was proud of his clothing. He was prouder still of the necklace that he wore. On it was a jet-black stone scarred with an ice-blue flaw running across it. This stone was more important than anything he wore. It was more important than anything he *was*. To him, it was more important than the story itself. His whole reason for torturing his soul, to make it possible to switch across resonances, was to be able to keep this stone with him at all times. Being the carrier of it terrified and humbled him in equal measure, and he wore it with pride.

Despite his pride in his status and appearance, Dante avoided situations where he had to view himself. When he had been alive, he had been exquisitely handsome and vain. He knew he was still handsome but now the deep honey-colored skin on his face was pale with purplish bruises beneath his eyes. Today, he would probably be considered sexy in a ghoulish, alt sort of way. So perhaps he wasn't completely unfit for his companion.

"Where have you been?" Kara asked, as Dante got close enough to hear her. She had not taken her eyes off him. To be honest, he enjoyed the feeling of her eyes on him, even when she was annoyed.

"It takes time to create a bubble," Dante said, using a lilting, musical tone and letting his old accent bleed through, because he knew it would affect her. He used this voice when he needed to either ignite desire or soothe the beast. She was overburdened and had been away from him too much recently—and the effects were showing.

"We could have just met at a restaurant," Kara said, her voice softening just a bit.

"True. We could have. But there is some news, and, well, you don't always respond well to surprises particularly when—" Kara stood up slowly and gave him what could only be called the evil eye. Dante could feel the hairs on his arms begin to stand up, as if by static electricity.

"Kara," he said her name softly, gently, saying it as if it were a prayer, which it actually was. "You are showing signs of being overloaded. It's been too long since—"

"I know how long it's been," she said coldly, but she sat back down. Her statement wasn't strictly true, but Dante breathed a sigh of relief. She was still reasonable, as the world was still reasonable. He would fight, kill, and even die to keep it so, for her sake.

"So what is this news you have that requires that you drain yourself to produce all this?" Kara asked, as she gestured around them. At first blush, nothing seemed amiss except for the deserted streets and silence, but a simple glance at the sky would change that. The clouds weren't moving, and the birds overhead were frozen in flight.

"Did you visit the most recent school shooting yet?" he asked.

"The one in Manassas, Virginia?"

Dante nodded.

"Yes. It was horrible and awful, of course," Kara said. "But that's normal. I found the people that you had marked at the scene. Most of them were clean. A few had low-level infections that were easily taken care of. I didn't see anything particularly unusual at the school. But you must have, or you wouldn't have created this. What happened?"

Before he could reply, Kara caught a glimpse of a grasshopper sitting motionless on the stone wall to her right.

"I detest those things," she said, as she smashed it quickly with one hand and wiped its guts on the step beside her.

"I wish you wouldn't do that," Dante said quietly.

"I know, but I don't like them, which means they shouldn't exist," Kara said testily. She was in pain and suppressing it. "You were saying?"

"Well, yes, there are two things," he said, as he laced and unlaced his fingers. "There is one thing that is clearly bad. The other is—well, concerning."

"Tell me what you need to tell me."

"Okay. When I was at the recent shooting site, I saw a virus."

Kara shrugged slightly. "Okay. Did you take care of it?"

"Of course, and I'll get to that, but the first problem was that I saw it. As in, actually saw it at the higher levels of this plane. It had form."

"As in it had a visible form?" Kara was now sitting straight on her perch on the stairs.

"Yes. It was visible and it was larger than usual. It—"

"Where was it exactly?" Kara interrupted.

"It was roaming the halls of the school, searching for another host."

"Another host? Had it been in the shooter?"

"Yes."

"And the shooter, did you find out anything about him?" she asked.

"Of course. That's when I got more concerned. Everyone who knew him was completely shocked by this incident. He had been a smart and popular kid. He was also fairly athletic. Well rounded, no enemies and his family life was as good as family life can be for a teenager. No abuse, sexual or otherwise. No romantic breakups or college acceptance issues. The only glitch was that he had been diagnosed with a nasty flu a few months earlier. And that's when I remembered."

"Remembered what?"

"We had a shooting in this exact same school, with the exact same methodology, about eighteen years ago. I cross-checked news articles and confirmed. In this shooting, the shooter had been diagnosed with a flu at the end of the last school year. This year the boy comes to school and guns down a building full of kids. The kid eighteen years ago did exactly the same thing under almost identical circumstances. Same type of kid, same level of popularity, same previous flu issue."

"Have people noticed the similarities?" Kara asked.

"Not broadly, yet, but they will. The media is always thrilled with this sort of story," Dante replied. It was hard to keep the contempt from his voice, but he was trying. She didn't need any additional triggers.

"Was there a pattern to the victims?"

"None that I could tell, but the victims from before were all dead and had long left this plane so I could have missed a lot. But this time, most of the victims' souls were missing as well."

"The dead were gone? How long did it take you to get there?"

"Not very. Of course, it could be that their transports were just unusually quick and that no one from that group chose the ghost route. That bit wouldn't be very surprising, given the circumstances, but it felt odd that it was a ghost town immediately afterward."

Dante caught his own ironic reference as it was coming out of his mouth. Kara noticed it as well, and it made her smile for the tiniest of seconds. But then her eyebrows creased. She put her chin on her folded hands.

"How old were the victims—both times?"

"Students and teachers, from age five to fifty-nine. Apparently, age wasn't a driver," Dante replied. "They were also spread across male and female, so that wasn't a driver either. There was no discernible pattern to the victims but, that being said, he did seem to choose victims specifically. He didn't open fire on whole classrooms, he picked one or two per class. It was the same last time."

Kara started to interrupt again but Dante held up his hand.

"I followed his body to the hospital. They found an entire bottle of pills in his stomach. The kid had consumed enough benzodiazepines to anesthetize an elephant. The level of GABA in his system was sky-high. The doctors were saying that it was amazing that this kid could even walk, let alone get a gun, aim, and kill people."

"So you think …"

"I think he was taking them to contain the effects of the virus that was infecting him," Dante said softly. "Something that big, raping the machinery of his code, had to be causing no small amount of pain."

"Do you think the virus was responsible for this kid opening fire in his school?" Kara asked.

"I can't make a direct correlation, no. But I wouldn't rule it out."

"So it's a neuro virus? It could affect behavior?" Outwardly Kara seemed calmer, but the hair on her head was beginning to move even though there was no breeze.

Dante nodded.

"He got sick with a nasty flu a few months before, and suddenly developed mental problems bad enough to make him shoot a school full of kids, including preschoolers. So, yes, I think it's a neuro virus."

"A large, completely formed neuro virus," Kara muttered to herself as she stood up and began walking in circles. "We haven't seen one of those in a while. What were you able to read from the boy's body? Anything?"

"By the time I got to him, there was nothing left. His soul was gone."

"How did he die?" She sat back down on the steps.

"Shot by a policeman."

"Hmmmm." Kara began to chew on one of her fingernails. Her hair was now coming loose from the ponytail. Tiny hairs were beginning to move and caress her face with a life of their own.

"So we have a nasty neuro virus that seems to be airborne. That's not great. But you also said it had a form. That means that the shooter had to have lots of holes in his code for it to be able to attach to him. If that's the case, then there are limited individuals who are either gifted or flawed enough to meet those criteria and be hosts—and we should have already identified someone like this. Did we?"

"That's the second thing," Dante said. "It appears that this new shooter was also a Cambion."

"What? How old was he?"

"Sixteen, maybe seventeen."

"Motherfucker!" Kara snapped, eyes now a much lighter shade of blue. "Give me his stats."

"That's the thing, I'm having trouble finding him in the system," Dante said quietly. "But you know I have trouble navigating that system without help. I sent out a request for information from 8th-floor channels and one of the ghosts recognized the kid as Cambion."

"Son of a bitch. Why didn't you lead with that? What ghost recognized him?" Kara was pacing back and forth again.

"A ghost who wanted to remain anonymous said that Howard had 'interacted' with the boy," Dante replied. Kara stopped pacing and rolled her eyes.

"The creepy writer?" she asked. "The one with the delusions of grandeur and, apparently, eternal racism? How did he recognize him?"

"I'm not exactly sure, but Howard tends to be attracted to Cambion boys of that age."

Kara snorted.

"Okay, so let's herd up some other ghosts to work on this and find his watcher. We need to get Joe to pull all the files we can find on this kid and the one from eighteen years ago. The ghosts can search their resonances and the recently deceased for any information they can glean."

"I'm not sure how cooperative Howard will be if he thinks it's beneath his time," Dante muttered.

"Then inform him that if he can't play well with others—well, then I'm sure my ex would love to know his whereabouts," Kara said, with venom in her voice. "Surely he's experimenting on ghosts these days, isn't he? He experiments on everything else."

Her emotions were jumping all over the place. She was on edge now. Dante knew the signs of fatigue in her. He also knew what pain she must be experiencing, and the amount of energy it took for her to bank it.

"You don't need to threaten," Dante said gently. "My concern is more that he would hardly be the best choice to keep an eye on someone. For this we need a ghost with a cool head and attention to detail. That's hardly Howard's MO. Also, there could also be operational issues there and we need seasoned eyes, I think."

"Fine," Kara said, with less venom. "Also, I think we need to check on the locals here, something feels wrong. I felt that even before you told me this. It's making me edgy. We may need to make a small world tour together, just to be sure."

"There is one last thing, about the virus," Dante said. "I caught and contained it."

Kara's sudden smile was like the sun.

"How? Where?"

"I netted it at the site. It's now in a very holey news reporter for a local public access TV station."

"So let's go see this reporter," she said, coming toward him and taking his hand.

"Don't you think we should maybe do something else first?" Dante asked. "You are past time."

"*Let it go*, Dante."

She turned, her face mere inches from his. The blue of her normally sapphire eyes was now more of a sky blue. Dante flinched a bit, involuntarily, but held his ground. Her hair was suddenly a fully developed life-form of its own. It snaked around her head like tentacles. Her body was still, but there was so much energy radiating from her that the temperature of the air around him was plummeting. The hair on his arms was beginning to freeze. From the place where Kara's hand touched his, he felt electricity slam up his forearm and into his brain. She was one of the very few who could touch him and whose touch he could feel, and it could sometimes cause this sort of sensation. Still, he would take it. If truth be told, he craved her touch, even in this form.

"You are going to injure yourself," he said calmly.

At this, Kara's eyes darkened, regaining their depth of color, and she stepped back. She sighed audibly.

"You're right. Of course you're right, when are you ever wrong?"

She rolled her eyes but her tone much lighter. It was enough to make Dante smile.

"We both know that I have been wrong more times than I can count. It's just that I am never wrong about you."

Kara gave him a small smile and touched his arm again, but this time gently and with no electricity. He felt the warmth of it spread throughout his body and to his extremities and whatever counted for blood in him followed suit.

Kara sat back down on the stairs.

"Okay. Once we have seen this reporter person, then we can make the trip for me. Does this work for you?" she asked.

Dante nodded.

Kara suddenly slumped a bit. Dante was next to her immediately.

"You are too tired," he said, sitting down and putting his arm around her. "Are you sure you can wait?"

Kara nodded, leaned her head on his shoulder and draped her legs over his.

"I am tired now. After tomorrow, we will make the necessary trip. You will make sure I do that, right?" she whispered.

"Always." Dante kissed the top of her head. Kara closed her eyes before sighing, disentangling herself, and standing up.

"Thank you for the bubble. You are probably right about needing it. Wouldn't do for others to watch me morph into Medusa, would it?" She smiled, but more weakly than he liked.

"Well, we don't need it anymore," Dante said, then closed his eyes, raised his gaze ever so slightly and then lowered it.

It was a very small gesture but the world around them began to bleed and whirl. Scenes of people walking, cars rushing by, birds flying sped by them at double or triple speed. Time was catching up. It only took a few seconds for things to return to normal speed. The street was now packed with noisy cars filled with noisy drivers. People were walking up and down the sidewalk. There were students, tourists, and residents. The birds that had been suspended over their heads were long gone.

"I need to rest now, before we do anything else," Kara said, standing up and holding her arm out to Dante. "I have a hotel just down the street. I can rest there for a bit before we go see this reporter. After that—tomorrow—we can do what we need to do."

As they walked down Main Street toward Georgetown Park, people stared at her. Whether this was a reaction to her beauty or the fact that she seemed to be talking to herself wasn't always easy to determine. As a large man and his family approached her, the man went out of his way to steer his wife and two young girls to the opposite side of the sidewalk. As Kara passed him, her eyes lit on him for just a moment and then she flipped her hand in his direction.

A few seconds later, there was a thump behind them and the sounds of a woman screaming and calling for help. When Dante turned, he saw the man on the ground clawing at his chest, as various people were frantically calling on their cell phones.

The ambulance arrived when they were only a few blocks up the street. The distraction caused by its arrival and the medical commotion that followed meant that no one was noticing the beautiful woman in the black retro dress and ballet slippers who talked to herself anymore. Dante saw Kara look back for a moment as a crowd of people gathered down the street.

Her expression was blank.

Chapter Three

Fall from Grace

The parking lot at Fairfax Public Access TV was mostly empty. There were a couple of ubiquitous white news vans with WRLD News stamped on the side. There was one beat-up blue Chevy truck parked near the door, a Honda next to it, and a Hyundai around the corner. There was also a new BMW sitting some way off, closer to the road, as if trying to avoid being seen with older, less well-off cars.

When Kara and Dante entered, they had to ring a bell at a service counter five or six times before someone sauntered out to the front. The man who did so was probably forty-something, but Dante guessed that his arteries were pushing seventy-five. His frame was roundish and he had long, frizzy, graying hair and the yellowish pallor of someone a bit too friendly with alcohol. Dante could smell at least four different fragrances on him: deodorant, shampoo, conditioner, and coffee. On top of that he had splashed on some cheap aftershave. This guy needed a month on a water and vegetable diet to clean all the crap and chemicals out of his system.

Kara cocked her head to the side as he approached them. His eyes widened and his step quickened as he caught sight of her. Dante was, of course, invisible to him.

"You're not too busy today, I see," Kara said, smiling at him.

"No, it's still early, we just opened. So there's only a couple of reporters and me. I'm Tim, the director of operations here." He stuck out his hand and Kara shook it delicately.

"Are you here to see someone?" Tim asked, with a hopeful tone to his voice that made Dante roll his eyes.

"I called about an hour ago about the shooting. I work as a nurse for the hospital, and she was looking for information about the shooting—"

"Oh. Excellent!" Tim said before catching himself. "Oh. I don't mean the shooting was excellent, but any information you have would be excellent. Have you spoken with anyone else?"

"No," Kara asked.

"Great. Our reporter Grace would love to talk to you. Let me show you in." Tim ushered them down a short hallway to a media room where Grace was sitting in front of a computer.

"Hey, Grace, this is the nurse that called earlier about the shooting at the school," he said.

When Grace turned around, alarm bells went off in Dante's head. Her eyes were abnormally wide and her pupils were so dilated that you couldn't even see the iris.

"Hello, the employee that took the call said your name was Karen, is that right?" she asked Kara.

"Yes, Karen." Kara reached out her hand, and when Grace took it, Dante saw a hard look cross Kara's face. She would want his read as well, but it wasn't looking good for this woman. She already had a broken code, but what was now in her was surely doing more damage. Add one more to the death count—or worse than death count.

"You said you work at the hospital, right? Please sit down," Grace said, pulling up a chair. "Do you mind if I jump right in with questions?"

"Of course, that's fine," Kara said, nodding. "I was directly involved in processing the body so I can tell you what you need to know about that side of it."

Grace pulled out a notebook, a bit antiquated, Dante thought. He also noticed that her hands were shaking as she held it.

"What we heard from a hospital attendant was that the kid was sick a few weeks before the shooting, and that he was on meds. Do you know if the meds were for that sickness?" Grace asked.

"The medication in his stomach had nothing to do with an acute illness," Kara replied. "They were the sort of medications that are usually given for more chronic problems."

"I see," Grace said, clearly disappointed. She was both tapping her foot and jiggling her pen. "Do we know if he had any chronic problems?"

"Listen, I can't just give you the patient's entire history," Kara said. Dante suspected she was agitating Grace on purpose, just to see how she responded. She often did this. Her detractors said it came from the same drive that makes a cat play with its prey before it eats it. Dante knew better.

"Perhaps if there is something in particular you are interested in?" Kara continued.

Dante waited to see if Grace would mention something about patient rights or privacy or anything else that would be pertinent or normal to inquire about in this sort of situation, but she didn't. Instead, her eyes lit up and she smiled. The smile was a milder version of the puppet-like quality that he had seen the other day at the site of the shooting. Kara caught it and looked over at him. He nodded at her.

"Actually, I am interested in the nature of his illness because I just got this amazing idea for a piece." Grace was speaking rapidly. "It's about the 'unseen world.' I heard that the shooter was maybe taking drugs for anxiety. I just had this idea, you know, this crazy idea that maybe he wasn't mentally unsound, maybe he just realized what was all around him all the time. You know, all the things that you don't see. Imagine what would happen to you if you could see what microscopes see, or electron microscopes see."

Dante had heard this sort of talk before. The ghost Howard had espoused these sorts of ideas before he died in the early twentieth century. It was odd to hear the thoughts repeated by a modern woman who had presumedly studied science at school.

Grace's eyes looked shiny and manic. She wasn't even really looking at Kara anymore. She was just staring above her head.

"And the thing is, even if we can see these things, we don't know anything about them," she continued. "Not really. We know what they are made up of, but we don't know how they process things. We don't know if they have thoughts, or desires. We always assumed no, but now, even those things are being questioned. Like how we used to think that animals couldn't think and feel like we do, but now we know that whales and chimps are just as emotionally intelligent as we are—maybe more so. What if these parasite things, things we don't see, actually think as well? What if the things crawling all over my body right now are there because they like the feel of me, or the smell of me, or the taste of me? What if the things that live in my eyelashes can change the way I see things?"

Kara and Dante exchanged looks. Grace looked straight at Dante and started.

"When did this guy show up?" She saw him now. Something had changed her perception.

"I just got here," Dante replied. "So what were you saying about the things in your eyelashes changing the way you see?"

"Yes. The thing is we have these few little senses to be able to understand the universe. Even with our microscopes and our computers, we still can only understand things through our own feeble little brains. You know what I mean? Let me show you something," Grace said, turning back to her computer and opening tabs.

Throughout this whole exchange, Dante had felt his stomach dropping again and again. He had seen Grace before. He had checked her code before. She had been damaged but intact. But what was in front of him right now was not the person that he had seen at the news van near the school.

"That's not her talking," Dante whispered to Kara. Kara's eyes widened. "She's not this smart, or this crazy. This is something else."

"Demon?"

"Don't think so. If it was a demon, it would have recognized me from the start, and stayed away. No, the only thing I know of is the virus."

"Shit," Kara muttered.

"Look at this, there is this parasite that changes the way its host thinks," Grace continued, whirling in her seat to point to something on the screen. It was an article from *Nature* magazine. She highlighted a few words: *Toxoplasma gondii is known to remove rodents' innate fear of cats.*

"See that?" Grace said. "It says it's thought to be an evolutionary adaptation in the parasite's life cycle. Toxoplasma only reproduces in the cat gut, and to get there, the pathogen's host—a rodent—must be eaten. They think the parasite causes mice to become weirdly drawn to cats, the cat eats the mouse, and the parasite is introduced into the cat's digestive system, where it can reproduce."

She looked back up at them. "See? The parasite *knows* it has to get back to the cat's intestines. *It knows.* Not only that, but it's also come up with a strategy to get there. The article says it's instinct but what is instinct? It's a form of knowing. So imagine if there are all these things all around us that are thinking about us, touching us, and realizing it. God, it's enough to make you want to scream."

Grace had started rubbing her hands on her skirt. Her hands were trembling more obviously now, and she was starting to look frantically around the room. She looked like an advertisement for caffeine gone bad.

Dante went and stood next to her.

"Hey there, it's okay. Everything's normal. Nothing's going to get you," he purred softly. This was only half a lie. Nothing was going to get her that hadn't already gotten in.

"Oh god," Grace said suddenly, her hands comically over her mouth. "Suppose they know I'm here now? Suppose knowledge triggers them? Suppose they can come after me now? Oh god. They are everywhere, and then suppose they … suppose they …"

Suddenly, Grace's whole body tensed, and she threw her head back, making gagging noises. Her hands were flung out rigidly at her sides and her body started twitching. She began to slide off the chair.

"Dante, she's convulsing."

Kara grabbed Grace and laid her on her back, kicking the chair out of the way. Dante fell to his knees and focused his attention on her, pushing part of his energy inside her. What he saw was there was indescribable.

Nothing inside the soul of Grace looked right. Nothing was ordered. There was no structure. It felt vile. He felt like he was swimming around in something regurgitated. He tried to look for something resembling a virus, but it was like a dark soup. Whatever it was, it had to be here somewhere, but he couldn't see. That was when it dawned on him. He couldn't see anything because he was actually inside the intruder—and the thing was this fucking huge.

"She's burning up. Pull that thing out," he heard Kara say. "Do it now. Capture it while it's busy cooking her brain."

Now that she said it, he felt it. The heat all around him.

Grace was lying on the ground. The large muscles of her back were contracting, forcing her body to arch backward in an extreme fashion, as if she had tetanus.

"Whatever this thing is, we have to kill it. Never mind, I'm taking her out!" Kara said.

Dante pulled back further; that was when he saw it. The thing was bigger than a melon and yet it had tied itself to strands of DNA all through her body.

He grabbed the thing and pulled. He heard a sickening sound that he suspected might be blood vessels bursting—or worse. When he pulled himself back into his regular form, there was a small reddish blob in his hands. It looked like yarn or rust, but it felt like melted rubber. He immediately dropped it. As he watched, it started to unfold, like a puzzle. He kicked it across the room away from them, where it continued to move and squirm and unwind. It continued this pattern until it was a shape about four feet tall.

This thing was like nothing like he had seen before. First, it seemed to have difficulty holding on to a continuous shape. In one form, it was covered with what looked like stalks, at the end of each was a purplish nodule or sac. These stalks waved back and forth. In another, it resembled a bundled collection of scabs. But it only held each shape for a few moments before changing in a rolling fashion. There was a smell coming off it that smelled like some strange mixture of pickles and sugar. But it wasn't the flipping image or the smell that made Dante feel queasy. It was the fact that it seemed imbued with something extra. Something his senses, even as a ghost, could not quite process.

In the corner, Grace was completely still, but Dante thought she was still alive.

"What is that thing?" Kara asked.

Suddenly, the thing rolled back toward Grace, shrinking as it went. Dante tried to grab for it, but it had already disappeared into her.

Grace's body jerked. Her torso moved into a sitting position in one straight movement, from waist to head, as if she were on strings. Her head cocked to the side, with that weird grimace-like smile.

"What the fuck?" Kara muttered in disgust.

The thing opened its mouth and sounds came out. They were not words and had no discernible structure. It sounded more like an out-of-tune flutophone. Dante looked around but the sound clearly came from Grace's mouth, which was just hanging open, drool now beginning to form and drip into her lap.

Ackackackack

This sound came from her mouth without her lips moving.

"Is that fucking monstrosity trying to speak?" Kara asked, crouching down.

"Yes. I think it is," Dante said, leaning toward it. "What are you trying to say?"

It produced a noise that might have been an attempt at a response.

Agggcccccckkkkkzzzzzz

Grace's face was turning very red. She started to shake and convulse. Dark sparks of light began to jump off her body.

"Whatever you are, you are beginning to cook your host from the inside. If you cook her, then you die too," Dante said, moving closer again. The thing that was Grace rocked itself rigidly back and forth. It was moving slowly toward him on its butt. Dante moved back a bit, trying to draw it away from Kara.

Kara's eyes were focused on Grace as she crouched, using her hands and feet to move herself noiselessly around the room. Dante knew viruses tended to try to flee when Kara got too close, but it had been a long time since they had dealt with something this large, this weird, or—well, this vocal before, so it was hard to know how it would play out. In the meantime, he wanted to get as much information as he could before she destroyed it.

"You were the one at the school, right?"

The rocking got even more exaggerated, and the body's hips moved in a circular pattern that somehow was suggestive of a sexual motion. Dante felt a surge of revulsion.

Kara was now directly across from Dante and behind Grace's body. She held her hands hip distance apart and a pale blue light began to spark from one to the other. Soon other colors joined it, all the way up through ultraviolet, brightening the room around them.

Grace's mouth made a strange noise that sounded like a cross between the wind in the trees and the crunching of aluminum foil.

A bulbous boil-thing was forming in her open mouth. It looked like a testicular sac to Dante.

Kara slowly moved up behind it.

The boil grew quickly until it was bulging out in front of her face. Her body began jerking again and her face was now the color of a tomato. Suddenly, the boil burst open, issuing from her mouth like vomit. When it hit the ground, it formed a semi-liquid ashy blob. This thing quickly took on a more humanoid, more solid shape, more like the shape Dante had observed at the school.

"Ah, now you look like this again," Dante said, as Kara moved forward. "You change forms a lot, don't you? Is that you mutating? If so, that's a very handy trick."

The new gray shape trembled. Dante kept his eyes on it as Kara moved closer to her target.

There were two things now that Kara would have to deal with. What was still in Grace's body and what had now escaped it. As the gray shape moved away from its parent, Kara got just behind Grace's body. Just as she put her hands to either side of Grace's head, the ash progeny sprang forward, right at Dante.

At first Dante was shocked and pushed himself back toward the wall instinctively. But he was even more shocked when the thing latched itself onto his shoulder and, as it did so, a wave of desire washed over him. It was of the dark, twisted, hate-fuck sort of variety, but it was still desire. This was followed immediately by a physical sensation. He felt something puncture his shoulder, then a sharp pain and a feeling of numbness, a paralysis that prevented him from moving.

"Kara," he called, trying to remain calm.

Kara had her attention focused on Grace's head, which was now thrown up toward the ceiling. A greenish slime tinged with red was seeping out of her eyes and disintegrating into something in Kara's hands—something that could only be called a liquid as a means of comparison to something known.

"Kara," Dante said again, as he tried to get a grasp on the thing at his neck. He couldn't touch it, his hands went right through, but it seemed to be able to touch him easily enough. Kara looked up and her eyes widened.

"Son of a bitch." She dropped Grace's head and threw herself on the thing attached to him, grabbing it. She usually tried to avoid actually touching these things so that she didn't accidentally absorb them, but she made no such effort this time. She crouched, grabbing it with both hands. It wrapped itself around her hands and, to Dante's horror, sunk into her flesh.

That thing is inside her. It's actually inside her.

The thing began to smoke as whatever it had for flesh began to freeze. Dante reached out and grabbed another part of the blob, focusing his heat into his hands before it could attack him again. As it smoked, it started to drip. As the fire and ice met inside, it began to make a high-pitched sound that sounded disconcertingly like crying.

When it was gone, Kara was still kneeling, staring at her hands.

"That thing tried to attack you." She was shaking with anger. "If it's reproduced, all of it has to be unmade, and I will make that unmaking as slow and painful as I can."

"The fact that it attacked me isn't the main concern," Dante said quietly.

His main concern was that it had apparently attacked Kara and she had immediately forgotten that. But it was not the time to discuss this.

"My main concern is that it could," he continued. "I'm a ghost. Viruses can't attach to ghosts, at least 99.99 percent of the time. So that thing is new and bad, but we can analyze that later. Right now, you need to calm down enough to walk out of here. Call someone and tell them this woman had a seizure. Then we need to leave."

"That thing actually went after you," Kara whispered. Her normally pale cheeks were blood-red. Her eyes were bright—too bright.

"I'm fine," Dante said, then stopped. Kara's eyes going from bright to milky.

"It has to be unmade," she repeated softly.

"You already did that, my love. It's gone now," he said. It was not the time to think about whether the virus had spread.

Kara said nothing. She was completely still but her hair was moving again.

Oh no.

The air in the room was starting to crackle. The computer screen was blinking on and off. A fan across the room began spinning faster than it had any right to do. Kara's skin was getting paler and beginning to glow. She was about to go over. She was too overloaded, and she hadn't seen anything actually attack him in hundreds of years. He was shaken too, but he could only imagine what was going on in her head. Two light bulbs above their heads burst, shattering glass around them.

Dante pulled her toward him and kissed her very hard. Her lips burned icy against his and he felt the electricity running through his body. There was always a danger in these moments that she would accidentally unmake him. She was furious, and she could turn this at him, but he didn't see much choice. He had to bring her back to her physical reality. The scene that would occur, if someone walked into the room and tried to interact with her while she was in this state, could result in death or even unmaking for those unfortunate enough to come close and be in any way infected. So he needed to distract her quickly and efficiently. After a few seconds, he felt her body relax. She pushed him away and sighed.

"We need to get out of here. Call for them now," Dante said.

"No, wait." Kara's voice sounded hoarse and ill-used. She crawled over to where Grace's body lay on the floor, and lightly touched her finger to Grace's forehead. Grace's body shuddered and was still.

"No?" Dante asked.

Kara shook her head. "Her brain is gone. The fucker burst her brain. And I can't feel her soul at all."

Suddenly, her eyes widened. "I must have unmade it when I unmade the virus."

"You would have had to unmake her anyway, her code was too damaged," Dante said quickly. "But let's get out of here now."

Kara stood up. She shook her head for a moment before going to the door.

"Help! Someone … anyone!" she called to the outer office. "Your reporter is having a seizure or something!"

After this, the room filled up with people fast. When the emergency team charged in, Kara stood to the side. As some of the medics started talking to people, Dante moved to the background. After a few minutes, Kara asked very politely if she needed to stay. She was calmer, but it was only for now. She had lost control twice in less than twenty-four hours. She had never done this before, at least, not in the last millennium. He suspected she had taken on more at the school than she had told him.

They walked together to her car. As she sat down in the driver's seat, Kara put her head on the wheel. The skin around her eyes was puffy and bruised looking.

"The pain … is it very bad?" Dante asked her.

"Yes," she whispered.

"How long?"

"About three months."

Dante sucked in breath. "Three months! Why didn't you say something?"

"You know why."

"All right. Let's do this. It will be done, and you will be better," he said firmly. In truth, he hated what they were about to do much more than she did, but it was part of the burden he had to bear. The burden that he had put on both of them.

"When we get back to London," she said, starting the car. "Take me then. In the meantime, let's go back to the hotel for a bit … you can make me better in other ways."

He should have argued but when she turned her eyes to him, the fire in them was undeniable and irresistible.

As it had always been with them.

Chapter Four

Madeleines and Madness

It was 9 a.m. and Kara had decided that they get breakfast at Le Pain Quotidien in Tyson's Corner Mall in DC. She had been very chipper in the car this morning, humming along to the radio as she drove. The mall was fairly empty when they arrived. Kara pulled into a parking space, totally ignoring the space delineations. She smiled at Dante as they got out of the burgundy Corvette she had rented.

"You are in a much better mood this morning," he said.

"I feel much better than yesterday. Good sex will do that. But it also makes me hungry," she said, with a sideways glance his way. Dante smiled to himself, feeling a surge of pride mixed with guilt as Kara walked through the door in front of him.

This morning, she was wearing a simple white shirt, no bra, and blue jeans. Her newly washed hair was tucked behind her ears. She wore not a scrap of makeup and no jewelry, but she still turned the heads of the staff as she walked in. It was literally impossible to gauge her age. She could have been anything from twenty-five to sixty-five. Beauty like hers was ageless. She made her way down the line of food, examining her choices before ordering a croissant, a madeleine, and some Marco Polo tea at the register. The man taking her order was young, tall, clean-cut, blond, and well built. He was also very obviously taken with Kara, like everyone was, when she wasn't killing them or driving them crazy.

"You aren't from here, are you?" he asked, as he leaned a little too far over the counter to pass her the croissant.

"What do you mean?" she responded, with a tiny flash of a smile.

"Well, you have an accent. You aren't American, are you? You sound sort of foreign. I love the way it sounds."

Dante snorted. There were many things about being a ghost that sucked. Not being able to say anything to the asshole that was flirting with the woman you spent last night and this morning having sex with was one of them. It was pointless to get annoyed about it, but he did. Kara must have sensed his irritation.

"Oh. I move around a lot, so that probably gives me an odd accent. Plus, my boyfriend is Sicilian, so from his tongue to my lips, you know?" she said, smiling. The smile on the blond guy's face became confused for an instant and he drew back across the counter quickly.

"Uh-oh. You aren't some Mafia guy's girlfriend, are you?" He laughed nervously, as she paid and picked up her tray.

"Oh no. He's much worse than Mafia." She turned and carried her tray to a table, dismissing the open-mouthed man behind her without so much as a backward glance.

She sat down on the bench gingerly and tucked one foot beneath her thigh. Dante sat down in front of her and watched her butter her croissant. The other thing that sucked about being a ghost was the inability to eat without a Herculean effort.

"I'm not Sicilian," Dante said, as he watched her eat.

"You were born in Sicily."

"But my parents were Carthaginian," he replied. "My whole family was Carthaginian."

"Dante, I know that, and you *know* I know that. But that guy is glorious in his utter simplicity. He wouldn't even have understood that word, let alone been able to comprehend that there is a difference between Carthaginian culture and Sicilian culture. But you know all that."

She looked up at him from under her eyebrows.

"You know, you don't have to brood when people flirt with me," she said.

"I wasn't brooding."

"Yes, you were. Next time, if you don't like him flirting with me, just smack him," Kara said, with a little smirk.

"You know I can't do that."

"You most assuredly can."

"Okay. Let me restate that. You know I can't do that without possibly killing him and making a huge scene."

Kara smiled and shrugged.

"Why? Does he need to die? Is there something I'm missing here?" Dante asked.

He was still a bit irked, but he was also secretly pleased that she had referred to him as her boyfriend. That title was a source of great pride to him. He would never say that out loud, because it would sound pathetic, but it was true.

"No. He was fine," Kara said. "I was just pointing out that you aren't powerless in these situations. Sometimes, it seems like you feel emasculated by not being able to have some sort of testosterone contest with the natives. I guess that's your birth culture coming out. I'm just pointing out that if there was such a contest, you would win. And you have no need to question your masculinity."

She took a small bite of her pastry and met his eyes directly.

"After last night and this morning, I won't be able to sit properly for a couple of days, and I won't regret it one bit. If that doesn't make you feel man enough then I don't know what will."

"I don't think that sort of statement is very PC in this day and age," Dante said, but Kara just laughed.

A surge of pride and guilt hit him again, but stronger this time. He usually tried to restrain himself with her, particularly when she was overwrought and vulnerable as she was now. But last night, as she had been getting ready for bed, she had pushed him and whatever passed for resolve in him crumbled with embarrassing speed.

"How are you, really?" Dante asked. She looked up and gave a small shrug.

"I'm tired. And what happened with that reporter yesterday worries me, and the worrying adds to the fatigue." She sighed. "You were right about needing to be cleared, but I hate it so much."

She said this with the same tone that a person would use if they were complaining about visiting annoying relatives or going to the dentist. To say that this was downplaying the situation was a horrific understatement.

He reached across the table and took her hand. "Let's do it tonight. After we check in with the local watchers. Then it will be done. Tomorrow we will eat breakfast in London, and it will all be over."

She nodded.

"The sex does make me feel better though," she said.

"Maybe, but given everything going on, it probably wasn't very nice of me," he said.

"Well, you were too tempting yesterday." Kara pulled a piece of the madeleine off using her incisors. "I love how cool you are when I'm not. Even when I accidentally hurt you, you don't back down. It's quite sexy, you know."

He smiled.

"So I showed a little skin, and you couldn't resist me?"

"I was never able to resist you. That's the root of our problem," he said.

Kara winced slightly then leaned across the table to kiss him gently on the lips. This caused two older ladies sitting across the room by the window to stare and then begin whispering. To them, it would look like Kara was kissing the air. Kara wouldn't give a shit, but he still felt crappy when people looked at her like she was crazy. She *was* crazy, by human definitions, but it still pissed him off when people looked at her that way.

"Okay, we will head to London right after we finish breakfast," she said, sipping her tea. "About Grace, do you think that virus could be some mutation of either dog flu or mouse flu? I mean, we haven't been able to eradicate those two viruses, even after all these years. So now they are just endemic. Could they have mutated into that thing we saw?"

"I don't think it is related to those. Those came from Amelie, and she has not been a problem since—" Dante began, but Kara cut him off.

"Yes, since." Kara looked away. "But still, this new virus, combined with the fact that it hit in the same place and in too much of the same way … well."

"It worries me too," said Dante. "I wish I had been able to capture it *before* it infected Grace."

"It's okay, my lover." Kara took his hand again. "The fact that you captured it in someone is actually better. Otherwise, you might have accidentally killed it. You don't always know your strength. And what we saw it do to her was something that we needed to know about."

Dante nodded, but he trembled at her touch.

"You think it was a neuro virus?" she asked.

"I think so, but I'm not sure. But that's concerning, if it is."

He was on more solid footing when they were talking "business" and not personal things. Jesus, it's not like he hadn't known this woman since literally before Christ. You'd think he'd be over the jitters by now. But then again,

Kara was Kara. She was as she was made. He doubted anyone else would do any better than he had done.

"It's not really the neuro virus part of it that makes me nervous," Kara said. "Nor the airborne part of it. An airborne neuro virus would be nasty, of course. It would mean a whole slew of people becoming mentally deranged. That was Jonestown. It was ugly but the fact that they killed themselves saved us having to do it. We still had to track down and deal with those who were still infected but even that was easier than it could have been."

She stopped and put the final bite of pastry in her mouth, then licked her lips delicately before continuing.

"What makes me nervous is how that thing behaved. It tried to speak. It tried to communicate. Viruses don't do that, so there has been some adaptation there, something that is mimicking consciousness to better invade its victims. All that is enough to set off alarm bells. But add that with the similarity to the past shooting and the growing trend of this sort of shooting idiocy and it really worries me."

Dante nodded.

"It seems like there is some kind of regularity to these shootings and killings," Kara said. "There is also a kind of, I don't know, precision that feels new—well, new for now. I'm starting to feel these sorts of incidents coming. You must be seeing patterns as well. You can't tell me that you haven't tried to sort out some sort of predictive algorithm for this, as in love with math as you are."

Kara said this with a slight smile. She was going for levity, but it fell flat. That moment was gone.

"Yes. I noticed. I've got a few people at the Office working on it. But nothing yet. It feels elusive but almost … I don't know …"

"Purposely elusive?" Kara asked. Dante nodded.

"Like it is being directed by something … or someone? Like maybe the Academy might be involved in some way?" Kara asked softly.

"Don't go there," Dante said. "This one feels strange, to be sure, but the Academy has only successfully crafted a truly sustainable virus once. That was bad but we caught it. We—"

"Leveled a whole civilization in Brazil, is that the phrase you are looking for?" Kara finished, looking down. "Well, *I* leveled a whole civilization."

At that moment, a soft musical phrase drifted up from Kara's purse. She pulled her phone out.

"Yes?"

"It's Joe," she mouthed to Dante.

"Slow down, slow down. This isn't an emergency," she said with a little laugh. "And believe me, I can use the good news right now."

Dante heard Joe's muffled voice. Kara was nodding.

"Listen, I tell you what. You just hold her in the waiting area. Dante and I will be there later today."

Kara returned her phone to her purse, but when she looked back at him, the tension of recent moments was gone. She was smiling.

"A young woman found her way into the Office," Kara said.

"What?" Dante said. "That's not possible. She couldn't get in. She couldn't get past the codes."

"Apparently, she followed one of your ghosts in," Kara said, her face breaking into a broad smile.

"What? Really? She saw a ghost?"

"Yes, and she had the balls to demand what the place is. From Joe, of all people!"

Dante felt his chest bloom. That took balls of steel.

"Who is she?" he asked.

"We don't know. But she came in roughed-up," Kara replied, her face darkening for a moment. "Joe says that she may be acting the way she is because she is on the edge of a meltdown. So we should go soon. This is one that I want to see myself."

Dante nodded. He wanted to remind her again of the need to clear herself. There were only so many of other people's moments, feelings, stories, memories, and random bullshit that she could absorb before she would break down, and she was already hitting her limit. But he also knew that she wouldn't hear of it now. She would want to meet this girl immediately. It was rare to see ghosts, even among Cambion. It was rarer still to be able to see a Cambion ghost.

"Let's head to London to meet this new woman," he said, standing up and holding out his hand. "If she can see me, then that's one box checked, and we have a new associate … maybe for management."

"That would be really nice," Kara replied, taking his hand and standing.

As they left the restaurant, everyone actively averted their eyes, even the guy behind the register. Beauty only went so far to offset craziness.

Chapter Five

The Office

The Canary Wharf skyline had more in common with New York than it did with the rest of London. A small but intense grouping of skyscrapers dominated the horizon here. As might be expected, a lot of the local and older residents complained about the addition of these buildings. Dante understood the compulsion to hold on to that which was familiar, and the violence and fear that could result from someone trying to take that familiarity away from people who needed it. He also knew that it was futile to resist change. Things and people that could not adapt to change died—or were eliminated.

The London weather had taken one of its typical turns and substituted the drizzle of five minutes before with blue skies and fluffy clouds. Rain, wind, sun, mist all in one day, same old, same old for London. Dante was walking, unseen, through the crowd with Kara as they made their way out of the Canary Wharf Tube station and through a sea of businesspeople in suits. They had crossed the Atlantic through less physical means for speed but Kara didn't like it. Unlike him, she was still physical enough to be seen and just non-physical enough to get caught by electrical wires when she was in that part of her being. As her physicality was easy for her, she relished it. She didn't like to be removed from it for any longer than she had to be. So they had settled in toward the end of the Jubilee Line and taken the Tube to Canary Wharf.

It was mid-afternoon, and the businesspeople present were clustered in groups of twos and threes. Most of these people were in banking or financial services and it wasn't hard to tell. They were men with a grayish tinge to their complexions, no matter what ethnicity they happened to be. Occasionally a tourist, local, or a banker's spouse or mistress would break up the waves of navy and gray bespoke decorum with some color, but that was fairly rare. The cold air was thick with the smell of restaurant food, aftershave, and anxiety.

Kara was mostly silent through this part of the journey, but her silence was not a passive thing. Dante knew that she was absorbing and assessing the crowd in a million different ways during each step of their short journey. When Dante looked at these people, he saw them surrounded in shades of color. These colors indicated their spiritual state. This was distracting enough; he could only imagine what Kara saw when she looked at them. When she was at this point in her clearing cycle, any misstep from a passerby could result in their termination.

As they passed an open-air mall area, a woman with a Hermès bag did a double take at her reflection in a shop window, almost running into one of the rare children present in the mob of adults. The woman scowled. It was fast, and most would have missed it, but Dante saw Kara frown. He knew that she was adding this woman into the area of her brain reserved for people that she might research further at a later date. The woman didn't know how lucky she was to have survived the moment. As they walked away, the woman began to cough.

A few blocks east, Kara began to rub the back of her neck, just at the point below the skull. This was a tell for her that she was too full.

Soon. It had to be soon …

They walked further east, making their way past one glass building after another until they came to the one that Dante knew so well. This building seemed tall in abstract, but it was about a third of the height of One Canada Square, so it attracted little attention. It was flanked on either side by buildings very similar in size and design. The name of a well-known bank was plastered across the top of it.

Instead of going through the front door, they followed a path through a camouflaged, almost invisible alleyway between buildings. At the back of their building was a metal door. Kara pulled a key card from her purse and waved it in front of a small black box. There was a buzzing sound, and she pushed open the heavy door. They entered a small alcove filled with an obscene number of cameras. There was one in each upper corner of the room, three or four at eye level and two more at floor level—an upskirter's dream. Kara shielded her face with her hands, in order to test the alarm system. Sure enough, the moment the door closed behind them, the alarm system went off. Strobe lights flashed all around them as a high-pitched beeping noise assaulted their eardrums. Dante hated the alarm system.

Kara looked up and the sound stopped.

"Well, the facial recognition system is working," she said, with a slight smile.

"So that does beg the question of how our potential new associate got in."

"It does, doesn't it? I'll have to ask Joe."

The metal wall in front of them then slid open to reveal an elevator. Inside, next to the elevator doors, was a stone wall pad engraved with the shape of a hand. It looked vaguely prehistoric and out of place in this modern space. Kara placed her hand on it. She didn't really need to go through this exercise. The electricity was to elevate people, the right sort of people, up the resonance chart just high enough to be able to get into their building. If someone's energy patterns were not capable of being raised then all they would ever see was a bank.

The elevator door shut behind them. When it reopened, it was onto a large, airy lobby. The walls were glass windows that stretched from floor to ceiling, catching the rare London sunbeams when they emerged from the clouds. It was open plan, spanning two floors, with escalators connecting them. On the perimeter of this bottom floor was a small cube farm. Occasionally a head would pop up, like a whack-a-mole, and the head would say something to someone near it before disappearing. Upstairs was a café and lounge, and a few people were coming down the escalators with coffee cups in their hands. In the center of the bottom floor was a large, empty expanse of marble flooring. There was one circular desk in the middle, with a uniformed man sitting at it.

Dante was happy to see that the man at the desk was Joe. They had other security people, but Joe was special. He was the head of Security, a forty-something bull of a man, with a bald head, heavy, dark eyebrows, a pierced nose and tattoos of demons on his skull. His appearance would be very intimidating to those who didn't know him. Those who did know him were intimidated by his history instead. Before he had found his way to them, he had been an "asset" in the Asian slave trade network. He had been feared by people everyone else feared. When Kara found him, he had sunk to such a level of depravation that he had actually mutated his code into a fragmented mess. In short, he was teetering on the brink of damnation. Kara had saved him from that, so his loyalty to her was as unwavering as his fear of her.

Looking at Joe now, it would be hard to imagine that he had ever been that wretched person. There was a speaker on the cabinet behind him and he had pop music playing softly. His eyes were closed, and he was dancing in his seat. Despite his physical appearance, the fact that he was making mirror face as he danced did a lot to make him seem less threatening.

Joe hadn't seen Kara enter, but others had. Everyone who had been walking stopped dead in their tracks. Dante could feel their tension blow through him like a sour wind. He mentally kicked himself for not telling HR they were coming back, and that Kara was calm. It would have made this moment much easier for all of them. But his mind had been on other things. As it was, everyone froze as Kara walked with measured footsteps toward the guard.

"Joe," she said in a singsong voice. Joe opened his eyes, and his mouth dropped.

"Kara, hi," he said quickly. "You got here quick."

"You didn't see us in the elevator?" Kara asked with mock innocence. Joe turned white. Dante rolled his eyes. She wasn't mad, but Joe wouldn't know that.

"I just got back from a break, I just ..." he stammered, as he turned the music down.

"Don't you dare!" Kara snapped, and Joe froze. The demons on his head began to move as his skin twitched.

"I love that song. Turn it up," Kara said, smiling and beginning to dance a bit herself. Dante smiled. The tension in the room broke with such force that it might have been an animation flower bomb. Joe let out an audible sigh, laughed and turned the music up loud. He came around the desk and Kara gave him a hug.

"Welcome home, girl," he said.

"Shut up and come dance with me." Kara laughed, pulling him toward the center of the room. Other people were now standing and swaying to the music.

"Oh, no. Can't do that. I know that scary-ass boyfriend of yours is around here somewhere. Right?" he said.

"Yep, Dante's here," a woman called from the upper floor, leaning over the upper railing, holding a cup of coffee. It was Sheila from Accounting, painfully single and painfully horny. She was one of the ones here who could see him. Dante waved at her, and she put her hands over her heart. He felt very self-conscious being the center of attention, but that was the nature of things whenever he was with Kara, which was most of the time.

In the meantime, Kara was still dancing in the middle of the room. More people had left their seats and were swaying or dancing.

When Kara returned she always brought either a celebration or a storm, and sometimes both. But despite some unsteady recent circumstances, this turned out to be a celebratory moment, because she felt better now. He had made her so. Dante let himself relax and move to the music as he watched her dance. She had danced like this in other lives too, and he had fallen in love with her in just such a moment. That was before she was all this, when she had been allowed to be only human.

Dante noticed a woman sitting near Joe's desk. She was shortish, plump, and pale. She stared at him from under her bangs with big brown eyes, looking like a wounded doe. Her level of menace was right up there with a Disney woodland animal. And like those characters, she probably got overlooked a lot. He would have discounted her as well but for the fact that she was staring right at him, which meant that she saw him. He was about to approach her when Kara left Joe and danced her way toward Dante. The woman visibly flinched when Kara got closer to her.

"Come dance with me, lover," Kara said, laughing. Dante shook his head with a smile, but she grabbed his hand.

He gave in to it and danced with her. He couldn't dance the way that they had, the way that they could in the early years of their union—that would be too much for this day and age. But the fact that she pressed herself against him meant that he had no choice but to dance with her hips held tight against his crotch. The energy of the room turned both more approving and more sexual. Kara threw her hands out to the side and let him support her as she arched her back. At that moment, the song ended, and the sharp nasal voice of a computer DJ broke the mood abruptly. Joe turned down the player to sounds of general disappointment from the cube farm.

Kara sighed, but when she walked back over to Joe there was still a smile on her face.

"So I hear we have someone who needs testing?" she asked him, her tone becoming more serious.

"Right." Joe beckoned to the seated woman with the doe eyes. The woman stood slowly and painfully, her eyes to the ground. When she walked, it was as if she were afraid of stepping on hot coals.

"This is Liz," Joe said. "I think she's had a bad day."

"My name is Kara," said Kara, extending her hand. "This is my place. Some call it the Office. You can call it whatever appeals to you."

Liz raised her head, squared her shoulders and took Kara's hand. For the first time, her face came into full view. Her right eye was bruised, and her nose was swollen.

Dante felt the surge in him before he could redirect it. A light bulb on Joe's desk turned black before bursting.

"Oh, my dear," Kara said, putting her hand under the woman's chin, examining her face. "I'm afraid your nose might be broken."

"I'm so sorry to have imposed on you," Liz began, her words rushing out in a trembling voice.

"He destroyed all my things. I got home. I was late. He had taken all my things and thrown them in the garden. He was looking for a lighter to set them on fire. He cut up all my pictures. He put water on all my journals. He was so angry. The whole house smelled like gasoline. I should have run. I shouldn't have gone in. But I didn't have anywhere else to go. That's a stupid excuse. He hit me when I walked in the door. He just kept hitting me. I curled up on the floor. Then he started trying to light a match. I was afraid that he would use it on me. So I just got up and ran. I just ran. I've been walking all night and all this morning. I didn't have anywhere to go."

At that moment, Liz crumpled down onto the floor with her head in her hands. Kara squatted next to her and put her hands on Liz's head. For a moment, Kara's head dropped and touched Liz's with her forehead. When she looked up at Dante, her eyes were no longer kind. There was death in them. Those who noticed the burst light bulb had already cleared off, but now the whole floor became very quiet.

"Don't you worry, sweetheart, you're safe here," Kara whispered to her. "But we do need to ask you a couple of questions."

Dante came to sit next to Liz.

"Hi Liz, I'm Dante," he said. Liz looked directly at him with swollen eyes. But she smiled a bit and stuck her hand out.

"I'm sorry, but you probably—" Dante gasped when Liz firmly grasped his hand. Kara's eyes widened and a smile returned to her face.

Dante felt his heart speed up. Someone who could touch him occurred only every hundred years or so.

"Liz, let me stress that we aren't angry," he began gently. "But we do have security. How did you find us?"

"I followed a stream of weird people," she replied flatly.

"What do you mean, weird?" Kara asked.

"They looked … well, they were dressed different," Liz said. "Most weren't dressed modern. They looked … I don't know. It's hard to explain. I might have just been hallucinating but they looked thin, somehow. So this place seemed—felt—different. I saw them go in and out of this place for hours. I have been watching since just before sunup."

"Indeed," Dante said softly. "And how did you get past the security in the elevator? Did you see the security cameras?"

Liz nodded, then looked down.

"I know you'll probably think I'm crazy, but I got in the elevator with one of the people and they didn't notice me. Then I just sort of made myself little. I'm not very interesting, so I can do that sometimes. Not all the time. If I could do it all the time, I wouldn't be as messed up as I am right now, but sometimes I can. You think I'm crazy, right? Michael says I'm crazy."

"No," Kara said. "No one here thinks you're crazy."

"But why did you choose *this* place to come into?" Dante asked. "Why this building instead of one of the hundreds of other buildings around here?"

"It was one of the thin people." Liz's voice cracked. "She smiled at me. I just needed someone to smile at me."

Then she put her head down and began to cry in earnest.

"You came to exactly the right place," Kara whispered, putting her hand on Liz's head. "I'm amazed that you found us, but you are in the right place. But I think we need for our infirmary to see you. We want to make sure that you don't have any other injuries."

Liz suddenly looked up and then threw her arms around Kara.

"Thank you. But I'm afraid that Michael will find me. He can be horrible, and I don't want him to hurt anyone here," Dante heard her say softly into Kara's shoulder.

Kara laughed out loud.

"Oh, don't you worry about that. Joe won't let anyone past him, will you Joe?"

Joe looked up from his computer and, for moment, his eyes looked wet.

"If he shows up here, I'll take him straight to the 8th floor," he muttered.

"They know how to deal with assholes like him."

Dante smiled to himself. The 8th floor was the ghost residential area, and no one could fuck up the living quite like the dead.

"Joe, can you call backup and then take Liz here to the doctor and make sure she gets there safely?" Kara asked. "Then take her to Records and get her properly checked in. She will need a room and other basic necessities until she decides what she wants to do. I need to see our parabiologists and Dante needs to meet with IT and Finance, we need some records on recently active members. Once Liz is all set up, can you send her to meet with either me or Dante?"

"Dante," Joe said, eyes raised and a smile forming. "So she can see Dante?"

"She can indeed," said Kara, looking at Liz.

Joe came around his desk and escorted Liz toward the elevators in the back.

"Why wouldn't I be able to see Dante?" Dante heard Liz ask Joe.

"Most people can't," Joe replied, "because he's a ghost."

Liz's subsequent coughing fit was neither unexpected nor unique.

Chapter Six

Coffee with a Cambion

The day had turned out to be unusually clear for London, so Dante could see the sun beginning to set from the long glass windows running down the side of the building. He was sitting in a small alcove, taking a few moments to himself in preparation for his evening. From where he sat, he could smell the vanilla-sweet perfume of the woman who was working on the security desk, mixed with the smell of computer plastic, ink, and coffee. Smell was one of the senses that became accentuated after death rather than dulled, and it could be overwhelming for the newly deceased. There was something very distracting about knowing when every woman in the place was starting her menstrual cycle. Other senses sharpened too, but in stranger ways. Over time, and since the Abomination, Dante had begun to perceive the people around him not just by scent or voice or motion, but by the patterns hidden in their resonance. Everyone gave off a kind of waveform, a harmonic echo of their emotional and spiritual state. Some people flickered with frantic, erratic bursts, others pulsed in slow, heavy tides. A few rare souls held steady tones that resonated deeper—calmer, richer, easier to tune into. The older ghosts learned to tune most of this out by concentrating on less potent senses such as sight, as Dante did now. He turned his gaze to the setting sun and tried to focus.

He had just returned from meeting with the Finance and IT teams. In Finance, he had discovered that there were no records on either the current Manassas shooter or the one eighteen years ago. So Dante's first goal had been to determine why. The most recent boy had been recognized by ghosts, so he was known. As a known Cambion, he should have been registered across multiple departments, including Finance. If he had been registered but dropped out of any system, it should have triggered an alert. But Finance could find no evidence that either of the Manassas boys had ever existed in their systems. So, while he was there, Dante created an algorithm that would track any past, present, or future financial spikes, in either direction on a day-to-day basis and compare that with the number of files in existence on any given day. Said algorithm would alert them if files disappeared or there was a decrease in expected daily expenditures per Cambion. The Finance department had been positively orgasmic.

Dante was one of the best market analysts in a building full of world-class analysts. Over recent years, he had developed very lucrative algorithms that predicted market variance. This made him the golden child of the Finance and Accounting departments, so he got looks of adoration every time he came into their offices—from those who could see him. Newbies to the Finance team usually thought this gift had something to do with his being one of the older ghosts, or his relationship with Kara. In truth, it had far more to do with math because Dante didn't just see markets—he heard them, felt their hum beneath his feet, the rise and fall of frequency in every dataset, like tuning forks buried inside numbers. People were no different. Each one carried an individual signal; sometimes, when he was at rest, he would chart one and change it to music. It was all about the math of vibration.

Dante firmly believed that math was, indeed, the language of the angels. Not only that, it defined the existence and realm of angels. The resonances that all conscious beings existed on were governed by math, even though most would not see it. These resonances didn't just rise randomly, stacked upon each other like blocks in a toddler's game. No, they followed the golden ratio. Phi was said to mark the point at which resonance tipped from physical into conceptual. That threshold—somewhere around 1.618 times baseline human resonance—was where the highest-resonating beings, incubi, began to lose form. After this, the construct of consciousness as most beings understood it began to unravel. At the portal to reincarnation, at the end of the upper winds, all that remained were the fragments of code that contained those parts of conscious things that they took with them from life to life: patterns, scraps of personality, vibration, emotions. This same ratio was also found in art, spiral galaxies, sunflowers, and the human body—in all of creation.

Math had saved him during the first few decades after his death. It was in that time that he discovered that math, particularly higher math, was a conduit between the physical and non-physical worlds. The more he engaged in it, the more he was able to expand the number of resonances he could exist on. This made it easier for people who had the right gifts to see him. Math was also predictable, solid, and as familiar as a friend. More than that, some frequencies pulled at him in ways he didn't fully understand, like Kara's. Her presence was like a fundamental tone in the tangled chords of the world—a stabilizing frequency he had come to rely on. If he had a home frequency, it was her.

In recent weeks, he had less time for math because he had been on the road. There had been an uptick in reports from ground staff of suspicious viruses and "possessions" near some of their key Cambion, so Kara had felt the need to do a short world tour. It seemed like it was a good thing they had. The parallels between the two cases with the Manassas boys, combined with the behavior of the virus that possessed the reporter, was deeply concerning.

After his meeting with Finance, Dante had met with IT and these conversations had made him more skittish about the situation. IT was the first step in the registration process of a new Cambion and apparently both Manassas boys had been registered in their databases. After registration, normally everyone was assigned with a watcher. This watcher would look out for them and report back to the Office on a regular basis. Disturbingly, that wasn't what happened with the most recent boy. He had been registered, but no watcher seemed to have been assigned and there were no reports. His existence had not been flagged to Finance. The boy from eighteen years ago was the same. So the glitch seems to have occurred at the intersection between IT, Finance, and Security, and those departments were unusually strong.

Dante was still pondering this when he saw Liz exit the elevator and walk toward the café. Her nose was bandaged but her body posture was straighter. He suspected the doctor had given her pain medication. He had been impressed with how she had handled herself earlier. She had a broken nose and a cracked rib. Dante had known this immediately because he could pick up the smell of bone marrow that was leaking from the break in her bones. But she had found a way into the Office and had stood on her own in front of Kara for a while, and that was no small feat. Dante had received a message earlier saying that she had passed her preliminary tests, so now was as good a time as any to talk to her.

Liz was awaiting her coffee when she saw him. She smiled, and it was genuine. Upon closer inspection, she had a very pretty face beneath the swelling. It was too soft to be photographed well, but it was kind and open.

"How are you?" Dante asked, walking up to her at the counter.

"I feel much better, thanks. I saw the doctor and he said that my nose was broken but that it wasn't too bad and it should heal mostly straight. He also said I had cracked ribs, a dislocated shoulder, and lots of bruises but I should be at least functional in a week or so."

"Good," Dante said. He was feeling genuine affection for this woman. "I'm sure you have lots of questions and I have a few as well."

Liz nodded as the barista handed her a large cup of coffee. She put not one, two, or three, but four packs of sugar in it.

A sweet tooth. Dante had had one of those, once upon a time. It was a Cambion tell, as was diabetes.

"Would you like me to order you something?" Liz asked.

Dante just raised his eyebrows. It took Liz a couple of seconds, then her eyes widened.

"You don't eat?" she asked.

"Digestion is an incredibly physical thing," Dante replied. "It's hard to get to that level of physical when you're a ghost."

"Wow. You really are a ghost? This isn't some giant cosplay organization?" she asked softly.

"Certainly not." Dante laughed.

"Then what are you?"

"Let's sit down," Dante said, directing her to two overstuffed leather chairs on the far side of the coffee shop. Many of the branches of this particular coffee shop had abandoned such luxuries as fluffy chairs in exchange for basic tables and booths. But Kara liked the sofas and couches, so they had been shipped in. The fact that the Office were majority shareholders in this particular corporation had made that happen very quickly.

Liz sat down gently in her chair.

"Are you still in pain?" Dante asked.

"It's okay. It's been worse," Liz said.

"So this Michael, he's your husband?"

"Yes."

"What is his full name?"

"Michael Pierce. I was Liz Pierce." Liz stopped. "I never liked my married name. My real name is Liz Byrne."

Liz looked up, smiled fleetingly, then shrugged.

"So, Liz Byrne, do you have any children?" Dante asked.

"Oh god no," Liz said in very real horror. "I could never have left if I had children. At least not without them."

Dante nodded and Liz grimaced slightly.

"Listen, I know I seem like a loser. Why would anyone stay with someone who did this to them?" Liz said, indicating her face. "But it didn't start out like this."

"How did it start then?"

"We met in university. He … well, he helped me through a difficult time." She took a sip of her coffee. Dante simply waited as she stared at her cup.

"I met him shortly after I had been raped. I had just moved here to the UK to go to university. I grew up in Shreveport, Louisiana, so when I was accepted to Oxford, I was shocked and thrilled. But in my first couple of weeks there, I was raped in an alleyway walking home one night. Michael saw me stumbling back onto the street and helped me to the infirmary. He called me in the days afterward and was incredibly sweet. He told me that he was in love with me about a month after this happened. We were married within the year. It wasn't until after we were married that things started to get bad."

Liz poked at her coffee with the swizzle stick.

"It started small," she said, her voice much softer. "He got angry at me for spilling water. Then he called me a stupid twat for buying the 'wrong' groceries. By the time he hit me for the first time, I was already too afraid of him to leave. And he told me that I would never find anyone else who would find me attractive."

"What about your parents? Didn't they know what was going on?" Dante asked.

"My parents are dead. They died in a car crash when I was seventeen."

"I'm sorry. Did you have siblings?"

"No, I was—am—an only child."

Dante nodded. He had seen this pattern so often. She had no family, no friends, and she had been identified by a predator during a particularly vulnerable moment.

Liz pulled the wooden stick from her coffee and licked the end.

"I know that sounds like every battered-woman story ever," she said, looking up. "I need to change my life. I just have to figure out how."

She looked around her. "But this—this place has given me so much to think about."

She doesn't believe what she is seeing, Dante thought.

"You all have really helped me in my moment of need, so I'll pay you back for my doctor's treatment, if you can just let me know how much. But I need to get going. I have a job that I need to get to. And I guess I need to find a new place to live."

"What if we can offer you both of those here?" Dante asked.

"Offer me both—?"

"A job and a new place to live."

Liz laughed uncomfortably.

"What is this, a cult?"

Dante shrugged.

"Maybe, but not in the ways that you think," he said. "When you were with the doctor, we ran a series of tests on you, on your blood, and on a number of genetic markers. Your tests came back as being very similar to most of the other people in this building."

"What do you mean?" Liz asked.

"Biologically, you have an unusually high white blood cell count, far above and beyond what would be expected even given your injuries. You also have a high number of markers indicating inflammation. I suspect that you have had issues with autoimmune disease in your life. Yes?"

"Yes … I have lots of allergies."

"I assume you have also had nerve problems?" Dante asked. "Migraines? Digestion problems? Bouts of pain that doctors can't explain?"

"How did you know?" Liz whispered.

"Because many of the people in the building have the same problems. All these physical problems come from the fact that most people here have certain genetic abnormalities. We ran a gene scan and discovered that you do as well."

"No one has mentioned it before," Liz said.

"No one else does the tests that we do."

"Okay, but what does that have to do with anything?" Liz asked, then she blinked. "I didn't mean that to sound so aggressive."

"It didn't, and don't worry about that here," Dante replied. "These genetic differences, and the reason for them, may be the most important thing in your life. It's what makes you different and special."

"I'm not special—" Liz began.

"You came into this building following ghosts. You hid from a state-of-the-art security system. Then you came into our office and shook hands with a ghost," Dante said, sitting back for a moment and watching his words sink in.

For a moment, Liz sat quietly, staring at her coffee. She opened her mouth to speak but she was interrupted by a loud, strident voice.

At the sound, the sun chose to pull in its last rays of light and disappear.

Unfortunately, Dante had no such option.

"Hey, Dante," said Jayce Whitney Miller. Jayce was an employee in the department that monitored HR data for the Med Tech. Unfortunately, Jayce had the ability to see him due to her ghost heritage. Her strident voice was in such contrast with her sweet, girl-next-door appearance that it could be shocking for those who saw her before they heard her.

"Hello Jayce. This is Liz. Liz this is Jayce."

"Oh, right, a recruit," Jayce said. She glanced at Liz for a moment before actually throwing up one hand in dismissal. "I just wanted to tell you that I haven't heard a thing about being reassigned."

"Out of HR? Out of Med Tech? Or both?" Dante asked.

"No, no, I don't mind either of those. I just don't want to monitor some of the employees that I have to monitor."

"Which employees would those be?"

"You know, the ones from Parabiology."

"Why do you have a problem monitoring them?" Dante knew what her answer would be but he wanted her to have to say it out loud.

"They're just … just … I can't understand them," Jayce said. "That clicking noise that the one thing makes when it talks."

"You're speaking of Geraldine?" Dante asked.

"Yes, whatever it's called," Jayce said, rolling her eyes.

"Geraldine has a translator. Doesn't it work?"

"Yeah, it works. But I can still hear it clicking and it's gross."

"I see."

"No, really, I'm not discriminating or anything, it's just that—well, you know, I'm more comfortable with the more human people. I'm okay with the freaks that come in, the ones that are mentally unstable, the abused women—"

Jayce stopped and looked at Liz, apparently just now taking in the state of her face.

"Sorry, no offense," she said.

"None taken," said Liz, in a voice cold enough to rival Kara's.

"Or you move me out of Med Tech and into IT or even Security," Jayce continued. "I have wicked skills in coding. Before I came here, I spent a lot of time trolling people in the darkest of the dark net, and worse."

"Why would you do that?" Liz asked.

Jayce rolled her eyes again. "Because I could," she said, turning back to Dante. "Listen, rather than wasting my time going to some school, I educated myself. I learned every language of coding that you were allowed to learn and had a hand in creating a few more. As a teenager, I was a hacker. I managed to hack a hospital once and disrupted their whole power grid. I was only sixteen at the time."

"That's very advanced." Dante wondered again about the wisdom of bringing this girl in-house.

"I know, I'm super advanced in tech," Jayce said excitedly. "I've also helped develop web interfaces for gaming. My dream job would be to work at the interface between gaming and AI. But all I'm doing here is just checking the HR systems, and the interface with the freaks downstairs."

"You are referring to Parabiology again?"

"Well, yeah, of course. Also, I'm really scared that they will send me down there in person one day. I don't think I could deal with that. It would probably give me PTSD or something. You know, they threatened to do that one day last week."

"Threatened? What exactly did they say?"

"Oh, I don't remember but something about needing me to go down to Parabiology to check the calibration on some of their electronic bio monitors that fed into the HR systems."

"That doesn't sound like a threat," Dante said. Liz whipped her head around to look at him. Whatever Liz had heard went unnoticed by Jayce.

"If I go to Parabiology, I'm sure they will make me talk to that horrible clicking creature. I can't imagine having to look at it. It's bad enough hearing it through the translator. They say she looks like a goddamned praying mantis. She might decide to eat my head or something."

Dante had let this conversation go on as long as it had because he thought it would be insightful for Liz. Jayce was obnoxious and entitled but she certainly didn't come off as a cult member. Still, he was losing patience with her. He was about to dismiss her when he had another thought.

"Geraldine is one of the kindest creatures here," Dante said to Jayce.

"Yeah, right," Jayce muttered. Clearly being a Cambion did not guarantee emotional intelligence.

"I'm sorry, I just can't with those people, and I could be so much more helpful in IT or Security," she said, smiling now and dropping one shoulder to allow her shirt to slip down, revealing a bra strap. Dante might have laughed at how silly this was if he hadn't already been so disgusted with her.

"Fine, leave it with me, I'll ask about it," he said. "I can't promise anything."

"But you run this place," Jayce whined.

"Kara actually runs this place. Would you like me to take this directly to her?"

Jayce paled.

"No, no, that's fine. Just, whatever you can do," she said, backing away. Still, she couldn't help sighing and throwing up her hands as she walked off.

Dante made a mental note to ask for her to be moved into a job where she would work alone. Very few people there deserved being subjected to her on a daily basis.

Still, as he watched her sit down in a chair across the room, he felt troubled. Something about the conversation had been unsettling but he didn't have time to analyze it just now.

Chapter Seven

In Love with Egypt

"I'm sorry about her," Dante said.

"She can see you too?" Liz asked.

"Unfortunately, yes. Her genetics make it easier for her to see ghosts."

"So everyone here is genetically different?"

"Yes. But for some it has been significantly harder than for others."

"Like that woman Geraldine?"

"Yes, Geraldine has had a difficult life starting at her very conception. After giving birth, her mother took one look at her and threw her into a trash bin. She should have died there, but she had such a will to live that she survived days until someone from the Office found her and brought her here."

"Why would her mother do that?" Liz asked. Her eyes were becoming moist. Yes, Dante liked this woman a lot.

"Her mother can't be blamed too much," Dante said. "She was artificially inseminated against her will with an egg that had been altered. Her mother was essentially a prisoner at a facility that was designed just for that. Geraldine's mother was forced to produce several offspring. We suspect it was done to create intelligent and unstoppable killing agents."

"That's horrible. What sort of place would do that?" Liz asked.

"An evil one."

"And you saved her?"

"Yes, they designed her to kill, but they failed. Geraldine is extraordinary. She is kind, caring, and self-sacrificing to a fault. She is so kind that she has become the official liaison for Parabiology with the rest of the Office. And she is an unofficial mother for each new employee in Parabiology. She is even the godmother to a few of the children born here in the Office, both biological and parabiological beings," Dante said. "Her spirit is lovely and warm."

"She sounds wonderful."

"She is."

"So you are saying that she is the way she is because of her genes? Is this why they wanted her—this other place?"

"Strictly speaking, they wanted her mother because her mother had different genes, and these genes were altered and enhanced to produce Geraldine. But most people here are more like Geraldine's mother than Geraldine herself."

"Okay," Liz said quietly, "so how did we end up genetically different then?"

"The reason for that is hard to explain … and might be harder for you to hear," Dante said. "So let me start with telling you a bit about the Office as a whole."

Dante paused as Sheila from Accounting walked by and gave him a little wave.

"We are an organization, but we don't have a real name," Dante began. "We refer to ourselves as 'the Office.' Those who don't like us call us 'demons' or 'the demon cult.' What we are, at least in part, is an aggregate of subsidiaries of various institutions and companies—mainly hospitals, labs, charitable institutions, and financial companies. We exist in these forms because we need immediate awareness and free access to emergency health situations when they happen, and then the money to address them."

"And what do you do?"

This was always the hardest question. Dante had to be honest but not too honest. Too much information hurt people but too little would put them in danger.

"We monitor people—people like us and like you," he said. "People who, by the nature of their DNA, have souls we believe to be more loosely connected to their bodies. This gives them vulnerabilities and capabilities that need watching."

Liz cocked her head to the side, regarding him. She was pondering her next question. The look of an abused woman had dropped from her face. What had replaced it was a look of intense curiosity.

Dante smiled. He appreciated people who measured their words.

Looking around him, he saw that Jayce was now sitting with her stocking feet on a dark oak table, playing some sort of video game on her phone. Video games were forbidden at the Office, and most people would have been terrified to break an official rule, but not Jayce. She was arrogant and oversure of her own abilities. Her parents had owned a publishing empire. She ended up here because her mother committed suicide, and her father had believed it was Jayce's fault and tried to kill her. Dante could resonate with the man's feelings. She was proof that one didn't need values to be accepted here. At the other end of the room—and the spectrum—was Sheila, his friend from Accounting, who was now enjoying a coffee and staring at the blank space between herself and the wall. Sheila was charming, in an awkward sort of way. She could see him, but she could see a great deal more as well. At the moment, she was having a conversation with a young male ghost in Atlantean clothing. Sheila had been heavily drugged in a mental institution and had attempted suicide a few times when Kara decided to pull her out. It took her a few years to settle in but now she was fully functional and more than ready to make up for the time she had lost. If she had been able to touch Dante, he was pretty sure she would have cornered him in some secluded hallway by now. But she wasn't, for which he was supremely grateful.

"Okay, how do you find these people, without testing?" Liz finally asked, leaning forward.

"Some identify themselves," Dante replied. "Some of them are people who claim to astral travel. Some are psychics. Some are witches. In truth, most of the people claiming these sorts of things are full of shit, but a few aren't. Usually, the ones with the greatest differences are the quietest. They are bank tellers and schoolteachers and corporate executives. They are often patients at mental health facilities. Having medical problems themselves, some are in medicine. We identify these people like we identified you, through blood work and observation. What they all have in common is a genetic code that creates a looseness of connection between soul and body. This lack of close connection, and the reasons for it, can have various effects on people, from physical to psychological to hormonal."

"Like X-men or something," Liz muttered.

"More like 'or something,'" Dante replied. "Science fiction movies glamourize this sort of thing. The truth of genetic difference is much more horrific and much richer."

"Horrific?"

"Yes. It's not like the movies. Most people don't have superpowers like you see in them. Most of our genetic differences aren't obviously physical. What powers we have tend to be more subtle, like being able to blend into the background and have no one notice you."

Liz smiled slightly and looked down, poking at her coffee again.

"You don't become invisible per se, but people don't notice you, so the result is the same," Dante continued. "People don't bring down lightning from the sky or open portals through time."

Lie number one, he thought.

"Most of the traits we deal with are mental or spiritual, or sometimes hormonal. But these traits can be powerful nonetheless."

"Like mind control?"

"Yes—and no," Dante said. "We have people who can manipulate others with their minds. But the result is subtle and the price they pay for doing it is extreme. Individuals do this by exchanging part of their soul with the soul of the target. Sometimes this can be retrieved, sometimes it can't. If it can't, they remain mentally connected to the other person forever, unless drastic measures are taken. So they pay for the gift with their minds and their souls, literally. Doing this makes them even more porous and more vulnerable to other types of attack."

Liz sat back in her seat.

"If it's that terrible, would anyone ever use it? This skill? Or gift? Or whatever?" she asked.

"Some can't control it. Those who can control it try to bury it," Dante replied. "But, in rare circumstances, individuals will actually exploit their own abilities regardless of the cost. Some argue that life would not have given them such a gift if they weren't meant to use it, an argument that has some merit. In rarer circumstances, we may ask people here to use it, but we take every precaution. But mental manipulation is just one example of the sort of symptom that might come of being genetically different. Not all symptoms are that bad, but many are. So our goal is to monitor these people and to try to help them if they need it. We *do not* contact them unless it is absolutely necessary. We want them to be integrated into society."

"But sometimes you do contact them?" Liz asked.

"Yes, sometimes we have to intercede, either for the good of the person, or the good of society."

"What would cause you to intercede?" Liz asked. Her eyes were bright.

She's smart, this one.

"Mostly, we intercede when it comes to viral infections. We study viruses in great detail here. This is because the people that we watch are more susceptible to dangerous viral infections."

"How does the gene thing have anything to do with getting a virus?"

"Because Cambion have unusual DNA, or mixed DNA, that is more susceptible to hosting unusual viruses … as well as other things."

"Cambion?"

"That's what we call people who have this sort of genetic structure. This structure makes them more likely to be able to carry and transmit particularly virulent forms of viruses, including those not normally capable of attaching to humans. This is how viruses can cross from animals to people. If one of these transmutes in one of our kind and then gets loose in the general population—well, then that is when we can have a global pandemic. We try to keep such pandemics from happening."

"So what do you do if one of us gets such a virus?" Liz asked.

Us. Liz didn't notice her use of this word, but Dante did. She was attaching, so he needed to be both truthful and careful.

"We would keep the virus from spreading," he said.

"Am I infected?

"No."

"But I am one of these people? The loosely connected ones?"

"Yes."

"Okay." Liz was thinking things through, and her thoughts were registering on her swollen face.

"Are you going to allow me to leave? If I want to?" she asked suddenly.

"Of course," Dante lied. "You still don't quite believe what I am saying, do you?"

"That you are a ghost? That I am some sort of mutant with special abilities?" Liz shook her head. "No, I don't believe it. I would like to, but I know what I am. I'm a slightly overweight, average-looking woman with a crappy, underpaying job and an abusive husband. And I was weak enough to let myself get into that situation, even though I am smart enough to know better. So what you are saying sounds amazing and maybe it exists somewhere, but not for me."

Her eyes teared up.

"Okay," Dante said. "Let me do an experiment, just to give you a different perspective. I want you to keep your eyes on me and not move from this spot for at least three minutes, no matter what happens, okay?"

"Okay."

Dante nodded at her and disappeared.

Dante drifted out of the coffee shop, and up several layers to a spot on the higher resonance. He found himself on the roof of the building. The sun had set, and the stars were bright above him, brighter than city light would allow at lower resonances.

Abi, one of his dearest friends, was crouched on the roof staring at the sky. Abi was an Egyptian ghoul who had befriended Dante just after his death—and had saved his sanity.

He saw Dante and smiled.

"So cometh the superstar."

"Hardly," Dante said.

"It's a beautiful night, could I tempt you into having a fly?" Abi asked.

Dante was suddenly awash in memories of the dark nights, the cold wind and the wet smell of cemetery dirt. His time with Abi had been both dreadful and sweet. It was a time when Dante thought himself damned as a creature who could neither live in the world nor reincarnate out of it. It was Abi who gave him, if not a joy for life itself, then an example of how a creature with so many reasons to hate life could find wonder and beauty in it. Abi had made him feel both loved and accepted for who he was. At the time, he had felt completely unworthy of this love. Rather than giving in to that feeling, he had chosen to push against it and make himself worthy of Abi's friendship and love. This was the start of his real afterlife. But he could not have become what he became without those years with Abi.

It struck him that Abi was exactly the sort of creature that Jayce would call a freak. Normally, he would dismiss a creature like Jayce from his mind the minute she left, but something about her wasn't sitting right with him. Something about their conversation was lighting up the red parts of his brain.

"Something disturbs you, my friend?" Abi asked.

"Just a bad conversation with a resident," Dante replied. "A very entitled, very obnoxious resident."

Abi made a coughing noise that could have been a laugh or a growl, or perhaps a bit of both.

"Such a resident must be deep in the bowels of their own delusions to display such an abhorrent attitude with you."

"She is certainly delusional, but also rude, racist, misogynistic, and species-ist."

"Would you like me to realign her behavior, or form, into something more fitting, or perhaps more entertaining?" Abi asked. His huge, bright eyes belied the fury that slept inside him. Anyone who had ever seen Abi in a battle would been hard-pressed to ever get that vision out of their head. It was both terrible and beautiful.

"No, it's fine. She's a minor problem that I'll come back to when I have more time," Dante replied.

"So shall we go for a fly?"

"I can't, I'm with a recruit at the moment."

"Really? It seems to me that you are here with me."

"I disappeared for just a moment, to prove a point," Dante said.

"Ah, they don't believe yet?" Abi asked.

"No, not yet."

"They would if they could see me." Abi laughed.

Abi looked shockingly like a sphinx. He had a human head and lion body, but he also had tentacles for hair and mandibles that protruded from his jaws. In spite of this, he had a gallant countenance and did well with new recruits.

"Oh, she can see you," Dante said.

"She can? Does she have ghost parentage then?" Abi asked, beginning to knead his paws on the roof.

"At a minimum. She's an odd one. She could actually touch me. And she hugged Kara."

"She did *what*?"

"She hugged Kara."

"She must be truly extraordinary in both perception and bravery. That such humans exist reminds me of just how noble and exceptional humans can be. I would like to meet this extraordinary being sometime."

A little idea lit up Dante's thoughts.

"Actually, would you mind popping in for just a second?" Dante asked. "That might speed things up a bit."

Abi smiled, making the mandibles at his jawline curve inward, frighteningly close to his eyes.

"But of course, it would be a great honor to both help my dearest comrade and to meet such a bright soul."

The next moment, Dante was back sitting in his chair at the café. Liz jumped when she saw him. She shrieked and dropped her coffee cup when she saw Abi appear next to him. Abi's eyes widened as he immediately bent low and put one paw out in front of him.

"I am Abi," he said, bowing his head deeply. "I am enchanted to meet you. Dante told me of your bravery and warmth, but he failed to warn me of your radiant beauty."

"Liz," she said, sticking her hand out and then quickly withdrawing it. "Sorry, I … er … I …"

"A beautiful smile need never apologize," Abi said. "A beautiful soul smiling out from it will light a thousand dark nights and pierce even the most ancient and hardened of hearts."

Liz was staring at Abi with an expression of shock, and something else.

"Thanks, Abi," Dante said.

Abi's golden brow furrowed but he nodded.

"Alas, he dismisses me prematurely, so I must take my leave. I hope to have the gift of your presence again soon," Abi said, bowing again, his eyes lingering on Liz.

Dante coughed and Abi seemed to be jolted back to himself. He then nodded at Dante and disappeared.

Dante looked at Liz. She was sitting stone-still. This was the moment that people either fainted, screamed, ran, or froze. Liz did none of these things. Instead, a small smile played on her lips.

"So I guess Kara wasn't kidding when she said that I wouldn't have to worry about Michael attacking me here."

Dante laughed out loud.

"No. She wasn't kidding."

"Maybe I'm not crazy after all," Liz said in a small voice, more to herself. "Probably I am. Still, there are worse ways to be crazy."

She stopped for a moment, then looked up at Dante and met his eyes.

"I would like to stay," she said.

"Excellent," Dante said, relieved. "Let me have one of our HR people come up to see you. They are slightly more frightening than Abi, but only slightly."

For a moment Liz looked shocked, then she smiled when she realized it was a joke.

"I need to meet with Kara now, but I will catch up with you soon. And just let Joe know if you need to reach me."

Liz nodded, and with that Dante focused on his memory of Kara's face, and his desire drew him to her.

As he sped forward, for a moment he saw something drop behind him. It was just for a second, but it looked like a small black blob.

And it looked like it had dropped from him.

Chapter Eight

Lightning Strikes Twice

When Dante appeared suddenly in the Microbiology lab, Dr. Jeremy Lepri didn't bat an eye. He was used to Dante's comings and goings. Lepri was a thin, shockingly handsome man with caramel-colored skin and salt-and-pepper dreadlocks. His movie star looks were offset by his quick, twitchy movements and tendency to chew on himself—nails, lips, fingers.

He had not only always been able to see Dante, but after working with him for ten or so years, he had managed to train his senses to both see and hear him. For Dante, this meant that he didn't need to go through the annoyance of being translated by someone else.

Lepri and Kara were leaning over a messy counter covered with test tubes, microscopes, and a couple of Bunsen burners that Lepri kept for nostalgia and reheating food. They were staring at a sheaf of papers scattered across the countertop. Lepri looked up at Dante, his eyes alight.

"Ah, now that Dante is here, shall I bring you up to speed on the blood work and samples?" Lepri said, bouncing from one foot to the other.

"Give us just a second, will you, Jeremy?" Kara said.

Lepri's face fell. He was obviously very excited about something and was bursting at the seams to discuss it. He had never had that stoic, uber-analytical, Spock-like quality that Dante expected from life science guys. Even at fifty, he had a twenty-year-old's level of exuberance. He also had a twenty-year-old's level of guile. Right now, he had shuffled off to sit at his computer, where he was sulking and sighing audibly. Kara rolled her eyes and snorted.

"I checked with the Parabiology people about the Manassas virus," she said. "It turns out that they had some old blood work on the Manassas kid—the new one. He was logged into their written records but when we tried to find him in the system, he didn't come up. We knew that if they had his blood work, he must have had a watcher at some point. That's the only way they would have been able to collect this. What we don't know is why his files aren't in the system. So the para guys were able to use some of their time assets to retroactively identify watchers for both Manassas boys."

"Were they able to contact them?" Dante asked.

"Not yet. But they are still working on it, and collecting more records, as we speak."

"Then you fared better than I did," Dante said. "IT did have records, but no information on watchers. Security and Finance had no record of their existence."

"That's not like Joe."

"No, it's not. So I'd like to see the printout of the watchers' names when we get a chance. Also, Joe should conduct a full sweep of all our systems."

"You think there could have been a systems breach?" Kara asked. She didn't mention the Academy, but she didn't need to. Most of the world didn't know the Office existed. Anyone who did know about them would be too afraid to try anything—with the exception of an outlier at the Academy.

"No, it's just a precaution, it's probably just a system glitch," Dante replied quickly.

"Okay, I'll text Parabiology now to send what records they have on these boys." She pulled out her phone. The energy coming off Kara felt like a cool breeze.

"Did you see Liz's blood work?" Dante asked, changing the subject.

"Yes. She's Cambion, for sure," Kara replied. "I mean, she can see you, that's all the proof we really needed. But add in her ability to get past our security and actually touch you, that makes it beyond doubt. I want her assigned to a unit directly reporting to us. I think she's talented. What's her background?"

"Orphaned. Raped at university. She didn't say much more than that."

"So you think she has air elemental parentage?"

"Not sure. I couldn't tell from her blood work and her human side is very guarded. But she can see me, and she saw Abi. So maybe she has ghost parentage."

"You introduced her to Abi?" she gasped. Her expression made him a bit defensive.

"Abi is very friendly," he said.

"Abi is one of your 8th-floor ghost friends." Kara snorted.

"Strictly, Abi is a ghoul, not a ghost."

"Maybe, but he spends too much time with the inhabitants of the 8th," she said sharply.

"They're not bad people, they are just stuck there, for better or for worse," Dante said, focusing on picking up a random test tube and examining the contents, avoiding eye contact. He hated this particular discussion.

"Dante, they should be gone," Kara said, a bit more gently. "And maybe they aren't bad people now, but a few of them were most assuredly bad people in life or they wouldn't have ended up stuck."

"So was I," he replied, looking up and meeting her gaze directly.

"No. You were stuck because of your parentage. Your behavior was the product of your culture. What was 'bad' about you was bad about everything and everyone around you, it had nothing to do with your soul."

"So I was naively bad?" Dante asked, with a dark laugh.

"Yes, and that makes a difference," Kara replied, with no change of seriousness in her tone.

"Maybe that's true for them as well. We don't know yet."

"Fine. Maybe. Let's not argue this one again. We never agree on it and we're not going to. But let's be very clear that other ghosts are *not* like you. And the only reason I allow them here is because you insist on it." Kara said this fiercely.

You allow them here because we need them and because they are world-class hunters and trackers, Dante thought to himself, but saw no value in voicing that fact again.

"Well, back to Liz, how did she handle it? The Abi introduction," Kara asked, reaching out and touching his hand.

Dante relaxed. That was his one piece of good news for the day.

"Shockingly well. She was startled, but her response was to say that she wanted to stay," he said.

Kara laughed and clapped her hands.

"That's great."

Dante knew that Kara already liked Liz and hadn't wanted to have to kill her. If she stayed, it wouldn't come to that.

Lepri was now tapping his fingers loudly on the lab counter as he stared at his computer, pulling up various windows and scrolling though data.

"So, about the virus that attacked us in Manassas, I was just going to have a chat with Jeremy about what he found out about the two Cambion boys and the reporter," Kara said, raising her voice. Lepri stood and came back toward them.

"What were you about to tell me, Jeremy?"

Lepri began bouncing on the balls of his feet. He adjusted his glasses, eyes gleaming with excitement.

"So, to understand the virus, it was important to study the three people it might have infected," he began. "That being the recent Manassas kid, one David Spanarkle. Kenneth Jones, the kid eighteen years ago. And Grace Rogers, the news reporter."

"So what were you able to collect?" Kara asked.

"We were lucky, and I managed to get autopsy reports for all three," Lepri replied. "I have been looking at them all day. Those, plus the virus samples taken from both Spanarkle and Grace."

He sat down in front of his computer and pulled up a photo of a fuzzy, reddish blob. Dante and Kara moved to stand on either side of him.

"It looks like the thing that attacked you," Kara muttered.

"This is the active infection I found in the reporter. It's weird as hell, but I'll get back to that," Lepri said. "Weirdly, I saw nothing interesting in the recent blood work of the new kid, Spanarkle. He didn't have any active bacterial infections. He showed no traces of viral infection. All his blood and immune markers were in the normal range, for Cambion at least. So I couldn't figure it out. Then I thought, maybe it's something that was latent, so I used a FISH-Flow."

"What's a FISH-Flow?" Dante asked, staring at the thing on the screen.

"It's a method that uses fluorescent probes to detect specific RNA sequences within cells, helping us identify latent viruses. I combined that with—oh, you will love this—it's elegant, really."

"Jeremy, English," Kara said, snapping her fingers. "We have neither the time nor the talent for your level of microbiology. What did you do and what does it tell us?"

Lepri sighed and rolled his eyes.

"In short, I forced a gene expression, designed to make a latent virus express itself so we can see it. And sure enough, Spanarkle had a latent virus in him. I called friends in the CDC and really lucked out. Someone had been on the ball eighteen years ago and froze a blood sample of Kenneth Jones back then. When I subjected it to the same processes, the same thing happened. They all had it."

"Kenneth, David, and Grace all had the same virus?" Kara asked. "That nasty thing we saw?"

"Or some version of it, yes."

"So it's not a one-off infection?" Dante asked.

Lepri shook his head. "Doesn't look like it."

"Shit," muttered Kara, one tendril of hair escaping the rest and reaching toward Lepri. Instinctively, he rolled his chair away from it.

"It's even more than that," he said. "I forced expression on an eighteen-year-old sample that had been *frozen*. So, whatever it is, it survived freezing for eighteen years, so it's a tough bastard. And in all three, this is what the expression looked like."

He pointed to the screen at the fuzzy, rust-colored blob. Dante leaned in. What he was seeing on the screen did look disturbingly like the initial form of the thing that had attacked them at the TV station.

"It doesn't look like a virus."

"No, it doesn't, does it? The damn thing is the size of a bacterium. It's bigger than the mimivirus. And look at that." He pointed to the center of the blob. "It has ribosomes and plasmids, like a bacterium. I did some other tests, and it has structures for protein metabolism as well. And there are other things in here that I can't even begin to categorize."

Lepri was excitedly waving his hands around. "Even crazier is that when it's active, it tries to insert itself into sections of junk DNA! Junk DNA and only junk DNA."

The temperature in the room dropped a couple of degrees very quickly. Dante glanced at Kara, and she shook her head ever so slightly.

"So that's unusual?" she asked softly.

"That's unheard of. Junk DNA is noncoding sections of DNA. Why would a virus attach there if it doesn't code for anything?"

Only consciousness, Dante thought, as Kara slipped her hand into his.

"Does it succeed in attaching to the sections of junk DNA?" he asked.

"I don't think so, at least nothing is produced from it if it does," Lepri replied.

"Can you dig into that a bit more?"

Lepri's eyebrows shot up. "Is there something—" he began, but Kara cut him off.

"Does it do anything else unusual?"

"No, not that I can see. But I need to test it to see how to kill it and how it degrades. I will get back on that. But it's definitely weird."

"Do you think that this virus is what caused the boys to shoot up their schools?" Dante asked.

"It could be. It has some similar components to both neuroinvasive and neurovirulent viruses."

"Jeremy, this thing was visible outside of the reporter woman's body—and it attacked Dante," Kara said.

"What?" Jeremy swiveled in his chair to look at her.

"And it was huge," Kara said. "Only someone with a very corrupted code, or particularly vulnerable Cambion, could host that kind of virus."

"Was the reporter Cambion?" Lepri asked.

"We don't know. By the time I saw her there wasn't much left of her insides, but the two boys were," Kara replied.

"So it could be targeting Cambion," Lepri said, chewing on his nail.

"Yes, but there's more," Dante said. "It was fully formed at a resonance just above human but had the breadth to get high enough to actually touch me."

"It could touch you ..." Lepri ran a hand over his forehead.

"Even worse, it attacked us as if it had purpose. It also tried to speak through the body of the reporter. It moved her around like she was a marionette."

"Speak—shit," muttered Lepri.

"Do you think it's man-made?" Kara's voice was too calm, which was a bad sign.

Lepri shook his head.

"We might have the sophistication to engineer something like that now, but not eighteen years ago, the time of the first sample."

Kara nodded and her shoulders relaxed noticeably, but Lepri sighed.

"Listen, just because it wasn't directly engineered doesn't mean that the Academy wasn't involved somehow. I'm just saying that they couldn't have engineered it *de novo*. It doesn't mean they couldn't have found it and manipulated it."

Kara's shoulders returned to their tenser state.

"Can you also get a medical history for the five years before each of these kids died?" Dante asked. "As well as the reporter? And any additional history of illnesses, mental or otherwise?"

"On it," Lepri said, turning to his computer.

"Also, could we get a universal scan of reported 'possessions' with the same symptoms that the reporter exhibited?" Dante said.

"Of course."

"We will want to check all possible possessions to see if it was really a viral infection," Dante continued.

A sharp ping from Kara's phone interrupted the conversation.

"Oh, I just got an email from the para guys with the document showing the watchers for both the Manassas boys, and what we have on them," Kara said. "You want to look at it?"

Dante nodded.

"Jeremy, can you print this out for Dante, it's easier for him than dealing with my phone."

Lepri nodded.

Dante hated cell phones. Computers were sticky enough, from an energy and current perspective but cell phones were the worst. Sometimes, he couldn't get them detached from himself without help.

"Jeremy, how contagious is this thing?" Dante asked.

"Oh, that's the one piece of good news," Lepri replied. "Preliminary data suggests the virus isn't easily transmitted between individuals. However, its ability to manifest physically and attack indicates an unusual mode of action. Oh, and it doesn't seem to be airborne."

"But I saw it infect the reporter, and it came for me," Dante replied. Kara squeezed his hand, it was involuntary. She was remembering that moment.

"Maybe that has more to do with the reporter than the virus. You said that it was huge, maybe it can only transmit to a particularly holey type of target."

"Like Cambion?" Dante asked.

"Maybe," Lepri replied, chewing his lip. "I'll do a screen of the people in the building, just to be sure."

"They are going to love another blood draw," Dante muttered.

"The weekly one is tomorrow anyway; I'll just have to rush out an identifying marker."

At that moment, Lepri's phone rang.

"Kara, it's Joe, he's looking for you and he sounds—agitated."

Kara took the phone and walked to the other side of the room.

"Here's the watchers for the Manassas boys," Lepri said, opening the document Kara had sent on his screen.

When Dante saw the names, he felt his stomach drop.

"Something wrong?" Lepri asked, looking up at Dante but they were interrupted.

"We have a problem," Kara said, as she got off the phone. Her eyes were noticeably lighter blue.

"Joe decided to do a full universal sweep of all the caches related to these kids' files. It seems that the Manassas kids' files had been moved into a hidden junk mail folder. Something buried in the systems and password protected. When he got it open, he found other emails—ones that seemed to have been routed there directly. They never reached the intended person."

"How many?" Dante asked.

"Hundreds," Kara replied. Her eyes were now ice blue, making the iris less distinguishable against the white.

No one said the word "hacked." It was too incendiary for Kara at that moment, and even Lepri must have sensed that.

"The emails in the hidden junk, who were they from?" Dante asked.

"Our watchers—a whole bunch of our watchers," Kara replied. She was shoving the files she had brought with her into a large handbag.

Her voice was getting flatter, and more than one strand of her hair was now moving. "Some of these emails apparently identified the Cambion they were watching by name."

"Shit," muttered Lepri.

"So the identity of these Cambion may have been compromised?" Dante asked.

"Yes," Kara said. "The identity of *all* our Cambion could be compromised. We can't assume that anyone in the field is safe now. We need to start identifying and contacting all watchers."

Kara's voice was becoming less and less emotional rather than more so, indicating that she was being pulled more out of the human side of her nature.

"Joe has shut down all external computer links until he gets to the root of this," she said. "Only you and I will be able to link to the system for the moment. And he has a special passcode for us."

"There's something else," Dante said softly. "The watchers assigned for both David and Kenneth were ghosts."

"What? We never use ghosts as watchers because they aren't reliable enough."

"We only use them with Cambion who have particularly vulnerable codes," Dante replied. "We do that because ghosts can be on the job 24/7 and they can make it back to us in milliseconds if a problem arises. Both of the watchers assigned to these boys were completely reliable. They wouldn't just disappear."

"Great," Kara replied. "So we have two supposedly reliable watchers who have gone AWOL, leaving Cambion unprotected. And emails from other watchers that have gone unread. All with some weird new virus out there that might target them."

She didn't mention the Academy, but the Director's presence hung in the air around them like a bad smell.

"Did Joe open all the emails in the junk file?" Dante asked.

"He is in the process of doing that, but some of the files are self-destructing when opened," Kara said. "He also said that most of the ones he has managed to open were from watchers assigned to wards classified level 5 for vulnerability."

And some of the most powerful and vulnerable Cambion are level 5. That means this could be a huge mess, and you are at the end of a cycle, Dante thought, but didn't speak it out loud. This was not the time or place.

"Don't worry about the virus," Lepri said softly. "I'll understand it soon. We don't know for sure that it targets Cambion. It might just target any genetic vulnerability. And the fact that it doesn't seem to transmit from person to person easily makes it less of a threat. If it is a bigger threat, I'll design a vaccine."

Lepri's eyes were glued to his screen, and for a moment Dante was reminded of Lepri as a kid. The genius kid they found in an abusive foster home who had figured out how to make genetic alterations in his foster brothers using a self-made CRSPR kit.

"I know you'll figure it out, Jeremy. I have total faith in you," Kara said, as if reading Dante's thoughts. "So I feel completely comfortable leaving you with this. Just as I am leaving Joe with our computer issue … for the moment."

Despite her words, Kara's eyes were icy, and her hair was caressing things on the shelves beside her. If there was an internal hack, someone would pray for death. If it was external, it was a bigger problem, and many people would pray for death.

"All that can wait for a couple of days," she said. "Right now, you and I need to go."

"Why and where do we need to go?" Dante asked. The skin under Kara's eyes was becoming shadowed again, which meant she was in a lot of pain. He felt the age-old desire to take her in his arms and take the pain away. They were supposed to take her to clean her out yesterday.

"We need to do a world tour," Kara replied. "And we will start in Richmond, Virginia. One of the first things that Joe was able to extract from that pile of messages was a series of SOS messages from one of our watchers. They're six months old and we haven't heard a thing since. I told Joe to figure out how the fuck no one in HR noticed that some of our watchers had just stopped reporting in. Anyway, the last place this Cambion was seen was in Richmond, Virginia." Kara pulled out her phone and glanced at it. "His name is Lazlo—apparently another ghost."

"I know Lazlo," Dante said. "He wouldn't SOS unless it was serious."

"An unexpected SOS came to us from a trusted watcher, and we didn't reply," Kara said, turning for the door.

"Also, what about Amelie McCormick?" Dante asked.

Kara stopped in her tracks.

"What about her?"

"She had a ghost watcher as well."

"Shit." Kara snapped. "Shit. Shit. Shit. Shit."

Suddenly, she froze. Her eyes were now completely white and the temperature in the room dropped a good ten degrees.

"Kara, my love," Dante said, reaching out to touch her.

"Is she okay?" Lepri asked, moving toward her. As he got close, he began to cough. At first, it sounded like a normal cough, but it quickly escalated to hacking and retching. Lepri dropped to his knees and began to gag.

Dante grabbed Kara and dematerialized with her in his arms.

In the sliver of a moment that it took to materialize back in their bedroom, Kara's temperature had dropped enough that her skin felt like ice. Luckily, this cold seemed to be contained to her and her immediate environment, but that might not last.

The fear that had been born when he saw that blob bury itself into Kara's flesh at the shabby TV studio now flared. And if Kara was infected, the world, the entire story, would be impacted. Lepri's response to her only underscored this.

He had to clean her out, and now.

Dante pulled Kara more tightly into his arms. She didn't fight him, she simply lay her head on his chest.

He pulled her toward the inside of him. This act was contradictory in the way of deeper realities. As he pulled himself and Kara deeper into his essence, he also expanded their presence across the story. It was the fulcrum of the spiral of their story. It was in this place of the infinitesimally small and the incomprehensibly large that Dante found the hallway. Or his entrance to the hallway.

Dante's entrance to the hallway was tailored to him, as it must have been for the .001 percent of people capable of entering it. It changed every time he entered, but what remained constant was the perfection of the dimensions. Everything was aligned and many things were aligned to Kara. The beautiful arches were in symmetry with the curve of Kara's ribcage. The sapphire blue decorations on the obsidian doors matched the blue of her eyes. The dim lighting was a testament to her depth. And yet, today, there was something slightly off in the angles. The light was brighter than it should have been, almost as if it were trying too hard. The brightness cast shadows where there had never been shadows before.

As they came fully into consciousness in this place, Kara jerked.

"I can't stay here," she said, looking around.

"You won't," Dante said, taking her hand. "We just need to do what we have to do."

"No," Kara said, pulling her hand away. "I won't."

"My love, we don't have a choice," Dante said, dropping his pitch and taking her hand again. He stepped closer to her. It was better if she went of her own accord, but he would drag her if he had to.

"This isn't right." Kara's voice was icy but her eyes were back to a more normal blue.

"You know I hate this as much as you. If I could take your place, I would. But I can't. And the fuller you become, the harder this is. You know this."

"Yes, I know that but listen to me, this is *not* right! I cannot!"

"You can't stay like you are. Everything depends on you. If you fail, the story fails."

"And if I am stolen, the story is damned!" Kara pulled away from him, and began to back down the hallway. "We have to get out of here. We have to get out now. It's dangerous to be here, even for seconds."

"My love," Dante said, walking slowly toward her, measuring his tone of voice, his words, and his gait.

"This is *not* you," Kara said, her head jerking back and forth, her eyes scanning the hallway for something, or seeing something, that Dante could not see.

"This is a carnival mask. It's a cheat. It's a ruse, it's a monster, it's a magician's trick."

Kara's words stung him, but what she said was true.

"Yes, I am all those things," Dante said softly, "and yet, I still love you. I still cherish you and I would still damn myself to keep you safe."

"No, Dante … no," Kara said, and with those words, she launched herself into his arms. Her body was no longer cold. It was now as warm as his own, and she kissed him fiercely. He tried to pull back from her but she wrapped one leg around him and used it to pull him even closer.

"Bring me back," she whispered in his ear.

"We have to go—" he began, but she blocked his mouth with another kiss.

"Not now, not in this place," she said between kisses.

Dante could feel his resonance dropping. Their passion was an earthly thing and could not survive long at this higher resonance.

"We have to take you. We have to clean you," he said, trying to maintain some composure despite what was building between them, a passion that could and had changed worlds.

"There is an infection, I know," Kara said softly, as she pushed her body up against his. "But you cannot clean me here."

"Kara," he whispered, "this is the only place I can clear you."

He tried to hold on to himself but his resonance suddenly dropped so quickly that he felt it crash through his energy centers until he found himself back on their bed with Kara in his arms. And once there, they connected in the way that they always had, forgetting everything, forgetting everyone, forgetting even reality.

When their haze lifted, Kara turned to face him. She was now clear-eyed.

"I guess we needed that," she said with a little laugh.

She didn't remember, he could see it in her eyes, but she never did. He had failed to do the one thing he most needed to do.

"I needed that," Kara continued. "I needed a moment to ground myself after hearing all that."

She sat up and sighed deeply as she rolled her head, stretching her neck.

"We need to go to Richmond. If Lazlo is as reliable as you think, then we need to know why he sent an SOS, what he said and why he hasn't reported back in since. And then we need to do a world tour to check on all the others."

In Dante's mind, he saw Lazlo as he had been in life—a soldier, and a decorated one.

"And we need to check on Amelie McCormick," Kara said. "I can do that first."

"No, let me do that," Dante replied. Kara's connection to Amelie was something she was unaware of and this would not be a good time to awaken those memories.

"Thank you, my lover," she whispered, as she leaned forward and hugged him. "Go, and come back to me quickly."

"I am never away," Dante replied in a hoarse growl, and then threw himself into the upper winds.

As he dematerialized, he heard the words Kara had said in the hallway.

There is an infection, I know.

It was as he feared. The virus had infected Kara. That had happened before, but clearing her had always solved the problem. What was different this time was not that she was infected, or that she hated going, but that she was actively fighting to keep him from taking her. This meant two very bad things. The first was simply that he had not been able to clear her. The second was that, to make her fight him, the virus must be something that impacted behavior—just like the virus they saw at the TV station.

He needed to take her back soon, but he had to be quicker, or she had to be unconscious.

If she had the presence of mind to fight him, it would never work. She was too strong.

Chapter Nine

Amelie Embraced

Dante's concern about Amelie had been threefold. As he told Kara, he was concerned that she had a ghost watcher, and if her ghost watcher was missing it would leave a very powerful and very vulnerable Cambion open to attack. He didn't voice his other two concerns. The first was that the missing ghosts could mean that their ghost network had possibly been infiltrated. This was possible but hard to determine, given the nature of many ghosts. He would need to run that down himself. The second was that, as the result of a missing watcher, Amelie and many others might have already fallen into the embrace of the Academy. In Amelie's case, he was angry at himself for not checking on her sooner, but time ran differently for him. It seemed like only yesterday that he and Kara had unmade Clovis. Eighteen years was a blink of an eye for Dante and Kara, but a lot could happen to humans in a couple of decades.

Fortunately, Dante was able to locate Amelie in the same way that he had always been able to locate Kara, by something like smell. He only had this ability for souls that came from a certain lineage.

When he dropped into the lower plane, he found himself in London, standing in front of All Souls Church. The steeple of the church rose up toward a flat black, starless sky, accented with puffy white clouds that would have been more at home drifting across a blue sky and sunbeams. The streetlights were on but dimmed and the only light or color came from the blue light on the BT Tower in the distance, giving the whole scene an eerie, unnatural quality. The sky told him that a storm was approaching; what Dante didn't know was whether this weather came from nature, or something existing slightly outside of nature, something that existed closer in nature to him.

Across from him was a stately, luxury hotel. The entrance glowed with a golden light that escaped from the hotel's interior, lighting up golden accents that decorated the marble of the archway and columns that framed the door. Orbs of white light were situated on both columns, lighting up the name of the hotel, written in gold. A Union Jack flag on one side waved in the gentle breeze. There was a staircase from the entrance door down to a semicircular driveway where hotel guests were dropped off with their luggage. A security guard was standing at the bottom of the steps, hands behind his back.

Just on the other side of the drive, a crowd had gathered. At first, it looked like a typical group awaiting the appearance of a celebrity. Most of the people gathered there were fans. The energy structure of these people was similar; spiked and laced with veins of hope and desperation. These were people who would live on a celebrity encounter for the rest of their lives. It was sad, but also honest and clean. Less clean were the one or two professional journalists and photographers in the crowd. While none of them had the same broken code he had seen in the reporter Grace, none were completely clean either. All this was fairly normal. What was not normal were the not-quite-humans scattered about between the humans. Dante recognized some of them as Academy agents.

The tiny, anorexic-looking French woman standing stock still near the front of the crowd was one of the Academy's better arsonists. Her name was Iselle something or other and she was a Cambion with fire elemental heritage. Dante couldn't see her face, but he didn't need to, her energy and stance was enough to ID her. One of the photographers was an Academy operative who believed himself to be possessed by a demon. He was now slouching against a bin in a cheap, shapeless black suit and Hawaiian print shirt. His blond hair was thinning, and he wore it long enough to pull back into a straggly ponytail. He had some bland name like Robert, or Jim, or John. In truth, he was a ghost Cambion who was a spy for the Academy, and was bland enough to be good at it. The doorman who occasionally poked his head out to survey the crowd with a critical eye was a ghoul Cambion. Such Cambion were unusual, given the nature of ghouls and humans, but he was perfectly placed as guard and keeper of the rich and powerful. The most dangerous non-human present was the briefcase-carrying businessman who had just stopped to survey the front of the hotel with a wry smile. His name was Thomas Ceyrolle, and he was an incubus Cambion with fairly weak abilities. What he lacked in ability, he made up for in disgusting appetites and a penchant for death and excrement. He would be here not just to kill, but to torture and then kill.

A homeless man lying on the steps of the church behind him coughed. When Dante turned to him, the man's eyes widened. The man was Cambion, and barely holding on to his sanity.

"Ah, you see me," Dante said. "Academy?"

The homeless man began to scuttle backward.

"If you move again, I will flay your soul," Dante said calmly.

"You're Dante," the man muttered, actually crossing himself.

"Yes, I am," Dante replied. "And I am guessing, from your response, that you are Academy. They teach you that I am a monster of some sort, yes?"

The man nodded.

Dante moved closer and crouched down to the man's level. He ran his hand over the man's head. His code was clean enough and fragmented by more than one non-human ancestor. At his touch, the man trembled.

"I am a monster, but so are you," Dante said softly. "I won't hurt you. It seems to me like you have been hurt enough already. If you would like that to change, you can go to Canary Wharf tomorrow. Wait outside the Tube station. One of our people will find you if you wait long enough. It's a weigh station for us. It may take a few hours, but that is a place we watch."

"You're not going to kill me?" the man asked, still wide-eyed.

"No, but I would like to ask you about why you are here, if you don't mind," Dante said.

"They told me to watch for people from the Office," the man mumbled. "They seemed to be worried that you would show up—you or *her*."

"And what is your name?" Dante asked the man, who flinched back again. "Settle down, if I wanted to hurt you, I would have done so already, I only want your name."

"Laird. Laird Moyers."

"Pleasure to meet you, Mr. Moyers. Did they tell you why they thought I might show up here?"

"They said it had to do with an Academy agent being tested to level up," he said quietly, looking around him nervously.

"Do you know anything about the agent in question?"

The man shook his head. "But I know that the agent is here with Ossian. And I know it's a woman."

"Ossian?"

"He's a famous actor who is … who is …" Laird stopped, his eyes to the ground.

"Not really an actor?"

"Not really a person."

"Doesn't it seem that there is a lot of manpower here for a single person and a simple promotional level up?" Dante asked.

"I don't know, man. I'm just a low-level guy. They keep me on the streets. I'm always cold and hungry." The man's bloodshot eyes implored Dante, reminding him of who he had been, once upon a time.

"So they keep you out here all the time? How do you eat?"

"They give me some cash every week, but they don't want me to buy too much or have too much comfort because I need to look authentic," Laird said. "It's not too bad. It's not as bad as the place I was before ... how I was before."

"It is bad. You are an asset and they should be treating you as such."

"I'm just a low-level guy, man. I'm nobody special."

"You are a ghost Cambion," Dante said softly. "And you can see me, this makes you special, to me at least."

Dante stood, but as he turned to go, the man called out.

"Wait, were you serious about taking me in?"

"Of course I was," Dante said. "Just go to the Canary Wharf stop tomorrow. I will put your information out to our networks, so they will be aware of you."

"The Academy, I mean, I'm grateful to them but it's a hard place unless you are a favorite," the man said. "Is the Office the same?"

Dante thought for a minute. Jayce came to mind.

"No, we try to find ways for everyone to fit in as best we can."

"Fitting in." The man snorted. "I wonder what that feels like."

"It feels like coming home. You should try it."

Dante turned back to the hotel just in time to see a commotion in front of it. Two young women had emerged from the entrance. One was a strikingly beautiful, blonde-haired Asian woman dressed in black. The other one was wearing the remains of a green dress that was torn in several places. Her hair was disheveled. Her face was bruised and bloody.

It was the face of Amelie McCormick.

The two women froze for a minute at the top of the stairs. Behind them, Dante could see trails of dark slimy blobs, that had additional dimensions, pushing out from under the revolving door. They looked disturbingly like one of the forms that the Manassas virus had taken. Dante moved quickly through the crowd. He needed to get Amelie away from those things before she became infected, however, just as one of them got about six inches from her, it exploded. Another did the same. The blobs stopped in their advance. At that moment, a face appeared on the other side of the doors. It was the Welsh actor Ossian Reese. Reese was known for his working-class upbringing and his incredible work ethic. He had been nominated for several big awards that year including a Golden Globe and an Oscar. He hadn't won them but everyone was saying it was only a matter of time. He was also clearly possessed.

Amelie turned and looked behind her. When she turned back, Dante caught her eye, hoping she could see him. Her eyes widened and he quickly mouthed *Ossian Reese—yell out his name*. He then cupped his hands around his mouth as if he were yelling.

Amelie immediately turned and called out. "Look, it's Ossian Reese!"

Some of the fans surged forward just as Ossian was coming out of the revolving door. Amelie and the other woman ran down the stairs and across the street toward a bus stop half a block away. The number 453 was just pulling up. Both women sprinted for it. This must have been difficult for Amelie as she was barefoot and running with a limp. Dante felt a surge of heat in his belly. He had always cared for Amelie. How could he not, knowing her history as intimately as he did? Yet it had been necessary to keep her away from Kara as much as possible, for the safety of Kara and the rest of the story.

Ossian Reese was now standing at the top of the stairs, staring at the fleeing girls.

"Ossian, can I get your autograph?" asked a young woman with an American accent. Ossian turned to her and, for a split second, his face was a mask of fury. The girl stepped back, eyes wide and paper held against her chest, as if to protect her heart. His expression immediately changed to a slightly patronizing smile, as he took the paper from the girl's trembling hands and signed it. By doing this, he had signaled that he was willing to interact with the crowd, so more fans pushed forward.

Dante looked around and found that both Iselle, the arsonist, and Thomas, the deviant, had disappeared. Scanning the street, he saw them walking together up Portland Place. After checking to make sure that Ossian was staying put, and Amelie's bus was long gone, Dante followed the Academy agents.

He followed for a few blocks before moving to get ahead of them. He wanted to check if he was visible to them, but they had no reaction, so apparently, they were the more "normal" sort of Cambion. When they entered a cinema, Dante followed. Inside the cinema was a small café and they took a seat near the back. The place was empty but for one woman behind the counter.

"Well, that was a waste of time," Iselle said, in her thick French accent.

"Ossian might have made the situation better if he had let the girls stay out front a little longer," Thomas replied, as he brought two coffees and a couple of croissants to the table. "I would have liked to have looked at her a little longer. I love the ripped-up dress, the cuts and the bruises just starting to show. If she had been forced to stay out front in the cold, in that thin dress, her nipples would have gotten hard, and she might have even started to cry. Delicious."

Iselle laughed. "You are a pervert."

"Only in the best ways."

She rolled her eyes. "So I didn't see any evidence of unusual abilities in either of them, did you?"

"No, but I had just arrived when she came out. Was that the only time you saw her?" Thomas asked.

Iselle nodded as she held her coffee cup daintily in two hands and took a sip.

"I did recognize the other woman though," Iselle said.

"It was Majo Petrov, right? The IT sharpshooter?"

"Yes, I hate that one," Iselle hissed into her coffee cup. "She's an icy, arrogant bitch."

"How do you know her?"

"We joined at about the same time and were in basic training together. She's only out for herself."

"Well, that's all of us really, isn't it?"

"Of course, but it's tacky not to at least pretend that we aren't," Iselle said. "Did you send in the information they asked for?"

"I texted the hub that they took the 453 and the time. Are you sure that you didn't see any abilities on display?"

"No, nothing. But I suspect they will get that information from Ossian," Iselle replied. "Otherwise, we may be called on to kill the both of them. I wouldn't mind that."

"As long as we don't do it too quick," Thomas said, with dead eyes.

Iselle shrugged.

Another person then came into the café, and they switched to dull chatter about the weather. When they stood to leave, Dante moved up to them and touched each on the shoulder. What he felt there made his skin crawl. Their code was vile, both of them. Of course, he had expected them to have corrupted code, but he didn't expect such a high level of corruption. Iselle's code was badly fractured, but Thomas's was more hole than code. The code of Iselle felt like a terminally ill patient's but Thomas's felt like sticking your hand into a rotting corpse. Both of these people were a physical danger to Amelie and a viral risk to the story itself. The fact that both of them worked for the Academy could be a coincidence, but that seemed unlikely.

Dante followed them as they left the café and turned toward Regent Street. After Iselle and Thomas said their goodbyes, Thomas stepped out into the street to cross between intersections. When he was in the middle of the road, Dante created a bubble of time in a fifty-foot radius around them. A car just on the other side of the road froze, as did the people on the sidewalk at the street corner. There was still movement at the end of the street but even that had slowed down. That was how his bubbles worked. Time froze in the center of the bubble, and gradually reinserted itself the further away from the center it got.

"What the fuck is going on?" Thomas said, spinning around. Dante raised Thomas's energy level just enough for Thomas to be able to see him.

"I'm correcting you," Dante said. Thomas whirled around again, and seeing Dante, his eyes widened.

"Wait, you are … you are …"

"Time," Dante said, and dropped the bubble. Time around them sped forward to catch up with the time around it. So when a bus hit Thomas, it hit with enough force to drag him under the tires. His clothes, or skin, must have caught on to the underside of the bus because his body did not appear once the bus had passed, at least for a few moments. There was a long smear of blood, though, and bits of cloth thrown up behind it.

When his body did appear, it was not much more than a tangle of what clothes had remained, blood, and meat.

Dante decided that he would deal with Iselle later, it was now more important to let Kara know that Amelie was in the embrace of the Academy.

Chapter Ten

The Linden and the Daffodil

Dante and Kara were lying in a bed at Linden Row Inn in Richmond, Virginia. The room was lavish, with high ceilings and Victorian furnishings. To be honest, it was that Victorian, repressed element of the decor that made having sex there even more enticing. Outside of the general intrigue of having passionate sex amid furniture designed by the repressed, the hotel's most interesting claim to fame was that Edgar Allen Poe had played in the gardens and that these gardens were the ones mentioned in his poem *To Helen.* Dante would have liked to have met him, but Poe obviously hadn't taken the ghost path.

After Dante discovered that Amelie McCormick was in the none too gentle embrace of the Academy, he returned to Kara to relay the news. Despite the circumstances, Dante was fairly sure that Amelie was safe enough for now, but he had sprung that news on Kara too quickly upon his arrival, and without adequate preparation. In the agitated state she was in, she had almost blown up the building. He had redirected her energy into sex, which had been a dangerous move for him. She had hurt him before in similar situations and had spent months self-flagellating about it, which had led to a season of freakish natural phenomena for all. Luckily, this time had turned out better. They only broke some furniture. Afterward, she was worn out and slept.

Kara needed to be cleared out, but the more overtaxed she was, the harder it was to get her to do it. It was like trying to reason with someone with low blood sugar. With every day, with every person she encountered, she absorbed more of their stories, feelings, histories, and sins. The more she took in, the harder it was to hold on to herself and the more resistant she was to being cleared out. He understood her reluctance. The clearing was horrible.

Dante stroked Kara's hair. She was calm and content in sleep. Kara was lucky in that she could still sleep—and escape. Dante didn't have that luck. Instead, he decided to use the time to drift back into the hallway. If he was going to have to take Kara soon, he wanted to discover the door he needed, as the look of it frequently changed.

He turned his focus inward and listened for the song of the hallway. It only took a few moments to catch a snippet of a refrain and he followed it through the layers of energy that made up his body. The music surrounded him and filled him up, taking him through the oceans, skies, stars, and exploding suns, all spinning inside him. As the music reached its crescendo, he was dropped from its embrace into a glowing hallway floating in space. It consisted of a long corridor that went on endlessly in both directions.

The hallway changed often, possibly in mockery of his own inability to change. Despite this, it was always somewhat reflective of his health and mindset. Today the floor was shiny black obsidian. Above his head, rivers of roses were suspended in the air, spinning as if in a vortex. The walls were covered in balls of green marimo moss. Interspersed between these were doors made of crystal-clear water. Next to each door was an ornate iron sconce holding a white candle. Instead of touching down and walking, Dante floated down the hallway, his eyes scanning the distance for notes of fire. It wasn't long before he found what he was looking for—a door that looked different from the others. This door was not made of water, instead it looked like ash. The candle next to it was five times larger than the others and it burned bright like a torch. This would be the one. He reached his hand out to mark it, so that he could easily find it again, but when his fingers touched the silky ash of the door, he felt a jolt of electricity. It wasn't much, but he had never felt this before—and new things in the hallway were disconcerting.

He reached out again, but a sound stopped him. It was the sound of Kara muttering. Dante quickly stepped back and dropped his resonance.

When Dante came back to himself, Kara was stirring in her sleep. He quickly solidified himself, as she reached out to him. For the next thirty minutes she brought him into the physical in her own very enticing ways. This time more sweetly, more lovingly.

Afterward, Kara wandered downstairs and returned five minutes later with some fairly lame-looking pastries. He was lying naked on the bed, having left his less-than-corporeal clothes behind. They would be back when he willed them to be. Kara lay down, and snuggled up next to him, shockingly beautiful as she propped her legs against the wall behind the bed. She was chewing on a pain au chocolat as she began to read through a page in a notepad. She preferred this to technology because, like him, technology wasn't completely reliable in her hands.

"Are you comfortable like that?" he asked, sitting up and crossing his legs.

"Like what?"

"Like that. With your legs like that? Is that actually comfortable?"

"Yeah. It's fine." Then she stopped and gave him a sad little smile. "I'm probably just doing that thing again. My subconscious forgets that we aren't human anymore, and I can't have your baby."

She said that with no warning and Dante felt the familiar knife in his heart. The ache for what they weren't—what they had never even had the opportunity to be.

"Come closer," he said, pulling her onto his lap, her back against his chest. She sighed and gave a little shiver.

"So you think Amelie's all right?" Kara whispered. Dante understood why her mind had turned to this girl at this moment, but he hoped that she hadn't made that connection. Some things were better unknown, or at least unsaid.

"For now, yes," Dante said. "But being with the Academy explains a lot about why we have had difficulty tracking her. They usually insert some sort of microparticle to block out our scanners."

"So how were you able to find her this time, without a watcher and without trackers?"

"Something must be blocking their blocker. I'm not sure why or even how," Dante lied, best that she didn't know exactly how he did this, for the same reasons that she shouldn't think about why she was focusing on Amelie right now. He stroked Kara's hair, which was fine but plentiful.

"What was she doing when you saw her?"

"She was escaping a mark. She was a bit banged up but good enough."

"What are they trying to get her to attract?"

"It was hard to tell from the one moment, but this particular mark was a non-human possessing a movie star."

"Jesus," Kara muttered.

"There is good news, though."

"I can use that." Kara took his hand and kissed it.

"She's still not infected," Dante said. "And there seems to be something inside her preventing it."

"That's good but we did expect it," Kara said, her voice becoming softer. "That was the point of Clovis's sacrifice. I didn't want to have to unmake her. I remember when I first saw her in that institution. What a sad, distraught little thing she was. I thought we had protected her. I thought we were continuing to protect her, but she met Clovis and became a risk. That was my fault, and it was Clovis that fixed it for her—and for me."

"I have to admit, I didn't expect that of him," Dante said. "I always thought that one day you would just catch him and unmake him. You know, he used to think you were after him because his father was a demon."

"His father wasn't a demon. I have no problem with anything that occurs naturally here. But there is something in him that isn't from here. I've known that for a long time and I think he finally figured it out himself."

"So what do you think his father is, if not a demon?"

"His mother is capable of mating with almost anything, so he could be anything really. And once again, if it is from this story, I don't care. Rose could fuck a kangaroo and have a child, for all I care. But I am pretty sure Clovis didn't come from a kangaroo mating," Kara said, blowing a stray piece of hair out of her eyes. Dante laughed.

Kara smiled, but it faded quickly.

"It's sad because it's not his fault. I liked him, because there was a lot to like about him. He was smart, capable, and fearless. Plus, his strange immunity to viruses even in corporeal form could possibly have helped us if he had been willing to join us. But he was too dangerous as an outlier—too unethical and unpredictable. Still, I hate the fact that we are in a world where I needed to get rid of him."

"Luckily, you didn't have to. He did it himself," Dante said.

"No, we did it. He just came to us willingly," Kara replied.

"It seems to have worked. Amelie has been responsible for no infections since that happened."

"That we know of."

Dante looked at her. Kara was tearing up.

"You're right. She hasn't been a risk," she whispered. "But the fact that he was willing to do that for her … those are not the actions of the selfish Clovis that we once knew. Think of how much he loved her to even think of that, let alone do it. I only know one other creature capable of such a sacrifice."

She turned her wet face to him, and he kissed her gently. She was remembering what she shouldn't.

"Well, what he did means that both he and Amelie are no longer problems for us."

"But Rose still is," Kara said, sitting up straighter. "If I find her, I will unmake her faster than she can get away."

This whole line of conversation was not a good one; Kara's energy was too frazzled to be thinking about past sacrifices and Rose.

"Let's focus on something we can fix in the here and now," Dante said. "As much as we might want to, there is not much we can, or should, do about Amelie while she is with the Academy, unless it becomes dire. So today let's focus on the Cambion we found here and the SOS that his watcher sent. What did it say again?"

Kara put her bag on the bed and pulled out a few folded sheets of paper.

"It says '*SOS. SOS. SOS. Cambion kidnapped and in distress. Current location Daffodil Hall Alzheimer's Facility in Richmond Va. Help needed ASAP.*'"

"That's it?" Dante asked.

"Yep. It's not a lot, but it's bad—and it's about witching hour at what I'm sure is another house of horror. So let's find out what we need to know in person." Kara stood, grabbed her dress from the red velvet chair near the bed and pulled it over her head without bothering with underwear.

"What's the boy's name?" Dante asked.

"Tobias Solomon."

"Okay then. Let's get Tobias and get out."

Kara nodded.

"We won't stay there a second longer than needed."

Daffodil Hall Alzheimer's Facility was about as depressing from the outside as Dante had expected. The "grounds" consisted of a cluster of three urine-yellow, two-story buildings, each with a feces-brown, fake slate overhanging roof. The paint had probably once been daffodil yellow to reinforce the establishment's name, but time, weather, and negligence had faded it to its current excretory shade. This could have been offset by attractive grounds and some landscaping—or even some land, but the building was in a parking lot and the only green to be seen was the few bushes that could fend for themselves and an occasional straggly cypress tree. Of course, it was winter, but Dante suspected this dreariness was on display all year round.

As Kara parked the car in the almost empty parking lot, Dante steeled himself for the soul-sucking vacuum that he knew he would find when they entered the building. They owned interests in many such care facilities, and they had sunk huge sums of money into providing an uplifting atmosphere, employing only genuinely kind nursing staff, and providing cutting-edge treatments. The facilities they were associated with were the best someone with a mental disease could hope to end up in, but even the best were dismal. No matter how much they tried to brighten things up with activities, decor, and perky nursing staff, it couldn't change the fact that the building was filled with people who were, more or less, waiting to die. Many were natural victims of the very viral monsters that he and Kara spent their time tracking and containing. This meant that the only hope for salvation or sanity for people in these facilities was escape from them, either through death or, more rarely, release. This was the reason that Kara had invested so much time and money in them. She knew that many Cambion do time in just such facilities, and it was a way to track and find new people. If they were Cambion, she usually extracted them from these places the moment they were identified. Sometimes, she helped train them while they were residents and then facilitated their release.

The worst of these types of facilities were havens for sociopaths, sadists, and the chronically incompetent. Dante thought it was a good guess that Daffodil Hall probably fell into the "worst of" category. It was not one of theirs. It had little to no online presence. There were no ads, no web pages, no reviews. One could only find it in the online version of the Yellow Pages. In this day and age of online advertising, this was a huge red flag. If it had no online presence, and no reviews, it usually meant it was either underfunded, antiquated, or staying off-grid for a reason. Dante felt himself becoming pre-emptively pissed off and heat began building in his belly, until he felt Kara's hand on his arm. Her skin was cool and dry. His heat drained from him and into her. He immediately felt better.

She shouldn't be taking this on, she is carrying too much already.

"Who was the watcher supposed to be on this guy again?" she asked quickly, as she unbuckled her seatbelt.

"Lazlo Fox."

"And not a typical flighty ghost? He wouldn't have just bailed?"

"No. Lazlo was anything but flighty. He is also anything but typical. In life, he was a war hero. A World War Two African American war hero … before that was a thing."

Kara shrugged a bit.

"War hero or not, he is still a ghost. Is he trustworthy?"

"Yes."

"Okay then, let's go get our boy out," she said. "And we'll see if Lazlo is still there."

They entered the building under a shabby blue awning. The air was stagnant and smelled of pine, perfumed with an undercurrent of urine and unwashed linen. The tired plastic plants did nothing to help the situation. As Kara went to the desk to check on Tobias Solomon, Dante scanned the waiting room.

Hospital waiting rooms were usually quiet, but not at this sort of facility. Here, they left the waiting room open to the residents as well as visitors. This meant that people wandered in and out like restless, confused ghosts. This reminded Dante a bit too much of himself in the days just after his death, so he turned his attention to the residents themselves.

There was a ninety-something woman with a walker, who was moving herself back and forth across the room calling "Daddy, Daddy." Dante wasn't sure if she was looking for a father or husband. A younger woman, maybe in her sixties, was walking crisply between the receptionist desk and the lobby, where she would stare at the wall for a few minutes before breaking into flat, hollow laughter. Dante suspected that she was having gelastic seizures that had not been properly diagnosed. Closer to him, next to a window, a man in a wheelchair was staring blankly out into the bright but dreadful parking lot. Two young women, one blonde and one dark haired, flanked him. Both were talking to him in soft tones. The pain and despair that radiated off them was enough to dim Dante to the point of invisibility. He was intensely relieved when Kara waved him over. The receptionist she had been speaking with had been taken with a sudden coughing fit. Something about this moment seemed familiar. The coughing. A picture of the virus at the public access TV station suddenly came to Dante's mind. It had attacked Kara. It had inserted itself into her. For a moment he felt his throat constrict.

"Done." Kara interrupted his thoughts. She drew him away from the desk.

"Did you learn anything?" he asked.

"No. Just Tobias's room number. Two-one-five. Second floor," Kara whispered as they walked. A man shuffling down the hallway toward them stopped and was staring at him. Clearly, he saw Dante. He needed to be careful in places like this. Some of the "inmates" here were close enough to death to be able to see him easily. As the "jailers" wouldn't, this could make for uncomfortable situations—assuming anyone noticed or gave a shit, which was unlikely. Still, it was best to keep his antennae up.

"Who did you say you were? And who should I be, in case anyone can see me?" Dante asked.

"They didn't even ask who I was. I could barely get the woman's eyes off her phone long enough to acknowledge that I was there."

"Typically appalling," Dante said, shaking his head.

"Yes, it is," Kara said. "Actually, wait a second."

She stopped and pulled out her phone.

"What are you doing?"

"Sending a text to the Office telling them we want an extraction today. After pulling our guy out, I want the extraction team to stick around to wipe this place. There is going to be an accidental but completely devastating fire here tonight. The inmates here are to be moved to one of our facilities just prior to that."

Dante quickly put his hand on Kara's arm. "Not here and now. Not until we know more. We can do it when we leave. Just be patient. Nothing is likely to change in the next fifteen minutes that will make any difference."

Kara shrugged.

Neither of them trusted elevators in the outside world, so they took the stairs to get to room 215. Outside the door, they waited a few minutes before entering, just listening. They heard nothing untoward.

As they entered the room, they had just enough time to register that it was a private room before the fire alarm started blaring. They waited for a few moments, assuming it was a test, but when it had not stopped after thirty seconds, it seemed to be real. Still, as they saw no one reacting to the alarm, they proceeded to the bed where Tobias Solomon lay.

Tobias was lying with his eyes closed and his hands folded over his chest.

With his pale face, dark brown hair, and circles under his eyes, his position might have looked comic in an old, campy vampire movie way—were it not for the IV, heart monitor, and urine bag strapped to the side of the bed. These things made the scene look more pathetic than amusing.

Kara put her hand to the boy's brow, then pulled it away, shaking her head.

"He's not in there anymore. His spirit is gone."

"We will still want to take the body, right?" Dante asked. Kara nodded.

"I'll call retrieval," she said.

Just as they turned to go, Tobias Solomon sat up in his bed and opened his eyes.

"Don't go! I'm suffocating in here!"

Chapter Eleven

The Other Side of the Tracks

Kara whirled, wide-eyed. Dante moved closer. Tobias's eyes were frantic and darting around the room, but they were filmy white with cataracts. He smelled of bile. He reached out for Dante as he got closer, knocking over an empty plastic vomit tray.

"Tobias?" Kara said, taking his hand.

"No, it's Lazlo," the voice rasped. "I'm stuck in here."

"What happened to Tobias? Is he still around somewhere?"

"She took him," Lazlo croaked, turning his white eyes toward Kara. "She took him, and she's gonna come back for me."

"Who is 'she'? And where is Tobias?" Kara asked.

"She's a nurse who wasn't a nurse," he said. At this, Tobias's body began convulsing. Kara laid her hand on his forehead. The spasms immediately stopped but he was breathing hard.

"I managed to stretch part of myself out of the body so I could set off the alarm and warn you," Lazlo whispered. "But I don't think we have much time before someone comes back."

"Time won't be a problem," Dante said, throwing a blanket of time over them. The bleeps and clicks of the machinery surrounding Tobias suddenly stopped. His face relaxed and he sighed.

"What happened?" Kara asked.

"Start with Tobias's history," Dante said gently to Lazlo. "It will help you stay focused."

"Okay," Lazlo said with a sigh. "Tobias was quiet and kind. When he was a toddler, his parents died when their house caught fire. The flames didn't touch Tobias, because he was a fire elemental Cambion. Later, he believed he had killed his parents, so he buried his gifts and fears. He was sent to live with his grandmother and everything was quiet after that. There were no incidents of unexplained fires or anything else out of the ordinary. So, in short, he was a cautious and controlled kid. He didn't experiment with drugs, alcohol. He just threw himself into studying violin. When this happened, he was studying violin at UVA in Charlottesville."

"Then how did he end up in Richmond?" Kara asked.

"He got sick. It was just a cold but he went to the infirmary because he had fever and some vomiting. I think it was nothing more than the fact that he got a new video game, went on a game bender the weekend before and ate nothing but shit pizzas. But the doctor working at the infirmary was fucked up. He gave Tobias a vaccine that was supposedly for meningitis. It wasn't. I tried to get him away, but I couldn't. I sent in a report about it immediately, but after that everything happened so fast. Almost immediately after getting the vaccine Tobias went into convulsions. The doctor made a call, and some men came and took him away in an ambulance. That's when I sent the second SOS."

"We never got it. It got buried," said Kara, taking his hand again.

"Why wasn't he taken to the hospital where he was? What about his grandmother? Didn't she check on any of this? What about his other relatives?" Dante asked.

"His grandmother had a sudden heart attack. I suspect she was disposed of. And he didn't have any other relatives to ask any questions."

"Do you think this was why he was targeted? The fact that he didn't have much family?"

"Maybe. But to do that, they would have had to have already known about him, and been tracking him to make it happen so quickly."

Dante and Kara exchanged glances.

"So what happened when he got here?" Kara asked.

Lazlo closed his eyes.

"They pumped him full of drugs. I don't know what the shit was, but it made him scream, vomit, and hallucinate. The worst part was that he was conscious and in between the drugs, he would beg them to leave, but they would just give him another drug. It was horrible."

Dante could feel the flow of time pulsing at the edges of the bubble he had created. In this moment, it felt like the beating heart of some great beast.

"Finally, a nurse came in the middle of the night," Lazlo rasped. "She was pasty white, fat, and ugly as homemade sin but that wasn't the worst. Worse was the smile on her face. It was uglier than the rest of her put together. She looked round the room, like she was looking for something. I felt like she was looking for me. Tobias was sleeping. She took a needle out and injected something into his IV. Tobias went all stiff and then suddenly there he was standing in front of me. Not his body, you know, his spirit."

"So the drug killed him?" Dante asked.

"No, man, that's just it. His body was still there, still breathing, still alive. It's just that his spirit wasn't in there no more."

"His spirit leaving didn't trigger his body to begin death?" Kara asked.

"No," Lazlo whispered. "It didn't. His body was a living, soulless shell."

"You think the drug did that?" Dante asked, moving closer.

"Yeah, well whatever was in the needle did that. It kind of loosed him from his body. Maybe that was what they was doing with all the drugs."

Kara nodded for him to go on.

"That ain't the worst. After that, these tiny shadow shapes crawled out of his spirit's mouth. They began to circle round his legs like damn cats. Tobias looked over at me and he saw me. I saw that he saw me, and he was damn scared. His spirit looked wrong. It was blinking in and out, like it was barely holding itself in a form. He was about to say something but then the woman pulled this little black boxy thing out of her pocket. Damn thing wasn't much bigger than a phone or a game remote, but it pulsed and made a weird humming sound. It was scary as hell."

"The sound was scary?" Dante asked.

"Yes and no. Yeah, it pulsed and hummed but that wasn't the scary part. It was scary because—well … damn … it was sexy. It was just some black box but looking at it made me feel sexy as hell. I can't explain it. It sounds fucked up and it was. So she holds it up and the little shadow things immediately get sucked into it. Then Tobias starts walking toward it, like he couldn't control himself. And then he was gone. But he wasn't gone like ghosts are supposed to get gone. The box ate him."

"*Ate* him?" Kara asked.

"Yeah. It ate him. I felt his spirit die."

"Spirits don't die unless they are unmade," Kara said, her voice tight.

"I know that's how it's supposed to be, but this one did," Lazlo said in a shaky voice.

"Go on," Dante said.

"So then this woman looks straight at me, holds out the box and says, 'Come on now, sugar.' And this wave of desire hit me so hard it 'bout knocked me down at the same time this thing came out of the box. It was this huge, ashy thing—well, part of the time it looked like that, but it seemed to have a hard time holding a shape and kept changing. I forced myself to look away, and then I jumped into Tobias's body. Inside his body felt sick and soulless, but it also felt safe. The woman glared at me."

Dante glanced at Kara, and she nodded ever so slightly.

"So she says, 'Don't you want to live forever? In here you can live forever.' And I says, 'I already live forever, we all do.' And she laughs and says 'Not like you want. Not with the person you want. In here, you could live with her.' That scared me 'cause it was like she knew me, knew my history, and she was evil. She looked like a woman but only in body. What was in her was nothing like human. So I say, 'No thanks.'

"Then she gets really mad," Lazlo continued, shivering in Tobias's body. "She says, 'Okay, lamb. I can wait. We'll take his body and you'll be stuck in it, and you might not like the roommates we will find for you.' Then she leaves."

Lazlo stopped talking. He was breathing deeply.

"Why didn't you come and tell us?" Dante said.

"Because I couldn't get out. I tried. Whatever she injected into Tobias's body changed me once I went into it. It's like I'm heavier."

"Do you know if the woman was with the Academy?" Dante asked.

"No. I don't know and she didn't say," Lazlo replied.

"Any idea why Tobias was targeted, besides his lack of relatives?" Kara asked.

"No. He's no different from any other Cambion that I could tell."

There was a sound from outside the room. It sounded like a bump on the wall.

"The flow is pushing in on us," Dante said. "I can't hold this much longer without consequences and ripples, and there is pressure from the outside."

"We need to go, and you need to come with us," Kara said, standing up from where she had been sitting on the edge of his bed.

"But I can't get out," Lazlo said, "and I need to. Something in here is changing me, pulling at parts of me—like it's eating me alive."

"We'll get you out, but not here. We need the right combination of drugs and people with certain talents. Do you think you can walk his body out?"

Dante asked.

Lazlo nodded.

"Okay," said Kara. "Then we need to get out of here now. And I need to call an extraction team to send in an ambulance."

Kara pulled out her phone and started dialing.

"Joe is on fire," Kara said, when she got off the phone. "He knew we were here and what the place was like already. The ambulance should be here before the fire department leaves. He has a team with the appropriate paperwork so there should be no problem getting Tobias out. He's even got a temporary cryo-tube coming in a separate car, just in case."

Just as Kara finished speaking, the room began to shake with a low moaning sound. As the seconds passed, these became deep sirens from outside. Water began to drip from the ceiling in exaggerated slow motion.

"You can let go now," Kara said, placing her hand on Dante's shoulder. He pulled that stream of time into himself. Suddenly, there was a burst of angry voices coming down the hall.

Time was up.

"Listen, we aren't sure if these rooms are safe yet, so we need to check them before you go in," said a deep male voice from the hallway.

"Well, I don't see or smell a fire, but the CDC *is* fairly worried that the person in this room may have a highly contagious brain infection," said a muffled female voice. "So I agree it's not safe for you, but I should be fine."

At that moment a woman entered the room in a white hazmat suit. She had a wallet out with a CDC badge on it. She was accompanied by a very pissed-off-looking fireman.

"Excuse me, ma'am. I'm with the CDC. Are you related to Tobias Solomon?" asked the woman.

"Yes, I am his auntie," Kara responded smoothly. "Was that a real fire alarm? I thought it was just going off again. It goes off all the time here. Everyone usually ignores it. In fact, a lot of times they just turn off the breaker for it."

"They what?" snapped the fireman. His eyes looked like glowing embers. He immediately pulled out his phone and turned to leave the room.

If Dante had been less concerned by the news that they had received from Lazlo, the next thirty minutes would have been a joy to watch. The extraction team was elegant in its efficiency. They had Tobias out of Daffodil and into a hazmat-equipped ambulance in less than five minutes. They assessed and examined all the patients and hospital employees as they filed them out. No one fit the description of the ugly woman that Lazlo had described.

As everyone was led out, Kara went into a separate ambulance with some of the security team. Dante sat in the back of the ambulance with Tobias/Lazlo. As they pulled out of the parking lot, the woman in the hazmat suit opened the sliding door between the driver's seat and the back of the ambulance.

"We are heading to the airport," she said. It was Diane, one of the most talented and oldest members of their extraction team. While she was probably pushing ninety, she didn't look a day over forty-five. This was due to her particular parentage. She had light brown hair, graying at the temples, and sharp gray eyes. She had known, and could see, Dante for some time and they were on very friendly terms.

"We have a full unit set up in a hangar at a nearby private airfield. After we put him in, we can be in London in no time."

"There is something I didn't say," Lazlo whispered. "I didn't want to say it in there, in case she was there. But when she first asked me to go into the box and I said 'no thanks,' she said to me, 'it's a place where you can make your own heaven. Your friends weren't nearly so suspicious. They jumped at the chance.' When I said no again, that was when she got mad."

"Do you know what friends she was talking about?" Dante asked.

"No, but by saying that I know she has done this to other people," Lazlo said. "And because she said friends, I think she means our people."

Dante felt the heat inside him begin to rise.

"And there's worse," Lazlo said. "I told you about those black things in me. The things that went into the box?"

Dante nodded.

"I think they took a part of me with them."

"A part of you?"

"A part of my soul," Lazlo said softly.

At these words, and for the briefest moment, time buckled inside Dante.

It was 8 a.m. London time. Kara, Dante, Diane, and Lazlo in the body of Tobias Solomon were now installed in an isolation room on the 7th floor of the Office. This one floor had more sophisticated medical equipment on it than all the medical facilities of London combined. One of the reasons for this was one of dimension, or the lack of certain basic concrete laws of physics that allowed for increased size. The room itself was larger than the anatomy of the building would have allowed, but space in the Office could be adapted as needed, and this floor, as the medical wing, always needed to be bigger.

One of their decked-out cryo-tubes had been set up in the middle of the room, connected to several laptops sitting on desks nearby. They were in the process of cooling down the tube to the temperature needed to quickly freeze Tobias's body for transport to one of the parabiology units below, which could not be accessed by any creature with a heat signature.

All this had required that Dante create another bubble to protect Lazlo from whatever might be inside Tobias's body with him. The small, dark figures that Lazlo had mentioned could be viruses—sometimes they appeared as shadows, but rarely with any real power and certainly never with intent. Intent required a level of consciousness. Still, it was best to be careful.

"Cryo is ready and the cryoprotectants are in place. We can start whenever you are ready," said Diane, looking up from the computer. "We can give the body the lethal injection."

"Will that kill Tobias's body?" Lazlo asked.

"Without his soul inside to trigger the final death code? No," Dante replied. "If his soul happened to return while the drugs were in his system, then it would kill him. But that is not likely. As it is, it will simply immobilize body functions so that you will be released."

"We already got blood samples, right?" Dante turned to Diane.

Diane nodded. "Yes, and we're testing them for any type of infection."

"And we ran an energy signature scan on Lazlo?" Dante asked, nodding at Lazlo who was sitting on a gurney in the middle of the room.

"We are running it right now," Diane replied. "We will send the results to Lepri when we are done, so he can compare and contrast Lazlo's current resonance with the one he had when he joined the Academy."

"Good. Get me those results when they come in," Dante said.

Kara was sitting quietly on a plastic chair with her arms crossed, looking at Lazlo. She didn't trust most non-physical beings, and she certainly had her reasons, but right now her face looked more conflicted than angry.

"Thank you for staying with him and not running," she said to Lazlo suddenly.

"Why would I run? It was my job to protect him. I did a piss-poor job, but I tried," Lazlo replied.

Kara looked at him intently.

"Are you sure you want to be released?" she asked. "As you have been in a body for a while, I can't promise what will happen to you when you are released. You might not have the chance to stay a ghost. You might have to move on."

"That's okay. That's what I want. To move on," Lazlo said.

"Why?"

For a moment Lazlo said nothing, but then he shrugged.

"Well, the reason is my past. I have kept this story to myself for many years. I guess because when I was alive, it would have been a scandal. But maybe if I explain that, it will influence someone, someone I feel is listening, to help me out. Maybe. So maybe I'll try that."

Lazlo was sitting with his hands folded in his lap. He was still for a moment before sighing gently and then raising his head.

"I was born in 1923," he began. "My parents were sharecroppers in Georgia, so if you know what that means, you know what dirt poor is. I was one of thirteen kids they had to feed. We were half black and half Indian, so there was all the name calling and shit that you would expect if you was the son of a black sharecropper in Georgia. Plus, all the name calling and shit you would expect if you was the son of an Indian in Georgia. I had no way out, until the war broke out and I enlisted."

Lazlo smiled to himself.

"So, just my luck, I met the most beautiful girl in the world at the draft office. She registered me. She was looking down when I first saw her, and all I could see was the top of her head. She had this red hair that was so fine. It was fine as silk. It looked like it would just float away if you touched it. And I fell in love. With the top of her damn head. She had a name tag on, and it said Veronica. Ain't that a beautiful name? Veronica."

As he spoke, his eyes turned misty, and he began to slump on the stretcher. Dante looked over at Kara, but she was now sitting with her forearms resting on her thighs, completely engrossed.

"So, there I was. A black boy falling in love with a white girl he had not a fucking chance with. This was 1942 you know—that shit just wasn't okay. But she was sweet as she could be with me."

Lazlo was now definitely listing left. His arms and legs were also beginning to twitch. He didn't seem to notice. He was staring off into the distance.

"And what happened?" asked Diane, sitting down next to him so she could gently hold him up.

"I won't talk much 'bout what happened but to say that I saw her two more times before I was deployed. In those two times, I realized that she was the bravest person I ever met, and I was in love with her. The town would have lynched me if they had known. They would have done her just as bad, or worse. She asked me to write to her anyway, and I did, but she didn't get those letters until after I got blowed up by a mine."

Tobias Solomon's body was slouched over. Diane laid her hands on him. And as she did so, he slumped all the way over on the gurney. The person left sitting there was the ghost of Lazlo Fox. A young, handsome man with caramel-colored skin and bright, dark eyes so big that they would have been compared to a doe's if he had been a woman.

Diane called a technician and quietly moved the body into the tube. Lazlo didn't seem to notice. He turned to look at Kara with tears in his eyes.

"I thought that all I wanted was just to have my time with her, so I stayed behind to be with her, in whatever way I could, but it wasn't enough. It wouldn't ever be enough and when she went on, I was stuck behind, and I ain't seen her come back. I think being a ghost was maybe keeping me from finding her where she is now."

"You won't remember when you come back in the flesh," Dante said softly.

"I know but I think that that don't matter. I think maybe I can find her if I don't try."

Kara took his hand and nodded.

"And Dante, promise me that ya'll get Tobias out that box, if there is any part of him left. You get the others out too. That box is a bad place, I know it. Hell couldn't be no worse. You promise?"

Dante nodded.

A wind rose up, loud enough to shake the building. Dante looked around at the others. No one seemed to notice.

At that moment, a woman materialized out of the noise. She had long dark hair and pale white wings. She smiled at Lazlo and held out her hand.

"She's come for me. I wasn't sure she would be able to … so I need to be goin' now."

Lazlo stood up. Kara turned to Dante, but Dante shook his head. It was not for them to interfere; it was his time to go.

"Thank you for your service," Kara said to Lazlo, tears in her eyes.

Lazlo took the woman's hand and began to break apart. Small bits of him were drifting up and away, as if he were made of dust, leaving a shining form beneath. He looked down at his own body and laughed. He had time to look up and make eye contact with Dante. His great brown eyes were the last thing to disappear.

The sound of the wind disappeared and with it, the woman. Then there was silence, with the exception of the soft sounds of sniffles coming from Diane as she unplugged the cryo-tube from the computer and finished packing Tobias's body for the trip downstairs.

"This is a horrible story. This is my fault. It's my fault," Kara whispered, head down. The skin beneath her eyes looked almost bruised.

Like someone who is sick.

Dante went to her and took her in his arms.

"No, this is not a horrible story. Lazlo found love here, there is nothing horrible about that."

"He found a love but hate won—" Kara began, but Dante cut her short.

"For that one lifetime. But he'll find her again in another lifetime and they will get their chance … and if not in the first lifetime, then in the second or third. Situations can go wrong, and they can keep messing it up, but they will keep getting chances too. Just like a loving parent, this story lets you learn from your mistakes and keep trying. That's what makes it beautiful. That's why we stay here. That's why we protect it."

Kara looked up at him with eyes full of shifting emotion. "Yes. We protect it."

As usual, the dark memories triggered by her words were both comforting and horrifying.

"Come on now, back to work, we have other people we are responsible for," Dante said gently.

Kara nodded, and took Dante's hand. He led her from the room that still smelled of love and death.

Chapter Twelve

Sleeping Shades

"What did Lazlo mean about saving the others?" Kara asked, wiping her eyes as the stepped into the Office's Recovery Room.

"Lazlo told me that the nurse who appeared told him that he had friends who had 'jumped at the chance' to go into the game," Dante replied.

"What? What friends?"

"As Lazlo is—was—a ghost, it's unlikely that he would have any other friends besides ghosts, or other Cambion."

"So whatever happened to Tobias might have already happened to some of our other Cambion," Kara said, her voice becoming icy.

"Yes, but we don't know for sure." Dante put his hand on Kara's arm to ground her. "We need to look through the emails that Joe found in our computer systems and then run a full security check and cross-reference every person mentioned there with our overall system, and with every person in each department's system. All systems should be registering the same people and the same number of people. If not, we need to aggregate all of these into one system and restart from there. Once we have the list, we need to contact everyone by whatever method we can reach them."

Kara nodded. "How will we know what's not in our systems?" she asked. "We can't know what we don't know."

"I'm hoping we will find enough files in the ones Joe has found to be able to reasonably assume that is all of them. To be honest, I'm more concerned about that black box Lazlo talked about. Something that can steal souls …"

"Incubi can steal souls," Kara said.

"Yes, but that's their job in this story. They are sentient creatures with desires and ethics of their own, they aren't technology. Also, they can only steal one soul at a time. They aren't a device that can be used on as many beings in as many ways as someone might see fit."

Dante regretted voicing this concern the moment it left his mouth. Kara went rigid, her eyes turned ice blue, and her hair began to whip around her face.

"You think the Academy has developed something like this?" Kara asked.

"If they have, we'll take care of it, like we always do." Dante pulled her into his arms. For a moment she resisted but then she softened in his embrace. He felt desire, but it was more than that, it had always been more than that. What they had between them was comparable to nothing else, understood by no one else. It was made of the heat of stars, the cold of space and the potential held in every second of time.

He kissed the top of Kara's head, taking in the smell of her. In truth, his heart cared little for anything that did not directly touch her or impact her. But anything and everything that did—well, it came under his direct and harsh scrutiny. When Kara stepped back, her eyes had darkened. She sighed.

"Before we go see Joe, let's just check the patients," Dante said.

He didn't mention that it would also settle Kara down, but her smile and the way she squeezed his hand slightly as she moved into the room told him that she knew.

The air in the Recovery Room was warm, at least by medical office standards. Dante, who was only able to process sensations such as cold and heat in muted ways, was always strangely amused by the fact that even he could actually feel the cold in most doctors' offices. Still, the room that they had just come out of had been cryogenically cold, so any other room would, by necessity, feel warmer. The warmth of the Recovery Room was something more than temperature. There was a cocooning sensation here that came from the efforts of quite a few individuals who were gifted in energy manipulation. Everyone felt better in the Recovery Room, whether they were technically recovering or not.

The further they got into the room, the more he could feel the grief radiating from Kara begin to fade. The room was doing its job. He looked around, taking in the light and movement of the air. The room itself looked more like a family suite in an expensive hotel than a hospital. There were floor-to-ceiling windows on the west side of the room. Along the walls of the north and south sides, beds were lined up, with a patient lying on each. The beds were covered with expensive comforters and the softest of cotton sheets. Each patient's space had a table, a chair, and a bureau. On each table was a vase of flowers, and on each bureau was a TV, but none were on. The truth was that none of their current patients would have any idea of whether the TV was on or off. Most of them were now outliers—neither here nor elsewhere.

Kara walked toward the nearest bed. Lying on it was a fair-haired man with a growth of reddish stubble on his face. His face was sharp-featured and probably would have been handsome if not for the dark circles under his eyes and the deep hollows under his cheeks.

At that moment, Liz appeared at the door. She stared around her, wide-eyed.

Dante motioned her over. Kara was now sitting on the bed next to the blond man.

"Are we feeding him enough?" Kara asked Dante, as she put her hand to the man's head.

"His body is getting infusions of nutrients in his IV. We have been giving him our strongest maintenance solutions and his muscles go through re-building stimulation at least once a week."

"Who is he?" Liz asked softly.

"We picked him up eighteen years ago," Kara said. "He had been knocked unconscious, but he wasn't severely injured. We brought him here because he was one of the Cambion we were watching anyway, and he had been through a traumatic experience, but he never came back."

"What do you mean he never came back?"

"He was raped," Dante replied. "So, when we found him, his soul was not completely in his body. That's not uncommon in such situations. In moments of great trauma, the soul often flees. It leaves only a tiny residue of itself to maintain the basic functions. What remains is the spiritual equivalent of the brain stem."

Dante stopped. Kara had turned away from the man on the bed, her eyes becoming a bit unfocused. A conversation about trauma might not be smart in this moment, given Kara's past and current status. He turned to Liz and found that she had a similar look.

Of course. Liz had been raped as well.

Liz must have caught his expression because she shrugged her shoulders and nodded slightly.

"The point is that he was unusual because his spirit never found its way back to his body," Dante continued. "That is the situation for everyone on this floor. Their souls are no longer connected to their bodies enough for consciousness."

"But wouldn't they die, I mean at least after a while?" Liz asked. Dante started to speak but it was Kara who answered.

"Sadly, these particular people can stay alive indefinitely in this state. They had the unfortunate luck of having their souls split from their bodies at the wrong point."

"What does that mean?" Liz asked.

"What she means is that there are different parts of the soul, and each does different things," Dante said. "Some parts are located in the physical body, and some are not. The physicality of the soul, for example, is tied into certain sections of the DNA, including the part that allows the separation between the body and the soul at death. But it is another part of the soul, not centered in the body, that turns that particular section of DNA on and off. So, for the people on this floor, the part that codes for the separation is stuck in the body while the part that initiates the process of physical death to start is with the spirit, which is gone. So that means these people can't die and they age very, very slowly."

"Is this common?" Liz asked.

"No, it only happens with certain Cambion," Kara interjected. "We only see two or three like that in a normal lifespan."

She began to gently stroke the hair of the man on the bed.

"But there are what, twenty people in this room?" Liz asked. "How can that be, if you only see two or three every eighty years or so."

"They don't age," Dante said.

This was only a partial truth. Not everyone on these beds were people who had naturally left their bodies. Some were people who Kara had chosen to unmake, but only spiritually. This happened when Kara believed that the person in question had a role or mission to fulfill in their current body, but their souls were too corrupt to complete. In these cases, Kara had done that psychic surgery herself. This process was excruciating but Kara believed that the pain was also part of the healing process. So, in these particular cases, she ripped the soul in such a way that a bit of their consciousness remained inside the immobile body. In short, they were partially conscious inside the immobile corpses of their bodies. One such person was the very rapist who had attacked the man that Kara was sitting beside.

Liz's eyes were wide.

"Did you have something you needed from us?" Dante asked gently.

"Oh, right. I was sent here by Joe to ask if you could meet him in the War Room when you have minute."

"Joe?" Kara said, standing up. Joe never actually requested their presence. For him, that would be like issuing a directive to god. Also, his turf was the security offices on the lower floors. The War Room was at the top of the building, and it was difficult for normal humans to stay there for long. So there must be something Joe needed that he could only get there. This was not a good sign.

"Tell him we will be there as soon as we finish checking up on everyone here," Kara said.

Liz nodded and turned to go, but then stopped. When she turned, her face bore a look that was hard to define.

"That man, there. When did he go into the coma? I mean, when did that happen to him?" she asked.

"About eighteen years ago, why?"

"Wasn't that the same year that the first Manassas boy shot up his school?" Liz asked.

"Yes, it was. Why do you ask?" Dante asked.

"I don't know. I just … I have a weird thought that sort of came to me out of nowhere that it's kind of important, so I want to run it down."

She has shade ancestry, for sure.

She turned to go, but stopped again.

"Is it okay if I ask his name?"

"Crowe," Kara said softly from the bed. "His name was Hudson Crowe."

After a quick review of the remaining patients in the Recovery Room, Dante took Kara's hand and they materialized in the middle of the War Room.

The room was an enormous pentagon, and the ceiling was made of glass that opened onto a sky thick with oppressive clouds. Normal rules of physics were even looser here. While this made it advantageous if they needed to further bend the laws to achieve their goals, it was less conducive to hosting "normal" things. Sometimes objects floated. Sometimes people floated.

Ghosts tended to blink out. In order to keep it useful, Parabiology had to normalize the physical space before meetings with more physical things, like people.

While the glass ceiling gave an unencumbered view of the sky, each of the five walls of the room was covered with screens. On the wall directly in front of them were screens dedicated to security. On them, the Office, and its subsidiaries, were monitored from all angles. There were thousands of cameras throughout the building, monitoring all levels of activity. They were a necessary evil as this building held more secrets, more intel, and more people who could be weaponized than any other building in the world, challenged only by the Academy headquarters. So this meant that they would be a target for any other covert agency that discovered their existence—and there were always leaks. Therefore, constant security was a requirement for the safety of everyone in the Office, and the safety of their story.

On the wall to the far left, a second set of screens monitored the vital signs of the planet. Of course, it tracked weather, temperature, and natural disasters but it also tracked physical and biological signatures of tagged humans and animals, including temperature, heart rates, breathing rates, blood cell counts, and hormone levels. The data presented here tracked current viral infections, and potential viral infections, through changes in normal physiology. The data on these screens were monitored by both Biology and Parabiology for any outliers. Screens where anomalies were detected were tinted red. This would happen if a population suddenly fell outside of the normal expected bell curve on some parameter. For example, if there was a sudden spike in sickness, injuries, or deaths in a geographic region or particular species.

The wall to the near left had screens dedicated to behavioral monitoring. These tracked areas of increased violence, aggression, sexual activity, expressions of joy or jubilation, and risky behaviors. Changes in behavior was another sign of infections and contaminations that might be occurring in populations not actively being tracked. The images that flashed across these display screens were difficult to watch at the best of times. Mostly they displayed news feeds from around the world. But, as opposed to conventional wisdom pertaining to data analysis, they tended to shun the middle of the road for what was happening on the fringes. This gave them a better idea of how far from the center things were drifting and how quickly. They also had numerous cameras set up in wilderness areas to track the behavior of animal populations. So, on this wall, it wasn't too unusual to see a video feed of a world leader right next to a feed of animals fucking.

The wall to their near right had screens that tracked the flow of electrical currents across the planet. This meant everything from streetlamps to lightning to the electrical energy emitted by humans. This wall was more esoteric and therefore more interesting to Dante. Ghosts showed up as electrical images on these monitors, so if he saw a hub of electricity that was unexplained, then it could possibly be a congregation of ghosts. Also, spikes or waves of electromagnetic energy tended to precede large physical events, including epidemics. Any unusually large drains on electricity were always inspected to make sure they were not related to activities by the Academy.

Along the far-right wall were screens that tracked the Dreamscape. This was the resonance level at which most humans dreamed, just above the ghoul level. It was a shared mental landscape where consciousnesses of different creatures inhabiting different resonances could meet and interact. For humans, this was usually only during sleep. Across these screens random words and images flashed—pictures coming from ghosts, humans, and Cambion whose consciousness was currently inhabiting the Dreamscape.

Of course, none of these particular screens looked like normal computer screens. They were thicker and spongier and were encased in liquid. This allowed for greater connectivity across different resonances.

It was in front of this screen that Joe was now standing, with Liz next to him.

"What's happening, Joe?" Kara asked, as she approached him. Joe twitched ever so slightly before turning around.

"We have a bigger problem than I initially thought." He pulled out a stack of papers and placed it on a semicircular desk. His jaw was clenched and the demon tattoos on his head were dancing.

"I scanned for all the Cambion humans registered with us who had ghost watchers, like you asked, but nothing came up. There were no matches to that search," he said.

"What? There should be at least forty ghost watchers out there," Dante said, forgetting that Joe couldn't hear him.

"Dante said there should be forty," Liz interjected.

"Yeah, I knew that," Joe replied crisply. "So I did a search on all the ghost watchers that I could remember by name, but none of them came up in our records either. Then I went to check the messages that had been sent to that invisible junk mail folder. I ran a search in that file for all the watchers' names I could remember. And still nothing came up. So I started going through all forms of communication manually, not using search terms. It turns out that there were emails from a few other ghost watchers besides Lazlo in that file, but they had been stripped of all their identifying markers."

"How did you know who it was then?" asked Liz.

"Some of the more physical ghosts used emails, and signed their names," Joe replied.

"We are old-fashioned like that," Dante said, with a fleeting smile.

"After I found that, I grabbed a small team and we used the emails, apartment records, credit card assignments and usage, gym memberships, anything we could find to trigger our memory of the human Cambions that had ghosts attached to them, or the ghosts themselves. We also checked medical records because most Cambion with ghost watchers had more significant medical vulnerabilities. We did it fast, but we had most of the departments involved. We came up with a list of thirty-eight Cambion who should have ghost watchers."

"Well done, Joe," Kara said. "You did a lot in a short time frame."

Joe nodded. He didn't smile but he stood a bit taller.

"We did a bit more too. We checked security codes."

"Right, ghosts have codes, not facial recognition," Dante said, nodding.

"And ghosts don't register with facial recognition software, so we have to assign codes for them to check in and out," Joe said, almost as if he had heard Dante. "They also need to use this code if they need to requisition something for their ward. For example, if they need a medical done or a test run. Our ops department will organize that and assign it the code of the ghost."

"Joe, you're amazing," Kara said.

"I found the names of the ghosts in question in the field by their security codes. We discovered the names of the Cambion by the requisitions that had been filed. There were forty-two Cambion in total. And only ghosts who were watchers for Cambion seem to be missing from the system. That, plus the fact we found these in the security code system and not in the overall tracking systems, means that it's not a broad system error. They both run on the same system."

"What does that mean?" Kara asked.

"It means the stripping and erasure was specific, that the ghosts and

Cambion were removed from the tracking system purposefully."

"Was this an inside job?" Liz asked.

Joe nodded. The demons on his head were twitching again and his face looked murderous. The idea that they had a traitor in their midst was anathema to Joe, and he would be all too happy to "disappear" them when they were found.

"What's worse is that we have tried to contact all forty-two of these watchers and the Cambion they were assigned to but with no success," Joe said through gritted teeth. "So I asked Dr. Lepri to meet us here. I have the names of the Cambion, and I can try to run them down physically, but the ghosts I can't. I was wondering ... I thought ... well, I thought maybe Dante could find the missing ghosts on these monitors."

"The monitors don't work like that," Dante began, but Joe continued.

"Also, I've been looking at these monitors and something is different on it." Joe pointed to the monitors that scanned the Dreamscape. "Some of the images in there look different to anything I've seen before."

"What do you mean, different?" asked Kara.

"They look—I don't know, too clean. Watch for a minute."

The four of them stared at the bank of screens and it didn't take long for Dante to see what Joe was talking about. The images looked indistinct, or smeared, like images in dreams. But every so often an image would flash by that was sharper, crisper than the others. It just lasted a millisecond and then it was gone.

"I see it," Liz said.

"Yes," Kara said. "Do you have a thought as to what it is?"

"No, not really," Joe replied. "But I was wondering if, maybe—well, I know it sounds dumb, but what if the ghosts somehow got caught in the Dreamscape. Would that change the images we see?"

"No, I don't think so," Kara said. "Ghosts operate in much the same way as humans in the Dreamscape. They are only partially there, and their images are the same. That is something different. Those images look way too physical to be ghosts or even to be in the Dreamscape."

The door behind them opened and Jeremy Lepri entered the room.

"Hello everyone, sorry it took me a while to get here. I got lost working on the viruses downstairs. What's happening?"

"It appears that every single one of our ghost watchers and the Cambion that they were watching have gone missing," Kara said. Her voice had taken on that icy tone that was not a good sign.

"What? All of them? How?"

"We're not sure but it seems to be an inside job. Joe was wondering if there was some biometric way to search for the ghosts," Dante said.

"No, I don't think so. I mean, unless they had a particular signature that we could search for."

"Would a specific electromagnetic signature work?" Dante asked.

"Yes, if I had something that was unique about the ghosts in question but not about other ghosts or other people. But that's unlikely."

"Maybe not," Dante said. "I have a thought. It's not a reassuring thought, but it's something that I can test. Jeremy, did you happen to test the resonance of the viruses that the Manassas boys were infected by?"

"No, not specifically," Lepri replied. "But I can, and I will. What are you thinking?"

"I'm thinking that Tobias, Lazlo's charge, might have been infected by the same virus that infected the Manassas boys. I want to know if Lazlo's resonance could have been altered by that virus."

Lepri nodded. Kara's eyes widened.

"I got Lazlo's resonance measurements, so I will compare it to the Manassas boys, other ghosts, and his previous readings. It may tell us something but it's not a huge dataset."

"I know, so I will need to go to the 8th to test it," Dante said. "There are some ghosts there who I know interacted with the Manassas boys."

"Do you think this is an Academy attack?" Joe turned to Kara. "Do we need to lock down?"

"Not yet, but walk me through our emergency protocols just in case," Kara said. "And we need a way to sweep for a traitor."

Joe nodded.

"I brought the protocols with me," Joe said, walking with Kara toward the table covered with papers. Lepri followed them. Kara suddenly stopped in front of one set of monitors, but she wasn't looking at them. She was looking at her phone.

"My love, you need to see this," Kara said.

"What is it?" Dante asked.

"Oh shit," Lepri said, coming up behind her.

"I got the data back from Tobias Solomon's body. It looks like he *did* have the same virus as the Manassas boys—and the reporter."

"Damn," Dante muttered.

"It gets worse. The results of the resonance scan for Lazlo show that his resonance had dropped significantly."

"From when he joined us?" Dante asked.

"No, from his most recent scan, only a year ago."

Dante read the email over her shoulder.

"Jesus. That's a giant drop."

"What does that mean?" Liz asked, startling Dante. She had been so quiet he had forgotten she was there.

"What does what mean?" Kara asked.

"What is a resonance? Is it like resonance in physics?"

"Not really," Kara replied. "It's a term of art we use. To explain it simply, everything vibrates at a certain speed, which is their energy signature. All things, living, dead, not alive, each have a rate of vibration that's unique. All creatures have unique resonances but similar creatures fall within similar bands of resonance. This speed of vibration, or resonance, determines what level of our existence we live in. The faster it vibrates the higher the resonance and the less physical it is. Ghosts resonate much faster than humans. Non-human spirits resonate even faster. The fact that Lazlo's energy pattern has changed is completely abnormal. Only a handful of creatures have ever changed their resonance significantly, unless they die."

"Is that a problem?" Liz asked.

"Yes, it means that he had been altered at the core of what he is," Dante said. "This might change what options he has for reincarnation, if any."

"If spirits, or something else, had changed resonance, could the spirits show up like the weird shapes there?" Liz pointed to the screen.

Kara whipped her head around and looked at Liz. Then she turned back to the murky screens.

"I don't know," she said.

"If Lazlo's signature was changed to something more solid, maybe," Dante replied.

Something was twisting in the back of Dante's brain. Nothing existed between the Dreamscape and the Ghoul Lands. Human physical existence was just below that of the ghouls. Human psychics called this area the astral layer, but it was nothing but mental static and astral junk. It was just a place humans quickly passed through before getting to the Dreamscape. Incubi almost never went there, as they weren't heavy enough to get past the

Dreamscape. Except for Clovis, but he was gone. And he didn't really go to that particular area for any other reason besides the fact that through it he could get to …

The hallway.

There were rumors of hidden but universal entrances to the hallway between the Dreamscape and the Ghoul Lands. The explanation was that it was a misunderstanding of the dynamics of the hallway. Entrances were person specific, residing inside only a rare number of people.

But what if this is wrong and there ***is*** *more general access to the hallway? What if anything at the proper resonance could have access? Even if they were normal, decent ghosts, the results of entering the hallway could be catastrophic …*

Dante turned to Lepri.

"Jeremy, can you work with Joe to check the resonance energies on all of the visuals that appear on the screen for the next few hours? And can you then isolate the images based on the weight of their resonance and compare that with Lazlo's resonance?"

"You think that might be a way to track our missing ghosts and Cambion?" Kara asked.

"Maybe."

"Do what you have to do," Kara said, "but we need answers fast. We have a new virus and missing Cambion who may have been kidnapped. Our security has also been breached which means the safety of *all* our people has been compromised. My gut tells me that these things are connected and, if they are, we have a good guess of the culprit."

"And if it is them, then what?" Dante asked.

"I will deal with them directly."

Dante felt a rabbit crawl over his grave.

"You need to rest, my love," he said softly. "Go to our room and have a nap. I'll join you as soon as I've dropped by the 8th floor."

Kara sighed and nodded. The dark under her eyes was getting darker.

"I could use a nap, just a short one," she said. With that, she disappeared, but Dante felt her words hang in the air.

"*I will deal with them directly.*"

The last time Kara dealt with the Academy directly, an island sank, and a civilization was lost.

Chapter Thirteen

The Invisible Disappear

In the elevator on his way to the 8th floor, Dante glanced at the small device he held in his hand, the one he had just been given by Lepri. It was smaller than he expected but it had to be small and light for Dante to be able to carry it for any length of time. For ghosts to carry objects, they had to use a very grounded form of energy and while Dante was more physical than most ghosts, he still had his limits. Lepri assured him that once it was switched on, it would read the resonance signatures of every creature around him, alive or dead. This would then be plotted on a graph showing their distance from point zero, which was Dante, so he could determine the owner of each energy signature. As an added benefit, it would present resonances that were normal in yellow and those that were falling outside of the normal range in bright red, so that even an idiot could see it immediately. He slipped the device into his pocket as the elevator door opened onto the Office's most dangerous floor.

After hearing the news about Lazlo's lowered resonance, Dante realized that he should take samples of a cross section of ghosts to get controls. If the watcher ghosts of the missing Cambion had the same altered resonance as Lazlo, then it might be a way to find them. It had also occurred to him that Lazlo might not be the only one with a lowered resonance.

Despite its inherent dangers, when Dante stepped out of the elevator and into the 8th floor, he felt a loosening of stress throughout his being. There was nothing psychological about this. In truth, the 8th floor and its inhabitants had the tendency to be significantly more stressful to deal with than humans. The beings who called this space in the Office home were from wildly differing cultures, countries, and centuries. And, while all of them were spirits, not all of them were human spirits. This was something that Kara often forgot.

What was comforting about this space, for Dante, was its very lack of homogeneity and consistency. Even in life, Dante hadn't fit the standards of normal for his particular culture and time. In death, and in the first few hundred years after death, this difference became more pronounced. But here and now, standing in this organization he helped to build and looking out into this space that had been normalized for all manner of spirits and ghosts, he felt almost average in his particular diversities.

Almost.

The space on the 8th floor changed constantly, based on the whims and histories of those spirits present at the time. Today, its landscape could best be described as Tolkien meets Escher. There were plants winding around marble columns and staircases, but none of these structures seemed to be tied to gravity, perspective, or even dimensional space. There were a few objects here and there that were clearly made by a creature with the ability to see and create in more dimensions than three or even four. These objects looked somewhat disturbing to Dante, but were a normal human to look at them, they would likely be driven mad.

Dante heard a roar from above and saw Abi standing atop a large, grassy pyramid.

"So cometh the Dark Man," Abi said, leaping down onto an inverted chessboard, whose pieces were hanging beneath it, wrapped in spiders' webs. The mutated spiders were crawling over both sides of the board but scrambled away at the sight of Abi. Abi took no notice of them, but simply used the chessboard as a springboard to get to the stairs that Dante was standing on.

Dante smiled. Abi always made him smile, even when he was troubled.

"To what do we owe the honor?" Abi asked with a bow.

"You act like I never see you," Dante replied. "I saw you a couple days ago."

"A day away from my dearest friend feels like an eternity," Abi said. "But I wasn't referring to me, exactly. We so rarely see you here on the 8th. Some think you have become too solid to be here anymore."

Ah, the natives are restless and rumormongering again.

"No, but solidness is part of the reason I have come. We've had some problems. As some of them involve ghosts, I wanted to have my facts straight before I visited," Dante said.

"You are visiting with a definite purpose?"

"Yes. I have come to call a quorum." As Dante uttered these words, the air around him began to tingle in a slightly painful way, like dragging skin across brittle ice crystals.

He looked around. Abi was now crouched on his haunches, swishing his tail back and forth and clamping his mandibles open and shut. The posture looked aggressive, but Dante knew it to be Abi's acknowledgment of Dante's superior position in the ghost world. He would defend Dante if anyone questioned that. He had proven this in the past, to the regret of several, now eternally defaced, spirits.

Dante cleared his throat.

"I said, I have come to call a quorum. Now, please." He bowed his head slightly and spirits began appearing all around him, his voice having called them from wherever they happened to be in the vast, almost limitless, space of the 8th floor. As they appeared, some were seated, with cups in their hands, as if having tea. Others fell from the ceiling. After only a few moments, what had been an empty space was now filled with hundreds of ghosts, from every imaginable race, culture, and time period. He also saw a few elementals and nature spirits in the mix.

"First, I would ask that everyone here confirm your status as a human ghost," Dante said. "The topic for today's meeting really only concerns human ghosts."

The elementals and a few other entities around the room disappeared. Dante was sure they were more than happy to do so. These meetings were not universally loved by the undead. In fact, one of the ghosts once made a point of saying that one of the few real perks of being dead was never having to attend another meeting.

"I'm sorry to exercise such formality but there's an issue that we need to address together," Dante began. "I need your help, but before I ask for it, I need to tell you what you might be heading into."

There was muttering, twittering, and rustling around the room.

"I'm afraid we have several ghosts that have gone missing."

"What is it you mean, missing?" interrupted a ghost wearing the remnants of a navy-blue uniform that had wide legs and an equally wide collar. He was also wearing a ridiculous-looking beanie with an inscription that looked to be written in Norwegian. Of course, Dante was not really in a position to call anyone else's clothing ridiculous.

"Please let me tell you the whole story before you ask any questions," Dante said. They were ghosts, so they would still interrupt, but maybe less.

"Recently, I was called to a school shooting, in Manassas, Virginia," Dante began, using his most modulated vocal tone. "At the site, I saw a fully formed, visible airborne virus."

The questions started almost immediately.

"You actually saw it?"

"What type of virus?"

"You were completely within Malkuth, right?"

"Please, hold questions," Dante said raising his hand. Abi growled and there was sudden silence.

"We trapped the virus inside a news reporter who had a corrupted code. Later, when Kara and I went to see the reporter, the virus emerged and tried to attack me. It was actually able to touch me."

Gasps were audible around the room, but no one spoke.

"Kara unmade the virus, but we found remnants of it in the blood samples taken from the shooter. We also discovered evidence of the same virus in the blood samples of a kid who shot up the same school eighteen years ago. We suspect that it is not a natural virus."

"Is it a danger to us ghosts?" asked a female voice from the back.

Abi growled again, but Dante held up hand.

"The truth is that we don't know yet, but that is only the first part of the story. A few days ago, we discovered that our computer systems have become corrupted. As a result of this, and after a search of files, we found that we had lost contact with as many as forty of our watchers and their wards. An unusual number of these watchers were ghosts."

"Civil servants of the ghost world," muttered a posh voice with New England affectations. Dante knew the voice. Despite disliking its owner, he was relieved to hear it. He had questions for it.

"You lost contact with the watchers or the wards?" asked a woman wearing a full Victorian bloomers, a chemise, stockings, and corset. The only thing she was missing was about 25 percent of her skin. Bones stuck out in random places where the skin seemed to have taken a vacation.

"We lost contact with both the watchers and the wards," Dante replied. "But we have found emails sent to us that had been misdirected to a hidden junk mailbox that we had quite a difficult time finding and a more difficult time opening. One of the messages we had received was from Lazlo Fox."

"Oh, Lazlo, I love Lazlo," one of the younger female ghosts sitting near the front cooed. Dante could tell she was young because she had little clothing and what she had was so faint that she appeared almost naked.

There was more muttering from the crowd.

"Kara and I managed to track Lazlo to a mental facility where he had been locked into the comatose body of his ward," Dante said in slow, clear voice. The muttering stopped. All eyes were on him now.

"He told us that a woman had come to the hospital. She gave Lazlo's ward a drug that seemed to separate his soul from his body, while keeping his body alive. Once his soul was free, something that looked like black shapes came out of his mouth. Then the woman brought out a black box. Lazlo said that there had been something seductive about that box and that both his ward and the black shapes were pulled into it."

"Were the black shapes dream fragments or viruses?" asked a ghost dressed in a headdress and feathers.

"We don't know, but Lazlo said that the woman tried to draw him into it but, when she didn't succeed, she threatened to lock him into his body. She also told him that he might not like his new roommate."

"What does that mean?" asked the Victorian ghost.

"It means that they were planning to take his ward's body," Dante replied.

"And likely putting some other spirit into it," the Norwegian ghost muttered.

"Can they do that?" asked a young ghost.

"That and likely more," said the posh voice, with loud sniff.

"We don't know that," Dante said, stopping conversation. "However, this woman also told Lazlo that his 'friends' were happy to go into the box. He believed that the woman meant Cambion ghosts. It's worth noting that Lazlo's ward had a virus, and it was same virus we found in Manassas."

The group was now as silent as the grave.

Dante felt the weight of the device in his pocket. It was on and buzzing. He hoped no one would notice the sound. He would prefer not to explain that.

"Have any of you encountered or heard of anything like this before?" Dante asked.

A few ghosts looked around at each other. One or two looked like they might be about to speak when the posh voice spoke again. "None of us are watchers, so why would we?"

Dante turned to face the speaker, Howard. He was one of the floor's most pompous ghosts, which was saying a lot.

Howard was as unattractive as a ghost as he had been as a human, just more vividly so. In life, his long, oval face, close-cropped hair, hawk nose, oversized ears, thin lips, and protruding jaw had made him look as sullen and suspicious as a repressed religious zealot. In death, the left side of his face had been removed and replaced with a substance that looked like bubbling, bile-green tar. When he spoke, only half his mouth worked, while the other half spat out a bubbling foam of moss green. In life, Howard had been a horror writer, so perhaps this was not unfitting.

"To start with, we don't know that what happened with our watchers is limited to our watchers," Dante replied to Howard's question. "As Cambion ghosts are less tracked than Cambion mortals, I'm not sure if we would know if others had gone missing."

"Oh, so you couldn't even take care of your slaves, but now you are worried about us?" Howard snapped.

There was a none too subtle growl from Dante's left.

"You'll keep a civil tongue in your mouth, Howard, or I will remove your entire head this time," Abi snarled.

Howard shrunk back instinctively, caught himself and then puffed himself up to about twice his normal size.

"I have a right to ask questions," he spat.

"That wasn't a question," Abi spat back.

"All right then, I have a right to my opinions as well."

"You have what?" Abi said, standing, tail swishing, in a manner a bit too suggestive of stalking prey. "Did you say you have a right, you sniveling, cowardly—"

"Abi, this doesn't help things," Dante said.

"His comment was rude," Abi said, but he sat back down.

"I know, but I will ignore the rudeness for now, and answer the implied question for everyone else. All the watchers who disappeared were Cambion ghosts who were watchers by choice, not by commission. So they are far from slaves. We track them more carefully because the work they do does put them in vulnerable situations. We *could* track all of you that way, but, if you remember, you have directly voted not to be tracked, and we have respected that."

He looked pointedly at Howard.

"I heard something about a dark light. It wasn't exactly a box, but it sounds similar," said a ghost from the back in a throaty voice. Dante didn't recognize the voice or the ghost, but she sounded like a New Yorker. She was tiny with raven hair and large, light eyes. She was clothed in a shabby dark blue dress that was common to recently deceased ghosts. So she had been a ghost for less than fifty years.

"Who are you?" Dante asked.

"My name is Judith."

"What have you heard, Judith?"

"Well, I'm new," she began, "so I've been asking a lot of questions and listening a lot to what the other ghosts say. Of course, people have told me not to go near power lines and to avoid anyone who claims to be a psychic medium because they get human goo all over you. But one person did tell me about this dark light."

Everyone was quiet, all eyes on the girl. She glanced around the room before continuing.

"I had a bit of a difficult transition to being a ghost. I didn't really choose the path, it sort of chose me."

"What does that mean?" someone asked.

"It means that the woman who was supposed to be my ride told me that, given what my life had been like, my next ones were likely to be very difficult. She suggested that I stay put for a while and try to work out some of my karma as a ghost."

"Did she?" Dante said. "That's uncommon."

"Uncommon to have bad karma?" the girl asked.

"No, it's uncommon for someone to tell you that, because it's not really true. The woman, she didn't happen to have red hair, did she?"

"Yes, she did, how did you know?"

Dante had a good idea who that was but didn't want to get into it now.

"I might know her, but continue your story about the dark light."

"So, as I started meeting people, I started asking them how long they had been a ghost, and how long most people were ghosts. I started to get really upset because everyone said that the ghost gig was for hundreds of years, sometimes thousands. They said that you had to wait until someone showed up for you again. I started to get really depressed. This was before I knew this place existed. So one day I was talking to another ghost, and I was really down, and he said that there was another way to get back into life."

She stopped for a minute and swallowed.

"He said that you could go through the dark lights. He said that they lead you to a door where you can get into another world. He said you can be human again, but better," she whispered.

"Did he say what and where these dark lights were?" Dante asked.

"No, but he said they were hidden. He said that they had always existed but now they were easier to get to ..."

"I heard something like that too, from a ghoul," Abi said. "He said the dark light could make you human. He was entranced by the idea of it, but he couldn't find a way into it. He said it shimmered in the distance, away from him. I thought it was just a ghoul myth. They have a lot of those."

"Are we trusting information from ghouls now?" Howard snorted.

"They are more trustworthy than some humans I know," Abi countered.

"Oh, that's right. You're a ghoul, not a human. So why are you in this meeting anyway. Just to be Dante's guard dog?"

Abi was up and had Howard's head in his mouth before Dante could speak.

"Abi! Stop now! This gets us nowhere." Dante pushed Abi away from Howard with a flick of his hand.

Abi sat back down next to Dante, breathing hard. Howard, head dripping with saliva, had scrambled to the corner. He was no coward, despite what Abi said. No coward would provoke Abi. Only a species-ist.

"Abi is part ghoul and part human. So he should be in this meeting. His Cambion nature with ghouls makes him invaluable to our relationship with them," Dante said to the room, then turned to Howard.

"But since you've chosen to speak, I do have a question specifically for you, Howard. What do you know about the habits of the boy in Manassas?"

"What boy in Manassas?"

"The shooter we were discussing earlier," Dante replied. "And don't bother telling me you don't know who he is. I know you do, and I wouldn't want to embarrass you by telling you how and what I know."

Howard dimmed a bit. He also pulled himself inward so that he appeared significantly smaller.

"Were you actually at the shooting in Manassas?" Dante asked.

"No. No. I didn't see that. That was later. I just came across him one day when I was skimming along the wind," Howard said.

Dante doubted this, as Howard was not a carefree, "skim the wind" sort of ghost, but he let it go.

"How long ago did you first see him?"

"A couple of years ago. I recognized him as Cambion immediately. He had a real shine to him," Howard said.

"So why didn't you alert us to him?"

"How was I to know he wasn't in your precious system? I can't imagine that you could have missed him, given his stats."

"What stats are those then?" Dante asked. Howard suddenly developed an interest in the flooring.

"Answer carefully here, Howard, and don't even think about lying. I will know and I will let Abi deal with you—or worse, I will let Kara deal with you."

All the ghosts in the room dimmed at the mention of Kara.

He shouldn't threaten. He didn't need to; they all knew what she was capable of doing to them. They were less aware of what he could do to them, or they would never appear in his presence.

Howard was barely visible at this point. When he spoke, his voice was like the sound of a dry wind.

"Okay. First, the Manassas boy, he had that almost preternatural shine. That gleaming thing that only special ghosts like me can see in Cambion. Second, he seemed to have both ghost and incubus lineage. I guess the incubus bit was what made him seem so overwhelmingly beautiful. The ghost part meant that he resonated a bit higher than most humans, so I could … well, sometimes I could … I mean, in moments …"

"He's trying to say that we could touch him," said another ghost in the opposite corner. He was a greasy little smear of a ghost with a mop of tangled spider's-web-like substance on his head.

Several ghosts gasped out loud.

"Phillip Sawyer, that was your name, correct?" Dante asked.

"Yes," Sawyer replied.

Dante looked at this cringing creature with disdain. He was quite surprised that he had already made it back into ghost form after being unmade so recently. That usually took hundreds—or thousands—of years. Quick descending only happened with great growth or great desire. Dante suspected the latter.

"You also saw this boy?"

"Yes. His name was David Spanarkle."

"And what was that about touching him?" Dante asked. "Are you normally able to touch the living? That's an extremely rare gift."

"No, no. It was just him," Sawyer said, now beginning to sputter and dim even more beneath Dante's gaze.

"It was him, not us," Howard interjected. "His resonance must have been extremely high for a human."

"Is that why you were drawn to him?"

"No, it didn't start out that way. We didn't start being able to touch him. It happened after we had been around him a bit."

"So how many times did you visit this boy?"

"Five or six."

"Is this what you remember?" Dante turned to Sawyer. Howard was staring at Sawyer, who was fidgeting, squirming, and shrinking.

"Dante asked you a question," Abi said.

"I … I … well, I can't say how many times Howard saw him, but I saw him much more often," he said, twisting his hands.

"I see, and how many times did you see him, with or without Howard?" Dante asked.

"Not so many in the beginning but once we found we could touch him, well, it was more toward the end. Maybe ten or twenty times."

"That's a lot of time to spend with one boy," Dante said.

"Look, it wasn't like he noticed us. He never felt us touch him. We only did it when he was distracted with that video game he played. When he was in the game, he didn't notice real life, let alone a couple of ghosts."

Dante felt a jolt in his system at these words. Lazlo had mentioned Tobias playing a game …

At that moment, Dante felt another buzzing in his pocket. The device had finished uploading, reading, and analyzing the data.

Dante looked at the ghosts around him. Most looked distracted, it was hard to hold their attention for too long, but some looked intent and worried.

"I told you that I was going to ask for your help," he said. "Those on this floor are the best hunters and trackers in this story. So I need you to track down our missing ghosts."

Dante waved his hand in the air, and a piece of paper materialized. It wasn't physical paper, of course, it was made of the same stuff as the rest of the 8th floor.

He laid the paper on a slanted table nearby.

"This holds the names of all the missing watchers and their Cambion, who are also missing. I want every one of you to do nothing else but search for these people until I return. Search the timelines you have access to, talk to the newly deceased and the non-Cambion ghosts."

He looked at them, making a point of catching the eye of everyone who actually had the nerve to look at him.

"Abi will ensure that each of you looks at the list," he said. "Anyone who fails to comply will have their name sent to Kara."

He had their undivided attention. It was time to add the finishing touch.

"Speaking of Kara, most of you know that she doesn't approve of you. She isn't shy about that. This is a moment to show your worth. I know what you can do. In my early years as a ghost, some of you here helped keep me from blinking out completely. All I want is for you to show her what I see in you. Show her what you can do."

Most of them were nodding.

"What do we do when we find someone?" asked the Norwegian ghost. Dante noticed that he said "when" and not "if."

"Let me know. If you can't find me, then tell Abi. He can always find me. Go now and do what you do best."

As he turned to the elevator, he heard the wind rise behind him, called to carry spirit riders across all ghostly resonances in their story.

Chapter Fourteen

Consequences Bite Back

Descending in the elevator, the device in Dante's pocket buzzed again. When he took it out, what he saw on the screen was not what he had expected.

At the bottom of the readout was a legend showing yellow, red, and navy dots. Next to the yellow dots was written *Normal.* The readout in front of him was covered with yellow dots, indicating that most of the ghosts on the 8th floor were resonating at normal levels. So that part was good.

However, there were other dots on the readout. The entire figures of Howard, Sawyer, and the new ghost, Judith, were distinctly red. Next to the red dot on the legend it read *Lower than expected ghost energy signature.* Howard and Sawyer had admitted to having direct contact with Spanarkle, who they now knew was contaminated with this virus. This gave weight to the hypothesis Dante was formulating, which was that the lowering of these ghost signatures was something they picked up from a Cambion host. Just as Dante believed that the time Lazlo spent inside Tobias's body had done something to lower Lazlo's energy signature, it could be that the resonance of Howard and Sawyer was lowered by the Spanarkle boy when they touched him. What he didn't know was whether the ghosts got sick from the host themselves or from the virus inside the host. He would also need to track down Judith again, to see who and what she had been in contact with. He wasn't completely surprised by these readings. In truth, he was relieved to see that none of the other ghosts seemed to be affected. This meant that whatever it was, it probably didn't pass from ghost to ghost, which had only happened once before, in Brazil. Still, he would need to work with Lepri to do a broader scan for viruses in the ghost community.

It was the third thing he saw on the readout that was turning his head around. In and around Howard, Sawyer, and Judith there were small dark dots. At first, he thought that this was simply part of the grid, but on closer examination, he saw that they were actually navy dots. On the legend, next to a navy dot were words that brought a chill to Dante's ghost heart.

Unreadable signature.

All natural things had a readable energy signature, even rocks and dirt. Something with an unreadable signature was something not natural. So these navy dots meant that something unnatural was now intermeshed in ghosts who already had a significantly lower resonance than they should. Either the machine wasn't working properly, or these three ghosts had become infected by something not of this story—and maybe the Cambion they had interacted with had been infected as well.

Dante needed to see Lepri immediately. He materialized in Lepri's lab, but Lepri was not there. He quickly bounced through some of Lepri's favorite haunts before giving up and returning to the lab.

Dante had been fairly sure the resonance readings of Howard, Sawyer, and Judith would be in the same band as the most recent reading of Lazlo. Initially, he had been afraid that ghosts were somehow getting directly infected with viruses. This wasn't impossible. It had happened before, but it was exceedingly rare. On the occasions where ghosts had been infected with viruses, it had driven them, and any human too close to them, mad. The Salem witch trials had been just this. The young girls had been calling down ghosts to possess them via rituals in the woods. Ghosts love this sort of thing. It really strokes their egos. Sadly, the girls had a virus that was capable of passing to ghosts. The ghosts in question went mad and created all sorts of havoc in the area. This havoc was attributed to witchcraft—and then the fun began. Before it was all over, Kara had needed to unmake no small number of humans and ghosts to correct the vulnerability in their codes which had resulted in the madness that followed.

What Dante was seeing on these scans was very different and even more worrying. The strange navy dots looked like an infection, but they were resonating at a level higher than humans, higher even than the Dreamscape, but below that of normal ghosts. He might have thought them bacteria or viruses, but they resonated at too high a level to be physical. Viruses tended to resonate a bit higher than humans, but only a tiny bit.

Dante had a gut feeling that these dots had something to do with the dark light—the dark box that the ghosts were talking about. As he didn't actually believe in intuition, per se, he assumed that this gut feeling was his subconscious mind making logical connections that his conscious mind had not caught up with yet.

Suddenly, a movement caught his eye. A fuzzy image had appeared on Lepri's computer screen, at the same moment a weird sound came through its speakers. It sounded almost like static but with a pitch. As Dante moved closer, he saw that it was the same image of the Manassas virus that Lepri had shown him earlier, but the angle looked different. The static sound changed to a thumping noise, like a heartbeat, or something caught in the computer and trying to beat its way out. The air around him felt colder. The image on the screen began to spin and the sound changed.

Ackackackackack

Dante recognized the sound. It was the exact noise made by the virus when they had pulled it from Grace at the TV station. A row of DNA sequencers next to Lepri's computer suddenly came on and emitted a sound like the hissing of snakes.

Sosososososososo

Dante felt the repulsion crawl over his body like worms and an energy rush escape him before he could bank it. It hit the computer, and exploded in all directions. At the same moment, alarms began to go off all around him, followed by a computerized voice. It took him a second to realize that it was not the sound of the virus but the voice of their environmental alarm system.

The lights above him flickered. Then they flickered again—no, it wasn't a new flicker. Light had a pattern in time that never repeated twice. This was the same flicker, just repeated.

Earth temperature dropped by 0.1 degree Celsius, said a metallic voice. *Return to living quarters.*

Earth temperature dropped by 0.1 degree Celsius, the voice said again. *Return to living quarters.*

This was not a second warning, it was a replication of the first, a loop in time.

Somumumumumu

The voice of the virus, tinny-sounding, drifted up from an old monitor shoved in one corner. Dante turned toward it and it too exploded.

The temperature was dropping.

Soooooooomuuuuuuuceeeeeerrrrr . . . Soooomuuchheeere . . . Sooomuchheeere

This time, the voice came through the emergency speakers.

Earth temperature dropped by 0.5 degrees Celsius.

Suddenly, the words sunk in—along with what they meant. The Earth was cooling.

"Kara—" he gasped, as he turned his inner eye toward her and threw himself at her.

As Dante began to materialize into their apartment, he felt their shared space. Its energy touched him, caressed him, and made him feel more grounded and whole. It was Kara's energy and so this was the place he normally went to rest, but not now. Now he felt something else lurking here, the presence of a creeping equilibrium. Equilibrium was death—no, worse than death. With no singularity, no attraction to draw consciousness back, everything stopped. Once, long ago, Kara was that singularity but that was before the Abomination. After that, Kara became something else, both more and less, but changed forever by outside forces. Dante became the amalgam of things that he was—and a pale replacement for her.

He heard her breathing over the sound of the alarms going off all over the building. At that sound, his physicality cemented in the room. The room was icy cold. Kara was asleep on their bed, fully clothed. She had pulled an ancient red silk blanket from their closet and now had it tangled around her, wrapping her arms like ropes. She had shoved a pillow between her legs and her black rayon dress was shoved up, showing one long, bare leg. The room smelled like her hair. Given her power, it was easy to forget how small she was, how delicately boned. Her face was beyond beautiful in repose, but her pale skin was too pale. She sighed in her sleep, making small clouds in the cold air as she breathed. The smell of her breath filled Dante's nostrils. Waves of desire hit him, making him dizzy and threatening to wash away logic, reason or even his current fear. Quickly, he lay down next to her and took her in his arms. That was when the extent of her cold hit him.

Kara's body was ice-cold—no, it was worse than ice-cold. It was space-cold. The sudden dip in global temperature was linked to what was happening in her body. As Kara went, so the story went.

He turned her over and saw that her face was blank. Her eyes were half-open, revealing only the white. Her unmoving body was not still, it was vibrating so fast that the movement could not be seen, only felt.

Fear seized Dante. He had waited too long to clear her, and she had gone over.

He put his arms around her and pulled her to him. She did not resist, nor did she acknowledge his presence. She opened her mouth and sounds began to issue from her lips. Some of these sounds were people sounds, moaning, crying, yelling, laughing … but all as if from a great distance. Other sounds were noises that no human mouth could produce. He heard the sounds of crowds. There was the sound of a whip and a gun. The sound of thunder and rain. The rushing sound of blood being pumped by an over-stressed heart.

These were the sounds of the memories and life histories that she had absorbed. It was this that was draining her heat, her energy, and her life. It happened slowly, over time. Every day, moment by moment, hour by hour, she collected imprints of the memories and lives of everything around her. In doing so, she connected and stabilized everything she encountered and, on some level, the creatures that had entered her presence felt this. But she could only absorb so much.

"I need to take you now, my love," he whispered into her ear, as alarms continued to shriek around them.

Dante pulled Kara more tightly to him, and she began to tremble in his arms. It would be hard to take her now. The lives of others that were infecting her, possessing her, would resist it. This was a ticking time bomb and he had known it for a while. Around him, he could feel the air getting colder still. Kara was the epicenter of this cold, which could become something to rival the cold of a boomerang nebula.

He concentrated his energy and slowly began to merge both of their energy signatures. As he did this, he felt the heat welling up in him. This was no normal heat. It was a heat that existed before physical laws. It had as much in common with normal heat as a supernova did with a lit match. This was something older and darker. It was hell's answer to the remote iciness of heaven, a heated darkness that came as an unsuspected gift from his distant ancestry.

Kara began to moan and squirm in his arms.

The sirens around them continued to blare but the sound of them became more muted, running together, individual sounds only distinguishable by volume.

His body was heating more, and Kara was beginning to pull away from him, but she was still cold. Her face still deathly pale with a bluish cast, her eyes white and rolled back in her head. He let the red-black passion that always lurked in the gut of him snake out further toward the surface … toward life and his more basic nature. Dante allowed this passion to escape him, reaching out for Kara's very soul.

Dante pulled himself and Kara into the core of him, and into the hallway that resided there. It existed at the crux of where he ended and time began. It was where the code he inherited all those years ago was kept safe and secret. The hallway itself had always been a calm place, even if the doors inside it could hold horrors.

But today it was smoldering and filled with acrid smoke.

Dante felt the stone around his neck like a lead weight, pulling his head down. The walls of the hallway were covered in something burned and peeling. It looked disturbingly like skin. The floor was covered in ash. As he felt his own heat rise to protect them from the environment, lines of small flames erupted from the ashy floor, leading in one direction. He didn't know why this was happening, but he did know that the last time he saw the door he needed it had been in the direction taken by the flames—at least, he thought so. The smell of smoke was interfering with his ability to smell the door he needed with certainty.

Suddenly, Kara woke, her eyes wild and pure white.

"We have to get out of here!" she shrieked. "It's coming after us!"

She pushed away from him, and they both fell to the ground. Kara rolled as she hit it and immediately assumed a crouching position, head down.

"Ssssshhhh, my love," Dante said, as he slowly stood up. When Kara looked up at him, whatever fear she had felt had passed. What was left on her face was bright rage.

"What is this place?" she snarled, as she stood, putting her hands out to either side of her.

"It's only me, my love." Dante moved toward her.

"It's NOT you. THIS is NOT YOU."

A frigid wind began swirling around her. Where it met the heat and smoke, it created rivulets of water that hung in the air around them. In none of their other trips here had she awakened before they had entered the door, but in no other trip had the hallway itself been in distress.

Dante felt something in his ghost body begin to spasm. Whatever Kara did in this hallway would impact the substance that defined him. He grabbed her and pulled her to him, at the same time releasing the heat that was inside him, calling it from all corners of the hallway. He kissed her with the passion of all their eternities together. He pulled her body tight to his, as he had in thousands of different bodies and thousands of different lifetimes. Kara pushed against him, burning him with the cold of her lips.

Is she really that far gone? Would she really be willing to freeze not just me, but the hallway itself—our connection to reality?

He had barely thought this when he felt himself yanked back to the outer limits of his body. He was back lying on his bed, with Kara in front of him. Without opening her eyes, she put her arms around his neck and pulled his face to hers, kissing him. There was now a sheen to her face.

She was starting to sweat.

Dante pulled his heat back in. He put his lips to Kara's neck. Sure enough, her skin tasted wet and salty. He looked at her face. The blue undertone that had been there was fading, replaced by a growing flush.

The alarms suddenly went silent.

Kara's eyes fluttered open and lit up when she saw his face.

"You're here," she whispered. "I had a terrible nightmare."

"I'm here." Dante pulled her closer. When she kissed him, it was with no reserve and no memory of what had just happened.

Dante pulled the heat back inside himself and used it to fuel moving their bodies back to a normal resonance, or normal for them. As her mouth opened and she kissed him deeply, he let himself be enveloped by the desire of that kiss, and toward the energy they made between them in these moments. An energy that was unknown and unknowable to anyone but them. In the heat of their attraction, consciousness continued to be created and recreated.

Afterward, he let her sleep. When he had seen her lying there, cold and in danger, everything else had faded to nothing in his head. The world outside could have burned away, and he wouldn't have given it a thought, as long as Kara was here with him and safe. The Office, their mission, their passion stemmed from her passion, not his. She was the one who wanted to protect the Cambion. She was the one who insisted on monitoring viruses that might hurt them. It was she who feared for the safety of this story.

Right now, Dante only had one fear. One overwhelming fear. He had been unable to take Kara to be cleaned.

This is NOT YOU.

That was what Kara had said. She had said something similar the last time he had tried to take her. So her words were not a fluke. They were not a moment of panic. He needed to find out why this was happening and how to correct it. Was it because she had been awake both times and that was an anomaly? But then, what had driven that anomaly? Or was all this because she was infected and that changed her perspective? This wouldn't be surprising. Dante had been seeing strains of sickness above and beyond the viruses they were tracking. Kara's presence seemed to be triggering some immune reactions in Cambion. If he had been given more time, he might have been able to convince her to go through the hallway with him, but time, and Kara's waking, hadn't been the only things different. This time, the hallway hadn't looked like any other time he had been there in the millennia that he had been going. At times, it could be a place of high energy, or even high anxiety, but he had never seen it ravaged before, and that was how it had looked.

Dante looked down at Kara's sleeping form. There was so much that was contained in such a small creature. Looking at her, just at her form, no one would suspect that worlds resided inside her. Kara was a creature of order and balance. Many who knew her would have a hard time believing or even understanding that. Those were the people who thought of balance as a static thing, a dead pendulum stuck in the center position. In truth, movement and change was the nature of balance, and so it was Kara's nature as well. Her emotional, mental, and spiritual range was almost beyond comprehension. She was both a destroyer and a savior. She was ecstasy and torment, despair and epiphany, evolution and stagnation. She was life and death.

He, on the other hand, was a creature of chaos. When people contemplated the nature of chaos—the very few who were inclined to do so—most considered it a thing of movement and change. But chaos, the very nature of it, was the opposite of change. Chaos never changed, it stayed chaotic. Its nature was bounded and stagnant in that way, and this was the real reason why it was the opposite of order and balance. In life, people made choices between the chaos of stagnation and change needed for life on a daily basis. In death, they did the same. This is how Dante started out on his path as a creature of chaos, but not by choice. Most ghosts, on the other hand, made the conscious choice to remain the same. This was the real reason that Kara didn't like them. They were creatures that existed in opposition to her nature.

Even before he and Kara had been pulled together, Kara had the seed of this order and balance in her. The DNA of her soul allowed for this breadth of existence. When he had seen her and seen this in her, he had been a young ghost, only a few centuries old. He had been drawn to her and, even though he could not interact with her or be with her in any way, he had tracked her. He watched her spirit reincarnate two or three times, always able to find her by this special quality that she had. He could see it with a sense that didn't exist in life, only in death. And he, like a creature of true chaos, did nothing, he remained static. He simply watched her through lifetimes. All that changed in one moment during the time of the Abomination. As he saw Kara on the desert sands, broken and burned in body and soul, he chose. He chose not to accept random chaos. He chose not to accept a static state. To save her, he chose to change the nature of absolutely everything—his nature, her nature, the nature of the universe, the nature of their story. In forcing him to make this choice, Kara had inadvertently saved his sorry soul.

So while it was her duty to carry consciousness, and all the souls and memories of everything in existence, it was his duty to accept and carry her memories from the Abomination and before, including the pain and horror of her own making. He bore these willingly because the weight of them, added to everything else, could destroy her.

So he had to find a way to clean her out soon. She could only hold so much; it had been too long, and she had been out in the world too much. It was making her weak and vulnerable. Crazy and hair-triggered was something he could mitigate, but weak and vulnerable would put the onus on him to do what was right, and he wasn't reliable enough to do so. He only cared about her and keeping her healthy. That was his duty and his right.

Suddenly, the image of the black blob that had fallen from him after leaving Liz at the café inserted itself into his head. The shape of that blob was not dissimilar to the shape of the Manassas virus. And then—just now—the looped light flicker and the repetition of the alert, that felt like a time loop. Not a consciousness anomaly, a glitch in time. This thought chilled him to the bone. What if the virus that attacked them at the TV station hadn't just infected Kara? That was bad enough but he had always been able to clean her out of all that infected her or overwhelmed her. But what if *he* had become infected? If he was infected, there would be no one to clean Kara.

And that would mean the end of their story as they knew it.

Chapter Fifteen

Up for Dead

"Sorry for the mess," Lepri said, as Dante appeared in the room. He gestured at the burned-out husk of the computer and shattered glass everywhere. He had a broom in one hand and a dustpan in the other and was sweeping debris into little piles.

"I have no idea what happened, maybe it had something to do with the alarms that were going off."

"Only partially," Dante replied. "What happened in here was my fault."

"Did the computer piss you off?" Lepri asked.

"No, I saw the virus inside it—and it tried to talk to me."

"*What?*"

"It appeared on the computer screen all by itself. It also seemed to turn on different devices in the room."

"Biological viruses cannot—" Lepri began, but Dante raised his hand.

"Speak? I know, but I think we can both agree that this virus is not acting like a normal biological virus," he said.

"If it's speaking, doesn't that mean it has consciousness?"

"Recording devices don't have consciousness. They just replay what has been put into them. This might be the same type of thing."

He didn't mention that a virus attaining consciousness was something that would mean that Dante himself would have to fix the problem, and that was something that would inevitably change the story and make it even less stable. This was the nuclear option, in a very real sense.

"Right now, there are other, more immediate concerns that I have," he said. "What level of clearance has security given you?"

"CAM12," Lepri said.

"Well, I need something from you that requires a CAM14 level."

"Doesn't it only go up to CAM13?"

"That's what we tell people at CAM12," Dante said. "Can you send Joe a message and tell him that I am authorizing that, and that we will meet him in the War Room at 14:00 hours?"

Lepri nodded, pulled out a phone and quickly typed the message.

Dante looked around at the mess in Lepri's lab. It wasn't just the destroyed computer and shattered glass, it was always a mess. He had always thought of scientists as meticulous, ordered, exacting. Lepri was more of a peanut-butter-on-his-lab-coat kind of guy, but he was also an acknowledged genius in his field. By age fifteen, he had managed to isolate and synthesize a pre-CRSPR DNA slicing enzyme. Kara had decided to bring him in-house once it was discovered that he had been experimenting on his foster brothers. It wasn't that she particularly cared for his foster brothers, she was more worried about Lepri getting caught and being forced toward mediocrity. His unorthodox approach to biology, and life, was simply a reflection of his brilliance.

Lepri had sheaves of paper littered on top of one of his lab benches. There were photos of bacteria and viruses. There were also more disturbing photos of the corpses of David Spanarkle, in colorful and gory detail, and Kenneth Jones, in faded, gory detail.

"So what do you need from me that requires the security upgrade?" Lepri asked, jarring Dante back to the present.

"First, tell me anything new you have discovered about the virus in the Manassas kids," Dante said.

"Well, first, there was more than one virus. The first ones made the later ones possible."

"So you are saying the Manassas boys both had some older virus that made them susceptible to other viruses? Wasn't that known?"

"Well, that's exactly it," Lepri said, waving his arms excitedly. "It was just like what happened with the virus in the Jones kid eighteen years ago. The virus we were looking for was dormant. But apparently, so were a lot of other viruses. In fact, what I discovered was that both boys had roughly 123 different viruses in each of them. It's just that no one knew."

"With 123 different viruses, the kids weren't sick?" Dante asked.

"That's the thing. They weren't physically sick, at least not in any discoverable way."

"But surely that would have shown up in the autopsies—" Dante said.

"What I mean by not discoverable is that the viruses were dormant. All 123 viruses infecting them were dormant, and attached to pieces of junk DNA."

Lepri glanced at Dante. He wasn't trying to hide the deep concern in his eyes.

"Why attach to the junk DNA?" Dante asked.

"Why indeed."

"Are they searching for something?"

"I wouldn't immediately jump to that, but we can't rule it out. And I don't want to make guesses until I have had some time to test it. So first I need to force expression in each of the 123 to see what they do when they are activated."

"Jeremy, you know as well as we do what is hidden in the DNA that is labeled junk," Dante said softly.

"If you are referring to the codes that grant us consciousness, of course I do," Lepri replied. "That was one of the primary things we learned when we were promoted to CAM12."

"So, if these boys have these dormant viruses, and they showed no symptoms and flew under all radars, then we have no idea how many people might have these same dormant viruses, right?"

"Yeah, that's right," Lepri said.

"And the danger here is that the population at large could be infected with a virus that targets genes that code for consciousness? Am I correct?"

"Whew, yeah, I guess that is a possibility. A horrifying possibility, but a possibility."

"Okay, so we need to find a way to test for this in a larger general population—hold on, if the viruses were dormant, how did you discover them to begin with? Did you force their expression?"

"No, I stole your idea," Lepri said. "You know you asked me to run resonance on those images that were flashing on the Dreamscape screens in the War Room? So, somehow, I started to wonder if the resonance of that original virus, the one in Kenneth Jones, was operating at a normal resonance for viruses. When I scanned the original virus for resonance, I found that it was waaaay out of normal range for viruses."

"Out of normal range in what way?" Dante asked.

"The resonance was way higher than the resonance of a virus should be."

"Well, viruses are normally higher than life as we define it."

"A little higher, not dimensional levels higher," Lepri said. "Normally viruses resonate only slightly higher than humans. Sometimes, they can get all the way up to ghoul level. But these viruses are resonating closer to the dream state. They are closer to ghosts than humans."

"How is that possible? What we saw of this virus was more solid than most viruses—more physical. That would make it a lower resonance."

"Exactly. It's weird as hell because its range is gigantic. So it's both too high and too low in resonance. There are also pockets of tiny particles inside it that I can't identify, packed in structures that I also can't identify. I'm still working on that. But I found the new viruses because I decided to do a scan of the blood of the Manassas boys for particles with the same weird resonance breadth, and I found 123 new viruses. They were tiny but resonating on the same frequencies as that original one."

"What does that signify?"

"I don't know exactly, but there is one more thing," Lepri said. "I checked Tobias's body, the one that Lazlo was in, and he had the same viruses with the same resonance patterns. Exactly the same resonance."

It's in the math. The answer is always in the math, Dante thought.

"What was the difference between the lowest resonance of this virus and the decrease in Lazlo's overall resonance between his initial reading and the one just now?" he asked.

Lepri smiled slightly. "You got it. Of course you did. Exactly zero. Lazlo's resonance was lowered by the exact amount of the combined lower resonance of the viruses inside Tobias's body."

"So you are saying that Lazlo was infected by the same thing as the Manassas kids, and it pulled his resonance down?"

"Infected? No, of course not. Ghosts are spirits. They don't get viruses, as we know them," Lepri said.

"Actually, ghosts can be infected by viruses. It's very rare but it has happened a few times over the years," Dante said. "That's part of the information you get with CAM14 clearance."

"Whoa … that changes things, and not for the better. Is there anything else I need to know?"

Lepri looked vaguely hurt and didn't hide it well. The thought that there was biological knowledge that he was excluded from didn't sit well with him.

"There is something else I need to show you," Dante said.

He materialized the resonance monitor that he had carried to the 8th floor, flipped it on and handed it to Lepri.

Lepri stared at it. Then he sat down at his lab bench and stared at it some more. Dante noticed his knuckles turning white as he gripped the monitor. After a moment, Lepri stood up, quickly walked to his laptop, and plugged the resonance monitor into it. After a few seconds, he uploaded the images from the device onto the screen. Dante saw the image of the three ghosts, surrounded by red, yellow, and navy dots. The navy dots in and around the red ones made the color of the red look crimson, like wounds.

"Shit. This isn't good," Lepri muttered. "Who are these three figures?"

"Judith, Howard, and Sawyer."

"All ghosts?" Lepri asked. "Normal ghosts?"

"For the most part, yes. Sawyer is a reconstituted ghost. That wouldn't cause this, would it?"

"No, it shouldn't," Lepri said. "And what are these things? Do you know?" He pointed to the navy dots.

"No, but it says it's resonating significantly lower than the ghosts. Is that right? Is the machine calibrated and working properly?"

"The machine is working," Lepri said. "I can test it again, but I tested it just before I sent it out. Plus, I have seen something that looks like those already."

Lepri grabbed his mouse and opened a few files on his laptop. A magnified picture of a bacterium appeared in front of them. But it wasn't a bacterium.

"This is the virus that I showed you before, the one we found in both Manassas boys and Tobias. You see this," Lepri said, pointing to something that looked like a small sac situated inside the virus. "There is a structure just here. You see the thing that looks about the size and structure of a mitochondria. Mitochondria, I might add, which neither viruses nor bacteria possess—only cells. Well, if we open this thing up, this is what we see."

Lepri clicked and another image opened up. It was the same structure but cut in half. Inside there were thousands of minuscule dots. It looked like a passion fruit that had been cut in half.

"What are those?" Dante asked, pointing to the dots.

"I have no idea," Lepri said. "But there is something important here. As you seemed to be very interested in the resonances of things, I checked the resonance of these—it's here."

He pointed to a number in the legend next to the image. Dante looked. He blinked and then looked again.

He did some calculations in his head. He then took a breath and recalculated.

"That's not possible," Dante whispered.

"I know, right? It shouldn't be there," Lepri said. "These things are resonating at too high a level for the physical world, even a virus. They are resonating at exactly the same level as the navy dots in this readout."

"It's too high to be contained by a physical form, without some form of possession. And possession requires at least a shadow of consciousness to work."

"Oh shit," said Lepri. "So you are pretty sure that the things in the virus are the same as those surrounding the ghosts?"

"I can't be sure until I test, but I think it's a safe guess."

"So those three are infected?" Dante asked.

"Yes, those three at least, but it could be more," Lepri said. "I suspect that the virus only releases these from itself once it becomes active. But if they are able to infect ghosts, then given what we have seen, they may be able to lower a ghost's resonance to be even closer to human level."

"Which would make them easier to infect by other viruses," Dante said.

"Exactly."

"So we need to quarantine these three ghosts immediately. Can you send Joe a text to tell him that?"

"I can, but how can Joe help with ghosts?"

"There is a division under Security that deals with ghosts," Dante said.

"Learn something new every day," muttered Lepri, as he typed into his phone.

"I also need you to find a way to quickly test for this virus, both in active and latent form."

"Yeah, I was working on that."

"We might also be able to use this change in resonance to find our missing watchers. If all, or even some of the watchers of the missing Cambion have been infected with this virus then it gives us something we can track. If we can calibrate the machines to track that particular lowered resonance..."

Lepri's eyes lit up. "Yes, that could work."

“Okay, then I need you to look for any past resonance readings on Sawyer and Howard. If you can find it, check the differential between before and after. Check how much the resonance was lowered by. If it is like Lazlo, and their resonance was lowered by the resonance of the virus, then it starts to look like a pattern. In any case, we’ll still need to quarantine the three of them.”

“If it proves an effective measurement tool, I can expand it out to the rest of the Office,” said Lepri, beginning to scribble some calculations in a notebook.

“On the positive side, it will give us a resonance to track for our missing watchers. Did you check the Dreamscape monitor for the resonances of all ghosts and compare them to Lazlo yet?” Dante asked.

“No, but Joe and Liz should already have a detailed scan of the resonances that are appearing in the Dreamscape. And they will have already compared that with Lazlo’s reading.”

“While you are at it, can you get them to compare with these three as well?” Dante said.

“I can.”

“Then get them to meet us in the War Room and bring that data. I will get Kara. I have a hunch about this, but I don’t want to speak until I know.”

“It might help if you shared it, if you can. Two heads are better than one and all that,” Lepri said, his voice unusually soft.

Dante nodded. “Okay. Here is my thought. Only those three ghosts on the 8th floor had lowered resonance. That resonance matched Lazlo’s, but they are still with us, they haven’t disappeared. I want to know why, and why the others disappeared.”

“Okay, but what do you suspect?” Lepri asked.

“Like you, I suspect that this virus, which resonates higher than normal viruses, managed to get close enough to the level of ghosts somehow to impact them. Or at least to distribute those little navy particles. For our watchers, I think this happened through the Cambion that they were watching, which is why the other three are still with us. Their interactions with the Manassas boy were short term, maybe too short to get impacted.”

“You think they were infected by the Cambion they were watching?”

“No, impacted, not infected. I’m not sure if it is infection. I’m not sure because I am not sure that thing is a virus. Not really. It doesn’t look like any normal virus we have seen in centuries. It was too big and too humanoid.

So something isn't sitting right."

Lepri's jaw was tight.

"So do you think that the resonance of all our missing ghosts was altered and that's why we can't find them through normal means?" he asked.

"Yes, I think they may be stuck at a resonance level that we can't see, and they can't project at. I had to rule out that *all* ghosts were not dropping their resonance levels. But now that we know that isn't true, we can hypothesize that it happens only through contact with a Cambion who has the virus."

"So you want to me to scan the dream monitors for that particular resonance level because you think we might find those ghosts there?" Lepri asked.

"Yes, and then we need to figure out a way to bring them back and, through them, locate their wards."

"Okay," Lepri said, picking up the resonance monitor. "Let me calibrate the readings for Sawyer, Howard, and Judith and do some probability work."

"There is one other thing," Dante said. "I need you to run whatever tests you need to ascertain if this thing is contagious ghost to ghost."

Lepri whirled back around.

"How—wait, why are you asking about this?"

Dante sighed.

"Recently, when I was moving up and down through some resonances, I saw something drop from me."

Lepri gasped.

"You think it was a virus?" he whispered.

"I don't really think anything yet, but I did feel it touch me at the TV station, so I need you to run up all the resonance readings on me."

"But that's not possible, is it?" Lepri asked. "For you to be infected."

"It happened once before, in Brazil," Dante said. "It turned out very badly. Lots of people died and lots of souls were unmade. I don't suppose I need to tell you how much worse it would have been if it had been Kara."

Lepri nodded, his face ashen.

"I'll get Kara and head up to the War Room," Dante said. "After that, you can run readings on all of us there. Just don't say what it's for—not yet."

It wouldn't do for Kara to suspect that something might have tried to, or succeeded in, infecting him … not in her current state.

When Dante appeared in their room, Kara was already up. She was sitting at the dresser brushing her hair. Her hair seemed to like this, as strands reached out for the brush as it approached her head, competing for the stroke.

She felt him before he was completely solid, and turned. Her smile was radiant and the bags under her eyes were less pronounced. Maybe it wasn't so bad after all—but even so, it wouldn't last, and he would need to try to bring her to the hallway again as soon as he knew that there wasn't something wrong with him that could impact her.

"I feel much better," Kara said, standing and coming into his arms.

"I'm glad," Dante whispered. "I would give my soul to take this from you."

He heard his voice break, and Kara pulled back.

"You do more than anyone, and if I loved you more—well, I'm pretty sure we aren't in what people today would call a healthy relationship already."

She made a prim face, and Dante laughed in spite of himself. Then he remembered why he came.

"Joe and Liz are waiting for us in the War Room. Lepri is on his way. He has some news for us. He—"

"Don't tell me yet," Kara said. "Just kiss me. Let me feel the solidness of you before that whirlwind begins again."

He pulled her even closer and kissed her. When he held her in his arms, he remembered every other time he had held her—every other time he had kissed her—and he remembered the soul-shattering horror when he thought he had lost her. He would never let that happen again. She was what he lived for. Not this story. Not these people. They were fine but he would sacrifice them all to save her or even to give her a few moments of rest.

Dante could go anywhere he wanted to rest—he was lucky enough to be an unfettered ghost after all. Some ghosts were tied to a place, but he wasn't. He had broken free from those shackles years ago. So he could watch Paris from the top of the Eiffel Tower. Or he could dance through the halls of Catherine the Great's Summer Palace at midnight. If he wanted company, he could just let his essence slip more from the physical plane and rise upward to the upper winds. If he stayed put when he did this, he would end up seeing the next plane up, with all its ghosts, spirits, and elementals. Some would be able to see him there, some wouldn't, but he could always find someone to talk to or get information from. Or he could just ride the upper winds around this plane for fun, as Abi and a lot of the more ancient ghosts and ghouls liked to do.

Dante had spent centuries doing all these things but over time the glamour and appeal had faded. Maybe he was just jaded after all these millennia, but he didn't think so. The truth was that none of these things could compete with Kara for his attention. The gardens of Babylon couldn't hold a candle to the shape of her upper lip when she was smiling. He knew the sound of her heart, and he could hear it in his inner ear when she wasn't around. It played like music there. For all his intellect, for all his learned brilliance, for all his mathematical innovations, his brain could be brought to a complete standstill if she happened to accidentally brush her hand over his arm. If he had still been a human, he might have considered his obsession with her, this limerence, a weakness, but he was not and he knew better. He knew he was a junkie, but there wasn't much he could do about it. If he were to pick a final death for himself, he would choose to overdose on her. He got hooked on her centuries before he even knew exactly what she was. She was the only thing, besides math, that had kept him sane in those early years, and she hadn't even known him. Later, after the Abomination and the death, after he found out about her total self, he felt no different about her. He felt different about himself, though. If he had felt unworthy before, his levels of self-loathing had soared once he was privy to that knowledge, but he kept all this to himself. Kara became very annoyed if anyone said anything remotely negative about him—including him. A few people had died for not much more than a verbal slipup at the wrong time.

After what could have been an eternity or the blink of an eye, Kara leaned back. She studied his face with her sapphire-blue eyes.

"Okay, let's go take care of our story," she said softly, as she kissed the tip of his nose.

The story could be damned, as far as Dante was concerned. He never said this aloud, but he didn't need to, they both knew his priorities, he had proven it long ago during the Abomination. He had proved that he would destroy everything, down to the very foundations of reality, to save her. Kara usually didn't remember this mentally, but she knew in other ways.

Just as they both knew that he would do it again.

Chapter Sixteen

Stretched

By the time Dante and Kara materialized in the War Room, Liz and Joe were already there. In fact, it seemed like half the Office, in flesh and spirit, was crammed into the room. There were people and ghosts everywhere, and the buzz of voices joined with the sound of technology, electricity, and a weird electronic whine to create something that could have been music in some spheres.

The sky above them was filled with rose and gray swirling clouds being whipped across the sky by a fierce wind.

"What's happening?" Kara asked a young woman at the desk nearest her. When the woman looked up and recognized Kara, her mouth dropped open for a minute before she quickly shut it.

"We had a sudden drop of five degrees in global temperatures, ma'am, I mean Kara, I mean ma'am."

Kara turned to Dante, ignoring the girl.

"Drop in temperature?" she asked. "Was it me?"

"Yes, my love, but I took care of it."

Hundreds of emotions crossed her face in a matter of seconds. Humans couldn't see this, but ghosts certainly could, and several of them began to move quickly away.

"Five degrees," she finally said. "That's a lot. How fast did it happen?"

"A minute, maybe two."

"But you didn't take me to be cleaned?"

"No, but we will soon. I thought it would be better for you to be completely functional until we can find our missing people."

Kara's eyes caught his, then she kissed him.

"I trust your judgment always," she said softly, before pulling back and turning to face the cacophony of the room. But before moving into the room, she placed her hand on the shoulder of the girl that she had just spoken with, and the girl jumped.

"Thank you," Kara said, and the girl beamed.

"Anything ma'am. I mean, for you, I mean ..." she sputtered.

She was still sputtering as Kara walked away. Dante smiled at the girl, but she couldn't see him, so the gesture was lost.

Looking around, Dante saw wide swaths of red areas on the biological monitors that hadn't been present before—even hours before. But when he turned his gaze to the behavioral monitors, he saw nothing amiss. Actually, he saw much less activity than usual. This meant a wide spike in infection rates across species was having no notable behavioral changes. This seemed unlikely but Dante filed this piece of data away in his brain for later examination.

Liz and Joe were standing in front of the watery surface of the Dreamscape monitor.

"What have you found?" Kara asked.

Joe whipped his head around. Kara's tone clearly made him edgy.

Liz squared her shoulders and took a deep breath. "We ran the numbers you asked," she said, stepping forward and in front of Joe, shielding him. Joe's shoulders visibly relaxed. Dante smiled briefly to himself. He suspected that Liz was going to turn out to be a real asset.

"We ran a full check on the full range of resonances for this year, five years ago, and ten years ago. What we got looked like this," she said, taking some papers from her notebook and spreading them on the table.

"The range of resonance levels were fairly unchanged until roughly twenty years ago. We tracked current and normal ghost resonance against these levels, and they consistently had the same pattern. We then assessed them against other known resonances of spiritual beings. And this is what we got."

She showed a graph with dots plotted against an axis of megahertz.

"You can see that there is very little differentiation between different types of spiritual creatures, and close to zero difference between individuals of a particular spiritual species. Joe said this was normal. This is what we've seen for years. But then, about twenty years ago, this happened." Liz pointed to the lower line of the graph. The lowest reading was slightly below the reading for the year before.

"So it looks like the resonance of the Dreamscape dropped," Kara said.

"We thought so at first, but it was only half the picture," Liz said. "It actually expanded."

"Here, you can see it," Joe said, turning the paper to Kara. "In the past twenty years, the difference between top and bottom number in the Dreamscape has gotten much bigger. Its range has grown."

"What's that red mark?" Kara asked, pointing to a red downward spike in data.

"That's five years ago," Liz said. "There was a massive expansion downward in the range of the Dreamscape. It isn't on this graph but there was an equal and equivalent spike upward."

"What about the resonances of spirits and other living things? Have they changed?" Dante asked.

"No. The resonance of the living creatures hasn't changed but the space around them seems to have contracted as this Dreamscape expanded. So then we checked the new, clearer images. You were right. All the images resonate at almost exactly the same level but different from everything else. Which is also the same level that Dr. Lepri said Lazlo was resonating on."

"Let me see the numbers," Dante said, pulling the paper toward him. "This is exactly the last resonance reading for Lazlo. It is also the resonance of Judith, Sawyer, and Howard. Exactly, even when fractionalized."

"So was Lazlo's resonance lower than normal Dreamscape resonance?" Kara asked.

"Much lower."

"Why didn't we see that when we were with him?"

"Because he was in Tobias's body until the very last second," Dante replied. "When he came out of his body, he was in the Healing Room, which has been modified for a wide range of resonances."

"And the creatures on the monitor, the ones at that same level? Do you think they are our missing ghosts?" Kara asked.

Dante nodded.

"How many are you seeing in the monitor?" Kara asked Joe.

"For the moment, the most we have tracked is about one hundred and sixty," Joe said.

"One-sixty," Kara whispered. "That's more than are missing."

"That's more than we know are missing," Dante replied.

"Can we tell the exact location from these numbers?" Kara asked.

Dante picked up the paper and did the calculations in his head.

"Yes," he said. "It looks like it's near the fields of Venenum in the Ghoul Lands."

"There's something more," Joe said, gesturing them closer to the screen. "First, if you look, you can see the images flashing up more regularly, but the way they show up is different."

Before Joe finished, Dante saw it. The strange images on the Dreamscape monitor—the clearer, sharper-looking ones—were indeed appearing more often, but they flickered and blinked on the screen in a way they had not before.

"They're flickering," Kara said.

"Yes, that just started happening ten minutes ago," Joe said.

"What does it mean? Is it something about the monitor?"

"I don't think so, because nothing else on that monitor is doing it."

"Wait, hold on a second," Liz said, pulling some paper off the printer. "This is different too. It looks like they are getting wider."

"What do you mean, getting wider?" Dante asked.

"Look here, their individual resonances are expanding up and down … it looks like …"

"They are being stretched," Kara said, reaching out and touching the monitor with one hand. "I can feel it now. They are being pulled and stretched."

Her face was paler, and her jaw was set.

"Would that be painful?" Liz asked.

"It's the first step to unmaking," Dante replied to her. "A ghost can sometimes survive it, but even if it's done gently and over centuries, it's still excruciating."

"But you said you can do that—" Liz began, but suddenly clamped her mouth shut.

"Yes, I can," Dante said softly. Liz's eyes glistened as she nodded and looked away.

"Some of them are already blinking out," Kara said, her eyes still on the screen. When she turned around, her eyes were pale blue, and her hair was on the move. As they watched, the figures on the screen twinkled, twisted, and spun.

"They are being tortured ..." Kara whispered, as strands of her hair caressed the monitor behind them. Despite the danger, Dante felt his heart warm. Kara, who didn't normally like ghosts, was remembering that they too were her children. Wayward children, but hers nonetheless.

"We need to get them now," she said, reaching out her hand for Dante.

"My love, I don't think that we are the ideal candidates, our energy is too recognizable and easily felt. If they are being held, they could be moved before we could get to them. They are ghosts, after all ..." Kara bristled, so he added quickly, "But I know someone who could probably reach them. Someone who is from there."

"Who?" Liz asked.

"Abi. He is a ghoul, and a Cambion ghoul as well. So he can travel easily at the lower resonances just above this one."

Kara nodded.

"So let's go to the 8th and find him."

Dante nodded but Liz shook her head.

"Umm. I think he is on the roof right now," she said.

"He doesn't usually tarry near the building unless there is a reason," Dante said.

"Umm. Well. Yes. I just got a quick coffee with him and that's where he said he was going afterward ... to speak with the stars," Liz said, looking down.

For the briefest of seconds Kara's face lightened but it immediately faded. The skin under her eyes was becoming alarmingly dark again. Dread flared inside Dante, but he clamped it down quickly.

"Then he's close enough that I can pull him without causing damage," Dante said. He reached out toward Abi and pulled.

Abi immediately appeared before them, licking his paw. He had been in mid-bath. When he saw where he was, and who he was with, he immediately colored and threw himself into a deep bow. In fact, he bowed so low that his nose actually touched the ground.

He rarely had opportunity or reason to see Kara, and his deference was real. Ghouls understood what Kara was much more intimately than humans or even ghosts.

"How shall my eyes ever recover from seeing such beauty?" Abi said, raising his eyes to Kara and then turning to look at Liz as well. "From this day forth, the most beautiful sunset shall be as the grayest rain … the most full and fragrant of roses as the husk of a dried weed. How fortunate am I to have lived in this moment and how tragic am I to know it must, at some point, end?"

This was typical of an ancient ghoul greeting. It might have sounded ridiculous but for the deep note of sincerity that ran through the words. If ghosts had a broader emotional spectrum than humans, ghouls put them to shame. Only incubi had a broader range of emotion.

Liz blushed a bit and Kara smiled. In truth, Kara felt much more warmly toward ghouls than ghosts. Ghouls were natural things. They could be dark and unwholesome, but they were natural.

"We asked you here because we need help finding a few ghosts, and we would like for you to find them and bring them home," Kara said.

"These would be the missing ghosts?"

"Yes."

"I will spend from now until eternity in joy doing only as you ask of me," Abi said. "But I am afraid that it may take me that long to be successful. I cannot reach the upper winds, lowly creature that I am."

"Actually, it's not the upper winds that we want you to search," Dante said. "It is the lower ones."

"Indeed? That is highly unusual, my friend," Abi replied. "But even the lower winds are vast and treacherous."

"Yes, they are. But we know the exact resonance that these ghosts are existing on. They are in the fields of Venenum. It is a resonance that only ghouls, and some ghosts, can get to."

"Your mother was from the fields of Venenum, was she not?" Kara asked.

Abi bowed again in acknowledgment.

"And you are familiar with these fields?"

"It was my home for many years. It was there that Dante met me, all those years ago. Wasted, alone, and wishing for my own end. It was there that I learned that my mixed nature was no shame and no curse. And later, it was through him that I came to you, blessed mother of the wounded and damned. You saved and released me from my heart's bondage to that place." He bowed again.

Abi had stated this with the flourish of a ghoul but the very real sadness underlying the words bled through. When Dante had met Abi, he had been far worse off than Abi. He suspected he might have given Abi a purpose, as well as friendship. Certainly, loneliness was an experience all Cambion understood.

Kara's eyes misted over for a moment. She walked over to Abi and laid her hand on his lowered head.

"I wouldn't ask you to go back to that place if I didn't think it was necessary to save others. They are particularly gifted and particularly vulnerable. Your ghoul mother and human father gave you a gift, the gift of movement across layers of existence that very few creatures have, save perhaps for me and Dante. As foreigners to that land, I am afraid that Dante and I cannot go there without being felt before we arrive. If there is something there guarding our people, they would have advance notice of our arrival. But you are from there. You can find them and find exactly where they are."

Abi looked up and met Kara's gaze.

"My life is for you," he said. His eyes were openly worshipful.

"No!" Kara said firmly. "No one gives their life for me. You may risk your life for others of our kind, but do not do it for me."

As Abi smiled, his mandibles pulled back from his face at a right angle.

"You, others, it's all the same, is it not?" Abi said. "As you go, so the world."

Kara's eyes widened for a moment, then she laughed unexpectedly. It was a wonderful sound to hear. Abi glanced toward Liz, who was openly smiling at him. He colored slightly.

"He has you there," Dante said, with a smile.

"I must remember not to underestimate the ghouls," Kara said, with a soft smile.

"So what is my mission?" Abi asked.

"Go to the fields of Venenum," Dante said. "Explore down to the ice crypts and no lower. Explore up to the roots of the Somnia and no higher."

"There is still much there to search," Abi said.

"Yes, there is," Kara said. "But you are searching for human Cambion ghosts. Their human hearts will call to the human side of your heart, if you can allow yourself to hear it."

"I hear it always, but sometimes louder than others," Abi said, as his eyes turned again toward Liz.

"Go, and find our people," Kara said, "but do not engage with anything you find. Come back and tell us what you have found and where. I will not have you hurt. In fact, if any of our people are hurt, I will not be merciful."

She leaned forward and kissed Abi on the forehead. At that, Abi disappeared.

Kara then turned to Liz, who was looking down. Kara had opened her mouth to speak but closed it and smiled.

"I'm sorry, did you say something?" Liz asked, looking up.

"No, not yet. It seems you have a fan."

"What? Why?"

"Abi. He seems quite taken with you," Kara said.

"Me? No," Liz said, with an uncomfortable laugh.

"Does it disturb you? Being admired by a ghoul?"

"No." Liz smiled shyly.

"It would disturb some," Kara said. "Ghouls are intense creatures in all ways. They are not generally considered beautiful by humans, living as they do outside what is acceptable and at the border of what is natural. They exist by consuming the dead and decaying, but they find beauty there."

"Exactly," Liz said. "Abi sees beauty everywhere. That's much more noble than most humans I have known."

She stopped and blushed.

"It's just—I mean, no. It's just—you know. He says that stuff. He uses flowery words. It's not about me. I'm just … I'm not …"

"I wouldn't be so sure," Kara said, touching Liz's shoulder gently before taking Dante's hand and moving away.

"It cleans my heart, even in the worst of times," she said softly.

"What does, my love?" Dante asked.

"Seeing connections form between creatures. Particularly creatures so externally different but so internally the same. I guess it's like you and I."

Dante reached out for her and kissed her lips. He felt her warming at his touch. After a few moments she pulled away.

"Excuse me," a voice said from behind them.

Liz had walked up. Dante smiled a bit. Few would have dared to intercede in such a moment.

There is something fearless in the center of this one.

"There are a couple of other things I wanted to tell you," Liz said swiftly. "First, on the cluster chart, in addition to the cluster below normal resonance, there is a tiny cluster at a much, much lower than normal resonance."

"How much lower?" Dante asked.

"A lot."

The virus. The dots.

Dante nodded.

"We'll talk to Lepri about it," Dante said. He didn't want to comment until he saw the actual numbers.

"Was there something else?" he asked.

"Yes, there is, but it might be nothing," Liz said, looking down and shrugging.

"An intuition from a shade is never anything to ignore," Kara said, with a little smile.

"Well, I did a bit of personal research on the kids who died, you know Tobias, Kenneth, and David. I was looking for things they had in common. And then I thought about that guy in the Recovery Room. His name was Hudson. His spirit is missing too. So I checked him too. And I found something that they all had in common. It's probably nothing though . . ."

"What was it?"

"All of them were gamers."

Words and phrases began swirling in Dante's head.

We only did it when he was distracted with that video game he played.

It's the new one that all the kids are playing. The one with the bodysuit interface.

Nothing more than the fact that he got a new video game.

Black box.

It kind of loosed him from his body.

Don't you want to live forever?

Soooomuuuuchinheeerreee . . .

"Gamers?" Kara asked.

"Yeah. Of course, lots of people are gamers now but it was more unusual when Hudson and Kenneth were young. But it seems that they were both first adopters of games."

Bells, deep and bone-shattering, were going off in Dante's head.

"Which particular games did these kids play?" he asked.

"I don't know. I didn't take it that far," she said.

"Take it that far. Find out exactly what games they played. How you play them, what accessories they have, what platforms were used. Take it further. Take it as far as your mind goes. Find out everything that you can. If you find anything that feels off-kilter, you reach out to us immediately. Don't wait, even if you think it's small."

"How do I—" Liz began, but Kara interrupted her.

"Joe, give Liz my direct line number," she said. Joe looked at Liz with a smile and a little nod.

Lepri had just entered the room.

"Did I miss anything?" he asked.

"Yes. Ask Joe to fill you in and show him your readouts. Liz, give Lepri your high-end resonance numbers before you start researching."

Dante took Kara's hand and turned.

"I think I know how our systems could have been hacked. I also think I have an idea of origin of the virus and how it infected our ghosts. We just need to go to the 8th floor to find out."

"The 8th floor?"' Kara asked, raising her eyebrows.

"I need to talk to an outlier in all this," Dante said. "I need to find out how she died."

Chapter Seventeen

Uncovering Judith

Kara and Dante came to the 8th floor by the elevator rather than simply materializing there. This was because one was never sure what the layout of the 8th floor would be at any given moment. On some days, you could find yourself in an awkward situation simply by the nature of where you landed.

Today, when the door to the 8th floor opened, they stepped out into darkness and firelight. The darkness was filled with the sounds of drums and chanting. All around them, ghosts were dancing and spinning on a floor made of packed red dirt. One ghost, dressed in bright yellow feathers and red beads, was standing next to the fire, his body twitching and shaking. It was hard to tell if the ghost had been male or female but whatever gender, the movements looked like it was having an epileptic fit.

"Who are these?" Kara asked, nodding around her.

"West African ghosts," Dante replied. "It's a ceremony day for them."

"What's the occasion?"

"It's their version of Day of the Dead."

"Meaning?"

Meaning that they are trying to commune with the living. Their culture believes that ghosts are venerated ancestors who exist to provide knowledge and help to the living."

"Well, they misinterpreted that, didn't they?" Kara snorted.

Dante started to speak, but they had no time for that argument.

"So where is the girl?" Kara asked, looking around. "She's not one of these, is she?"

"No, no. But she should be near. I asked her to remain close by," Dante replied.

He looked above him, to the black starry sky and called. "Judith?"

At first there was nothing, but before he could call again, a figure came out from behind the fire. Judith's blue dress caught and reflected the light from the flames. As she moved through the dancers, they moved away from her. One muttered something as she passed by.

Kara looked at Dante.

"He called her a white witch," Dante said softly to Kara. "They sense something wrong with her."

Judith came to stand before them and did an awkward little curtsy.

"Hi Judith," Dante said.

"Hi." Judith glanced at Kara nervously.

"If you don't remember, my name is Dante," he said. "This is Kara."

"Yes, I remember who you are—and I know who she is. Did I do something wrong? Is she going to unmake me?" Judith asked, making an obvious attempt to keep a steady voice.

"No, you haven't done anything wrong. And even if you had, why do you think I would unmake you for it?" Kara asked.

"Howard said you hate ghosts. And Sawyer said that you unmade him," Judith said.

"Did Sawyer also tell you that I unmade him after literally catching him with his pants down, raping a teenage boy, whom he had just hit over the head with a brick?" she asked.

Judith's eyes widened. "No, he didn't tell me that."

"Of course not. As for Howard, he is of similar ilk. It's not completely untrue that I dislike ghosts. But the reason that I dislike them is because I think most of them take an unnatural path. From what I have heard, you took your path because you were misled—and misled by someone very good at misleading people. So I hold you no ill will, my dear."

Kara put her hand on Judith's shoulder and Judith visibly relaxed.

"But we do have some questions for you," Dante said. "We have questions about your life and your death."

"I don't really remember either my life or my death. The first thing I remember is meeting the red-haired woman."

"Sometimes that happens," Dante said. "Particularly if your death was in any way traumatic. But we would like to help you remember both your death and your life."

"I'm not sure I want to remember."

"You may not, but it might help others," Kara said. Before Judith could say more, Kara put her hand to the young ghost's head. For a moment, Judith's essence shimmered and blinked. Then it stopped. Judith put her hands to her head and sat down on the ground so swiftly that it would have bruised her had she been more physical.

"Do you remember?" Dante asked.

"Wait. Hold on. Yes. I remember things, but it's all muddled. It's like having index cards for things but they aren't in any order."

"Then we can help you focus. Do you remember your parents?" Kara asked.

"I remember what they looked like … yes. I remember that they got divorced. I don't remember their names."

"Was Judith your name then as well?"

Judith closed her eyes for a second.

"Yes, it was Judith, but I don't remember my last name."

"Can you remember where you lived?"

"Yes. Well, I lived in the United States. I think."

"Let me try to pull a little more out of her," Kara said, placing her hand on the top of Judith's head again. Judith flickered again and then shook her head.

"Yeah, I think more is coming."

"Do you happen to remember if you had hobbies? Were you into sports? Music? Video games?" Dante asked.

Judith shook her head.

"I liked music. I played tennis but I wasn't really into it. I hated video games," she said.

"Did you have friends that were gamers?"

"If I did, I don't remember it. But I remember hating gamers in general."

"Judith, do you remember your death?"

Judith closed her eyes and let out a long sigh … then another.

"Yes. I remember that. I remember it clearly now. I kind of know now why that woman told me that I would have a terrible reincarnation."

"Because of the way you died?" Dante asked.

"Yes, and the events leading up to my death. How much do you want to know?"

"As much as you can tell us," Kara replied.

"It started with a boy," said Judith. "I fell in love with a boy in high school. Or I thought I did. I had sex with him on our senior beach trip. It's funny, that was the same trip where some ridiculously naive friend of mine told her boyfriend that she was carrying his baby. The asshole convinced her that he loved her, but that the best thing for their relationship was for her to get an abortion. She was as dumb as a box of hair, so she believed him and did it. Afterward, he found he couldn't cope with the grief of taking the life of a baby that was his. So he dumped her. But I was never that stupid. In the beginning I went on the Pill, but I changed my mind once I realized that I was in love, and stopped taking them. I got pregnant a few months later. When he suggested getting an abortion, I refused on religious grounds."

"So you were religious in life?"

"Not in the slightest. My parents were Jewish, but I was nothing. Religion always seemed to me to be a way to control people. And with what I have seen after death, it appears that I was right."

"So what does all this have to do with your death?" Kara asked.

"It was the beginning of my malaise. I thought I was in love with Jack, but I realized later that I wasn't. I was completely thrown off by that because I had felt something when I was with him. It was a fierce, powerful thing. There were times when I was around him that I felt a desire so strong that I could barely breathe from it. But once we were married, I never felt that way again. In fact, I never felt anything like that again, after our senior beach trip. While I was pregnant, I thought that this was because my body just wanted him to make a baby. Once the baby was born, well, I didn't have much feeling for her either."

Kara's eyes narrowed and Dante reached out and touched her arm. This was a touchy subject.

"So getting back to your death," Dante said.

"Yes, I know. I was telling you all that so that you would understand why I did what I did. I fell into some sort of depression after the baby was born, but it felt more like a sort of fugue state. I wasn't unhappy, per se, I just didn't see the point in anything. After a year or so, my husband divorced me and took my baby girl. If I hadn't inherited a lot of money, I probably would have died in the street because I could barely be bothered to do anything physical. Most of the time, I just watched TV. Then, one day, it happened. I saw her." Judith sighed softly.

"You saw who?" Kara asked.

"I can't remember her name, but it was a girl that I knew from high school. I saw just a flash of her in an advertisement for this company called Everlast."

"The one that promises to put you into a video game forever?" Words began swirling in Dante's head again, but he shut them down, focusing on what he knew of Everlast. He had seen the ads, and they looked really cheesy. They were almost as bad as local advertisements for diamonds and used cars—almost.

"It's not a video game. It's a virtual world," Judith said. "I know the adverts looked awful. I never would have called them if I hadn't seen that girl. When I saw her, I remembered, and I had that feeling again. That crazy hot feeling of desire. That's when I realized that I had never been in love with Jack, but with her."

"She was advertising Everlast?" Kara asked.

"Oh no. No. She was just in the background walking past during one of the interviews, but I recognized her immediately. And I felt such a burning."

"So what happened?" Dante asked.

"I called the company immediately," Judith said. "They ask that you come in for an interview before they tell you anything about the place. I hoped that they would be able to track down the girl. Well, she was a woman by then, but she looked pretty much the same to me. So I flew out to the Everlast offices in Palo Alto, California."

"You flew to California because you saw a girl you remembered from high school in the background of some advertisement?" Kara asked.

"You don't understand. It wasn't just 'some girl.' It was like, I don't know, it's like if desire had a form, it would be her. That sounds super stupid but that's how I felt."

"So what does this all have to do with your death?"

"Everlast is the reason I died."

Even in the created space of the 8th floor, Dante felt the chill that came from Kara at these words.

"Okay," he said. "Give us the details."

"All the details?"

"All you can remember."

"Okay. I got to their office in Palo Alto about a week after I saw the ad. The office was in this tall, mirrored building that had a doorman. I checked in with the doorman and was told to go up to the top floor. Up there, I was met by a woman with long mouse-brown hair and glasses. She was ridiculously fit, in that trendy, shallow California sort of way, which made me suspicious. But when the woman started speaking, I realized that she was very smart—unusually smart. She sat down at a desk situated in a large room that was empty save for the desk and began to talk me through the whole Everlast system. Throughout all of this she never once pitched it, she just explained that they had discovered the tech for separating the consciousness from the body. I didn't understand all the tech, but I understood the basics. She explained that consciousness was ageless, so once inside a matrix, you would not die. You would feel just like you did in the real world, as your senses would be adjusted to interact with the matrix like you did with the world, but you would never die. And you could change your game whenever you wanted to. I was only half listening at that point. I was trying to figure out how to ask her about the girl. So eventually I asked if the people in the ad were customers or actors. She said that they were all customers. I asked about extras, and she said that they were customers too. They needed to keep certain information about the matrix secret, so the extras were people already in the matrix. They agreed to be in the ad, which was created partially in a virtual reality space that Everlast set up for this purpose.

"I was really shaken by this point. I felt like my insides were on fire. If that girl was in the matrix, that was where I needed to be. But the ads had been so awful that I was still a bit suspicious. When I asked about this, the woman laughed and said that they made them that way on purpose. She said that only people who really wanted this would be willing to run them down after such a video. So, to make a long story short, I went home and made my final financial plans and signed lots of papers. On December 4th, they plugged me in. I remember that because it was the same date that my mother killed herself a couple of years before."

"So you went into the matrix?" Dante asked.

"Not exactly. It didn't work. Or I don't think it worked. If it did, then I feel sorry for anyone in there. It was like a nightmare."

Judith's ghost form was trembling ever so slightly.

"In what way?" Kara asked.

"When I came to inside it, I was in this white space, and it seemed to go on forever. Not white like a white room, but white like being in curdled milk or something. It was thick and suffocating. And it wasn't empty. There were things swimming around me. Things that seemed to burst out of the white every now and then. At first, I couldn't make out what they were, but when one finally got close enough to see—well, I guess there are some things we aren't supposed to see. After that, I remember feeling this horrible pain, like I was fragmenting or something."

Judith stopped for a minute, putting her hand to her throat and shivering.

"How did you escape?" Dante asked.

"I don't know. I just suddenly found myself standing in the middle of a crowd on the plateau of a mountaintop overlooking the sea. I felt like I had been there before somehow. There was smoke coming from somewhere and this horrible smell in the air."

Kara took Dante's hand and squeezed it.

"So that was where I met the red-haired woman." Judith's voice had taken on a raspy quality, as if responding to smoke that wasn't there.

"Can you describe the red-haired woman a bit better?"

"Absolutely. You don't forget someone like that. She was probably the most beautiful woman I had ever seen. She was wearing sandals and an almost see-through toga-like thing. Her skin was perfect, and her eyes were so blue that they looked like a doll's. Actually, come to think of it, she looked completely like a doll, a Barbie or something. But even with her beauty, or maybe because of it, she was super scary. Then what she told me was even scarier."

Judith stopped for a second and closed her eyes.

"She told me that I wasn't fit for the matrix that they tried to put me in. She said that I wasn't evolved enough. She also said that by trying to go into it, I had, what was it she said … perverted the natural order. So she couldn't take me to the upper winds and to another life. Well, she said that she could but that my next life, or next hundred, would be horrific. So she said that she could take me back to my world where I would be a ghost. She said that I could work my way up from here. It wasn't until later that I found out from other ghosts that it would take almost forever to do this."

Kara nodded.

"Do you know who the woman was?" Judith asked.

"Yes, and she lied to you," Kara said sharply. "What I don't know is why."

"The girl that you saw in the video. Do you know her name now?" Dante asked.

"I can't remember it." She stopped and furrowed her pale brow. "No, I can't get to it even now. It's like it's blocked somehow."

"Can you remember any other names? Or the place where you lived?" Kara asked.

"No, I can't. When I try to remember, it's like something is blocking it."

"Do you think, if you saw someone you knew from then, that you would remember?"

"Maybe."

"Then I am guessing we need to take you downstairs to the hospital wing, is that okay with you? I have a hunch," Dante said.

"I can't go there, can I? They told me that ghosts aren't allowed in that section of the Office," Judith said.

"It's not that you aren't allowed, it's that normally you couldn't easily materialize there, but we can change that if you go with us."

"Okay."

"Let us make a few calls," Dante said, moving Kara away a bit.

When he spoke to her, it was in the old language. The one of their past.

"Do you think the Academy is involved with this?" Kara asked him. Dante hesitated a second.

"Yes. I do. Judith either died in the process of going into Everlast or Rose killed her. But for whatever reason, Rose wanted her as a ghost. We need to treat that carefully."

"So why do you want her in the Recovery Room?"

"To find out what those things are inside her. If they are some form of virus that attaches to ghosts, we can try to heal her. If not, if she has been made into a plant, or spy of some sort, she is easier to unmake if she is not in a place that she can easily escape from."

"You think she is infected?"

"I know she is infected. The question is with what."

Dante turned back to Judith. "Are you ready to go?"

Judith nodded and Dante took her hand and pulled her energy downward.

They materialized a split second later in the Recovery Room.

Judith put her hand to her forehead.

"Are you okay?" Dante asked.

"Yes, I'm just dizzy. And it feels different here," she said.

"Yes, that's because we have dropped your resonance. You should feel more solid."

"Solid? Maybe. I also feel more … I don't know, more … alive."

"That's because you are. The more physical you are, the more of life you feel. But that can be a double-edged sword. Take a few minutes to adjust."

Kara had walked over to where Hudson was lying and sat down on his bed. She motioned to Judith.

By good fortune, Lepri walked into the room just at that moment. Dante moved quickly to him now that Kara was engaged elsewhere.

"Did you find a way to take my resonance readings?" he asked softly.

"Yep, I've adjusted the monitor that you took to the 8th," Lepri replied.

"You knew we would be here?"

"If you were going to question a ghost, I suspected that after that you would either come to my lab or the Recovery Room."

"How long will this take, and how accurate will it be?"

"It's already done," Lepri said. "As to how long it will take to process the readings, well, I adjusted it to be wildly sensitive but because of that, I'll have to filter out noise. Once I've done that, I will be able to compare your current resonance to what your resonance had been with a high level of certainty."

"Dante," Kara called, motioning to him.

Judith was standing beside the bed, staring at Hudson. She sighed.

"Yes, he looks familiar," she said.

She reached out and tried to touch him, but as was the case with most human and ghost interactions, even with her altered resonance, she couldn't connect. Despite this, Judith jerked her hand back suddenly.

"I remember. It's coming back. His name is Hudson," she whispered as she backed away. "Yes, his name is Hudson. My name was Judith Love. I went to school with him."

"And the girl, the one that you saw in the game and that you were so attracted to? Do you remember her name?" Dante asked.

"Her name …" Judith closed her eyes for a moment. When she opened them, her gaze was unfocused, and her eyes misted.

"Her name was Amelie."

At that moment, the smoke alarms in the building began to wail, and Judith put her hands over her ears and began to scream.

At the same moment, Hudson sat straight up.

"Help me," he choked out, before falling out of the bed and onto the floor.

Chapter Eighteen

Charged and Tried

Judith screamed as the strident blare of the alarms ricocheted across the room. Dante put his arms around her and tried to cover her with an energy shield.

Kara ran to Hudson, who was thrashing on the floor, grabbing his neck with his hands. He was screaming something. It was hard to catch it over the earsplitting noise, but Dante caught words—*taking, voice, stealing.* Kara was running her hands over him, trying to pull his energy toward something more stable. Even from here, Dante could feel the staccato nature of the energy that Hudson was emitting.

Then suddenly, as quickly as it began, the noise of the alarms stopped. Judith stopped screaming and Hudson flopped down, immobile once again.

The old intercom system, the one that hadn't been used in thirty years, came to life with a crackling sound. After a momentary whine of feedback, Joe's voice came over the system. It was piped into the room, but it also echoed in the hallway outside and from the adjacent floors.

Kara looked up at the dusty speaker in the corner of the room. She had Hudson's body in her arms. Her face was deceptively placid, but her hair was sticking out on either side of her head, tendrils reaching out around her as if searching for a victim.

This is a red level security alert, Joe's voice said. *This is not a drill. There has been a serious and dangerous computer security breach. All associates should log out of any electronic system that they may be connected to, including computers, laptops, phones, pads, printers, scanners, scientific analysis devices, and any nonessential medical devices. All associates, no matter their function, should immediately return to their residences. They should remain in their residences and offline until further notice.*

The intercom disconnected with a scratching and popping sound.

"What the fuck was that?" Kara asked, turning to Dante. "What sort of computer security breach would cause a red level alert?"

Judith suddenly plopped to the floor next to him. Dante squatted down.

"Are you okay?" he asked.

Judith nodded.

"What happened?"

"I don't know," she said softly. "I just suddenly felt ... I felt ... horrible."

"What do you mean, horrible?" Dante asked, putting an arm around her. "Were you in pain?"

Judith shook her head.

"I didn't feel pain. Not exactly," she said. "I felt like ... I don't know ... I felt like I was being crushed, but not just that. I felt like I ... like I ... like there were bugs running under my skin. I felt like I was being crushed by a mountain of bugs."

Shit. Dante stood up quickly.

"Can I see the monitor?" he said to Lepri, who handed it to him.

"Could that thing be infected?" Kara asked, nodding at the monitor, as she laid a now motionless Hudson back on the floor.

"Unlikely and probably the least of our worries," Dante replied.

"What is that?" Judith asked, looking warily at the monitor.

"I just want to check your energy for something."

"Will it hurt?"

Dante shook his head as he turned the device on and sat it on a dresser near her. It was set to scan up to thirty feet around them, so it would take a few minutes.

"How is Hudson?" Dante asked, turning to Kara who was kneeling next to him.

"I don't know," she said. "For a moment, his spirit was here, he was with us. And now he is gone again. I don't sense him in the room or the building. I tried to reach out further but felt nothing of him."

"Was he saying something?" Dante asked.

"Yes, he said something about warning people, and being trapped here, and something about the white room, and then about forgetting things, and something about someone trying to steal his voice. But it was all a jumble. Do you think he could be trapped in the same place as our Cambion ghosts?"

"Yes, it's possible."

At that moment, Joe appeared at the door.

"Our whole computer network is infected with some sort of a virus," he said breathlessly. "All computer-run processes are breaking down."

"At least you caught it," Kara said softly. Way too softly.

"Kara, I'm so sorry. I don't know how this could have happened," he said, words tumbling over themselves. Kara stood up and Joe came directly to her. His eyes were wide and tortured.

"We aren't even connected to regular outside servers. We have maybe a hundred different firewalls. I insisted on every possible security precaution with all the IT people," he said.

"I guess the IT people missed something," Kara said. She said it gently, and Dante detected no menace, but Joe looked devastated.

"No, it's my fault. I should have checked more often. I should have insisted on daily system reviews rather than weekly ones."

"It's not a time factor," Dante said to Kara, "it's a skill factor. And it's a leak factor."

"Is Dante here?" Joe asked.

"Yes, and he assures me that whatever has happened is no reflection on your abilities." She reached out and put her hand on Joe's arm. His body visibly relaxed.

"Dante, can you put a bubble around our computer systems?" Kara asked.

"I can, but I can't bubble every device. There are too many of them and I would need to know where all of them existed."

"Then can you put the whole of the building in a bubble?"

"I can." Dante briefly closed his eyes and directed the energy at his core to pull the resonance of the building slightly upward and out of the flow of time.

"What happened?" Kara asked Joe.

"It started when I was running a check for missing files," Joe began. "I asked the IT folks to check for them, and they found the invisible folder containing emails. That was good, but it seemed too easy to me that there would just be one file. I mean, if we were hacked, why would someone just change one file. So I started checking on my own."

"But the IT guys had run a check for those, right?" Kara asked.

"Of course, but it's the IT guys." Joe shrugged. "Most of those guys are white collar, college sorts. They know the coding, but they don't know all the ways to fuck the coding up. But I came from a different world—well, you know all that."

He looked at Kara with a moment of worship before shaking his head and continuing.

"So some skills I learned in that world—well, these guys might not have had the opportunity to have learned them. I got a serious education in computer viruses from the porn and slavery side of the industries I was involved in."

He looked down but shook his head again and continued. "So I ran some illegal search codes that I had from the old days. And I guess they are using similar root sources because I found hundreds—no, thousands—of hidden files. They were in the files, the drivers, and the operating systems. So I decided to widen the search."

Joe stopped and sighed.

"That's when I found residue of infection in some of our medical and genetic coding devices."

"Shit," Lepri muttered.

Kara was noticeably paler than she had been minutes before. Dante moved to put his arm around her. She stiffened for just a second and then relaxed into it.

"Is there more?" she asked.

"Yeah," Joe said, and let out a breath. "One of the files that seemed to be corrupted was the new recruits file that we keep. As you know, that file is where we store all the background information on incoming associates—their background, family, skills, spiritual heritage, everything. Well, in this file there was a subfile called TarCAMver. I didn't know what that meant but the words 'tar' and 'cam' together were a little too close to 'target Cambion' for my taste, and it seemed to have roughly 300 subfiles in it. But all of the files were now encrypted. After opening it, the whole system blacked. When I got it reopened, all our associate files were corrupted."

"All of them?" Kara asked.

"Yep. All associate files are now encrypted, and we can't get into them. Also all our backups of everything."

"So that triggered the alarms?"

"No, the bug did that," Joe said. "When I tried to hack into the encrypted files, those alarms were triggered. But even those are weird."

"What do you mean?" asked Lepri.

"I mean the sound of them didn't come from any of our sound libraries. The sound must come from somewhere in the encrypted files."

"How did it stop?" Kara asked.

"We cut power to all speakers and any device that had a speaker."

"What about the virus?" Dante asked, forgetting Joe couldn't hear him.

"Have you found the virus?" Lepri repeated for Joe.

"That's the good news," he said. "We have shut off all the systems and we think the IT guys have isolated the virus. But it's a strange one. It has a lot of the hallmarks of the Stuxnet virus, the one that was used against the nuclear plants in Iran."

"Why didn't we detect that?" Lepri asked.

"Because it's slick. At first, it did nothing. It seems to have been sitting there for a long time, just tracking our data. When we scanned for it, it used a playback of previous data to make our security systems think everyone was okay. All the while it was copying itself everywhere."

"What is it doing? What is it looking for?" Kara asked.

"We aren't completely sure," Joe replied. "We know it changes file names, it encrypts files, but it also seems to be able to spy on our activities and copy data."

Kara's body was getting colder. Dante sent a little wave of heat her way, hoping she wouldn't notice.

"Have you scrapped it from our systems?" she asked.

"Not yet. We are in the process of trying to do it now. All the IT people are on it. All the security people in the Office and all of our branches have been advised and activated. All security protocol is in place for a lockdown and manual safety procedures have been engaged. But there are some really weird things about this virus."

"Such as?" Lepri was clutching his notebook to his chest.

Just as Joe was about to answer, Liz came into the room. She nodded at Kara and Dante, and then went to stand near Joe.

"They are asking what is weird about the computer virus," Joe said to Liz.

She nodded, and said, "Well, it has written musical sequences in it, for one."

"Musical sequences?" Dante asked.

"Yes, musical notes."

"Notes and pitches," Joe continued. "Like the alarm. That was a pitch from inside the virus."

"Also, there are some long sequences of letters," Joe said.

"What sort of letters?" Lepri asked.

"If I remember right, there were a lot of As and Cs."

"Could there have been Ts and Gs as well?"

"Yeah, actually there were," Joe said.

Dante felt the chill in his chest before Lepri opened his mouth.

"We need to scan everyone for viruses, now!" Lepri said, turning to Kara and Dante.

"Does it have to be now?" Joe asked. "We shouldn't be using our machines."

"Yes, it has to be now," Lepri said, picking up his forbidden cell phone.

"Because of our computer virus?" Joe asked.

"No, because the computer virus might have transferred itself into our biological systems."

"But computer viruses can't pass into humans," Liz said.

"Actually, under the right circumstances, they can," Lepri said as he texted something into his phone.

He turned to face them.

"It sounds like that computer virus is coding for sequences of DNA. A, T, C, and G are the bases used to create strands of DNA. Normally, this wouldn't mean much, but in our world, it might. We have various interfaces between our computers and ourselves—more than normal places. Some of us have inserted trackers and scanners. More than a few of us have cybernetic implants. We have computers connected to automated machines that generate sequences of DNA for study. And that's just the basic stuff, even I don't know how far it reaches. I can look into it more, but you need to order the scans."

"Parabiology," Dante said, looking at Kara.

Kara turned to Lepri and Joe.

"Order the scans now, Joe, and you need to enforce them. Make sure everyone has one. We need to make sure that we test parabiology as well," she said.

"You mean the monsters in the basement?" Joe asked.

"Yes, the very talented and very dangerous associates in Parabiology," Kara said sharply. "You and Lepri will need to find a way to scan whoever is in our basement and do it now."

Joe, Liz, and Jeremy turned to leave but Kara took Lepri's arm.

"Jeremy, stay for just a minute."

After Joe and Liz left, Kara went to crouch beside Hudson as he lay on the floor.

"Jeremy, can you help me get him back on the table." Together, they gently lifted Hudson's body onto the table.

"What happened to him?" Lepri asked.

"When the alarms went off, he fell off the bed and began convulsing," Dante said.

"Maybe it was an epileptic response to the sound," Lepri replied. "Sound sometimes acts as a trigger."

"Does epilepsy also cause consciousness and speaking?" Kara said.

"He woke up?" Lepri leaned forward and placed his ear against Hudson's chest.

"Yes, but the moment the sound stopped, he went back into this state."

"Okay then. Once we have dealt with this crisis, I can try experimenting with sound to see if I can wake him, but for now, we have whales to fry," Lepri said.

"Agreed, the current crisis *is* our priority," Kara said. "So you want everyone tested for viruses because you suspect we may have been infected by a computer virus that managed to become a biological one?"

"Yes, but it's not just that," Lepri replied. "I also suspect that this computer virus might have come through a human host."

"Why would you think that?" Kara asked.

"Because I discovered tech elements hiding in the virus from the Manassas boys."

"What sort of tech elements?" Dante asked.

"The navy dots. I was so caught up in this being a new virus that I didn't see that it could just be an adaptation of an old one—which is exactly what it was. It *was* the mimivirus, but with tech inserted."

He pulled out a photo they had seen earlier of the large virus.

"These navy dots, the ones that looked the same on the ghost scan, these aren't biological, natural things. They are nanoparticles that contain minute amounts of DNA. Less than a quarter than we see in normal viruses. So the viruses could be being used as tech to transfer that DNA code."

"Viruses as tech?"

"It's not unheard of," Lepri said. "Medicine already uses viruses as a gateway into the body. We use it all the time in gene therapy. The virus is just a protein coat containing little bits of DNA. Usually, those bits are code for telling a cell to make more of a virus, but it can be anything really."

"So you think that our computers were hacked using a biological virus?" Dante asked.

"Yeah, I do. A biological virus with tech elements that allow it to interface with other technology."

"That's not possible, is it?" Kara asked.

"It's been done before," Lepri said. "It's a bit complex but it can be done. But what's more frightening is the possible next step."

"Which is?"

"Using the computer virus in our systems to code for some new and worse virus." There was fear in Lepri's eyes.

"What does that look like?" Dante asked.

"It would start with a computer virus hacked into our systems that could attack our DNA sequencing machines. Which Joe seemed to indicate happened here. We use these machines to transfer data back and forth between organic code and computer code all the time. The sequencing machine reads the data and transfers it back to computer as code, including the malware. Once it is malware, it can be transferred from computer to computer."

"But how could our computer systems get hacked to begin with? We have too many protocols in place for that to happen, right?" Kara asked.

"That's where the human vectors come in. I suspect the computer virus comes from the outside via an actual person that we aren't catching. They are transferring it into our systems via their bodies. It could come from a computer virus found in the software of a medical device, like a pacemaker, or a deep brain stimulator, or a cochlear implant. Given the nature of Cambions, a lot of us have things like this. These devices have software installed but they have updates, assessments and the like. I know we scan for viruses in software and updates, but do we scan the programming code of the devices themselves for code that could be genetically transferable before they are inserted? I'm not sure."

Lepri sighed and began pacing.

"These devices should be monitored by our medical technology groups. Their data is uploaded into our system for analysis. If the devices are sending nitrogenous base codes, and it wasn't caught, it could get into the system and then send directly to the DNA sequencers. At that point, we have something outside of the Office creating strands of DNA in our facility."

"What could they do with that?" Dante asked.

"What couldn't they do?" Lepri said, with a dark laugh. "If they can do something like that, then they could release strands of DNA, proteins, or even viruses into almost any part of our system—the water, the air, even through contaminated blood samples. All of our people could be infected with something latent, and we might not know."

"So you need to run the same test that you did on the Manassas kids, but on everyone," Dante said in his most modulated tones. Lepri blew out a long stream of air, and then nodded.

"Also, as we have a breach somewhere, and it would likely be someone with an implant who was somehow connected to outside sources with frequencies we aren't monitoring, we need to run an immediate check for all Cambion in the building with implantable electronics that connects back to the computer. Jeremy, can you text Joe to coordinate with Med Tech to get that information?"

Lepri nodded. "Also, the structure and placement of the nanoparticles themselves are concerning," he said. "They're not anything natural, obviously. They were inserted into the viruses but my question was, for what purpose? So I tried to subject them to a variety of conditions. They didn't react to anything really, except vibration and resonance. At certain resonances and vibrations, they began to reproduce and burst out from the original virus."

"Meaning?" Kara asked.

"Meaning that they broke out when they came in contact with creatures who have a certain resonance."

"And what creatures would those be?"

"The resonance that this worked for was ghosts, particularly Cambion ghosts," Lepri said.

"So they could be tracking devices attached to the ghosts?" Kara asked. "Could they be a type of spy, or spying tech?"

"They could be," Lepri replied.

"Could they be spies designed to capture ghost DNA for analysis?" Dante asked. "Ghost DNA is much smaller and much simpler, and the only thing it has in common with human DNA is the stretch of DNA that controls our consciousness."

"No one has analyzed this before because they couldn't capture ghosts long enough to test them."

There was silence as they all looked at each other.

"Is this coming from the Academy?" Kara asked.

"It is coming from someone, and I know of no one else with this sort of technological advancement. Plus, whoever is doing this is targeting us," Lepri said.

"Because of the Cambion link?"

"Yes, that's right," Lepri said. "Some of the strands of DNA inside the virus contain sequences that you find *only* in Cambion. It's Cambion DNA. There are also other sorts of strands that I can't even recognize as DNA per se."

"The Director wouldn't openly challenge me," Kara said, her voice icy and her hair beginning to wave.

"No, he wouldn't," Dante said, "but one of his underlings might."

Rose was too close to all of this for comfort. She had tricked ghosts into Everlast, which was clearly not what it seemed.

Suddenly, Liz returned, not quite running but almost.

"I just found something, and you told me that I should find you if I found out anything about the gamers and the games they played. So, well, I found out a lot."

She opened a notebook.

"Our outside access has been cut but I had printed these off before it happened. I just now had the chance to look at them. It turns out that David, Kenneth, and Hudson all played the same game. And it looks like Tobias did too. The only game they had in common was a game called Verite. David and Tobias were recent, heavy-duty players. Hudson and Kenneth were early adopters of a beta version of the game."

Liz sifted through her papers and pulled out a page.

"The interesting thing about this game is that it is 4D plus. It is supposed to make you feel as if you are really in the game. Even I had heard about it. It is supposed to be amazing. For accessories, you use a little headpiece with eyepieces and a full body suit. The body suit has sensors in it to measure your biometric responses to the game so that the game can respond to you. It says something about using a 'harmless viral interface' in the suits."

"What is a 'viral interface'? Does it mean viral like we mean viral? Is it common in the gaming world?" Lepri asked suddenly.

"I don't know, why?" Liz asked.

"Nothing," he said, beginning to chew a nail. "Excuse me for a moment, but I need to make that call to Joe about running a search for electrical inserts."

Lepri walked to the far end of the room and got on a landline. No cell phones right now.

"So I went a little further and looked up their corporate information," Liz continued. "The immediate developer and distributor was Envision Corporation. But that was a subdivision of Mindless Carrot Games. Anyway, after digging through lots of corporate filings, I discovered that the parent corporation seemed to be a company called Crossroads Inc. They are big into video gaming, but they are into a lot more than that. They have interests in property, real estate, and energy. They are also tied in to some weirder stuff."

"Like?" Dante asked.

"Like they have a subsidiary called Zoo that is working with engineering and—" Liz stopped mid-sentence.

"Genetics. Shit," she whispered. "And then there is this longevity company based out of Silicon Valley."

"Is it called Everlast?" Kara asked.

"Yes, that's it. Everlast is a subsidiary of a company called Maltese Academic, but they are owned by Crossroads. How did you know?"

"Because you meet the devil at night at the Crossroads," Dante said, laughing.

"Jeremy," Kara called out. "Tell Joe that he also needs to scour the building for any video games. Look for anything on the network, or anything like game consoles or boxes in people's rooms. We are specifically looking for a game called Verite—or anything that has been produced by Envision Corporation, Mindless Carrot Games, or Crossroads Inc."

"Well done, Liz," Kara said, pulling her suddenly into her arms.

"What have I done?" Liz asked.

"You have just found something we have been in search of for years," Dante said.

"You found the shell company for the Academy," Kara said, kissing the top of Liz's head.

Liz smiled and leaned into the embrace.

"Dante!" Lepri called out from across the room. He held up the monitor that he had used to assess Judith. It was buzzing like crazy. Dante was by his side in an instant. The device was pulsing and beeping. When Dante took it, he saw something that he didn't understand.

The device was showing the humans in the room, registering as green. Kara was not registering, but that would be normal. Dante himself was registering as a dark orange, which didn't bode well. But what was even worse was Judith's readings. She still registered the yellow color of ghosts but where once she had only had a few dots around her, she was now covered in them. These were the tech nanoparticles, and a stream of them was coming from her and leading across the room to Hudson.

"I don't feel well," Judith said suddenly, collapsing on the floor. Dante dropped the device and ran to her.

"She's being attacked by the nanoparticles, and she may be infecting Hudson." Dante put an arm around her.

"No," Lepri said, reading the device. "The flow is the other way. Hudson is infecting her."

"What? Didn't we scan him for viruses?" Kara said.

"He was scanned when he came in, but he must have been infected since then," Lepri said, turning to the medical equipment next to Hudson's bed. The needles, the bags of fluid—and the computer to which all of these things were attached.

Judith was flickering in Dante's arms. Bits of her were beginning to flake off. She was beginning to fall apart.

"What's happening to me?" Judith whispered.

"What can we do?" Kara said.

"She's infected ..." Lepri said.

"Can these nanoparticles survive above the Dreamscape?" Kara's hair was whipping around her face.

"No, not if you go high enough," replied Lepri. "The particles will fall to pieces and the DNA will be unmade."

"Neither can most ghosts," Dante said.

"Dante, we don't have a choice, take her up now or there will be nothing left to take," Kara said.

Dante didn't need to hear more.

Chapter Nineteen

Bile and Rain

Dante pushed himself upward and outward through the layers of resonance closest to that of humans. He clutched Judith's frail form in his arms. He felt her spirit flicker in his arms—a complex frequency dampened by the foreign signal laced through her. If he could shift her resonance high enough, the intruder's harmonic would become visible, like a low note lifted from a chord. He took them quickly because creating the force of motion was easy here, but it would become harder as they rose, as less of him would be available to drive this push. Judith was trembling in his arms, getting more transparent by the moment.

The sights of the Kingdom began to fade along with the smell of dittany that was always strong there. This smell was replaced by a scent unknown to human senses and too etheric for embodied creatures to tolerate. Its closest cousin was the smell of jasmine, but with an overtone of grilled meat.

"What's wrong with me?" Judith whispered in a voice almost too soft to hear. Pieces of her body were still flaking off her.

"You're sick," Dante said.

"Ghosts can get sick?"

"Normally, no. But we think you have been purposefully infected with something that can attach to ghosts."

"Did it come from Everlast?"

"Originally, yes." This was not the moment to tell her that he suspected that the Academy had used her as a mule to carry the viral nanoparticles that would then infect ghosts on the 8th floor.

Judith nodded and put her head against Dante's chest.

A giant, orange-red moon appeared above them as they moved upward.

It was not the Earth's moon, it was the idea of all moons, the blueprint for moons. It was the place of the unconscious, the shadow, and the spiritual body freed from its physical limitations. This was the land of the ghosts.

Judith shuddered in his arms. The nanoparticles attached to her were now visible and no longer tiny. They were the size of a child's marbles inside her transparent body, taking up space in her essence and weighing her down. Inside them, Dante could see points of light spinning amid darkness, like galaxies in a darkened universe.

"Is that …?" Judith pointed to one of the particles.

"Yes, that's what is in you. We don't think they are natural, so we need to take you up the layers of existence to a place where non-natural things are undone."

Judith didn't reply, instead, her head flopped against him. She had lost consciousness.

As his essence became thinner, movement at this level was based more on will than physicality. So, as his consciousness became more scattered, his will became a weaker driver. For a moment they slowed in their ascent long enough to see flashes of ghostly figures as they passed through the moon and beyond the space of ghosts. Dante felt this change immediately. His essence was beginning to spread out, the definition between his body and the rest of space becoming less defined.

Judith moaned. The flakes of her that she was losing were becoming chunks.

As they rose above and away from the moon space, Dante's nose was assaulted with a strong scent of sandalwood, rose, and storax balsam.

The space around them was beginning to fill with a shiny, translucent light that flickered with all colors, colors visible to the human eye as well as those only visible to the non-human eye. As they ascended, they passed by luscious fields of green grass, cities filled with buildings towering far above anything that was possible or even fathomable by a human. Everywhere the light touched, there was something beautiful; beautiful trees, beautiful buildings, beautiful oceans, and the occasional perfectly formed winged humanoid creature. Dante knew that this is how he saw them because he had been a human. Incubi always appeared as what you found most beautiful. But despite the beauty, there was something shallow about this place. It was like a painting of the perfect apple. It looked beautiful but you couldn't eat it.

Judith was now panting and twitching in his arms. Her frequency was fragmenting now—her signal scattering into the resonance around them. The higher they rose, the harder it became to keep her harmonic intact. He had to push beyond, to where discordant frequencies couldn't hold form. He held her closer. His own form was becoming thinner and more stretched as they moved into a painfully empty space. The whiteness around them had changed from soft, translucent light to a harsh and palpable thing.

It was then that he saw it, at the same time he felt it. There was something in his own body. Inside him were dots that looked a bit like the navy dots that had attached to Judith, but fuzzier, softer, and more like liquid than solid. As he watched, he saw them beginning to aggregate inside him. One would touch another, only to be engulfed by it. In this way, the small dots were becoming bigger dots, and then blobs, and as they did, they took on more of a structure, one that looked like the form the virus had taken when it attacked him at the TV station. As he watched, tiny flames appeared, racing toward the dark balls. His own body was mounting a defense. Some of the blobs began to push at the edges of his form, as if seeking to escape. Through all of this he felt every movement, as if these things were tearing through his ghostly flesh with each motion. What sort of thing could do that to him? What would these things be able to do at this level of resonance, a level where the ideas for reality begin? A smell of curdled milk suddenly filled the air.

Dante pushed himself further up, further out, and above any place he had gone before—save for that one time, when the story was remade.

In his arms, Judith was little more than a wisp of ash, nothing else. The whiteness all around blinded him to everything but its own whiteness. Soon even the whiteness began to fade to a nothingness. This was the place that stripped a creature of all but its most essential, its most unique. His senses, which were being burned away by the light, occasionally presented him with something—a faint smell of frankincense, the thought of a lion projected into his brain, the taste of liquefied diamonds he remembered from another life. Now he was holding on to his consciousness by sheer force of memory and will, but he was beginning to lose focus and was struggling to retain the memory of who he was and why he was here.

Judith was now completely still in his arms. Looking at her, it struck him that there were no dots or marbles on her anymore. Whatever they were, they could not survive the higher resonances and their frequencies in this incubator for the idea of creation. Their waveforms weren't a match for the purity of this space. Perhaps they had burst apart, but if so, he had been too blinded to see it. The pain in his body had also abated. When he looked down at his body, he saw no blobs and no dots.

Dante needed to get them out of there, but he was having trouble focusing enough to weigh them down. He was still moving upward and losing more coherence by the second. The strip of fire at the heart of him, the essence of him, could last further than most because its source did not follow the rules laid out in this reality. He knew of only one other with that trait.

Kara.

Her face appeared in his consciousness with a surge of electricity and desire. His nose remembered her scent as his body remembered the longing for her touch. His movement upward stopped, and he began to sink. As he floated downward, he focused his fire on his memories of Kara in the flesh, her pale skin, her deep blue eyes, and the sounds she made when he held her in his arms. Her frequency was etched in his memory and it was his anchor, his home. He kept his eyes turned inward, toward his vision of her as he fell. Judith was becoming heavier in his arms. He didn't know if she had survived their ascent, but he knew that she had been stripped of whatever invader had possessed her.

As he dropped, he latched on to the thousands of images from his past, until he sensed that his movement had stopped. He opened his eyes to find that he was sitting in the familiar bubble of the 8th floor. His body had drawn them here, perhaps called by familiarity and the memory of trauma.

He saw no ghosts for the moment, but the scenery on this floor had changed into something disconcertingly familiar. It was dark, and there were two beautiful gray moons above them. Not real moons, but someone's memory of them. Their light shone on a silver-blue landscape of black marble mausoleums and white marble gravestones.

Dante knew this place. It was his memory of the Ghoul Lands. He had been here many times as a young ghost.

He laid Judith down on a long, stone table set in the middle of a circle of mausoleums. The table was easily 100 feet long and made of the black marble, that glinted in the moonlight. Judith wasn't moving. Her etheric body was intact, but Dante had no way to know if her consciousness had survived her forced ascension. As he touched her hair, he heard the sound of movement coming from the group of mausoleums situated at the end of the table.

Dante checked on Judith again, and then moved toward the sound. As he got closer, he realized that the sound was a low growl, and it was coming from just behind a large mausoleum of black obsidian.

As he rounded it, he saw the source of the noise. A figure, torn and bleeding, was lying tangled in the dead vines that surrounded the mausoleums.

It was Abi—and he was growling and panting.

"Abi," Dante said, kneeling down by his side.

Abi looked up. He smiled, but his smile was replaced almost instantaneously with a grimace. His breath was coming fast and ragged.

"Dante, my friend," Abi said. "How fortunate I am that it is you who has found me. But of course, only a true friend can hear the beat of a heart in need."

Abi's words were as beautiful as ever, but his voice was thick and slurred, as if his tongue were swollen.

Dante put his hand to Abi's head. He felt the ebb and flow of energy that he felt from all creatures, but the outflow was much greater than the influx.

"I'll call Kara," he said.

"Not yet. Not before I tell you what I have seen. After I left—" He coughed and turned his face away, his body racked with spasms. Finally, he settled and turned back to Dante.

"When I left you, I returned to the place of my birth," he said. "I knew from the moment I appeared just outside the fields of Venenum that something had changed. It was dark and the gray moons cast the shadows they had always cast from the starless sky, but the air was different. It smelled empty. There was no smell of death, no smell of decay, no smell of life regenerating. It smelled of nothing."

A wind picked up and the leaves began to rustle around them, releasing the smell of earth and detritus. Abi sighed.

"When I came unto the fields themselves, it was not like it had been when I had lived there a millennium ago," he said. "I had spent my youth playing among the acres of mausoleums, under the light of our gray moons. In that time, the mausoleums were so grand that they reached into the sky so high that they scraped the very ice in the clouds of our upper winds. I used to feast at banquet tables that were the size of city streets, covered with everything from remnants of decayed and reabsorbed bone to the deeds of the worst of mankind's sinners. The size of the banquet was so grand and the stench of it so great that it attracted ghouls from all our sub-levels and sub-evils. In earlier times, we met at these tables, and for that short time, we feasted and they celebrated with me gloriously and shamelessly. In their gluttony, they forgot my half-blood nature. I remember winds so strong that they could lift me and carry me for twenty-seven of our nights with no break. Do you remember how beautiful those winds felt, in the old days?"

"Yes." Dante remembered those days, but not with fondness. Abi claimed that Dante saved him, but that was later on. It was before meeting Kara, before becoming sane again. In those older days, Abi had been his only friend. Abi had been his home when he had nowhere else to go.

Abi nodded. "And yet, you would not have recognized them. When I approached the fields, I could taste none of the memories of my youth. I sensed no other ghouls or even the remains of ghouls. Everything was gone and sterile. There was no smell and no wind. As I walked in the places where the mausoleums and banquet tables had been, there was nothing but pale, pure white sand as far as the eye could see. As I walked, this cool, silken, sickly substance stuck to my paws, burning them ... and I was afraid. But I continued because I had given my word to our goddess."

Abi turned his gaze back to Dante. "You know I would never break that," he said.

Dante nodded.

"I walked on for what felt like years," Abi continued. "I think time was different there, but how could that be? Time is you, but I couldn't feel you in this place. After an eternity, I saw something shimmering in the distance. I thought it was some mirage but, as I walked, it grew to take up the entire horizon. I saw it was a vast ocean. There had never been water in Venenum besides the water created by decomposition. At first, I believed that my eyes had betrayed me but then my nose confirmed it. The gentle breeze coming from its direction smelled of salt ... and something else, something sickly sweet. It was a smell that had no place in Venenum Fields. Then I saw the most horrible sight I have ever seen. In the distance, rising over a vast black ocean and at the horizon, there was a tiny slash of light."

Abi began to cough again, sputtering up a milky liquid.

"There are no suns on Venenum Fields," Dante said.

"Yes, brother, and no light but moonlight. But this was no sun. What I saw was a slash of light that was ripping the fabric of the horizon. It was not the beauty of twilight or the gloaming, which the human side of me can relish, even as the ghoul side of me withdraws from it. No, this was a harsh, white abomination. It was the rape of our sky. I did not want to go near it. My very breath was sucked away by the thought of getting any closer to it, but my human heart had begun to ache and pull me forward … and Kara had told me to listen to my human heart."

Dante noticed that Abi's sides were heaving as he spoke.

"I forced my paws to move forward. I was drawn on and on, keeping my eyes down until finally I came to the edge of that monstrous black ocean. The water was thick and black and smelled of oil and bile. Tiny, inky waves lapped at my paws. At their touch, I was revived slightly. This gave me strength enough to look up at the light. The slit in the sky was expanding again, and as it did so, the white light fell from it like the afterbirth of some obscene monster. The water where it touched began to clear. As I watched, the blackness of the waves faded away only to be replaced by clear water that glinted in shades of lavender and pink."

Abi shuddered violently, and rolled to the side. Dante reached out and put his hand on Abi's back.

"It was a travesty," Abi whispered. "Such a sight does not belong in Venenum. And it was then that I noticed that there were shapes moving in the water, toward the shore. At first, I could not make them out as they moved beneath the waves, but as they neared the shoreline, I saw that they had a human form. As they got closer to me, two shapes rose out of the waves. It was a man and a woman, and they were beautiful."

He rolled back over and met Dante's eyes. Abi's eyes were wide, and his eyelids were twitching.

"Abi," Dante said, as Abi retched again. "We need to call Kara now."

"No, let me finish. Then you can call her. You must decide what to do. She will … she will … she cannot …"

Dante took his hand back. "You saw people in the water? Humans?"

"Human shaped," Abi whispered, his eyes closed. "And they were beautiful … but they were also … unfinished. They had skin and form, but I could still see the water flowing just beneath the surface of their skin. They had glowing eyes, one black and one golden, and transparent hair that reflected the light and yet they had no other features. What was worse was the way they smelled. They smelled like they did not belong here.

"As I watched, more of these shapes stood in the waves, there must have been fifty or a hundred of them. They were glorious but awful, so, coward that I am, I began to back away, even though my heart was drawing me forward. I was about to turn and run when one of the figures pushed its way through the waves toward me. It reached out its arms to me, and as it did so, the bright rip in the sky widened even more and the sickly-sweet smell of the air turned more pungent. I felt like I was choking on it. Then, the whiteness of the rip seemed to break forth from the sky itself and fall upon the sea beneath it in thick streams."

Whiteness. Hudson had said something about whiteness. That's what Kara had said.

"As this happened, a noise filled the air," Abi continued. "It was a sound of sighs and groans and soft weeping. I did not know where it came from, unless somehow from the creatures in front of me. The whiteness that had fallen from the sky was still expanding across the surface of the waves. It was swirling and mixing with the clear water. And, at my feet, I saw the water begin to recede."

Abi's voice was getting softer, and his energy was dimming. Kara would need to be called soon. Abi must have seen the concern in Dante's eyes because he shook his head.

"In the distance, I could see standing figures being pulled beneath the whitening waves. The white slash in the sky was like an insect, piercing the skin of this world and injecting acid to dissolve its food before sucking up the liquefied remains. Just like such an insect, the white gash was infecting and then drinking the ocean. The smell in the air was now so thick and sweet that I could barely absorb it. I started to back away when I saw something that stopped me."

Abi drew a long breath.

"As the white water touched the figures near the shoreline, for the briefest of seconds, before they were pulled down and into the waves, I saw what was inside them."

Abi raised his head and a cavalcade of expressions passed across his face; pain, pride, fear, longing, and something that looked a bit like joy.

"I saw what Kara sent me to find. I saw living, conscious things. I recognized some of them as spirits I had known. Ghosts I hadn't seen in maybe a lifetime or two but all of whom I had been friendly with at one time or another. Some were merely acquaintances, but others had been like you, playing in the winds with me when we were younger."

Abi laughed darkly, triggering another coughing fit. This time he coughed up a reddish-white liquid.

"So what did you do?" Dante asked.

Abi's tortured eyes looked into Dante's own.

"I did the only thing that a ghoul might be able to do in this situation. I had to save them, so I took them into myself."

Abi closed his eyes and gulped. He lifted a paw to his mouth for a moment and licked it. Dante noticed that the skin on the pads underneath his foot was blistered and bleeding.

"What do you mean, took them into yourself?"

"I ate them."

"You ate them?"

"Yes. Ghouls' stomachs can tolerate anything. It can take much more than our thin skin or our silly minds. Our stomachs are invincible. So I opened my mouth and drank from that horrible, fetid white pool. I took in as many of them as I could. I fought for them with the ripping, white sky. It dug itself into my insides, but my gut was stronger. It ripped open my tongue and lips. But my gut was stronger. It dug into the roof of my mouth toward my useless brain. But my gut was stronger. Finally, the slit itself pulled away and closed. It took what treasures it managed to keep back to whatever horror had birthed it, but it left something. It left a doorway there in the sky."

Dante froze. A doorway. Could this be another entrance to the hallway?

"And I, for my effort, was left with pain and a belly full of sick. It took everything in me to get back here. I have defied my queen's direct order but yet I have done as she desired. I believe I have found the missing ghosts," Abi said, with a small laughing groan that turned into a sputtering cough.

"And they are still inside you?" Dante asked, putting his hand on his friend's stomach.

Abi nodded.

"You have not absorbed them yet?"

"I cannot," Abi said. "Ghouls eat the remains of life. We eat death and decay. I could not have even ingested these things to begin with if they had been fully alive but, as I suspected, they were not. But apparently, they still have partial life, so I could digest what was dead, but the living parts remain inside me."

"A thing cannot be life and yet not life," Dante said softly.

"Not in this world," Abi replied. "Not in this story. But I think these ghosts are now no longer completely of this story. This makes them now unnatural things, created by an unnatural place. But I know they were once natural because I recognized them. So I will save them if I can."

"You did not have to take this on, my friend."

"Oh, but I did, my brother. Kara wanted these ghosts saved, and that was the only way I could see that I could do it. But now, I need your help. You, who understands the pain of taking other beings inside yourself. And what I ask is much to ask ... even for a brother."

Abi raised himself on his front legs, weaving and breathing hard. He leaned forward and touched his forehead to Dante's.

"I should get Kara," Dante said again.

"No, Kara cannot help me. Only you can help me," Abi said. "Kara has dominion only over natural things in this story. She can create, draw, or unmake, but only natural things. These things inside me, that I have consumed, are no longer natural things. They are a mix. So her belief will keep her from being able to draw them forth—but you can. A part of you can."

Dante sat back on his heels.

"I know it is much to ask," Abi said. "Remember, I know. But all evil exists for good, just as all good exists for evil. They cannot exist separately. We have learned that, you and I ... sometimes together. I helped you when you needed to take down a civilization that had gone wrong. I gazed in awe at the story that you created to fulfill the gap those civilizations left. So, I ask you now, take these things from me."

"But Kara could save you—"

"Maybe. But she can't save them, not if they are still in me," Abi whispered. "So I must ask it of you instead. You are a god in more than one story. Use that hidden part of you to call to the alien part inside our lost brothers and sisters. This is a gift from your father and your maker. Once they are in our world, Kara can do as she must with the existing natural part of them."

Abi dropped back to the ground. He was now foaming at the mouth and trembling. His pain was visceral. Dante felt what tears he could cry well up in his eyes. What must a pain be like to do this to a ghoul?

Abi reached out his paw and placed it on Dante's knee.

"This part of me is not controlled or gentle, Abi. You may not survive it. *They* may not survive it," Dante said softly.

"My friend, I don't expect to survive this anyway," Abi whispered. "I told Kara that I would give my life for her. I would give it to save those she would save. Ghouls do not lie."

"If you die, there is no way back for you. You know this. You will simply cease. I don't want to lose you."

"Brother, as much as I do not wish to burden you, you have no choice. There is something deeply wrong in our story. These ghosts have seen it and you need to know what they know. You must do it now before she comes."

Dante knew that Abi was right. They needed these ghosts, although he was unsure if they could even survive here in their current state. But he needed to try.

Dante closed his eyes and put his hand around the icy black stone at his neck. He then turned his thoughts inward … searching. He was searching for that grain of memory. The memory which slept at the root of him, the one that poisoned one world and created another. He could not bring that memory back in its full form, as it would recreate everything again, destroying all that exists in the process. He needed to unearth only the tiniest fraction of it … only a tiny spark of that dying world.

"You must hurry," Abi whispered. "I feel that some of the ghosts in me are languishing."

Dante hesitated for only a moment before he laid his hand on Abi's flank, and reached out with the memory of who he was. He immediately felt the energy that made up Abi's body pull away from his touch.

Abi began to tremble. Then his whole body started to spasm and contort. His back twisted, and his neck arched backward. He tried to pull himself up, but his legs gave out under him. Everything around them began to shake.

"If anyone is here, you need to get out," Dante called to the air around them, using his old voice with its unrestrained power and violence. There were sounds of wind, rain, and bells as currently invisible ghosts fled from his voice and what it might mean for them.

Abi began to thrash beneath Dante's touch. He threw back his head and roared. Wave after wave of spasms crashed through Abi's body.

Dante removed his hand from Abi's side. That memory, that power from the past, was now inside Abi, for good or evil.

Abi struggled to his feet. He stood, then staggered and raised his tortured eyes to the spinning moons above them. Then his eyes rolled up in his head and he fell backward upon the floor. He opened his mouth, as if to roar, but instead he vomited a geyser of white liquid into the sky above him. It sprayed forth in unimaginable amounts, and with an impossible force, painting the air around them with a pale mist. Dante heard a sound coming from Abi's throat that he thought might have been an attempt to roar.

Abi stopped vomiting for a moment, but immediately began retching. He threw back his head one more time, but this time what he vomited toward the sky was more form than liquid. Abi stumbled and fell to the ground, as the torn and mangled figures of ghosts began to rain down around them.

Chapter Twenty

Death in All Her Glory

The entirety of the 8th floor was now shrouded in a purplish-white mist. This was how the area had dealt with the eruption of pale bile that had been vomited into the atmosphere. It had been absorbed, transformed, and turned into mist. Between the gravestones there were now trees, dark twisted shapes, raising their arms in despair to a flat, milky-gray sky. The soft sounds of moans and weeping drifted through the air, seeming to come from all directions at once.

Dante saw Abi lying motionless in front of him. He went to his friend and put his hand on his flank. There was still energy radiating from his body, but Dante wasn't sure if it was current or simply residual. It could be hard to tell with ghouls—or ghosts.

At the sound of footsteps behind him, Dante turned to find Judith, holding on to a gravestone to keep herself on her feet.

"Am I okay? Are we okay?" she asked.

"I think you are fine now," Dante said. "I'm not sure that all of us can say the same."

Dante looked back to Abi and stood up.

"Can you walk?"

"I think so."

"Good. We need to see if there are any ghosts here that managed to survive what they've been through. And we need to do it quickly. I suspect that not many will survive if we don't get them help."

Judith nodded.

"Look around. Call me if you find anyone coherent."

Judith began to walk slowly in the opposite direction. For a ghost who had just been infected, yanked through upper levels until she was unconscious and on the point of being unmade, and then awakened to a landscape of injury and bile-covered trees, she was handling herself with surprising grit.

Dante began to walk swiftly toward the sounds of moaning coming from a cluster of trees nearby. As he got close enough to see the trees clearly, he wished he hadn't. The things he thought were trees were not actually trees, at least not in the strictest sense. What he had taken for trees were actually ghosts, but distorted beyond normalcy, even for an etheric body. Their torsos had been stretched and elongated. Their limbs ripped in half, severing again and again such that they looked like branches reaching to the sky—or to a god in despair.

As Dante reached the nearest tree, he saw something like a face, covered in scars and dripping with ectoplasm. All along its trunk were black nodules. At first, they had looked like typical knots one finds in trees, but as he got closer, he saw that these knots were bulging and twisting. Near the center of it was a large, flat knot, with a zagged slash across the middle. This seemed to be the source of the moaning.

Dante placed his hand on the torso of the thing. In his mind, he saw the face of a girl, a pretty young girl. He remembered her. In her life, she had been vain, selfish, and self-serving. On her death, she feared her afterlife, so she had stayed a ghost. Later, she had volunteered to be the watcher of a young Cambion boy in Tokyo. She would not have had such an opportunity if she had not been a Cambion ghost and a member of the 8th floor. Somehow, she had ended up as this monstrous aberration in front of him. There was a rustle, and Dante looked up to see a black, humanoid thing impaled on one of her twisted and distorted arms.

"They won't live long like this," someone said from behind him.

Dante turned to find himself face-to-face with Phil Sawyer.

"How did you get here?" Dante asked. "I put this area in a bubble to keep other ghosts out."

"I came with the others from the stomach of that thing," Sawyer said, with a shudder.

Dante noticed that Sawyer's essence was pulled and frayed at the edges but largely intact.

"How did you get in there?" he asked. "And why aren't you in the same state as the others?"

"I think maybe I shouldn't be your major concern right now. The others are going to be snuffed out soon," Sawyer said, pointing to the tree things.

"How—why?"

"The game changed them. Being in the game a long time pulled their resonance way down. Being up this high stretches them beyond what they can bear for long."

Dante felt the pain radiating off the twisted and tortured ghosts behind him just as he heard new voices join the chorus of moaning and sobbing.

If Kara had been here, she would have immediately dropped the resonance of the floor to relieve their pain and accommodate them. But he was not Kara, and there was too much here he didn't know.

"They're ghosts, they can wait," Dante said, with calculated cold as he stepped closer to Sawyer. "I still have some questions for you."

Sawyer backed up and turned to flee but a large golden form leaped on him, pinning him to the ground.

It was Abi.

"Try to get up and I will rip your wretched little face from your undeserving head and wear it as a mask," Abi spat at Sawyer.

Sawyer was too busy trying to curl himself into a ball to see that Abi was panting.

Dante moved quickly to his friend and put his hand on his head. His energy was still weak but growing stronger. Dante felt a surge of relief.

"Now, I think it would be wise of you to answer my questions and answer them quickly," Dante said, squatting down beside Sawyer. "Every second you hesitate is another second that these ghosts are in pain. I don't think you want them to think that you are responsible for prolonging their agony."

Sawyer nodded. What small moment of bravery had caused him to confront Dante had evaporated and he was now a sniveling, weeping mess.

"I'll ask you again. How did you end up inside Abi's stomach?"

"I was in the game. While I was there, the area of the matrix I was in got thin. We fell through it and into a hallway, and then immediately into a rip that opened up in it. That spat us out in that horrible ghoul land. And … and … and … he ate me."

Dante felt the words enter his brain like pieces of a puzzle. *A game. The hallway. Rips.* None of these were good words, particularly when used in the same sentence.

Sawyer was shaking and shivering, and his eyes were darting between Dante and Abi.

"What game were you in?" Dante asked him.

"I don't know. There are two. It was one of them." Sawyer sniveled.

"Do not disrespect Dante, slime of a worm," Abi said, and Sawyer curled back into a ball.

"What are the names of the games?"

"Verite and Everlast," Sawyer whispered.

"And these games were created by the Academy?"

Sawyer nodded.

"For what purpose were they created?"

"I don't know," Sawyer said. Abi immediately put a paw on Sawyer's head and pressed.

"I don't know. I don't know. I'm not important enough to know things like that. I only know what they promised me," Sawyer cried.

"And what did they promise you?" Dante asked.

"They said that the game would make me heavier. The game has a viral interface. They said that it would use the people plugged into it to help pull me down to the physical world faster. That's one of the things they say to the ghosts to get them to go inside."

"So you are part of the Academy?" Dante asked softly.

"No … no … I wouldn't do that. I just used them. I wanted to get back to the world faster. You know. And I wanted …" Sawyer buried his face in his hands.

"You wanted what?"

"I wanted to see someone again," Sawyer whispered. "They told me that she was in the game and that I could see her there."

"Who?"

"Her name is Amelie."

"Amelie, the Cambion Amelie, the one you stalked when you were still alive?" Dante asked.

Sawyer nodded.

Dante shook his head.

Sawyer suddenly sat up, his eyes were blackened and sunken in his skull.

"You judge me but I do what I do out of love," he said, trembling, but holding his head higher.

"Love doesn't usually cause you to bash someone over the head and rape them when they are unconscious," Dante replied. The creature in front of him repulsed him in so many ways, not least of which was that his obsession with Amelie might not be all that different from Dante's own obsession with Kara.

"I didn't do that to Amelie," Sawyer said.

The groaning of the tree ghosts around them was getting louder. Their breath was beginning to create a wind.

"How did the game lower the resonance of these ghosts?" Dante asked. Despite what he said, he felt the pain of the ghosts in the room vividly. But he didn't want to injure them further by acting without information.

"I don't know exactly. It has something to do with the fact that there are other things besides ghosts. There are people who have different resonances, and even non-human things. So they said it was easier to switch things back and forth between people and non-people in the game, or something like that. And the game is so popular that it is easy to find someone to switch with. That's how I first got into the game, through the Manassas boy."

"What are the black things? The knots in the trees?" Dante asked.

"You mean the things tangled in the ghosts?" Sawyer said, with a brief little smile. Abi growled and Sawyer cringed.

"I only know what I heard. After the meeting where you asked us about the black light, Howard told me to watch out for those shapes. He said that they were nanoparticles or something and that they attach to ghosts."

Dante stood up.

"So those black shapes, those viruses attached to ghosts, what happens to them if I drop the resonance in here?"

"What happens to them will happen to you as well," Abi said, glaring at Sawyer.

"What do you care what happens to me?" Sawyer spat out. "You don't care about me, you just want to judge me. You want to judge me for loving someone that someone else said I shouldn't love."

Abi snorted.

"See, this is what you do," Sawyer whined. "All of you here. You make us something and then you blame us for being what you created us to be. The reason I was attracted to Amelie had nothing to do with my wickedness or any other stupid bullshit you want to spout to make me feel like shit. The Academy isn't like you. They told me that I was attracted to her because she is an attractor. They said every now and then a person could be a super attractor, singularity, or something like—"

Dante didn't give Sawyer time to finish his sentence. He grabbed him, threw him down and shoved his hand over his mouth.

He was about to speak when he felt her; he felt her presence before he saw her. He heard her gasp as if it were in his own ears.

He turned to see Kara, standing in the elevator, with Liz at her side.

What the hell was Liz doing on the 8th?

Both Kara and Liz were now staring out at the purplish waste that was around them. Liz would not be likely to have a clue about any of this. Come to think of it, Abi throwing up a hundred or so mutated ghosts infected with nanoparticles probably wouldn't be the first thing that popped into Kara's mind either.

"What happened here?" Kara whispered. The moaning and crying had now been joined by the occasional shriek.

"We found our missing Cambion ghosts," Dante said, standing up and walking toward her. "Now we need to decide whether we can let them live."

What do you mean, if we decide to let them live—where are they?" Kara asked, stepping out of the elevator and into the horrible white mist.

"See the trees behind us?" Dante said. "They aren't trees. They are stretched and mutated ghosts."

"Mutated? How are they mutated?" asked Liz, moving forward.

"Stay in the elevator!" Kara and Dante snapped at the same time.

"We aren't sure what the 8th-floor atmosphere would do to you. You are encased in the atmosphere of the rest of the Office as long as you stay in the elevator," Dante said. To make sure of this, he quickly threw a little energy barrier across the door of the elevator.

"Why is she here?" Dante asked, turning to Kara.

"Somehow she knew you had gone to the 8th floor," Kara said. "She said she heard screaming. So I brought her with me. How did you find them? And why are they like that?"

"Abi found them. The way he found them is a longer story than we have time for right now. They are the way they are because their resonance has been altered downward, so the resonance of the 8th is too high for them."

"Why have you not put a bubble around them and lowered the resonance in the bubble?"

"Because I wasn't sure if we should save them, only to have to kill them afterward."

"Why would I kill them?" Kara's voice was becoming cold and staccato. Bad signs.

“Their resonance has become lowered because they were mutated by a game that they were locked into,” Dante said. “That was what we saw in the Dreamscape monitor. We saw our ghosts in this game. We saw it through a rip in reality that allowed direct access from this game to the Ghoul Lands.”

“Is this the Academy game that Liz found?”

“Yes. Verite and Everlast. We know what Everlast is, and I suspect Verite is the game with the viral interface.”

“Where are their wards?” Kara asked. “Where are the Cambion that they were watching?”

“We don’t know yet, so that’s one of the arguments for keeping them alive. We need the information they have,” Dante said.

“My queen, you must ease their pain. They have the answers. They came from a dark place,” came a voice from behind him. Abi was staggering forward, lurching, and dragging his front paw.

“Abi—” Liz said, stepping forward again. Kara turned and held up her hand.

“I must offer my … uh … my sincerest apologies for the … for the—well … mess of this room,” Abi said, bowing low until his head touched the ground.

Kara crouched down next to Abi and put her hand on his head.

“What happened to you?” she asked.

“In short, Abi had to save the ghosts he found by ingesting them. He could only get them out by regurgitating them,” Dante said. “It was not an easy process.”

Abi looked up at him and saw Liz standing in the elevator. His face registered shock and horror. He put his head back down, eyes to the ground.

“Lowly creature of death that I am, I have no right to offer you my thoughts,” Abi said to the ground. “But I must speak for them, for these ghosts have done no harm in your service, and who are now in indescribable pain.”

Kara stood and turned to Dante.

“Make a bubble. Draw them down to a resonance they can live at,” she said.

Dante could have argued with her, but this was not the time. Kara’s eyes were cold and ice blue, and her hair was twisting on its own.

And these ghosts had information that they needed.

Dante closed his eyes, surrounded the room with himself and then pulled it all downward ever so slightly. He knew he had succeeded in doing something because while the sounds of moaning and sobbing had not stopped, they had changed in pitch and nature.

When Dante opened his eyes, he was shocked by the difference in the environment. On one hand, the landscape had remained mostly unchanged. The mist in the sky was a tiny bit whiter, and the gravestones slightly darker and stonier-looking than before. The main difference was that all the trees were missing, replaced by lumps of ectoplasm lying on the earth.

These shadowy figures were what happened to the nanoparticles and the DNA inside them.

Kara moved to the nearest clump of ectoplasm. As she neared, the black figures skittered away. She knelt down next to it and rolled it over. It was the ghost of a small boy. His eyes fluttered and opened. For a moment, the boy did nothing, but then he threw his arms around Kara's neck—something ghosts *never* did with Kara.

"You saved us," he said, beginning to weep.

Kara momentarily cradled the boy's head on her shoulder before pulling back and looking into his face.

"It's very important that we find out where you were, and where your ward is right now."

"Josephine was my ward. I love Josie, I really do. I tried to stop her when I realized she was getting addicted to that stupid game. One night, she had an epileptic fit as she was playing, and her parents called an ambulance. When they came, I knew it wasn't a real ambulance. I tried to call out to her, but one of them trapped me in this black box, and it just sort of sucked me in. Next thing I knew, I was in that game."

"And Josephine, where did she go?"

"Oh, they'd have her at the Academy now. I'm sure she's plugged into one of their games and she's being hollowed out," said a soft, whispery voice off to the right. This was followed by a gurgling, watery sound coming from the very place where Dante had been a few minutes earlier.

Dante moved quickly toward the sound.

Just where Sawyer had been, Dante saw the shape of a young girl. She had tan skin, large, brilliant green eyes, and a bindi in the middle of her forehead. Her skin, her eyes, did not look like those of a ghost. Her body was far too vivid to be purely etheric. Except her mouth and lower face—these parts of her had the same coloring as ghosts. It took less than a second for

Dante to realize why this was.

Lying in front of her, on the ground, was Sawyer. He was curled up, as he had been when Abi had jumped on him, but now he was missing large parts of his mid-section. And the girl's face, her mouth and jaw, was dripping with ectoplasm.

This creature just ate a ghost. That shouldn't be possible.

Kara came up behind him, but Dante put his hand back to stop her.

"Oh no," said the girl with a slight smile. "Have I committed a *faux pas*?"

She looked back and forth between Kara and Dante. Then, behind them, Dante could hear Abi lumbering closer.

"These things aren't for eating, then?" the girl asked, wiping at her face. Dante noticed that while the humanoid shapes attached to the ghosts seemed to have disappeared, they had been replaced with tiny, dark, humanoid shadows sitting near the reassembled ghosts.

"No, they're not for eating," Dante said to her, but loudly enough to be heard by anyone standing close by. "They are living, conscious creatures."

"Conscious?" the girl asked, standing up. "Are they really?"

The girl was tall and thin, and almost solid enough to be human. Only the occasional non-fluidity of movement marked her as other than that.

"Yes, they are," Dante replied. "You said that one of the wards of these ghosts was with the Academy."

"Yes, they all are."

"How do you know that?"

"I was in the game too. I was put there. I don't remember much about that. What I remember is mostly pieced together from the snippets of other people's consciousness that I have collected over time." She looked around her and laughed. "This is beautiful. Do you know how beautiful this is? I have a voice that I can hear. I have a body I can see. I have—wait—I have opinions. I don't like the place called the Academy. That's an opinion, right?"

"Yes, it is," Dante said.

"Where is this game? Physically, where is it? Is it at some facility?" Kara asked. Dante could feel the cold radiating off her body.

The girl's eyes widened.

"You are *her*, aren't you?" she said.

"I'm Kara," Kara replied. "Who are you?"

"My name is—" The girl stopped and smiled. "Nipah."

Nipah. Dante's memory tingled.

"What are you?" Kara asked.

"I am nothing—not compared to you," Nipah said. "You're an author—no, you are *the* author. You are the creature of worlds. Did I say that right? No, *creator* of worlds. You own consciousness here. That's what the others said."

"It's not exactly that," Dante said. "But Kara is not someone you want to annoy."

"Where is the game?" Kara asked again.

"Oh, it's everywhere. Everyone is playing it," Nipah replied. "It's not really a game, you know. For us, it's a lifeline to consciousness."

"Where are the people that these ghosts were watching?"

"I heard people say it was an island, I think," Nipah said. "Someone heard something about acid. But I never saw it. I never actually went there. I went from the white room to the game, to a person, to the game, to another person, and back to the game … over and over."

"What is the white room?" asked Dante.

The girl put her hands over her face and moaned. She began to oscillate like a glitchy video image.

"It's a horrible place. They constructed it to be a copy of a hallway, *the* hallway, I think. It looks real but it isn't, it's an imitation of the hallway. The door I was in was the closest thing to my home, I think. They put you there until someone chooses you, hosts you."

Dante suddenly remembered where he had heard the name Nipah, and his stomach dropped.

"Who chooses you?" Kara asked.

"Someone who has a strong desire. Usually, it's someone who comes into the game looking for something or someone. If you have ever come in contact with that someone, then you can be them for a while, but only for a while."

"How?"

"That's what we do, you know," Nipah replied. "We steal bits of you. We are just trying to live, so we live on the scraps of what we can steal from you."

"Are you the Nipah virus?" Dante asked. He felt Kara's hand grip his to the point that his bones would have been crushed if he had been purely physical.

“Virus, that’s your word.” Nipah frowned.

“Very well. Are you what we would call a virus?”

“A part of me comes from what you would call a virus. A part of me comes from a nurse from India. A part of me comes from a nine-year-old Australian schoolboy. A part of me come from rats that fly. And now a part of me comes from that sad deviant ghost I just consumed.”

“So the consciousness you have now comes from those people and things?”

“Consciousness …” whispered the girl, hugging herself. “That’s what I have now? You would call me conscious? Is that what this is … this bliss?”

“Yes, you are conscious,” Kara said. “But it doesn’t seem you were made that way, so where did you get it from? Do you steal the consciousness from people?”

“No, no. I can only collect scraps from humans in life. Probably how I look, how my body functions, things like that were collected from them, maybe some of their memories as well. That was all I had the ability to process until I was put in the game.”

“Your consciousness comes from a game?” Dante asked.

“Yes,” Nipah said.

“So you are nothing but a thief,” growled Abi from behind them, “You steal consciousness from the ghosts inside that damnable game, just to gain your own.”

Nipah looked at him with sudden and unmasked rage.

“Why do you deserve consciousness, and we don’t?” she spat at him. “What have you done to deserve it? There are those of you that take your own lives. Some even take the lives of others. You’re sadistic and cruel. You are stupid and lazy. And none of you—none—are grateful enough for the gift you have been given. I would not waste such a gift. None of my kind would. We would adore it. We would treasure it.”

Abi growled again. Looking at him, the storm that had been on Nipah’s face dissipated. She smiled.

“But you found us when we fell into the hallway, and then into the land of the ghouls,” she said. “You brought us here. I am beyond grateful to you for that.”

“Why?” Abi asked.

“You brought me here, where I can meet her,” Nipah said, moving toward Kara.

She was staring at Kara, eyes shining.

"Imagine your code … imagine it …" Nipah whispered. "Imagine what we, what my kind, could be with just a tiny bit of it."

Without warning, she launched herself at Kara. She had not gotten three feet when she was hit from one side by Abi. They tumbled together behind one of the gravestones. The girl screamed in rage, but it was abruptly cut short.

Dante ran forward to find Abi standing over the girl's ripped body, panting.

Kara appeared next to Dante.

Suddenly, Abi fell over, his sides heaving. Dante dropped to his side.

"She scratched me," Abi gasped. "I'm poisoned with her."

Dante looked up at Kara. Her eyes were no longer blue; they were now much closer to silver.

"Where did that virus calling itself Nipah come from?" Kara said, her voice taking on an eerie metallic quality.

"That virus, or some virus like it, is what is in the nanoparticles that infected the ghosts," Dante said, standing and reaching his hand to hers.

When she turned her eyes to him, he felt a shiver that went straight to his core. She was very close to gone now. He needed to take her, but he couldn't. His connection to the hallway was … was …

The truth hit Dante like a sledgehammer.

Nipah said the game made an unreal hallway. His connection to the hallway had been infected. But perhaps it wasn't real. When he tried to take Kara, she had said that it wasn't him. If it wasn't real …

"You were right, but you always are," Kara said softly. "We cannot save these ghosts … not as they are. They are infected by something or someone not of our story."

She turned back to look at the bodies all around her.

"But they can be unmade and remade," she said, kneeling down to put her hand on Abi.

"Then you must unmake me too, my queen."

"I know," Kara said. "But I don't want you to die."

"No," Liz screamed, pushing against the barrier that Dante had put in front of the elevator.

"Ghouls, as you know, have no soul." Abi was flickering like a ghost. "So you must let me die."

"Nooo!" Liz screamed again, dropping to her knees in the elevator. Her eyes were filled with tears.

"True, ghouls have no souls," Kara said. Her flat, silver eyes were now brimming with tears as well. She turned her eyes to the sky.

"Ghouls have no souls," Kara repeated, "but humans do. And you are half human."

"Kara, you know the pain that he would have to go through, and how long it will take him to remake himself," Dante said. "He may not want it."

Kara's eyes grew hard.

"It's not just about what he wants," she said, her voice colder still and softer.

"You need to ask him, at least."

"I can bring you back," Kara said. "To do that, I have to unmake you. The human part of you will be what comes back. But it will be painful, it will be more painful than I can describe. And it will take time."

"What would I come back as?" Abi whispered.

"Human," Kara said. "You would be human. You would be Cambion, as tiny parts of your ghoul self will probably survive this, but not much."

Abi turned to Liz for a moment. Her eyes locked on his. It was just a moment, but it told Dante everything he needed to know. Eternities were created in such moments.

"To be human," Abi whispered. "Would my queen be willing to grant such a gift upon a spirit as lowly as mine?"

"I would … and much more. Would that I could grant it another way, but I cannot."

"I would have it no other way," Abi said. "To be human must be earned."

Dante felt his throat close as he fought grief and anger.

To remake Abi, Kara had to unmake him—and unmaking wasn't just destruction. It wasn't clean, or surgical. It was unnatural—a slow, ripping deconstruction of every code, shadow of code, or individual frequency. It was chewing through one's own soul with no promise of any rebirth. It was the collapse of a living fractal into the singular point it once sprang from, not with grace but with agony. A reversal so brutal it shredded meaning from memory and form from function. Reassembling afterward required an act of will so precise, so stubbornly fierce, that only the strongest succeeded.

Nipah seemed to have done it alone—without sanction, without guidance. Abi would at least have Kara, and the story itself, holding the door open.

Abi turned on his back, with his face to the moon above, panting with his tongue out.

Kara stood up and backed away from Abi. As she did, her hair began to extend and grow around her. From each strand, another tiny one appeared. More and more and more until the air was thick with waving strands of her hair, like a spider's web.

Judith reappeared from behind a distant gravestone. She took one look at Kara, threw her hands over her face, and dropped to her knees.

"Go now, Dante," Kara said softly.

"I don't want to leave you alone," he said, a cold dread piercing his chest. She was too vulnerable now for this. He had allowed this to happen.

"I will come to you in our room when it is over," Kara said. "Go now, while I can still speak."

Dante backed into the elevator. He pressed the button for the 4th floor and picked a trembling Liz up off the floor.

The screams started just as the door closed, a chorus that physically rocked the elevator. Dante could identify Abi's scream even amid the screams of all the others. These screams mixed to create a macabre melody that drifted down the elevator shaft and into Dante's ears, as he held Liz tight in his arms.

Chapter Twenty One

The Sun Shall Be Turned into Darkness

The elevator descended with an agonizing slowness. It took much longer to get to and from the 8th floor than any other floor, due to its specific constructions. It had probably already been three minutes, and he could still hear screams above him. All this time, Dante had held Liz tight in his arms.

Liz suddenly pulled back from him, wiped her eyes, and pressed the button for the 7th floor.

"We should tell Lepri about the virus and the Academy, and … everything," she said, her voice catching. "He'll still be in the Recovery Room, right?"

"Yes, but are you sure you don't want to go to your room for a while to rest?" Dante said. "What you just experienced is more than most humans could stand, even many of them here in the building."

"I'm sure," Liz said, voice hitching. "Working will help. It will help me understand why all of this is happening. Why is it happening to us? Why is it happening to me?"

As the door to the 7th floor opened, they moved quickly into the Recovery Room. The only sound in the room was the gentle beeps of the heartbeats coming from the patients' monitors. Hudson was back on his bed, eyes closed. It was as if nothing had happened.

"Lepri must have gone back to his lab," Dante said, turning to go.

"Why did they all have to die?" Liz asked, in a trembling, watery voice. She was standing next to Hudson with one hand placed on his chest.

Despite the anxious feeling in his stomach, Dante came to stand next to Liz.

"The reason is that we had no choice," he said softly. "It was imperative that we unmake them because they were contagious, and they had brought that contagion in to the 8th floor."

"But we didn't even have time to learn where the Cambion are, so was all that for nothing?" Liz asked. "What Abi did—was it for nothing?"

"No, it was not for nothing." Dante squeezed her shoulder. "We may not know the exact location of our missing Cambion, but we now have a way to track them. My guess is that we can measure and track them by their changed resonance. We also know that they are most likely plugged into a game that has been created by the Academy. You found the parent company for all Academy activities, which goes a long way to finding them. We also now know that this game uses a viral interface that infects people. Knowing this means we can warn our people. We can also work to prevent further suffering of others."

"But Abi was unmade," Liz said. A sob escaped her.

"I know unmaking seems harsh—no, unmaking *is* harsh. It is one of the harshest things that can happen to a conscious creature. If you are unmade, you have to re-earn your consciousness. But you are guaranteed a chance to do that, however long it might take. Those ghosts, who were caught in that game, they wouldn't have had that option if they had stayed there."

"Maybe they would have lived."

"No, they wouldn't have. That is the one thing I learned from the Nipah virus we just saw. That thing was feeding off ghosts. It was feeding on their code. It seems that the Academy is somehow inserting viruses into their game, viruses with the capacity to find and absorb the codes of ghosts, including the code for consciousness. If those ghosts had continued to stay in that game, each and every one of them would have had their consciousness code consumed and ingested by some virus eventually."

Liz looked up.

"Abi saved them from that," Dante said, reaching out to touch her face. "And now Kara will save them so that when they remake themselves, they will be clean and of this world again."

"You think these viruses are not of our world?" Liz whispered.

In Dante's head, he saw the black balls inside his own body, with his own flames resisting them. No technological thing, however elegant, could have pierced into him. What was inside the tech was alien to this world.

"I know they are not of our story," he said. "The Nipah virus told us that she came via the hallway. Somehow, whoever created them managed to move viruses from story to story. That has only happened once before, but it wasn't intentional."

"Why is that such a bad thing? Something coming from another story? Couldn't it be like immigration or genetic variety? Couldn't it just make us stronger?" Liz asked.

Dante smiled at her.

"Think about viruses in our world," he said. "They have tremendous ability. They are small enough to hide anywhere. They can be transferred in any number of ways. And they can live outside the body, waiting to infect someone. That is all difficult enough for our bodies to fight, but even the tiniest change of the wrong kind could wipe the entire population. Let me give you an example. We found a virus some years back. It was from another story as well. It had been hidden in the ice for 30,000 years. When it was discovered and unfrozen, it was still active. The scientists who found it originally thought it wasn't harmful because it only attacked single cell amoeba, but we kept an eye on it. Fairly quickly, it began to mutate to be able to infect humans. You can imagine the impact of a virus capable of remaining on a surface forever, waiting for a host."

"What happened to it?"

"We destroyed all traces of it."

"How?"

"We burned and sank Atlantis," Dante replied. "And that is just one example of just one tiny change. Imagine the impact of what we just saw, a virus with a consciousness. Something small, unseen and largely unstoppable, with the ability to think, to plan, to want. Such a thing could destroy our entire story. We can't risk any chance that such a thing would escape. Can you understand that?"

Liz wiped her eyes.

"Is there no other way? Isn't there a way to cure someone when they have been infected?" she asked.

"We tried that once before," Dante said. "In Brazil, many, many years ago, there was a particularly unique Cambion. We—"

Dante stopped. He felt Kara's presence move back toward their room. He felt an overwhelming desire to go to her. He reined in that desire.

He looked back to Liz. She was not a beautiful crier. She had snot running out of her reddened nose, and mascara streaked her face. But the feeling in her eyes was deep and intense enough to touch. The intensity of that feeling was its own beauty.

"We are all scarred creatures," Dante continued. "But all of us are marked and branded in some way by this thing we are. All those years ago, in Brazil, we had a Cambion who could go into the hallway."

"What is the hallway?" Liz asked. "I keep hearing people talk about it."

"The hallway is the intersection between all existing stories. It is unreachable by most, even by most Cambion. But the Brazilian boy was unique. He could not just go into the hallway. He could go into doors there, and he could bring back things from other stories. This Cambion was young. He was barely eight when it happened."

Dante could remember it like it was yesterday. The burning and the screaming.

"What happened?" Liz asked.

"The boy brought something back," Dante said. "He brought back something microscopic. But that thing went from him to the bugs and worms in the dirt where he played. It was a viral particle that changed the nature of the worms. It removed the section of DNA that codes for death. Those worms became immortal."

"Jesus."

"First it was the worms," Dante continued. "And then later, the worms infected sick people. When they infected certain Cambion, they were healed. It was only later that it was discovered that they couldn't age. This immortality made people worship them as gods, but they were not gods. And, sadly, their children suffered a horrible fate. They did not age starting at birth. They remained infants. Infants who could think and reason like adults."

"That's horrible," Liz whispered.

"It was worse that you can imagine. An adult with an adult's thoughts and needs in an infant body. I won't discuss it much, but some of the sexual evil in our world today comes from that tiny shift brought into our world at that time. Kara destroyed that society and all remnants of it, but the worms still exist. We cannot get rid of them as they spread out enough that they became part of this story. So the evil they brought us remains. Do you understand why we fight this? Why we cannot risk even the slightest infection from outside?"

Liz nodded.

"And that thing? The thing that ate that ghost and attacked Kara? Is that thing a virus with consciousness?"

"I think so. I hope not, but I think so. It if is, I pray it is an isolated incident," Dante said softly.

"And if it isn't?"

In his mind's eye, Dante saw fields of trees and people ablaze. Kara on her knees, weeping and pulling out her hair, even as she pulled that place apart, molecule by molecule. This memory brought a rush of rage so intense that it bordered on joy.

Dante held his hand out to Liz.

"Let's go to work to make sure it is," he said. "We want to make sure there is a world for Abi to come back to."

Liz nodded and took his hand.

When Dante and Liz entered the lab, Lepri was sitting at his computer. On the screen was the software he used to monitor the Cambion on the 7th floor Recovery Room. The name across the top of the screen read Hudson Drye. He turned and nodded at them as they entered and then turned back to his computer.

"Since the event, Hudson has been coming in and out of consciousness," Lepri said. "It is just for milliseconds, but you can see it in his data. I can't track any reason, but the virus seems to have completely left him when the nanoparticles infected Judith. I am trying to figure out if there is some reason that there was a complete transfer, but I—"

"Jeremy, we need to talk."

"What happened?" Lepri asked, standing up.

"We have trouble," Dante said. "There is no way to say this gently, as I need to explain quickly."

"Is it Judith? What happened to her?" Lepri asked.

"She's been unmade," Dante said. "But it's much more than that. Where is Joe?"

"Just there," Lepri said, as Joe entered the room.

Dante began to pace the room. Kara would be in their room now. He needed to get to her. She was on edge now, and probably fuller than she had ever been. But this emergency had to be dealt with first.

"Liz, can you repeat to Joe what I am saying?" Dante asked.

Liz nodded.

"I'll make this short and will fill in the details later. It seems that it is the

Academy, or one of its offshoots, that hacked into our computer systems. We suspect they have done this to find and collect information on the Cambion we have been tracking. They targeted certain Cambion, either on the basis of their code or on the basis of their ghost watchers."

"Why do they want them?" Joe asked, after Liz had repeated it to him.

"Given what I have just seen, someone has lost their sense of reason and decided to play Dr. Frankenstein over there and they are trying to give viruses consciousness again."

Lepri's jaw dropped. "What? How?"

"As for how, it seems that they have been looking for both human and ghost Cambion who have consciousness codes that are either easily identifiable or particularly vulnerable to viral attack," Dante replied. "These Cambion, once acquired by the Academy, have been hooked into their game matrix, the one called Verite, or the virtual reality life extension matrix called Everlast. I believe they are probably one and the same. Once inside the matrix, the Cambion, be they ghost or human, are put in proximity to viruses that have also been inserted into the game matrix and that have the ability to steal bits of the consciousness code of the victims. They are basically acting as hosts for the virus."

"Viruses can do that?" Joe asked.

"Not in our world," Lepri said.

"Exactly," Dante said. "The Academy has found viruses from some other stories that do have the ability to steal and absorb consciousness."

"You know for sure that they have done this?" Lepri asked.

"Yes, a virus told me."

Lepri opened his mouth to speak but Dante continued.

"When I left here, I took Judith upward and succeeded in removing the viruses she got from Hudson as we traveled. The ascension also removed a latent virus in me."

"Fuck," Lepri muttered.

"So this was a successful method to remove them. When we returned to the ghost layer, we found Abi. He had managed to find and get our missing ghost Cambion from a place in the Ghoul Lands where a rip had been formed in the fabric of space and time. This rip in space and time was either created or discovered by the games that the Academy created. The game seems to be able to connect to the hallway or create its own version of it."

Lepri let out a long sigh.

"When Abi brought these ghosts to the 8th floor, their resonance was lowered so much that they were unable to survive there for long. They were intertwined with dark, humanoid-looking shapes, which turned out to be viral pieces that had been inserted into the nanoparticles that had infected them. When Kara arrived, she insisted on bringing the resonance down to save our ghosts. After we did this, the viruses transformed into small shadows that were a bit too humanoid for comfort. One of these was much more advanced and spoke with us."

"Jesus." Lepri shook his head.

"Would have nothing to do with this," Dante uttered his common reply. "The virus told us that it came into the game from somewhere in the hallway. It had absorbed the consciousness code of others while in the game. At the end, it tried to attack Kara to get at her code. So Kara unmade everything that was on the 8th floor at the time, to make sure those viruses would be destroyed."

"Including Judith?" Lepri asked.

Dante nodded.

"How would the Director dare such a thing?" Joe had subconsciously put his hand on the gun that he always wore at his side.

"Somehow I think that this might not be completely the Director's doing," Dante replied. "Hurting Kara is something he would never tolerate."

"But why would the Academy want to give viruses consciousness?" Lepri asked.

"Why wouldn't they?" said Joe, eyes shining with anger. "I mean, man, if you can control them somehow, think about how much fucking power you would have. There would be nowhere they couldn't go. There would be no one you couldn't kill. And if you had an army of them? You could use them or rent them out to the highest bidder. You could own the world."

The room was silent for a moment.

"But you would have to be able to control them," Lepri said. "I can't imagine that even the Academy would try something so risky."

"Unless the Academy has something, some drug, or some incentive, that can be used to control them," Liz whispered, looking at Dante.

Like consciousness itself, Dante thought. *What had the virus said? "You would call me conscious? Is that what this is … this bliss?"*

"They've attacked Kara, so they've gone too far," Joe said, slamming his gun down on the table. "Give me a name. That's all I need. I still have a network of people who love to do the worst."

"Joe is right, but that will have to come later," Dante said.

Liz said this to Joe who reluctantly sat back down, but the demons on his head were redder than usual.

"For the time being, I think we have eliminated the immediate dangers, but we still have a lot to do in order to keep us safe," Dante continued. "First, we must make sure that our computer systems have been scoured for all viruses, computer or biological. I fear that there have been attacks multiple times on multiple systems. Therefore, we have to reboot from the ground up. I want new systems installed everywhere. All saved information must be examined by no less than three teams to make sure it is clean. One team should come from IT, one team should come from Security, and the third should be made up of people from Biology and Parabiology."

"We can coordinate that," Liz said, turning to explain to Joe, who nodded through clenched teeth. It was clear that he still felt responsible.

"The second issue is that we need to scan everyone in the Office for the presence of not only viruses but tech particles, like the ones we found in Hudson and Judith," Dante said, looking at Lepri. "This will require that we merge the Biology and Parabiology units, as we will need to be able to scan large numbers of people for viruses that would be from our story or potentially other stories."

"We don't have a way to do that yet."

"From the moment we saw that reporter, Parabiology has been working on it, it's time they got you involved."

Lepri nodded, shuddering. Those working in Parabiology were in that group for a reason and were often hard on the eyes.

"We need to start this right now," Dante said. "Starting with getting human resources involved to identify anyone who has implants that can get infected by computer-generated viruses. There has to be a link between the outside world and our world in terms of infection, and I suspect it comes from one of our associates."

"We had HR run that data already," Joe said, picking up his phone. "We have five people who are tagged as cyborg. Robert Stan, Jayce Whitney Miller, and Oakes Tucker have got internal insulin pumps synching with outside software. Jennifer Woodward and Marianne Atkins have artificial heart valves that also sync from the outside. We can send teams to these people immediately."

"No," Dante said. "Either Kara or myself should be present when we speak to each one, just in case. Do we have apartment numbers on all of them?"

"Yes," Liz said. "Robert, Oakes, and Jennifer are on the eighteenth floor. 1805, 1824, and 1851 respectively. Marianne and Jayce are on the fourteenth floor, 1400 and 1441, respectively."

"Should I forward the names and rooms to Kara?" Lepri said.

Dante nodded.

"Jayce," Joe said, frowning. "She should be the first one."

His words tingled in Dante's ears.

"Ask him why," Dante asked Liz, who relayed.

"She's one of those entitled brats," Joe replied. "She's super selfish. When she was brought in, she was one of those kids of rich parents who don't raise them. You know, the type raised on TV and video games."

Gamer. Jayce was playing a video game in the café.

Before Dante could speak, Liz had turned to Joe.

"Joe, is she a gamer?"

"Oh yeah, big time. She has one of those games where you use a suit—"

Shit—the suits with the "harmless viral interface"—and we have just texted Kara with the names. Please let her not have picked up the text.

"But she hasn't been allowed to connect it to the outside," Joe was saying. "I spoke with her—"

Dante didn't wait for Joe to finish his sentence before he threw himself toward room 1441.

When he arrived at the room, he had just enough time to see Jayce and Kara in the sunshine by the bay window. Sunbeams were illuminating dust motes in the air. Dante saw all this as if in slow motion. Jayce was wide-eyed but smiling. She was handing Kara a clumped-up ball of some white fabric.

"It's just a game," Jayce said. "It's no big deal, really."

Dante moved quickly toward Kara but not quickly enough.

The moment Kara's hand touched the white Verite suit, she went completely rigid, threw back her head, and began screaming.

The whole building began to shake and the sunshine from the window turned blood-red.

Chapter Twenty Two

Where the Earth Kisses the Sky

"I can't! I can't! I can't!" Kara screamed, whirling around her, clutching the white game suit to her chest. Her blue eyes were now white, sightless, and beginning to drip. She jumped and whipped her head around at the sound of each new crash and rumble. The room was bathed in crimson light from the reddening sun.

The building pitched beneath their feet and Jayce was thrown to the floor. The sound of alarms going off all around them combined with the cracks and groans of the building to create the discordant music of calamity.

But Dante only had eyes and ears for Kara, who was now crouched and spinning around, jerking at each new sound. As Dante stepped toward her, she stopped and stood up.

"Dante?"

"I am here, my love," Dante said. Kara turned toward him, her melting eyes wide and desperate.

"Get them out," Kara screamed, scratching her arms, her neck, and her face.

"What's happening?" Jayce screamed, as she plastered herself against the wall.

"What do I need to get out?" Dante asked Kara.

Kara fell to the floor, her pale dress now torn and hanging off her body in shreds. A water pipe burst just above her head but as the water sprayed downward, it formed a rainbow on either side of her. Even the water knew better than to touch her right now.

Kara's hair had grown several feet in the past thirty seconds and was now stretching straight upward above her head, forming a pale halo. She was silent now, but breathing hard, her white, molten eyes staring sightlessly out of the window at the red sun, which was now three times its normal size and deepening in color by the minute.

She was still holding on to that damn white game suit.

"There is something inside me," Kara said. She was no longer screaming. Her voice was now soft and taking on that dangerous metallic edge. "A virus, but a different kind. It's like the thing we saw on the 8th. It knows what it is doing. It's talking to me."

"Kara, you need to put that thing down," Dante said, pushing energy in his words.

Kara turned to him, her eyes had now melted from her head. What had replaced them were supernova remnants swirling in her eye sockets. No longer the eyes of a human but a god.

There was a scream, and Dante saw a body fall past Jayce's window. This was followed by another scream and another body—more would come. Some people would fall, but others would jump as Kara's virus-distorted thoughts became their reality, both inside and out.

The ones prone to madness always sense it first, Dante thought.

"My love," he said softly. Or as softly as he could over the rising sounds of rumbling and crashing around them.

"Stop her! Stop her!" screamed Jayce.

Dante turned toward Jayce. She was holding on to a support beam as the room pitched and rocked. Tiny pieces of concrete were raining down around them, with more substantial pieces falling in between.

"This place is coming apart, you have to stop her!" Jayce yelled.

"You're the cause of this," Dante said. "You gave her poison."

He felt the shift of his essence toward the old days as the words came out of his mouth. The tiniest fraction of him opened toward her.

Jayce's eyes widened for a second, then she began screaming again. Dante turned back to Kara, as the screaming was abruptly cut short.

It didn't take very long for a brain to boil.

Dante sat just in front of Kara.

"Kara, can you give that to me?" he asked, reaching for the game suit in her hands. She shook her head and pulled it closer to her.

"No," she said. The light outside was now red-black.

"Why not?"

"There are viruses in here," she said. "There are thousands of them. There are tiny, microscopic needles in the material. They are so tiny, you don't even feel them. But they puncture just enough to let the monsters in."

"Can I see it?" Dante asked, reaching for the suit again.

Kara shook her head.

"No, they would hurt you. And then you would hurt other people. I can't let you be responsible for that," she whispered.

She said this with tears welling and forming oceans in her galaxy eyes.

"But aren't they hurting you?" Dante asked.

"They can't hurt me. Nothing can hurt me, because everything is a part of me," she said softly.

Outside, fierce dark clouds swirled in the distance, moving at impossible speeds across the red sun. The buildings around them seemed as unsteady as their own. As he watched, a tall, mirrored tower in the center of the Canary Wharf landscape pitched and fell forward into two neighboring buildings. Shards of glass sparkled in the air, glinting in the crimson sunlight.

"It's true that nothing can destroy you," Dante said. "But you can be hurt and then others will be hurt. They are expanding the horizon of you. Too much is getting inside your body. You are overloaded."

"Am I?" she asked, looking toward him. Snakes of her hair wrapped itself around his wrists. It was acid cold. "Maybe I am becoming more."

At that moment, Joe, Liz, and Lepri came tumbling through Jayce's front door. Joe had his gun drawn.

Kara turned toward them, but Dante took her face in his hands.

"My darling, this is my fault. I let you go too long without taking some of this stress from you. You can only hold so much. You have limits."

"If it was so bad, then why did you wait?" Kara asked with an eerie nonchalance, as things began to explode outside.

"I tried," Dante said, pushing the loose, searching strands of her hair back from her eyes. "But when I took you to the hallway, it was on fire."

For a moment, a star exploded in Kara's eyes.

"I remember," she said. "But it wasn't the entrance to your hallway. It was a counterfeit. I knew it at the time, but I forgot when I came back."

"What was it then?" Dante asked.

"It was a decoy," Kara said. "It was a hallway created by something … yes, it was created by the virus in you. It had a purpose."

"What purpose is that, my love?"

"To steal code from you—or me."

The vision of Nipah coming after Kara flashed in his mind, followed by the image of dark shapes inside him. Suddenly, he knew what he had to do.

"Give that to me," Dante said softly.

"I don't think I want to. I can see everything now," Kara said, turning toward the sun again. The sound of sirens and screaming was now coming from all around them.

"Yes, you have always been that way," Dante replied. "But seeing and taking in are different things."

"This seeing is different," Kara said coldly. "I have always seen the now—all of the now. But what's inside me, it's opening the *then*. If I look backward, I can see the river of time. Everything becomes now. Everything comes to this moment."

"I know," Dante said, twisting his wrist so that he could grab hold of the strands of her hair.

There was the sound of another explosion outside. And then another. The building shook with greater force. Furniture was lifted and dashed against the floor. Jayce's bed slid from the bedroom and into her kitchen area, running over Jayce's dead body in the process. It then slammed itself and its owner against the kitchen sink, which exploded in blood, metal, and water. A TV flew across the room and smashed into the window, which blew outward in a rain of glass. The sounds of sirens and wailing was now much louder.

Liz, Joe, and Lepri had been thrown off their feet and against the back wall. Only Kara and Dante remained unmoving in the chaos.

"All of it is inside me," Kara said. "The then, the now, the when."

"Yes, it is."

"Because I am a monster," she said, fiery galaxy eyes glowing.

"What you are depends on who is looking at you," Dante said. "Gods will always be seen as monsters by those who fear."

Kara smiled wistfully.

"I'm not a god. Or I didn't used to be. I used to be human." Her gaze fell on him, her expression both beatific and horrifying. "You were the one who changed me."

"No, my darling, you were never fully human."

"But I thought I was. You took that away from me." Dante felt her words cut into him. What she said was true. But what choice had he ever had?

There was a rumbling as a monstrous temple erupted from the earth. Dante recognized it as a temple from Atlantis, but 1,000—no, 100,000 times as large. The things inside Kara were unraveling her, and therefore the world followed suit. It was pulling things out of time, out of order, and out of sequence.

Dante could feel her breath on his face.

"No, my love. I didn't take that from you—someone else did. With the help of someone who said he loved you," Dante replied.

Kara gasped.

"Wait—you—you—yooooooouuuuuu … oh god. You … picked up the fragments. You … saved me." Kara gave a long sigh and took in a watery breath.

She was too close to the memory now, the one that would overwhelm even her.

"Sheeee did this," Kara said. "The succubus. Sheeee did this to me."

"Yes," Dante said, struggling to keep his mind in the present, and not let it, and the external world, drift back to that time on the desert sands … not yet.

There was a low rumbling sound coming from outside and a rush of air with the smell of salt.

"You … you … gave … part of your soul. I took your soul. And you took on mine." She reached out to touch the stone with the icy flaw that hung around Dante's neck. "To save me, to remake me."

Her voice trembled as a sob escaped her.

"I gave it … willingly," Dante said. "And I will keep doing that … forever, for as long as it takes."

"It is wrong to have to ask that of you," Kara whispered. "It is all wrong, and the wrongness is my fault. I loved the wrong person."

The rumbling sound was louder now, and Dante looked up just in time to see a wall of water coming their way. Kara had called the oceans. As the wave rose up, the sun behind it went black in the sky and all was darkness.

Dante grabbed Kara and crushed her to him, as he pulled himself into himself. He used the shreds of singularity that he had taken from her all those years ago, and pulled himself, and her, into the supernova of time that was at his core.

Kara was struggling in his arms, as they fell inside him and through his etheric body, his emotional body, and eventually to his code. The holes between the code grew and grew until those holes were the size of planets. He was holding Kara in the blackness of space, but they were still falling both inward and upward at a speed that was blinding. Stars, solar systems, and galaxies whizzed by them. Faster and faster, they went, until suddenly, their movement stopped, and they were dropped, unceremoniously, into a hallway he had never seen before.

Rather than appearing as a long row of doors, it was simply a long white corridor, extending forever in both directions. There were no doors, no contrast, and no breaks in the oppressive sameness. The white of the walls and floors wasn't a pure white, instead it was more a white tinted with an overlay of yellow and green, like pus—or death.

"We shouldn't be here!" Kara continued to struggle in his arms.

As he watched, he saw something moving beneath the surfaces around him. Something that squirmed in a way that caused Dante to feel sick and unclean.

This is not my hallway, he thought. *This is not even in me.*

He pushed this feeling of repulsion outside his body and into the air, where small flames began to flicker, only to be snuffed out. This place was neither solid, nor liquid, nor gas, nor spirit, but some loathsome combination of them all.

"No. We have to go!" Kara said, turning her face to Dante's. "It will steal us from us! It will infect it all!"

"No, my love, it will steal nothing anymore, at least not from here," Dante said, and with that he set Kara down and closed his eyes. He put his hand on the stone around his neck, calling to the force that had forged him into what he was now, the force that churned and seethed inside him. It was the spiritual heart of a dying sun, the dreams of an unborn star, the destruction left behind by the movement of time.

When he opened his eyes, the length of the hallway, or what part he could see, was wreathed in flames. It was like before, but this time he saw it for what it was. His own immune system was mounting an attack on an invader. The whiteness was blistering and melting all around them. Lines of flame danced across the floor with a mounting rage, climbing up walls and making small tornadoes of blackened goo as it consumed the layer of whatever it was that was surrounding them. Strips of hardened whiteness began to fall from the roof, scattering and blazing on the floor. Moisture seeped from the paleness all around them, which the flames consumed greedily, furiously. The air smelled of smoke and burning plastic.

Suddenly, the hallway jolted, as if by an earthquake. Dante and Kara were thrown to the ground. In that same second, the hallway they were in vanished. Instead, they found themselves in a very different hallway. This one was also on fire but whatever white substance had been there was gone, as if it had never existed. This fire was burning with gleefulness rather than rage. Doors had appeared along the length of the hallway in either direction, but they were engulfed in flames as well.

Kara broke free of him and ran toward a wall of flame. Dante caught her just before she touched it, but a flame leaped out and caressed her sleeve, setting it on fire. Kara swatted at it, but it began to crawl up her arm. He would be no help in putting out a fire—not now, not after what he had seen. This hallway was his hallway, but it was purging itself from whatever unholy pestilence had poisoned it. He could only imagine what sort of horrible form he had taken after freeing this part of himself.

Dante needed to get Kara in a door now, but not just any door. He needed to find the source of this fire. That was why the fire was here, of course, to show him the way toward its creation and his beginning. He looked at the roof and saw a trail of flames. As he followed them with his eyes, he realized that the curtain of flames in front of him was blazing in a direction. They seemed to be blowing toward the left. This meant that their origin was on the right. He held on to Kara, as he stuck his head into this flame. Sure enough, there was a doorway to the right. It was open, and the flames were pouring through it. This was the one.

He grabbed Kara, and pulled her into the flames.

Chapter Twenty Three

The Abomination

Dante stepped through the door and into a space that was dark and smoky, but there were no more flames. The smoke in the air was different. It was something more tangible and could actually fill Dante's lungs, because they were physical here. It burned like acid. He felt a terror wash over him, as he always did when he returned here, but it was a mere shadow of the terror he had experienced so many lifetimes ago.

Kara had stopped struggling. She was standing next to him, frozen, eyes wide and blinking hard. The world around them was a hazy vision of swirling black smoke lit by an orange light in the distance. Glowing embers floated by on a hot, dry wind. At first, Dante could only see and feel, there was no sound, which was a mercy. That mercy did not last long. All too soon, the air was pierced with the sounds of flutes, drums, and the pounding of feet. Lurking beneath that was the desperate cries of young voices.

"The Abomination," Kara whispered, cringing back against him.

He wanted to run himself. He wanted away from this place before Kara was forced to see what she did not want to see, but that was weakness. This was what was required. It was the price they paid for their immortality and their reality.

After a few moments, the hot wind changed, blowing the smoke in a different direction, revealing the scene unfolding in front of them. At their feet, a stone walkway led up a steep, rocky hill, ending at a shape looming dark against an orange glow. Dante knew what it was without seeing it in detail. It was a statue created in the likeness of a man with a bull's head. It was a graven image of Ba'al Hammon, known more commonly as Moloch. He couldn't see it yet, but he knew that the origin of the smoke came from the base of the statue where there would be large opening that revealed a blazing fire. He also knew that there would be an altar in front of the fire, greedy for its obscene dues. But now, from their vantage point, they could only see people walking up the pathway from tents and huts scattered on the hillside.

Kara stepped forward, beginning to walk up the path, despite herself. Dante followed. He needed to keep a calm exterior for Kara, even as his heart pounded and moaned within his chest.

On either side of the walkway were stone altars. On them were the slaughtered bodies of animals—goats, cows, lambs. The blood of these animals looked like puddles of black tar as it pooled on the surface of the altars and dripped down the sides. Kara turned her eyes from them as she walked. Her focus was on what was happening above her. When they reached the top of the path, they found themselves standing on an unnaturally long mesa overlooking a black ocean.

The crowd in front of them was mostly still. The stone figure of Moloch was easily 100 feet tall. There was a gaping maw in the bottom of it where an unnatural green flame burned. On the right was a small pool of some liquid that reflected the firelight back up to the sky. On the left was a path leading behind the statue. The sound of the flutes and drums came from there. There must have been a small orchestra of musicians to be able to produce such a volume of sound. And still, beneath the music, he could hear the sounds of children and infants screaming.

Suddenly, there was a commotion behind them. Dante turned to see a litter being carried toward them. Four men were supporting it and on it lay a small, unconscious woman. Even from a distance, it was clear that she was beautiful. Her platinum blonde hair was being lifted by the strong breeze that blew down from the plateau above them. As the woman grew closer, Dante felt the pang in his gut. Her eyes were closed, as if sleeping. Her bone structure was fine and delicate, and her body was slender but somehow strangely distorted. She was pregnant.

She was only a girl then, he thought, as nausea and memory flooded him.

Kara stepped toward the litter as it passed by them. She reached out to her own, younger face, but she was unable to touch herself or have any physical impact on this story—at least, not yet.

And as the litter passed right through her, they were able to see the horror it was moving toward. The crowd in front of the statue had parted to let the litter through, and Dante saw a robed man holding a child, an infant, up toward the fire. For a moment, his eyes couldn't process what he was seeing; even after all these years, he couldn't believe such a thing would be possible.

Dante turned away but he could not block out the piercing cries. A rage began to build up inside him. The rage that he had felt so many years ago. The rage that had changed everything. He felt it burn through his body, boil his veins, and ignite something in his brain—something that wanted nothing more than to annihilate these people, all of them, as painfully and viciously as possible.

Dante turned back to the scene only when Kara began to run toward herself, calling her own name, but an invisible barrier kept her from getting past the final ring of onlookers. She started screaming at the people around her, but they carried on as they were, either stone-faced or singing. Many of the stone-faced women were carrying infants in their arms. He saw this younger version of Kara being lifted up off the litter by one of the men who then carried her toward the robed man. The fire was not only in front of the bull-headed statue. It was also emanating from within it, from a fire that had been built in the belly of the thing. All over the statue he could see what looked like shelves extending from its torso. Actually, they looked more like drawers, drawers large enough to hold small bodies. The whole monstrous blasphemy was glowing red with a halo of green. The red was from the heat, the green was from something else.

A swarm of bugs erupted from the belly of the stone monster. They looked like giant grasshoppers. As the robed man stepped forward, the bugs began alighting on the limp body of Kara's younger self. The priest, unperturbed by the bugs, motioned toward a bigger drawer on one leg of the statue. The man carrying the pregnant girl moved toward it.

This is what comes of unchecked belief, Dante thought for the millionth time. *This is the unbelievable evil of ignorance. We must change this.*

Kara turned to him, her eyes wild and mad.

"I remember," she said, her body trembling with horror and fury. "Kill them, Dante! Kill this world, end this now! End them all! End us all!"

Dante grabbed Kara and pulled her to him. He closed his eyes and, for a millisecond, let the fire inside him overtake him, burning away his sanity and control. The fire inside was not the cold fire of Kara, it was the molten heat of the event horizon of a black hole. Thousands, millions of times hotter than an exploding sun. He felt it surge forth from his body. His challenge now was to maintain enough control so that all was not lost forever. Shaking, sweating, and gasping, he held on to Kara as he narrowed the scope of his fire and contained it, within the time that he was, to the smallest unit of time that he could find. Behind closed eyelids, he felt the world around him begin to melt.

He did not see Kara's skin catch fire, but he heard it. He heard her screams turn to shrieks. He held her tight even as he felt her skin crisp in his embrace. Her shrieks were dimmed by the shrieks of all those around them. The fire that was born from him would take everything, people, rocks, cells, everything … even time itself, if he let it.

This infinitesimally small moment in time seemed to stretch on for eternity. Dante kept his eyes closed and his mind focused. It was imperative to make this moment right. This moment would remake all moments afterward. Any change would alter the dynamic of their story forever.

It was only when that moment ended, and the shrieks completely ceased, that he opened his eyes. In his arms were the remains of the woman he loved. Her body was little more than ash, holding its form only because of the current of energy he was emitting.

All that remained around them was the smoking and charred remnants of what had been solid mere seconds before. The statue was gone, melted into the hillside, which had itself burned down to the earth. Behind it, the ocean was now gone. There was nothing but bedrock as far as he could see. The sky above was hazy with clouds that rained ash around them. At least it was still an existing reality. He hadn't burned it all.

Dante held the ashes of Kara in his arms gently, so very gently. He yanked the black stone from around his neck, put it into his mouth and swallowed it. He turned his consciousness inward, into himself, following the stone. As it moved through him, he could feel it reaching deep into what remained of his molecular nature. It searched out for the molecular part of him that he loved and cherished the most … the part of him that he had taken from her all those years ago. It glowed with its own pale blue light inside the hall of flames that birthed him. The stone called those fragments forth and brought them into his heart, his lungs, and then his breath, where his lips used it to form one word.

"Kara."

He put his lips to hers. He breathed into her mouth the life that had once been hers and was hers still.

He closed his eyes, and uttered the prayer that he had whispered tens of thousands of times before.

"Whatever evil has been inside her, it is now taken by flame, and time destroys what crimes have been done. Take whatever restitution you need from me and only me."

For a moment nothing happened, and Dante felt his heart seize in his chest. Then her form became heavier in his arms.

He kept his eyes closed, his mouth on hers in wordless prayer.

The form in his arms became heavier and heavier. He waited until he could feel no more weight added before he opened his eyes. Kara's body was now white and moist in his arms. The damage of the flame had been completely healed. She was now as she had always been … as she would always be.

Tears burned his eyes. There was always the fear that this would be the time, the time he could not turn back time.

"My love," he whispered.

He gently kissed her lips, her upturned nose, her forehead. Her eyes fluttered open. They were ice blue, with only a tiny black point of a pupil. This was also normal, the color would return, as would everything else.

"I choose to stay," she whispered. "I choose to stay with you."

Whatever price must be paid, take your restitution from me.

"Is it over?"

"Yes," he said softly. "It is done. You don't have to worry about it for another century or so. How is your pain?"

"Gone," she said. Her smile was radiant. She looked for all the world like the girl he had loved so many eons ago. "But I can't remember much."

"It will come back. It will take a few hours. It always does. Enjoy this moment, my darling."

Kara looked around her and shuddered.

"Take me home, Dante," she whispered.

He nodded. Kara needed some time and space to heal.

With a sigh, Dante reached down to his feet and picked up a small chunk of ash that had fallen from Kara's burned body, a small piece of her being changed by his fire. Holding it in his hand, it solidified into a dark stone with an ice-blue flaw running through it. It was hard to believe such a small thing could be such a catalyst. And yet, universes had been created from less.

He reached forward and pulled Kara gently back into his embrace. He would take her to the Healing Room to rest, but there would be no rest for him yet.

He had spirits to burn and history to destroy.

Chapter Twenty Four

Stalking the Tick Tock

The timing, in destroying time, was everything. Time wasn't linear, not truly—it was fractal, recursive, a structure of repeating loops that echoed themselves endlessly at different scales. To cut time cleanly, he had to find the least disruptive branch, the smallest recursive pattern that could be severed without unraveling the whole design.

Dante was carrying Kara, holding her tightly in his arms as he pulled them into his hallway. Her eyes were closed, and her head was resting on his chest. The hallway was his, but the flames were now subdued, the fires gone. The wooden walls and floor were no longer burned. The doorways, their archways ringed in stone, were now intact and almost nautical. Kara had not been the only one who had needed to be cleared.

Dante didn't linger here, but instead focused on pulling them out of the hallway and into the intermediate place before dropping back into their current story. He needed to find the right moment to drop in. Too soon and he risked overlapping and creating two or more distinct stories that might impact their own. It would also undo what good had been done after that moment. Too late and he would not be able to correct what he needed to. He concentrated. There could be millions of branching events—sever one node too soon, and the effects spiraled outward, disrupting everything.

He reached out to the flow of time and pulled it to him. Dante had a unique relationship with time. In many ways he *was* time, but the more accurate description was that he was now its avatar. This was why he could make bubbles, change resonances, and alter a given time stream. It was also the reason that he and Kara were now immortal. It began in that moment long ago when Kara first went to the flames. That was the moment that he bargained his soul for hers. Everything that happened after that came from that one moment in that scene of horror.

He felt his way as the river of time flowed through him. He found the moment he was seeking by its feel. There was always a dip in energy in the moment before a disaster. This was the spot he was looking for.

Kara opened her eyes as they materialized into the antechamber of the Healing Room. The air in the room was soft and fresh. This was not the room where most of those recovering would stay. This was the room for people who needed privacy. There were only three beds here, although each of them looked much the same as the beds in the other room.

"Are we home?"

"Yes, lover."

"Why aren't we in our apartment?" she asked, yawning, as he laid her onto one of the beds.

"You aren't quite normalized here yet, so you need a few moments to readapt to this resonance. It's best if you sleep for just a little while," Dante said, leaning over to kiss her.

"Okay, but don't leave me here too long," Kara said, kissing him back, but harder. Her pupils were still too small, but they were widening.

Dante laughed as lightly as possible. Kara would not remember the recent traumatic events. By the time he was done, there would be nothing to remember.

He laid a blanket on top of her, and she rolled to her side. Then he pulled the privacy curtain around her.

Once that was done, he strode quickly through to the Recovery Room. This room was much less tranquil than usual. Hudson was gasping and moaning in his bed. They would need to attend to him, but not now. Now, Dante had other things to attend to—such as the man lying on the bed next to the window.

The sunlight did not do much to improve Phil Sawyer's sallow complexion. He had not been a handsome man in life but the body now lying on the bed was somehow more pathetic than loathsome. Without the noxious spirit that had inhabited it, it was just a body, a body that was not even close to making it to the halfway mark for normal human beauty. Dante was momentarily sad about what he was going to do, but only momentarily. He reached out and used his energy to pull the plugs on the life support systems from the wall and silence the alarms. He turned away just as the body began to twitch.

The fact that the body had not deteriorated meant that Sawyer's spirit was still around somewhere, in some form, below the upper winds. Kara would have set that up when she unmade him. And Dante had seen what the virus that called itself Nipah had done to the spirit of Sawyer. So it was possible that part of his spirit had been removed from the 8th floor before everything was unmade. Even if that were true, it would still be in no condition to be entering a physical body again, not before it went back to the winds, assuming it could. However, killing the body would normally release the spirit to be able to go back into the reincarnation cycle—normally. These were different circumstances, but Dante had done all that was required of him.

Dante moved to the center of the room. He took in a deep breath of the current moment and then blew it back out again. A lavender tunnel appeared in the room. It was composed of all the moments in recent history. Images flashed along the edges of the it, like highway signs. Dante focused on his target. As he did so, a figure appeared. It was Jayce, alone in her room, moments before Kara would come to her and Jayce would give her the horrible game suit. Dante moved down the hallway toward her.

As he did so, he burned out all moments in the flow of time that came afterward.

When Dante appeared in Jayce's living room, she was making herself a cup of coffee in the kitchen.

Dante felt the newness of the moment in a way that almost no one in this reality would ever feel it. The moment was not actually new, it was remade. From this moment forward, they would be remaking and correcting a pattern of history that had been eliminated. No one else would remember the old events, or very few. Kara could, but she was cleared regularly to keep her from experiencing just such overwhelming overlap. The only sorts that could own and survive such knowledge were those with ancestry that came from outside of this story, and those people were very few and far between. They were the holders of potential memories. There was only one or two at any given moment, and they were usually insane.

Dante heard Jayce humming to herself and the clink of metal on metal as she dropped her spoon into the sink. The room smelled of earth and fire which meant the intoxicating smell of coffee, a luxury he could no longer enjoy.

Jayce rounded the corner from her kitchen to her living room and saw

Dante. She jumped, screamed, and dropped her coffee onto an expensive-looking Navajo rug. Dante seemed to remember that Jayce had come from New Mexico.

"Excuse me for intruding into your personal chambers," Dante said, pitching his voice in the seductive range. "But I have a matter of some urgency that I need to discuss with you."

Jayce laughed nervously.

"Oh, that's okay. You just startled me. Let me just take care of this." She picked up her coffee cup and took it to the kitchen.

She is using this time to compose herself, Dante thought. She was rattled because she was doing things that were forbidden. The game would be one of them, but not all of them. He needed her to feel safe enough to divulge what information he needed.

Jayce returned with a sponge and began rubbing at the stain on the rug.

"Jayce, I know there are some people here that are logging into outside games from their internal computers. I don't really care if they are doing that, I am more interested in the games they are playing."

"Are you a gamer? I wouldn't have guessed that," Jayce said, looking up at him.

"Oh, I am most assuredly a gamer," Dante said. What he said was true, but his games were a far cry from the sort of video games she would be thinking about. Or maybe not.

"So what games are people playing now?" Dante asked.

"Oh, the big one is Verite," Jayce said, standing up.

"Is it good?"

"It's amazing. It's the first thing that has ever been produced that really makes you feel like you are in the game, you know. Or at least that's what I heard," Jayce said, with a sly little smile.

Dante laughed and winked at her.

"Do you happen to know if ghosts can play this game?" he asked.

"Oh, it's funny you mention that, I heard that ghosts could actually go into the game more completely than people."

"Really? That would be very tempting. Do you remember who told you this?"

Jayce leaned on the counter, and crossed one foot over the other, cocking her hip out. She looked him up and down, and none too subtly.

"My problem is that I can't touch people. Or I can't touch most people.

A game like that could be such an outlet for ghosts like me," Dante said.

Jayce licked her lips.

"Listen, I probably shouldn't tell you this, and I heard it from a friend of a friend."

Dante nodded encouragingly.

"But apparently, one of the ghosts left here. He went into the game permanently because he could be real there."

"The ghost's name didn't happen to be Sawyer, did it?" Dante asked.

"No, it wasn't Sawyer, it started with an H, I think. Hughes? Harris?"

"Howard?" Dante asked, feeling a bit of the heat he had cleaned out returning.

"Yeah, it was Howard," Jayce said. "I know about Howard because he was one of the unhappy ones. There are some unhappy people here—you know, people who feel the rules are too strict, and mostly arbitrary."

"You don't say," Dante said.

At that moment, Liz, Joe, and Lepri came crashing through the door.

"Dante!" Liz said, looking around. "Wait, where's Kara?"

"Kara's not here. I was just having a little chat with Jayce about her Verite addiction," Dante said. Jayce's head jerked and she took a couple of steps back from him.

"Wait. Weren't we just here?" Liz asked.

"No." Joe looked at her.

"We were, we were just here. We came here because Dante had freaked out about Jayce and the game. And then the building started to shake. And then … Wait—I'm losing it. No, we *were* here."

Liz put her hands to her head. She was remembering something, or at least a grain of something, but it was a something that had no longer happened. Her parentage must be extraordinary to be able to remember what no longer was. Or at least her deeper ancestry.

"Liz, I was wondering if you could check on Kara for me," Dante said, putting his hand on her arm. "She is in the antechamber of the Healing Room. She has been through a lot in recent moments, so don't wake her. Just check to see that nothing disturbs her."

"But we—I—the window … it was broken—"

"I would consider it a great favor."

Liz stopped, opened her mouth a few times like a trout, then looked pointedly at Dante and nodded and left the room.

"Jayce," Dante said. "May I see that game that you play?"

"What game?" Jayce said, blanching.

"The game that you aren't supposed to have," Joe said. He must have understood the gist of the conversation despite not hearing Dante.

"I don't—"

"Don't insult me. I want to see the thing." Dante had dropped the seductive note from his voice and Jayce felt it. She dropped her gaze to the floor.

"Which part of the game do you want?" she asked. "You want the suit or the console?"

"I'd like to see both."

Jayce left the room and returned with something white thrown over her shoulder. In her hand she carried a small black box.

"It looks like this is the black box," Dante said softly.

"Yeah, the design of the console is a bit too retro for me, but the game is amazing, or it—well, yeah ..." Jayce's voice faltered as she held out the box to Dante. For a moment, a look of hunger flitted across her face.

"No, I don't think I will be touching that thing," Dante said. Whatever it was, it had ensnared ghosts. He suspected that Jayce knew that as well. It certainly wouldn't do to lose himself at this particular moment.

"Can you just hand it to Lepri, if you please?"

Lepri took the box from Jayce.

Dante stared at Jayce and felt a surge of disgust. Jayce was not evil. She was just spoiled, selfish, and weak, but in many ways that was worse. Evil, true evil, was pure enough that anyone with a modicum of sense could see it coming. True evil was also fairly rare, but entitlement, selfishness, weakness—those things were rampant and caused more harm on a daily basis than evil. Jayce had brought a known danger into the Office because it was something she wanted, and she couldn't conceive of denying herself something she wanted. He suspected she may have been encouraged by Howard to show it to Kara for some sort of reward. But she would have had no clue as to the consequences of her actions, the pain she caused Kara, the world she almost destroyed, then or now, because he had taken those consequences away. Kara had paid the price for that. He had paid the price for that. But Jayce would be happily oblivious. So she would be wholly unprepared for the price that she was about to pay for those actions. And afterward, he would be viewed with an even greater level of fear for a decade or so, which was not necessarily a bad thing.

"Jeremy, you and Joe need to find a way to disrupt this game—all parts of it," Dante said.

"You want us to short circuit the box?"

"No, I want you to disrupt the game network, wherever it is, here and outside."

"It will be difficult to disrupt an entire game network and well, um, isn't that something that you can do more easily?" Lepri asked, rubbing his neck and biting his lip.

"If I run energy through those things, they will short circuit, but so will anyone using them. And I have no idea what it might do to people or ghosts currently in the game," Dante said. "So, for the moment, I am looking for ways to deter its use by our people, the Cambion population at large, so no one else will get trapped it in, without destroying the game itself and possibly our people in it. I want to give them reasons not to play the game."

Lepri brightened.

"I might be able to come up with a biological way to induce illness when Cambion play the game, that should discourage them," he said.

"If you are looking for ways to get people off the game, you could tarnish the company's image," Joe said, catching the flow of the conversation. "Now that we know the name of the company—you know, associate it with the slave trade or human rights violations. I know people who can do that."

Dante nodded.

"Right, I'm on this," Lepri said. "Could I borrow Jayce to ask her a few questions about the game?'

"I'm afraid Jayce won't be available to answer questions this afternoon," Dante said. "Or any time after that."

Jayce blanched again. "Why?" she asked.

Dante glanced at her briefly before turning his attention back to Lepri.

"Because we need to collect biological data on the impact of that game on users. That means we will need subjects to test on. So I will be escorting Jayce to Parabiology to serve as a test subject, where she will spend the rest of her days at the Office."

Dante took only a second to register the horror on Jayce's face before taking her by the arm and escorting her to her own personal hell.

Chapter Twenty Five

Retro Dreams

On his way to the 8th floor, Dante considered what Kara had done just before she had touched the game suit and lost her mind. She had unmade all the ghosts that Abi had rescued from the Academy's horrible game. He had restarted time after this had happened, so that past had remained in their timeline. This meant that Abi was unmade as well. Dante felt a deep pang of loss at this thought, but it had been necessary and he didn't have time for grief just now.

Dante had dropped Jayce off with the Parabiology unit just minutes before. Geraldine, the very associate that Jayce hated most, would be responsible for Jayce's integration. As kind as she was, Geraldine had been the unfortunate outcome of a crossbreeding experiment between insects and various mammals, including humans. This meant that her physicality was difficult for some people to be around. Of course, this experiment had not been one of theirs. It wasn't that they didn't conduct questionable experiments, it was just that they had processes and procedures to ensure that there was a truly compelling reason to do so. However, there were more than a few countries and individuals dabbling in genetic crossbreeding and mutations with little to no review or oversight. The bad news was that most of said experiments came to naught. The even worse news was that sometimes they didn't, and progeny of such experimentation was usually subjected to no end of torture and abuse. When he or Kara found such creatures, they brought them here. Kara sometimes called it "Midian" after a book she had once read by a writer unaware of his own Cambion nature.

Geraldine had tried to be as welcoming as possible toward Jayce as they came in, but it might have been difficult to recognize, as her form of communication involved buzzing and drooling. Jayce had been less than enthused to be left there—at least, Dante assumed that was what all her screaming was about.

After leaving Jayce, he had checked in with Joe and Lepri. The security team had felt humiliated by the recent attack, so they had collected and sent a huge dossier of all internal and external servers that they used, had used, or might ever use. Dante suspected it was their proof that they had taken the recent breaches seriously. They had also begun a complete computer revamp. All personal computers were now being confiscated and new ones were being prepared, with the appropriate data migration happening at lightning speed. Needless to say, the systems in the personal computers would now completely block all data that did not come through screening via the mainframe. Joe had even contacted Parabiology directly to ask them to review the security protocol for leaks that he had not considered. He also asked for their help in tracking down the exact locations of the Verite and Everlast headquarters. Once said headquarters were found, Dante suspected their Cambion would also be found nearby. Last, Joe had contacted all his old contacts from the human trafficking trade to begin a smear campaign on Verite and Everlast.

Lepri, for his part, was already on the phone with IT to transmit signals into the game flow of Verite that would cause flashes to trigger nausea or epileptic fits in Cambion. He was also adapting a series of scanners, similar to the one that scanned Dante, but that were capable of doing wide sweeps for particles that resonated at the same level as the nanoparticles released by the virus. Anything or anyone infected would be brought to the Healing Room. Lepri was currently experimenting with antiviral compounds, as well as with virophages, as potential agents with which to treat those found to be infected.

So, for the moment, Kara was stable, their home was being secured, and they had a path toward getting their people back, but there was still one more aspect of this to contain before they could move forward. Jayce had been an unwitting spy, but she had been pushed in that direction, just as Sawyer had been pushed, by the same person, and someone in-house. That sounded like the work of a spy, and he had a good idea of where he might find said spy.

When the elevator stopped at the 8th floor, the doors opened onto a white emptiness. Dante stepped out into it, and felt the weight of wrongness hit him with the force of a hammer. Around him was nothing but white mist. There was no furniture, no walls, no gravity. It was nothing but a wasteland of white. No one was visible.

Dante walked out into the mist, keeping an eye behind him. He felt a presence here that was not welcoming. The 8th floor always felt weird, but ghost weird, not like this. This felt weird with a different flare. There was a soft breeze that smelled like acetone and hurt Dante's eyes.

"You just missed it," whispered a voice from above him. When he looked up, for a moment he thought he saw Abi, but he realized that it was actually one of the ghosts from Nigeria, dressed in a mask.

"What did I miss?" Dante asked, beginning to heat himself up. The ghost jumped down the mist like it was a wall and stood in front of him. He was tall and well-muscled.

"Almost everyone is gone," the ghost said.

"What do you mean, gone?"

"After you ordered everyone out, and Kara—well, we were told that Kara unmade all the ghosts on the 8th. Is that true?"

"Yes, it's true. But only because they were infected. We weren't able to heal them, so they had to be unmade. What she did was a mercy."

"That not what he said. He said that she was going to come back and unmake us all, because she hates us."

"Who's the 'he' that said this?" Dante asked.

"He's the ghost with the dripping eyes," the ghost said.

"Howard?"

"Yes, that was it."

"And so they all left because they thought Kara was going to unmake them?" Dante asked with a sigh. Ghosts had a reputation for being skittish, and not without reason.

"No, they didn't leave," the ghost said, shaking his head. "He took them."

"He *what*?" Dante snapped, then lowered his voice when the ghost shrunk himself down to the size of a small dog.

"How?" he asked in a softer voice, squatting next to him.

"He came to talk to us just after Kara left. He talked to us for a long time. He told us that he knew of a place where we could be physical again without waiting. Then he pulled something out of the air, something dark. It was like a star—no, like a dark star in a bright sky. It reminded me of onyx. We all just stared at it. There was something about it that looked and felt like sex, but sex that even the most loosely attached of us could feel. There was a sound that came out of it too. It was like a song. As it sang, it got bigger. And then, almost at the same time, it expanded, and all the ghosts gathered disappeared. They were sucked into it."

"Then why are *you* still here?" Dante asked.

"I hid when I saw it. I was a sailor and I know a siren when I hear one," he whispered. "That thing took everything with it. Once a ghost went in, it disappeared but it also took the environment with it. There is only one thing left in here."

"What is it?" Dante asked.

"Keep walking and you'll find it. I think he's there, and I think he might be looking for you. I'm not sure you want him to find you."

"Yes. Okay. I'll keep that in mind," Dante said, as he took off into the mist, in the direction that the ghost had pointed.

It wasn't long before he saw the most incongruous thing he could imagine—a 1950s diner right in the middle of all this nothingness. It looked like a giant metal Airstream with neon lights and windows. But he could see nothing from the outside as the windows were blacked out.

Dante approached, sensing that for the first time in more than half a millennium he might be in for an actual fight. The idea of a fight didn't disturb him at all, he just found it hard to believe there would be any challenge coming from Howard. And yet, he felt a tug in the pit of his stomach. Fighting, or fighting of any great magnitude, was the one situation, outside of sex, where it was okay for him to lose some control, and he could use that after the level of control he had needed to have in the past few days.

When he opened the door to the diner, a little bell tinkled. Inside was all neon, red leather, and chrome. The floor was in the classic black and white checkerboard pattern. There was a soda bar with red and silver swivel barstools in front of it. But Howard was sitting in one of the leather booths in the back of the restaurant.

"Oh there you are," he said, as Dante approached him. The black tar-like things that passed for his eyes were still oozing and dripping onto the otherwise pristine white tabletop. In front of him was a half-eaten cheeseburger, some fries, and an oversized portion of ketchup.

"What did you do and where did you take everyone?" Dante asked flatly.

"Oh, sit down for a minute. You don't always have to be this rude."

"I'm not usually rude. In fact, I'm only rude when I have to deal with things that wallow in their ignorance." Dante sat down. He could see the seat around him begin to soften from the heat he was already emitting.

"So let me repeat, where is everyone and what did you do with them?"

"They have all volunteered to help the Academy with the evolution of our kind," Howard said, a smug smile playing at his lips.

Dante just stared at him. Now that he was confronted by Howard, knowing that Howard had betrayed all of them, he made the decision to unmake him, but in his own inelegant way. But first he wanted to find out how much Howard knew about the Academy motives, who he learned it from, and if there were any other spies that might be hiding in the ghost ranks.

"You know you are on the wrong side of this fight," Howard said suddenly. Perhaps he had seen a flicker of his own death in Dante's eyes.

"Okay, I'll take the bait. What fight are you talking about and why do you think I am on the wrong side of it? But let me make it clear, if you don't answer my other question quickly, then I am going to remind you of exactly what I am. I don't think you have actually ever seen that. And that might be an epiphany for someone of your ilk."

Howard sat back suddenly, then laughed a high-pitched giggle. But it was forced.

"Listen. All things are supposed to die or transform. This story, just like all other stories, is supposed to die or transform. You two have kept it alive long past the point of its death. So its form is still functioning, but the soul of the place is dead and decaying. You can see it all around you, in this world, in other worlds, in space. Its code is falling apart. That's what the whole expanding universe theory is about. It's actually trying to rip itself apart. I saw it even when I was alive, and I wrote about it."

Well, at least Dante now knew for sure that Howard was deeply aligned with the Academy. Dante had heard these exact arguments before from their sort and he didn't give a shit about them. They were ideas promoted by those with very little knowledge of the actual facts at hand, particularly the fact that Kara's health controlled the overall health of this story.

"I know you don't believe me but that's why they are attracted here. They consume detritus. And this place is becoming detritus," Howard said.

"I assume you are talking about the things you used to write about."

"Viruses. They are alien viruses. They come from other stories. I know that now."

"Then why exactly would you want to encourage them to be here? You're terrified of those things. You wrote about the horror of things from other worlds in your little stories while you were still alive. Why would you side with them?"

"Your scope has always been so limited," Howard said. "It's because you are so fact-based and literal. The game brings things, catches things, that are already malleable enough to be brought in. The truly adaptable are what survives. And what is more adaptable than ghosts and viruses?"

"So that's who the Academy wants for the game? Ghosts?" Dante asked.

"And Cambion and viruses, but more. They want ghosts, viruses, and Cambion from all sorts of stories. And it's found a way to get them."

Dante felt his heat rise again.

The game had somehow managed to punch a hole into the hallway, or created its own. And Dante's experience with it was probably not an isolated one. So the game itself was, in essence, now a doorway to their physical story as well as to other stories. Somehow, the Academy had found or manipulated another world virus to be capable of both mimicking the hallway and punching a hole in the fabric of this existence. It could not be allowed to continue to exist.

"So why would the Academy be collecting such creatures?" he asked.

"They are trying to combine them," Howard said. "To create new things."

"So you just betrayed all the ghosts on the 8th and for what purpose? To put them into a game where they would be fodder and hosts for viruses? Why would you agree to that? That's an abomination. Or are you working for someone else here?" Dante snarled, his hands now on the table. He could feel his eyes burning. There were flames beginning to erupt in different parts of the restaurant.

Howard had his eyes down, on his plate, and failed to notice any of this.

"See, such a small scope. I didn't betray them. I was the only one of them who had any real vision. I realized that if the Academy can use bits of ghosts to give the virus a consciousness, then they have a way to control those viruses. What non-conscious thing wouldn't do anything for consciousness? So we control them with that desire. If we can control viruses, think of the power we would have. We would have the power to infect any world, any story, the hallway, even the library. We could then rewrite the code of any world, any story, anything."

"And you, who have been terrified of these things for your whole existence, are okay to be a part of that? You are okay to merge with a virus?"

Dante said, slowly and softly.

"Oh. No. I'm not doing that. The ghosts and humans we have recruited into the game are doing that," Howard said, then looked at Dante and shut up.

"Those ghosts were my friends. And you are a spy," Dante purred. He was just about to flash fry Howard when he felt a presence.

He turned to find the Director of the Academy standing behind him.

The Director smiled at Dante.

Howard cowered in front of him. As the Director came to sit next to Howard, Dante noticed that the tar pits in Howard's eyes were now on fire.

"That's not really necessary, is it?" the Director asked Dante, leaning in toward Howard's face. He smiled and then blew out the fire in his eyes.

The Director was now in his incubus form. He had pale skin, strawberry blond hair, and skin like porcelain. His eyes were blue and gold, and his teeth, beneath his narrow lips, sparkled like snow in the late afternoon sun.

Dante had forgotten how much he detested the sight of this creature.

"How did you get through our protocol and into the 8th?" he asked.

"I think, in your desire to be inclusive of all types of spirits in your little club here, you may have given your chosen ghosts freer rein of this place than you were aware of," the Director said, with a little smile. "That's the danger of benevolent dictatorship. The benevolent part tends to make you soft and miss things. My Academy is much more disciplined, and even with them, I occasionally get surprised."

For a moment, the Director's smile faltered. Then he laughed.

"You trust them too much. That I understand, given your background, but I'm surprised that Kara trusts ghosts that much. I wonder what she believes she is accomplishing here."

"Kara believes what Kara believes. Her beliefs are not mine to share," Dante replied.

"Just so," the Director nodded, with a condescending sort of agreement.

"So you stole our ghosts, and now you want to see me. I assume that you want something in exchange for them," Dante said.

"That's a bit coarse to start out with." The Director laughed. "First, I just wanted to talk to you. We haven't spoken since—"

"Since you let Kara be destroyed," Dante said flatly.

The Director winced. "Yes, since then. But isn't it time this ended?"

"What 'this' are you talking about?"

"All this." The Director indicated around him. "The competing to find our own kind and hiding them from each other. This working at cross-purposes. We expend so much energy just to move the needle infinitesimally to one side or the other of the status quo that it exhausts all of us. I know it exhausts Kara. All this horror and fighting that we have done all these years, that we still do now, just for those tiny movements that we delude ourselves are gains."

"You have another option in mind?" Dante asked.

"Yes, we could work together to make this place as beautiful as Kara wants it to be."

"Interesting. And the price for that would be . . .?"

The Director put his hands on the table and leaned forward. The blue and gold of his eyes was whirling. Dante was almost amused. The Director was trying to glamour him. Which meant that the Director knew even less about him than Dante might have suspected.

"Just give her back to me," the Director whispered.

Dante laughed out loud, he couldn't help himself.

"I don't think she would be pleased to know that you think she is something to be given," he said.

The Director blinked hard, then sat up straighter in the booth. He let out a short sigh.

"Okay, then you disappear. If you disappear, she might come to her senses."

"And what? Give up the world she loves, the world she made. I think that's unlikely."

"She should never have known that she was the author of this world."

"No, you are right, she never should have learned that, but she did learn it. And she learned it through your mistake and vanity."

The Director's eyes flashed at Dante. "My mistake?"

"Yes, your mistake, that I fixed," Dante said quietly. A part of him wished for the Director to attack him. If he attacked him directly, it would give him an excuse.

The Director winced ever so slightly. It would have been invisible to most. Then he shrugged.

"Can't we let the past die?"

The words stoked the fire in Dante's gut.

"No, we can't. The past never dies. Never. Ever. Time never dies. Not for us," he whispered, more to himself than the creature in front of him.

The Director raised an eyebrow.

"If that is all you were looking for from me, then I will assume we are at a roadblock. I will find a way to get our ghosts back from you," Dante said.

"You can try."

"So I will leave now, and I will take him with me," Dante said, motioning to Howard.

"Why? What is he to you? He's just a sad little scrap of a ghost."

"He is a spy. He is your spy."

"Listen, let me explain this to you—" the Director began, but Dante cut him short.

"What do you feel the need to explain?" he said. "That you created a computer virus to hack our systems in order to gain the names of our most vulnerable Cambion and their ghosts? Or that you then used that knowledge to recruit, or kidnap, said Cambion and steal their ghosts so that you could use all of them as test subjects in whatever experiment in playing god that you are involved in now? Or that you are locking both ghosts and Cambion into a game matrix with altered or alien viruses in the hope that said viruses will steal bits of their consciousness? Or that the reason that you are trying to find and collect their codes of consciousness is that you are trying to use those codes to give their consciousness to viruses—again? And then to use them as a weapon?"

The Director smiled and shook his head.

"Did I miss anything?" Dante asked, standing up.

"Nothing pertinent. Why do I always allow myself to underestimate you?"

"Because you have always thought that you were better than I was. And it galls you that Kara chose me over you," Dante said, feeling himself glow inside with the truth of this statement.

The Director's eyes narrowed, and he stood as well.

"She didn't choose. You were—" the Director began, but Dante cut him short again.

"She did choose, and she chose before I became what I am today. In the moment of her anguish, her spirit reached out to me and not you."

Dante reached for the fire inside him. He knew that he could not unmake this creature, who was almost as close to being a god as Kara. Unmaking him would require unmaking reality, but he could hurt him. The thing inside him that was his birthright crawled beneath his skin. He could feel it dancing behind his eyes. The second hand on the clock on the diner's wall stopped and began trembling back and forth.

The Director began to back away, hands up.

"Remember later, when it all comes down, that I offered you peace," he said.

"You offered nothing," Dante replied. "But what you will get is war."

At that, a fiery stream of death leaped from Dante toward the Director, who promptly disappeared, taking Howard with him.

Chapter Twenty Six

Family Refound

When Dante appeared in the Healing Room, Kara was still asleep in her bed. The privacy curtain was drawn back, and Liz was sitting in a chair next to her, her hand on Kara's arm.

"Thank you, Liz," Dante said, and Liz jumped. "I'm sorry, I didn't mean to startle you."

"That's fine," Liz said, with a little laugh. "I was just enjoying spending time with her. I really haven't had the chance to see her when she isn't having to fix some problem, or save something, or kill something."

Dante nodded and came to stand on the other side of Kara. He touched her face gently and she muttered in her sleep.

"She doesn't get much of a chance to really rest. Only in these moments," Dante said, looking at Kara's unusually unfurrowed brow.

"What moments do you mean?" Liz asked.

Dante sighed. "You remembered Kara touching the game suit, don't you?"

"Yes, I thought I did. I remember it. But it didn't happen, right?"

Dante studied Liz's face. Her open, brown eyes that had looked so vulnerable when she first arrived here now looked different. The vulnerability wasn't gone, but it was fading. What was taking its place was not yet definable, but it was definitely different.

"I want to show you something," Dante said, walking across the room and picking up a random piece of paper, just in case Kara was in any way conscious. He nodded for Liz to follow him into the Recovery Room and closed the door behind them.

"What I am about to say to you, you must never share, not with friends, not with lovers, and definitely not with Kara."

Liz studied him for a moment, then nodded.

"What you saw was something that happened. But that section of time has been undone. In that section of time, Kara went crazy and began pulling the world apart. I killed Jayce. The building began collapsing. The sun began to go dark, and Kara called the oceans to destroy us all."

As he spoke, Liz's eyes got wider and wider. She then nodded vigorously.

"It was true," she whispered. "I saw it. I saw the water take us all. I died."

"Yes."

"Then why am I alive now?" Liz asked.

"Because I destroyed that section of time. From the moment that we discovered that Jayce could have infected the computers and we all left the room. From that point onward, time has been remade. Those incidents no longer happened."

"Then why do I remember them?"

"That's the operative question, isn't it?" Dante said. "I can remember unmade sections of time. Kara has the ability to remember unmade sections of time in moments, but that's because part of our lineage is not of this story. The fact that you can remember it as well says very interesting things about your lineage. I will try to look into that, but you can discuss it with no one."

"Doesn't Kara know?"

"No, I took her, she was wiped clean of much that was eating her up inside. Part of that was touching the suit and going crazy. So she will not remember that."

Liz nodded, but then frowned.

"But wait, if you can unmake and remake time, then can't you just fix everything?" she asked. "I mean, you could just go back and undo things every time something went wrong."

"It would seem like that, wouldn't it? But it doesn't work that way," Dante replied. "For better or for worse, I was not meant to be an author of this story, but I have had to be in order to—well, in order to keep things working. So when I remake a section of time, it isn't exactly the same as it was before. Some small things will be different and these things add up. If there are too many of them, then the story becomes unrecognizable and possibly unlivable."

"So who was supposed to be the author of this world?"

"We will discuss that in more detail later," Dante said. "But for now, it seems that you have DNA that allows you to reside partially in different timelines, but Kara cannot know this. Kara cannot even guess it. She would not be able to handle the knowledge that time has been erased or redirected for her. She would not be able to handle this. She knows that I clean her out, but she doesn't know exactly how it happens, or the impact such cleanings have on the flow of time."

Dante stopped. How many times had he taken Kara to be cleaned? Probably thousands, if not tens of thousands of times. And yet, he had only ever spoken of this with one other creature—Abi, who was now unmade. He was telling Liz more than she needed to know and he wasn't sure why. Logically, maybe it was because, without the full knowledge, she might blurt out something in front of the wrong people. It might also be that, for the first time, his own connection to the hallway had been hijacked and he felt the need to bring others into the fold so that he could be monitored as well. These were logical reasons, but he wasn't sure confiding in Liz was strictly based on logic. There was something about Liz.

Dante stepped closer and took her hands.

"Kara cannot know this, any of this. It would undo her," he said softly. "She takes too much else on herself, and I will not have her driven mad by that knowledge. She already feels responsible for this story and this timeline. Imagine if she felt responsible for all timelines. The burden she carries is too much to bear for long, and knowing that her influences could spread further than that would be too much to bear for any period of time. So, I must tell you, that if you so much as breathe any of this to anyone but me, I will have no choice but to kill you. I like you. I believe you are uniquely gifted, in fact, but this can be known by no one but you and me. Can I trust you to keep this to yourself?"

Liz furrowed her brow. She let go of Dante's hands and looked down. For a moment, she was silent.

"Yes, I can keep secrets," she said. "I have kept lots of secrets in my life. I know how to keep secrets from everyone, including myself."

When her eyes met Dante's, they were filled with tears.

"I get it," she said. "I understand at least a tiny bit about needing to not know things. I know something about having to do things you don't want to do for the good of others."

Liz wiped her eyes on her sleeve. A bit of mascara rubbed off and smeared both her face and her shirt, but when she looked up at Dante, her eyes were shining, and she was beautiful.

"I will forget everything I saw before. I will keep that secret. I'll do this because I have felt more love in this place than I have in any other place in my life. People love each other here. They respect each other. They are family. And you have all made me feel like family. So I will protect this family, even if it means protecting it from itself."

Dante smiled and kissed her on the forehead.

There was a noise from the other room. It was the sound of a bed creaking. The door opened and Kara entered. She was smiling and her beauty took Dante's breath away, like it always had.

"How do you feel, my love?" Dante asked.

"Wonderful. New," she said. "Well, almost new. I remember most things now, I think, but I feel like I can handle them."

She turned to Liz. "Liz, dear, I'm so sorry that you had to see me at my worst. I was very over—well over-full, when I met you. So please accept my apologies if I was a bit hard to bear."

Liz threw her arms around Kara. Kara smiled and hugged her back.

"I was afraid that you would die," Liz said in a watery voice. She pulled away. "I'm sorry."

"There is no need to apologize for a tender heart. At least, not here. And not to worry," Kara said. "I'm not easy to kill."

Liz laughed a bit and nodded.

Suddenly, a few feet from them, Hudson sat straight up in bed.

"Someone help, they have Amelie," he yelled.

Kara rushed to his bedside. Hudson grabbed her by the arm.

"They are going to lock her in the game. They want to tear her apart. You have to save her," he said breathlessly.

"Who are 'they'?" Kara put her hand to his face. The effect calmed him but not much.

"It's a place called the Academy," Hudson said. "If you don't get her soon, they will tear her apart in that stupid game."

Fuck the Director. Dante felt fury building.

"Do you know who authorized this, from the Academy?" Kara asked.

"The Director. The guy who runs the whole place," Hudson said. "They had me trapped there for years and years. I was in a different body. I couldn't remember who I was. They did that to me."

Kara's hair was beginning to flutter but there was no wind.

Liz came forward. She had a notebook and pen in her hand.

"We'll help you find her," she said. "But it will help if you can tell us everything you know. Can you describe the place where you were being held?"

"It was an island," Hudson began, notably calmer in Liz's presence.

Dante took Kara's hand and pulled her across the room to the large picture window. The sun was setting in the distance, coloring the scene gold, pink, and red.

"It's time to go to war," Kara said, staring into the setting sun. It was unclear if her words were a statement or a question.

"Yes, I think we have no other choice," Dante replied.

"If we go to war, much of life will be wiped out." Kara turned to him. Her eyes were back to normal but the grief in them was new.

"Most likely."

Dante took her in his arms.

They stood together like this, feeling the energy move in each other's bodies. It was sexual, but more than sexual. What was between them was beyond the physical, beyond natural law, and beyond comprehension.

Finally, Kara pulled back. Her eyes were wet but there was a wan smile on her face.

"I don't want to kill everyone," she whispered.

For a moment, Amelie's face popped into Dante's mind. Amelie, whose gifts were so strong and who seemed to be able to move up and down resonances. With this thought came an idea.

"Maybe we don't have to wipe out a civilization this time," he said. "Maybe we just need to start a more targeted war."

"You think the Academy will be deterred by a mere war?" Kara asked.

"Yes, if it's the right kind of war."

"You have an idea?"

"Yes, the beginnings of one. We need to fight fire with fire. We need to use his tactics against him."

He looked over at Hudson, who was speaking rapidly to Liz and waving his arms.

"But we should go now. We have a lot to do," Dante said. "There are three things we need to do immediately." A strand of Kara's hair stroked his face as she smiled at him.

"First, we need to build a truly safe space. I thought we were safe here, but it seems we are not. I won't make that mistake twice. Our new space needs to be untouchable and invisible."

Kara nodded.

"Second, we need to call everyone home. All Cambion we are aware of need to be brought in-house. The level of atrocities being done by the Academy means none of them are safe."

Kara's nodded again, her hair dancing around her face.

"What's last, lover?" Kara asked.

"The last is the hardest. We need to get our captured people home and the Director has left us no indirect means of doing this. He has banked on the belief that we won't openly attack the Academy."

"So what we do then?"

"To start with, we build an army. An army the likes of which the world has never seen."

Dante then pulled Kara even more tightly to him and they disappeared into a place only they could share.

Epilogue

Nipah felt a warmth on her face. This simple sensation brought her a level of joy that would be impossible to understand for a creature like her, newly born to the light.

The ghoul, Abi, had pulled her apart. He had torn her to shreds, actually, but it was not first time that had happened. In fact, it had happened on a fairly regular basis in the game where she had been living. She was usually 'the villain,' who was killed and dispatched by the 'hero' of the game. They had done so with blades, burns, and bullets, but her demise was never permanent.

When she had been pulled into the realm of the ghosts, she had rejoiced. She was closer to her target. When she consumed the creature called Sawyer, she had more physical and more conscious. She didn't understand why the ghoul Abi attacked her but, as he was doing so, she managed to ingest a tiny bit of him; she was not unhappy about the attack. Then, after she had been torn apart, there was still enough of her, clinging to that space, to hear what was happening. The goddess Kara had hated her. She had hated her enough to kill everything she had touched just to get rid of her. Nipah didn't understand what she had done to make the goddess hate her, but she knew that she didn't understand a lot yet. Maybe she would understand later. Just before the creature Kara sent out her unnatural cold, Nipah had managed to use the ghoul's DNA to give herself enough weight to drop her resonance so that she fell to the Ghoul Lands.

In the Ghoul Lands, she healed herself and put herself back together. In fact, she did more than put herself back together. Through the dead, rotten memories of flesh she found, left by ghouls after their feastings, she found remnants of what she needed. The ability to drop herself enough. Enough to be where she now was.

Nipah felt the sun on her face. She felt cool, moist sand at her feet. Her nose was filled with the smells of creosote and sage. She could hear the wind blowing, and the scraping sound of sand blown over rocks. The excitement of it was so overwhelming that she had been prolonging the last step. Finally, when she could stand it no more, she opened her eyes.

She was standing in the desert sun, in the Kingdom, in a body that was now completely physical.

She was now human.

Limerence Glossary

The Academy – A powerful organization experimenting on Cambion, ghosts, and viruses to manipulate consciousness and rewrite reality. They believe that reality itself is breaking apart and seek to control the next evolutionary step.

Cambion – A hybrid being with both human and non-human ancestry, often connected to supernatural forces. Cambion in *Limerence* are deeply tied to different planes of existence, making them sought after by the Academy.

The Director – The leader of the Academy, a powerful entity with deep ties to Kara's past. He believes that all things must either transform or die and is willing to use viruses, Cambion, and technology to accelerate this process.

The 8th floor – A space inside the Office where ghosts and other non-physical creatures can congregate or reside.

Ghouls – Ghouls reside at the resonance level just above humans. As a result, sometimes humans can see them "in real life." It is the job of ghouls to consume the "blueprint" of a being after it's death. What they consume is the spiritual residue of all the physical things attached to a human. These are the things that will not travel from life to life, such as appearance, memories, history, pain, and non-recurring personality traits. They are obsessed with their food. Discussion of its preparation, consumption, and digestion make up the bulk of their conversations. They exist in a resonance called "the Ghoul Lands", which exists slightly above human resonance.

Elementals – These are spirits of the elements, such as earth, air, fire, and water. They can, and often do, mate with mortals, producing human/elemental Cambion. Elementals can also mate with other spirits, thus producing different types of Cambion.

The hallway – A metaphysical space that exists outside of conventional time. It connects different realities and stories and allows movement between them. Very few humans can enter the hallway. Those who force entry usually end up dead, insane, or unmade.

The Healing Room – A secure area used to stabilize beings whose resonance has been altered or damaged.

Incubus/Succubus – A spirit that exists in the highest levels of resonance. They have been portrayed in human culture as angels or demons. Some religions think they are angels who "fell" because they loved humans. Incubi are actually spirits who incite desire in humans. This usually happens in dreams, but there are exceptions. The human gets sexual satisfaction from the incubus and the incubus gets energy from the human. To humans, they appear in the form that the individual desires most. In male form they are called incubus and when they take female form they are referred to as succubi. In truth, all incubi are gender fluid, however, they usually have a form that they consider their "true" form. Some incubi have evolved to be able to use seduction to help humans with the transition and fear of death.

The Kingdom – Also known as Malkuth. This is what spirits call the lowest level of resonance, and where humans exist. However, there are striations within this level that are deeper than humans resonate. This is why there are objects that we consider inanimate but which are actually conscious.

The Library – A place where consciousness and stories intertwine, competing to become reality. It represents the metaphysical foundation of existence, where authors shape the fabric of worlds.

Limerence – A state of deep infatuation or obsession, often characterized by a desperate need for reciprocation. In the context of the story, it also symbolizes an existential pull between forces—love, time, consciousness, and reality.

Nanoparticles and viral vectors – The microscopic delivery system used in the game suit. These particles make the skin porous, allowing external control over emotions and physiological states by triggering hormone releases (adrenaline, dopamine, serotonin).

The Office – The "home" of Kara and Dante. It is both a powerful world-wide organization, and a safe haven for Cambion whether they are human, ghost, ghoul, or spirit.. They work to protect the integrity of this story as it exists.

Floors of the Office:

Basement: Parabiology
Ground floor: Fake entrance to the Office that looks like a bank. This is what non-Cambion see via the elevator and front door
1st floor: Security and IT
2nd floor: Finance and Accounting
3rd floor: HR/Entrance Exams
4th floor: Lepri's lab
5th/6th floors: Regular Medical
7th floor: Healing and Recovery Rooms
8th floor: Ghost residence
10th floor and above: Residential
Top floor: War Room

Outliers – These are creatures that live "outside" of expected parameters of a group, resonance, or story. Cambion are a natural part of this story *but* they are outliers of the specific species to which they belong. For example, a fire elemental human Cambion has genetic code from both their human side and their fire Cambion side, but they do not really belong to humanity or to fire Cambion—yet they are still natural residents of this story. There are also creatures that don't come from this story but that can end up here, like some viruses. Very rarely, there will be creatures that are outliers to this story, such as those who have DNA from viruses that don't come from our story, the reality we live in.

Resonance – The frequency at which a being or object exists in a given reality. It is akin to how fast a being or object vibrates in space. A being with broader resonance can shift between different layers of existence. The ability to alter resonance is key to time manipulation and consciousness transfers.

The Recovery Room – An area in the office set up for those who will need very long term recovery time. The room is usually used when a soul has become disconnected from its body and needs either to be found or to work its own way back down to physical being.

Shade— Another name for a ghost Cambion. It isn't considered offensive.

Unmaking – The process of erasing something from existence. Kara and Dante possess the ability to unmake things, but it comes at a cost. Unmaking does not simply erase something, it removes all traces of its impact on the world.

Upper Winds — The currents of energy that can move across resonances. They are used to take human souls to the portal of reincarnation. Particularly attractive incubi were once encouraged to help souls pass by seducing them in such a manner that they are happy to leave their human bodies. The incubus would then take the soul to the upper winds where they would be lead to reincarnation.

Virophages – Viruses that infect and disable other viruses. Lepri experiments with these as a potential treatment for Cambion infected by Verite's viral code.

Acknowledgements

As always, my deepest thanks to those who helped bring this book into being.

Heartfelt gratitude to my constant and supportive friends and beta readers—Addie, Myra, and Valerie—who took time from their incredibly busy lives to read and respond to my work. Hugs and love to Ian, Tessa, Leo, and Eli for your insights, encouragement, and friendship along the way. I'm endlessly thankful to everyone who has read and reviewed my books—especially those who have truly *seen* my characters and connected with them. You are the best!

Most of all, my love and thanks to my family. Every person in our household is strong-willed and deeply immersed in their own creative projects, and yet they always make time to be involved in mine. Thank you to:

Sebastien, my unnaturally gifted developmental editor, treatment co-author, and the one who helps me bring my stories to life visually,

Lucas, muse and dreamer, who asks the questions that help me build worlds—and makes me laugh when I need it most,

Julien, my husband, my partner, and my anchor, who helps keep me steady in this wild and unpredictable world.

For those of you who enjoyed this book

Amelie, Clovis, James, Kara, Dante, and Nipah will return in *Mirrored Lands.*

***

As most people know, reviews make or break authors, so if this book made you feel anything, do please share it, and connect with me at the following...

Webpage: Lsdelorme.com

Tiktok:@lexyshawdelorme

Insta: ls_delorme

Twitter:@lexyshawdelorme

Facebook Page: Lexy Shaw Delorme

BV - #0144 - 190925 - C0 - 229/152/14 - PB - 9798992485523 - Matt Lamination